"Some writers have it, and some don't. C. J. Tudor has it big time—*The Hiding Place* is terrific in every way."

—Lee Child

"Dark, gothic and utterly compelling, *The Hiding Place* pulls off a rare combination—an atmosphere of unsettling evil along with richly nuanced characterization."

—JP Delaney, *New York Times* bestselling author of *The Girl Before*

"Deliciously creepy, impeccably plotted and laced with both wicked humor and genuine shocks, *The Hiding Place* is the kind of read-under-the-covers thriller you didn't think people wrote anymore. Lucky for us, C. J. Tudor still does. An absolute corker of a book."

—Riley Sager, *New York Times* bestselling author of *Final Girls* and *The Last Time I Lied*

"C. J. Tudor has proven that she is a true master at creating perfectly dark, highly propulsive and tightly coiled mysteries that are utterly impossible to put down. From page one, the reader is pulled in with a gathering sense of dread and taken on an addictive, thrilling ride to the very last page."

—Aimee Molloy, *New York Times* bestselling author of *The Perfect Mother*

"Tudor's 2018 *The Chalk Man* was a standout mystery novel with a fresh voice and a spooky plot. *The Hiding Place* is even better."

—*The Washington Post*

"Tudor maintains a tone of creeping dread throughout the book, of something lingering always in the background, coyly hiding its face while whispering promises of very bad things to come. In the last quarter, however, she goes for broke with outright horror, giving readers an effective jolt of adrenaline that will carry them all the way to the terrifying conclusion. Readers won't know what hit them. Tudor came out swinging with *Chalk Man,* but this one puts her firmly on the map. Not to be missed."

—*Kirkus Reviews*

"Devastating . . . Sharply drawn characters illustrate the cyclical natures of violence and victimhood. Joe's dark humor may balance the grim plot, but the epilogue is the stuff of nightmares. Tudor casts a searing light on the long-term damage wrought by grief, guilt, and regret."

—*Publishers Weekly*

"Confirms Tudor as Britain's female Stephen King. There is a creeping dread on every page and, as you start a new chapter, a dark shadow over your shoulder. . . . Tudor's punk prose style and her great eye for menace make this a book no one should read at night."

—*Daily Mail*

"Gripping and dark, *The Hiding Place* descends like its very own mine shaft, getting creepier the further you go. You'll race to the finish."

—Roz Nay, internationally bestselling author of *Our Little Secret*

"Razor-sharp writing and masterful plotting drive this dark story about a small town, buried secrets and ghosts from the past. Witty and compelling all at once, *The Hiding Place* is a must-read page-turner!"

—Wendy Walker, bestselling author of *All Is Not Forgotten*

"Delicious in every way. A deliciously creepy story, deliciously told. Storytelling like a siren's song: your hair will prickle and stand on end but you won't be able to tear your eyes from the page. If you like Tana French, you will love, love, love C. J. Tudor."

—Alma Katsu, author of *The Hunger*

"Wow! Wow! Wow! C. J. Tudor's follow-up to her impressive debut is superbly chilling and delightfully creepy. Smartly written and brilliantly plotted, here is a book that crawls under your skin and hooks on until you reach that jaw-dropping ending."

—C. J. Cooke, author of *I Know My Name*

"Tudor has crafted another fantastic horror-tinged thriller in the vein of John Connolly and Brendan Duffy."

—*Booklist*

BY C. J. TUDOR

THE CHALK MAN
THE HIDING PLACE
THE OTHER PEOPLE

THE
HIDING
PLACE

A NOVEL

C. J. TUDOR

BALLANTINE BOOKS
NEW YORK

2020 Ballantine Books Trade Paperback Edition

Copyright © 2019 by C. J. Tudor
Excerpt from *The Other People* by C. J. Tudor copyright © 2020 by C. J. Tudor

Published in the United States by Ballantine Books, an imprint of Random House, a division of Penguin Random House LLC, New York.

BALLANTINE and the HOUSE colophon are registered trademarks of Penguin Random House LLC.
RANDOM HOUSE READER'S CIRCLE & Design is a registered trademark of Penguin Random House LLC.

Originally published in hardcover in the United States by Crown, an imprint of Random House, a division of Penguin Random House LLC, in 2019.

A portion of this work originally appeared in *The Chalk Man* by C. J. Tudor, published by Broadway Books, an imprint of Random House, a division of Penguin Random House LLC, New York, in 2018.

This book contains an excerpt from the forthcoming book *The Other People* by C. J. Tudor. This excerpt has been set for this edition only and may not reflect the final content of the forthcoming edition.

ISBN 978-1-5247-6102-8
Ebook ISBN 978-1-5247-6103-5

Printed in the United States of America on acid-free paper

randomhousebooks.com
randomhousereaderscircle.com

9 8 7 6 5 4 3 2 1

Book design by Jen Valero

*Writers are like jigsaws. We need patience, perseverance
and occasionally, someone to pick up the pieces.*

This is for Neil, for completing me.

PROLOGUE

E ven before stepping into the cottage, Gary knows that this is bad.

It's the sickly-sweet smell drifting out through the open door; the flies buzzing around the sticky, hot hallway and, if that isn't a dead giveaway that something about this house is not right, not right in the worst possible way, then the silence confirms it.

A smart white Fiat sits in the driveway; a bike is propped outside the front door, rain boots discarded just inside. A family home. And even when a family home is empty it has an echo of life. It shouldn't sit, heavy and foreboding with a thick, suffocating blanket of silence like this house does.

Still, he calls again. "Hello. Anyone here?"

Cheryl raises a hand and raps briskly against the open door. Shut when they arrived, but unlocked. Again, not right. Arnhill might be a small village but people still lock their doors.

"Police!" she shouts.

Nothing. Not a faint footstep, creak or whisper. Gary sighs, realizing he feels superstitiously reluctant about entering. Not just because of the rancid aroma of death. There's something else. Something primal that seems to be urging him to turn and walk away, right now.

"Sarge?" Cheryl looks up at him, one pencil-thin eyebrow raised questioningly.

He glances at his five-foot-four, barely-breaking-one-hundred-pounds companion. At over six foot and almost two hundred eighty pounds, Gary is the Baloo to Cheryl's delicate Bambi. At least, in looks. Personality-wise, suffice it to say, Gary cries at Disney movies.

He gives her a small, grim nod and the pair step inside.

The ripe, rich smell of human decay is overwhelming. Gary swallows, trying to breathe through his mouth, wishing fervently that someone else—*anyone else*—could have taken this call. Cheryl pulls a disgusted face and covers her nose with her hand.

These small cottages are fairly typical in layout. Small hallway. Stairs to the left. Living room to the right and a tiny kitchen tacked on the back. Gary turns toward the living room. Pushes open the door.

Gary has seen dead bodies before. A young kid killed by a hit-and-run driver. A teenager mangled in farm equipment. They were horrible, yes. Needless, most definitely. But this. This is bad, he thinks again. Really bad.

"Fuck," Cheryl whispers, and Gary couldn't have put it better himself.

Everything conveyed in that single appalled expletive. *Fuck.*

A woman is slumped on a worn leather sofa in the middle of the room, facing a large flatscreen TV. The TV has a spiderweb crack in its front around which dozens of fat bluebottles crawl lazily.

The rest buzz around the woman. *The body*, Gary corrects himself. Not a person anymore. Just a corpse. Just another case. Pull it together.

Despite the bloating of putrefaction he can tell that in life she had probably been slim, with pale skin, now mottled and marbled with green veins. She is dressed well. Checked shirt, fitted jeans and leather boots. Telling her age is difficult, mainly because most of the top of her head is missing. Well, not exactly missing. He can see chunks of it stuck to the wall and the bookcase and the cushions.

Not much doubt about who pulled the trigger. The shotgun still rests in her lap, bloated fingers bulging around it. Quickly, Gary assesses what must have happened. Gun inserted into her mouth, pulls the trigger, bullet exits slightly to the left, as that's where the worst damage is, which makes sense, as the gun is in her right hand.

Gary is only a uniformed sergeant and doesn't have a lot to do with forensics, but he does watch a lot of *CSI*.

Decomposition probably occurred quite rapidly. It's hot in the little cottage, stifling in fact. The temperature outside is mid-seventies, the windows are shut and, although the curtains are pulled, it must be creeping up to ninety. He can already feel the sweat trickling down his back and dampening his underarms. Cheryl, who never loses her cool, is wiping her forehead and looking uncomfortable.

"Shit. What a mess," she says, with a weariness he doesn't often hear.

She stares at the body on the sofa, shaking her head, then her eyes shift around the rest of the room, lips pursed, face grim. Gary knows what she is thinking. *Nice cottage. Nice car. Nice clothes. But you never really know. You never really know what goes on inside.*

Apart from the leather sofa the only other furniture is a heavy oak bookcase, a small coffee table and the TV. He looks at it again, wondering about the crack in the screen and why the flies are so interested in crawling all over it. He takes a few steps forward, broken glass crunching beneath his feet, and bends down.

Closer, he spots the reason. The splintered glass is covered in dark, crusted blood. More has run down the screen to the floor, where, he realizes, he has only just avoided standing in a sticky puddle that has spread over the floorboards.

Cheryl moves to stand beside him. "What's that? Blood?"

He thinks about the bike. The rain boots. The silence.

"We need to check the rest of the cottage," he says. She looks at him with troubled eyes and nods.

The stairs are steep, creaky and streaked with more trails of dark blood. At the top a narrow landing leads to two bedrooms and a tiny bathroom. If possible, the heat on the landing is more intense, the smell even more repugnant. Gary gestures for Cheryl to go and check the bathroom. For a moment he thinks she'll argue. It's obvious that the smell is coming from one of the bedrooms but, for once, she lets him play the senior officer and walks cautiously across the landing.

He faces the first bedroom door, a bitter metallic taste in his mouth, and then, slowly, eases it open.

It's a woman's room. Clean, neat and empty. Wardrobe in one

corner, chest of drawers by the window, large bed covered with a pristine cream duvet. On the bedside table, a lamp and a solitary picture in a plain wooden frame. He walks over and picks it up. A young boy, ten or eleven, small and wiry, with a toothy smile and messy blond hair. *Oh God*, he finds himself praying. *Please, God, no.*

With an even heavier heart he walks back out into the corridor to find Cheryl looking pale and tense.

"Bathroom's empty," she says, and he knows that she is thinking the same thing. Only one room left. Only one door to open to reveal the grand prize. He angrily swats away a fly and would have taken a steadying breath if the smell hadn't already been choking him. Instead, he reaches for the handle and pushes the door open.

Cheryl is too tough to be sick, but he still hears her make a retching noise. His own stomach gives a good solid heave but he manages to fight the nausea back down.

When he thought this was bad, he was wrong. This is a fucking nightmare.

The boy lies on his bed, dressed in an oversized T-shirt, baggy shorts and white sports socks. The elastic of the socks digs into the swollen flesh of his legs.

Bright white socks, Gary can't help noticing. Blindingly white. Fresh-on white. Like a detergent ad. Or perhaps they just seem that way because everything else is red. Dark red. Streaking the oversized T-shirt, smeared all over the pillows and sheets. And where the boy's face should be just a big mushy mess of red, features indiscernible, crawling with busy black bodies, flies and beetles, wriggling in and out of the ruined flesh.

His mind flicks back to the splintered TV screen and the puddle of blood on the floor, and suddenly he sees it. The boy's head being smashed into the TV again and again, then hammered into the floor until he is unrecognizable, until he has no face.

And maybe that was the point, he thinks, as he raises his eyes to the other red. The most obvious red. The red it is impossible to miss. Big letters scrawled across the wall above the boy's body:

NOT MY SON

1

Never go back. That's what people always tell you. Things will have changed. They won't be the way you remembered. Leave the past in the past. Of course, the last one is easier said than done. The past has a habit of repeating on you. Like bad curry.

I don't want to go back. Really. There are several things higher up on my wish list, like being eaten alive by rats, or line dancing. This is how badly I don't want to see the craphole I grew up in ever again. But sometimes, there is no choice except the wrong choice.

That's why I find myself driving along a winding road, through the North Nottinghamshire countryside, at barely seven o'clock in the morning. I haven't seen this road for a long time. Come to think of it, I haven't seen 7 a.m. for a long time.

The road is quiet. Only a couple of cars overtake me, one blaring its horn (no doubt the driver indicating that I am impeding his Lewis Hamilton—esque progress to whatever shitty job he simply must get to a few minutes sooner). To be fair to him, I do drive slowly. Nose to the windshield, hands gripping the steering wheel with white, peaked knuckles slowly.

I don't like driving. I try not to whenever possible. I walk or take buses, or trains for longer journeys. Unfortunately, Arnhill is not on any main bus routes and the nearest train station is twelve miles away. Driving is the only real option. Again, sometimes you have no choice.

I signal and turn off the main road onto a series of even narrower, more treacherous country lanes. Fields of turgid brown and dirty green sprawl out on either side, pigs snuffle the air from rusted corrugated huts, in between tumbledown copses of silver birch. Sherwood Forest, or what remains of it. The only places you're likely to find Robin Hood and Little John these days are on badly painted signs above run-down pubs. The men inside are usually more than merry and the only thing they'll rob you of is your teeth, if you look at them the wrong way.

It is not necessarily *grim up north*. Nottinghamshire is not even that far north—unless you have never left the hellish embrace of the M25—but it is somehow colorless, flat, sapped of the vitality you would expect from the countryside. Like the mines that were once so prevalent here have somehow scooped the life out of the place from within.

Finally, a long time since I've seen anything resembling civilization, or even a McDonald's, I pass a crooked and weathered sign on my left: ARNHILL WELCOMES YOU.

Underneath, some eloquent little shit has added: TO GET FUCKED.

Arnhill is not a welcoming village. It is bitter and brooding and sour. It keeps to itself and views visitors with distrust. It is stoic and steadfast and weary all at the same time. It is the sort of village that glowers at you when you arrive and spits on the ground in disgust as you leave.

Apart from a couple of farmhouses and older stone cottages on the outskirts, Arnhill is not quaint or picturesque. Even though the pit closed for good almost thirty years ago, its legacy still runs through the place like the ore through the earth. There are no thatched roofs or hanging baskets. The only things hanging outside the houses here are lines of washing and the occasional St. George's flag.

Rows of uniform sooty-bricked terraces squat along a main road, along with one dilapidated pub: the Running Fox. There used to be two more—the Arnhill Arms and the Bull—but they shut down a long time ago. Back in the day (my day), the landlord of the Fox—Gypsy—would turn a blind eye to some of us older kids drinking in there. I still remember throwing up three pints of Snakebite, and what felt like most of my guts, in the filthy toilets, only to emerge to find him standing there with a mop and bucket.

Next door, the Wandering Dragon fish-and-chips is similarly untouched by progress, fresh paint or—I'm willing to bet—a new menu. One glitch in my total recall: the small corner shop where we used to buy bags of penny candy and Wham bars has gone. A Sainsbury's Local stands in its place. I suppose not even Arnhill is completely immune to the march of progress.

Except for that, my worst fears are confirmed. Nothing has changed. The place is, unfortunately, exactly as I remember it.

I drive further along the high street, past the run-down children's play area and small village green. A statue of a miner stands in the center. A memorial to the pit workers killed in the Arnhill Colliery Disaster of 1949.

Past the village's highlights, up a small hill, I see the gates to the school. Arnhill Academy, as it is called now. The buildings have been given fresh cladding, the aging English block, where a kid once fell from the very top, has been pulled down and a new seating area put in its place. You can roll a turd in glitter, but it's still a turd. I should know.

I pull into the staff parking lot around the rear of the building and climb out of my worn-out old Golf. There are two other cars in parking spaces—a red Mini and an old Saab. Schools are rarely empty during the summer holidays. Teachers have lesson plans to write up, classroom displays to organize, interventions to supervise. And sometimes, interviews to attend.

I lock my car and walk around to the front reception, trying not to limp. My leg is hurting today. Partly the driving, partly the stress of being here. Some people get migraines; I get the equivalent in my bad leg. I should use my cane, really. But I hate it. It makes me feel like an invalid. People look at me with pity. I hate being pitied. Pity should be saved for those who deserve it.

Wincing slightly, I walk up the steps to the main doors. A shiny plaque above them reads: "Good, better, best. Never let it rest. Till your good is better and your better is best."

Inspiring stuff. But I can't help thinking of the Homer Simpson alternative: "Kids, you tried your best and you failed miserably. The lesson is, never try."

I press the intercom beside the door. It crackles and I lean forward to speak into it.

"I'm here to see Mr. Price?"

Another crackle, a piercing whine of interference, and then the door buzzes. Rubbing at my ear, I push it open and walk inside.

The first thing that hits me is the smell. Every school has its own individual one. In the modern academies it's disinfectant and screen cleaner. In the fee-paying schools it's chalk, wooden floors and money. Arnhill Academy smells of stale burgers, toilet blocks and hormones.

"Hello?"

An austere-looking woman with cropped gray hair and spectacles glances up from behind the glass-fronted reception area.

Miss Grayson? Surely not. Surely she'd be retired by now? Then I spot it. The protruding brown mole on her chin, still sprouting the same stiff black hair. *Christ.* It really is her. That must mean, all those years ago, when I thought she was as ancient as the frigging dinosaurs, she was only—what?—forty? The same age I am now.

"I'm here to see Mr. Price," I repeat. "It's Joe . . . *Mr.* Thorne."

I wait for a glimmer of recognition. Nothing. But then it was a long time ago and she's seen a lot of students pass through these doors. I'm not the same skinny little kid in an oversized uniform who would scurry through reception, desperate not to hear her bark their name and rebuke them for an untucked shirt or non-school-regulation trainers.

Miss Grayson wasn't all bad. I would often see some of the weaker, shy kids in her little office. She would apply bandages to scraped knees if the school nurse wasn't in, let them sit and drink juice while they waited to see a teacher, or help with filing, anything to provide a little relief from the torments of the playground. A small place of sanctuary.

She scared the crap out of me.

Still does, I realize. She sighs—in a way that manages to convey I am wasting her time, my time and the school's time—and reaches for the phone. I wonder why she's here today. She isn't teaching staff. Although, somehow, I'm not surprised. As a child, I could never picture Miss Grayson *outside* of the school. She was part of the structure. Omnipresent.

"Mr. Price?" she barks. "I have a Mr. Thorne here to see you. Okay. Right. Fine." She replaces the receiver. "He's just coming."

"Great. Thanks."

She turns back to her computer, dismissing me. No offer of coffee or tea. And right now my every neuron is crying out for a caffeine fix. I perch on a plastic chair, trying not to look like an errant student waiting to see the headmaster. My knee throbs. I clasp my hands together on top of it, surreptitiously massaging the joint with my fingers.

Through the window, I can see a few kids, out of uniform, messing around by the school gates. They're swigging Red Bull and laughing at something on their smartphones. Déjà vu swamps me. I'm fifteen years old again, hanging around the same gates, swigging a bottle of Coke and . . . what did we hunch over and giggle about before smartphones? Copies of *Rolling Stone* and stolen porn mags, I guess.

I turn away and stare down at my boots. The leather is a little scuffed. I should have polished them. I *really* need coffee. I almost give in and ask for a damn drink when I hear the squeak of shoes on polished linoleum and the double doors to the main corridor swing open.

"Joseph Thorne?"

I stand. Harry Price is everything I expected, and less. A thin, wrung-out-looking man somewhere in his mid-fifties in a shapeless suit and slip-on loafers. His hair is sparse and gray, combed back from a face that looks as though it is constantly on the brink of receiving terrible news. An air of weary resignation hangs about him like bad aftershave.

He smiles. Crooked, nicotine-stained. It reminds me that I haven't had a cigarette since I left Manchester. That, combined with the caffeine craving, makes me want to grind my teeth together until they crumble.

Instead, I stick out a hand and manage what I hope is a pleasant smile in return. "Good to meet you."

I see him quickly appraise me. Taller than him, by a couple of inches. Clean-shaven. Good suit, expensive when it was new. Dark hair, although rather more shot through with gray these days. Dark eyes that are rather more shot through with blood. People have told me I have an honest face. Which just goes to show how little people know.

He grips my hand and shakes it firmly. "My office is just this way."

I adjust my satchel on my shoulders, try to force my bad leg to walk properly and follow Harry to his office. Showtime.

"SO, YOUR LETTER OF RECOMMENDATION from your previous head is glowing."

It should be. I wrote it myself.

"Thank you."

"In fact, everything here looks very impressive."

Bullshit is one of my specialties.

"But . . ."

And there it is.

"There is quite a long gap since your last position—over twelve months."

I reach for the weak, milky coffee that Miss Grayson eventually slammed on the desk in front of me. I take a sip and try not to grimace.

"Yes, well, that was deliberate. I decided I wanted a sabbatical. I'd been teaching for fifteen years. It was time to restock. Think about my future. Decide where I wanted to go next."

"And do you mind me asking what you did on your sabbatical? Your CV is a little vague."

"Some private tutoring. Community work. I taught abroad for a while."

"Really? Whereabouts?"

"Botswana."

Botswana? Where the hell did that come from? I don't think I could even point to it on a frigging map.

"That's very commendable."

And inventive.

"It wasn't entirely altruistic. The weather was better."

We both laugh.

"And now you want to get back to teaching full-time?"

"I'm ready for the next stage in my career, yes."

"So, my next question is—why do you want to work here at Arnhill Academy? Based upon your CV, I would have thought you have your pick of schools?"

Based upon my CV, I should probably have a Nobel Peace Prize.

"Well," I say, "I'm a local boy. I grew up in Arnhill. I suppose I'd like to give something back to the community."

He looks uncomfortable, shuffles papers on his desk. "You are aware of the circumstances in which this post became available?"

"I read the news."

"And how do you feel about that?"

"It's tragic. Terrible. But one tragedy shouldn't define a whole school."

"I'm glad to hear you say that."

I'm glad I practiced it.

"Although," I add, "I do appreciate you must all still be very upset."

"Mrs. Morton was a popular teacher."

"I'm sure."

"And Ben, well, he was a very promising student."

I feel my throat tighten, just a little. I've grown good at hardening myself. But for a moment it gets to me. A life full of promise. But that's all life ever is. A promise. Not a guarantee. We like to believe we have our place all set out in the future, but we only have a reservation. Life can be canceled at any moment, with no warning, no refund, no matter how far along you are in the journey. Even if you've barely had time to take in the scenery.

Like Ben. Like my sister.

I realize Harry is still talking.

"Obviously, it's a sensitive situation. Questions have been asked. How could the school not notice that one of their own teachers was mentally unstable? Could students have been at risk?"

"I understand."

I understand Harry is more worried about his position and his school than poor dead Benjamin Morton, who had his face caved in by the one person in life who should have been there to protect him.

"What I'm saying is I have to be careful who I choose to fill the position. Parents need to have confidence."

"Absolutely. And I completely understand if you have a better candidate—"

"I'm not saying that."

He hasn't. I'm bloody sure of it. And I'm a good teacher (mostly). The fact is, Arnhill Academy is a shithole. Underperforming. Poorly regarded. He knows it. I know it. Getting a decent teacher to work here will be harder than finding a bear that doesn't crap in the woods, especially under the current "circumstances."

I decide to push the point. "I hope you don't mind me being honest?"

Always good to say when you have no intention of being honest.

"I know Arnhill Academy has problems. That's why I want to work here. I'm not looking for an easy ride. I'm looking for a challenge. I know these kids because I used to be one of them. I know the community. I know exactly who and what I'm dealing with. It doesn't faze me. In fact, I think you'll find very little does."

I can tell I've got him. I'm good in interviews. I know what people want to hear. Most important, I know when they're desperate.

Harry sits back in his chair. "Well, I don't think there's anything else I need to ask."

"Good. Well, it was a pleasure meeting—"

"Oh, actually, there is just one thing."

Oh, for fuck's—

He smiles. "When can you start?"

2

THREE WEEKS LATER

It's cold in the cottage. The sort of cold you get with a property that has been shut up and unlived in for some time. The sort of cold that gets into your bones and lingers even when you pump up the heat to max.

It smells too. Of disuse and cheap paint and damp. The pictures on the website didn't do it justice. They conveyed a shabby kind of chic. A quaint neglect. The reality is rather more careworn and dilapidated. Not that I can afford to be picky. I need to live somewhere, and even in a dump like Arnhill this cottage is the only thing I can afford.

Of course, that isn't the only reason I chose it.

"Is everything okay?"

I turn to the slick-haired young man hovering in the doorway. Mike Belling from Belling and Co. Rental Agency. Not local. Too well dressed and well spoken. I can tell he's itching to get back to his city-center office and wipe the cow shit off his shiny black brogues.

"It's not quite what I expected."

His smile falters. "Well, as we state in the property's description, it's a traditional cottage, not a lot of modern conveniences, and it has been empty for some time—"

"I suppose," I say doubtfully. "You said the boiler was in the kitchen? I think I should get the place warmed up. Thanks for showing me in."

He continues to linger awkwardly. "There is just one thing, Mr. Thorne . . ."

"Yes?"

"The check for the deposit?"

"What about it?"

"I'm sure it's just a mistake, but . . . we haven't received it yet."

"Really?" I shake my head. "The mail just gets worse, doesn't it?"

"Well, this is why we prefer bank transfers, but it's no problem. If you could just—"

"Of course."

I reach into my jacket pocket and pull out my checkbook. Mike Belling hands me a pen. I lean on the arm of the threadbare sofa and scribble out a check. I rip it out and give it to him.

He smiles. Then he looks at the check and the smile snaps off. "This is for five hundred pounds. The deposit, plus the first month's rent, is one thousand."

"That's right. But now I've actually *seen* the cottage." I look around and pull a face. "Quite frankly, it's a dump. It's cold, it's damp, it smells. You'd be lucky to get squatters. You didn't even have the courtesy to come up here and turn on the heat before I arrived."

"I'm afraid this really isn't acceptable."

"Then get yourself another tenant."

Bluff called. I see him hesitate. Never show weakness.

"Or perhaps you can't? Perhaps no one wants to rent this place because of what happened here? You know, that small murder/suicide you failed to mention."

His face tenses, like someone has just stuck a hot poker up his backside. He swallows. "We're not legally obliged to inform tenants—"

"No, but morally, it might be nice?" I smile pleasantly. "Bearing all that in mind, I think a substantial discount on the deposit is the very least you can offer."

His jaw clenches. A small tic flickers by his right eye. He'd like to be rude back to me, maybe even hit me. But he can't, because then he would lose his cozy twenty grand a year plus commission job, and how would he pay for all those nice suits and shiny black brogues?

He folds the check up and slips it back into the folder. "Of course. No problem."

IT DOESN'T TAKE ME LONG to unpack. I'm not one of those people who accumulate things for the sake of it. I've never understood knickknacks, and photographs are fine if you have a family and children but I have neither. Clothes I wear until they wear out, then replace with identical versions.

There are, of course, exceptions to this rule. Two items that I have left until last to remove from my small suitcase. One is a pack of well-worn playing cards. I slip these into my pocket. Some cardplayers carry good-luck charms. I never believed in luck, until I started to lose. Then I blamed my luck, the shoes I was wearing, the alignment of the fucking stars. Everything, apart from myself. The cards are my reverse talisman—a constant reminder of how badly I screwed up.

The other item is bulkier, cocooned in newspaper. I lift her out and place her on the bed, as gently as if she were a real baby, then I carefully unwrap her.

Small pudgy legs stick upward, tiny hands are clenched at her side, shiny blond hair fans into crumpled curls. Vacant blue eyes stare up at me. Or, at least, one does. The other rattles around in the socket, staring off at an odd angle, as though it has caught sight of something more interesting and not bothered to inform its companion.

I pick up Annie's doll and sit her on top of the chest of drawers, where she can regard me with her lopsided gaze every day and every night.

FOR THE REST OF THE AFTERNOON and evening I potter, trying to warm up. My leg bothers me if I sit still for too long. The cold and damp in the cottage aren't helping. The radiators don't seem to be working too well—probably air in the system somewhere.

There's a wood-burning stove in the living room but an extensive search of the cottage and the small shed outside doesn't reveal any logs or kindling. However, it does reveal an old electric heater in one closet. I switch it on, the bars crispy-fry a thick layer of dust and the air fills with the smell of burning. Still, it should throw out a decent amount of heat, if it doesn't electrocute me first.

Despite the vague dilapidation I can tell this was probably a cozy family home once. The bathroom and kitchen are tired but clean. The garden out back is long and football-friendly, fringed by open countryside. A nice, comfortable, *safe* place for a young boy to grow up. Except he never did.

I don't believe in ghosts. My nan was fond of telling me, "It's not the dead you need to be scared of, love. It's the living." She was almost right. But I do believe you can still feel the echoes of bad things. They imprint on the fabric of our reality, like a footprint in concrete. Whatever made the impression is long gone, but you can never erase the mark it left.

Perhaps that's why I haven't gone into his room yet. I feel okay about living in the cottage, but the cottage does not necessarily *feel* okay. How could it? A terrible thing happened within its walls, and buildings remember.

I HAVEN'T GONE SHOPPING for food, but I'm not hungry. Once the clock slips past seven I open a bottle of bourbon and pour a quadruple. I can't use my laptop because I haven't sorted out an Internet connection yet. For now, there's not much to do but to sit and adjust to my new surroundings, trying to ignore the ache in my leg and the faint, familiar itch in my gut. I take the pack of cards out and place it on the coffee table, but I don't open it. That's not what the pack is for. Instead, I listen to some music on my phone while reading a much-hyped thriller that I've already guessed the ending of. Then I stand at the back door and smoke a cigarette, staring out at the overgrown garden.

The sky is darker than a pit hole in hell, not a single star piercing the blackness. I'd forgotten what countryside dark is like. Too long living in the city. It never gets properly dark in the city, nor this quiet. The only sounds are my own exhalations and the crinkling of the cigarette filter.

I wonder, again, why I really came back. Yes, Arnhill is isolated, a half-forgotten dot on the map. But abroad would have been safer. Thousands of miles between me, my debts and people who do not take a losing streak kindly. Not when you can't pay.

I could have changed my name, maybe got a job bartending in some shack on a beach. Sipping margaritas at sundown. But I chose here. Or perhaps, here chose me.

I don't really believe in fate. But I do believe certain things are hardwired into our genes. We're programmed to act and react in a certain way, and that's what shapes our lives. We're incapable of changing it, just like our eye color or propensity to freckle in the sun.

Or perhaps that is just so much bullshit and a handy excuse to avoid taking responsibility for my own actions. The fact is, I was always going to come back one day. The email just made the decision easier.

It arrived in my inbox almost two months ago. Surprising, really, that it didn't get shunted straight into junk.

Sender: ME1992@hotmail.com
Subject: Annie

I almost deleted it immediately. I'd never heard of the sender. It was probably a troll, someone playing a sick joke. There are some subjects that should remain closed. No good can ever come of opening them. The only sensible thing to do was to delete the message, empty the trash and forget I ever saw it.

That decided, I clicked Open:

I know what happened to your sister. It's happening again.

3

Parents shouldn't have favorites. Another stupid thing people say. *Of course* parents have favorites. It's human nature. Right back to the time when not all your young would survive. You favored the stronger chick. No point getting attached to the one who might not make it. And let's face it, some children are just easier to love.

Annie was our parents' favorite. It was understandable. She was born when I was seven. My cute-toddler phase was long behind me. I had grown into a serious, skinny little boy with permanently scabbed knees and dirty shorts. I didn't look sweet anymore. I didn't even make up for it by enjoying a kick-about with a football in the park or wanting to go and watch a match with my dad. I'd rather stay in and read comics or play computer games.

This disappointed my dad and annoyed my mum. "Get outside and get some bloody fresh air," she'd scowl at me. Even at seven I felt fresh air was overrated, but I would reluctantly oblige and inevitably end up falling over or into or onto something, come home filthy and get yelled at all over again.

No wonder my parents hankered for another child: a sweet little girl they could dress in pink and lace and cuddle without her frowning and squirming away.

I didn't realize back then that my parents had been trying for another baby for a while. A little brother or sister for me. Like it was some sort of special gift or favor they were bestowing. I wasn't too sure I needed a brother or sister. My parents already had me. Another child seemed, in my opinion, surplus to requirements.

I remained unconvinced after Annie was born. A strange shrunken pink blob, her face all kind of squished and alien-looking. All she seemed to do was sleep, shit or cry. Her high-pitched wails kept me awake at night, staring at the ceiling, wishing my parents had bought me a dog or even a goldfish.

I continued in a state of apathy for the first few months, neither loving nor disliking my baby sister that much. When she gurgled at me or clutched my finger until it felt like it was turning blue, I remained unmoved—even as my mum cooed in delight and screeched at my dad to "get the bloody camera, Sean."

If Annie crawled after me or touched my stuff, I would walk faster or snatch my things back. I wasn't unkind, just disinterested. I hadn't asked for her so I didn't see why I had to pay her any attention.

This continued until she was about twelve months old. Just before her first birthday she started to walk and babble things that almost sounded like words. Suddenly she seemed more like a small person rather than a baby. More interesting. Amusing even, with her foreign-sounding gibberish and wobbly old-man steps.

I began to play with her and talk to her a little. When she began to mimic me back an odd feeling swelled in my chest. When she gazed at me and gabbled, "Joe-ee, Joe-ee," my stomach glowed with warmth.

She started to follow me everywhere, copy everything I did; laugh at my silly faces, listen intently when I told her things she couldn't possibly understand. When she was crying, one touch from me and she would stop, so eager to please her big brother that all her other woes were instantly forgotten.

I had never been loved in such a way before. Not even by Mum and Dad. They loved me, of course. But they didn't look at me with the same unabashed adoration as my little sister did. No one did. I was more used to being looked at with pity or scorn.

I wasn't a little boy with many friends. I wasn't shy, exactly. One teacher at my junior school told my parents I was "standoffish." I guess I just found other little boys, with their dull pursuits like climbing trees and fighting, a bit boring and stupid. Besides, I was perfectly happy being on my own. Until Annie came along.

For my sister's third birthday I saved up my pocket money and bought her a doll. It wasn't one of the expensive ones you could buy in the toy store, the ones that made noises and peed themselves. It was what my dad would call a "knockoff" from the market. It was actually a bit ugly and creepy with its hard, blue-eyed stare and odd pursed lips. But Annie loved that doll. She took it everywhere with her and cuddled it to sleep every night. For some reason (probably a name misheard) she called it "Abbie-Eyes."

By the time Annie was five Abbie-Eyes had become consigned to a shelf in Annie's room, replaced in favor by Barbie and My Little Pony. But if Mum ever suggested taking her to the rummage sale, Annie would snatch her back with a cry of horror and hold her so tight I was surprised those blue plastic eyes didn't pop right out of their sockets.

ANNIE AND I REMAINED CLOSE as we grew older. We read together, played cards or computer games on my secondhand Sega Genesis. On rainy Sunday afternoons when Dad was at the pub and Mum was busy ironing, the air full of static warmth and the smell of fabric softener, we'd curl up on a beanbag and watch old videos together—*E.T.*, *Ghostbusters*, *Raiders of the Lost Ark*; sometimes a few newer, more grown-up ones Annie probably shouldn't have been watching, like *Terminator 2* and *Total Recall*.

Dad had a mate who pirated them and sold them for 50p. The picture was a bit fuzzy and sometimes you couldn't always make out the actors' words, but as Dad was fond of saying, "Beggars can't be choosers" and "You don't look a gift horse in the mouth."

I knew Mum and Dad didn't have a lot of money. Dad used to work down the pit but, after the strike, even though they didn't close our pit right away, he left.

He'd been one of the miners who didn't walk out. He never spoke about it, but I knew the bad feeling, the tension and fights—coworker against coworker, neighbor against neighbor—had been too much. I was pretty young when it all happened but I remember Mum scrubbing the word "SCAB" off our front door. Once, someone threw a brick through our window when we were inside watching TV. The next night Dad went out with some of his mates. When he came back he had a cut on his lip and looked all messed up. "It's taken care of," he said to Mum in a hard, grim voice I'd never heard before.

Dad changed after the strike. He had always been, in my eyes, a giant of a man, burly and tall, with a shock of thick, curly dark hair. Afterward, he seemed to shrink, become thinner, more stooped. When he smiled, which he did less and less often, the lines at the corners of his eyes sliced deeper into his skin. Gray started to shoot through his hair at the temples.

He decided to leave the pit and retrain as a bus driver. I don't think he really liked his new job. It paid a decent enough wage, but not as much as he had earned down the pit. He and Mum argued more, usually about how much she was spending or how he didn't realize what a growing family cost to feed and clothe. That was when he'd go down to the pub. He only drank at one in the village. The same one the other miners who'd gone into work drank in. The Arnhill Arms. The miners who'd downed tools drank in the Bull. The Running Fox was the only place that was kind of neutral ground. None of the miners drank in there. But I knew some of the older kids did, safe in the knowledge that they wouldn't run into their dad or their grandad.

My parents weren't bad parents. They loved us as much as they could. If they argued and didn't always have much time for us, it wasn't because they didn't care but simply because they worked hard, had little spare cash and were often tired.

Of course, we had a TV and a cassette player and a computer, but still, without wanting to sound like a cheesy ad, a lot of the time we made our own entertainment: I'd play tag and football with Annie in the street, we'd draw chalk pictures on the pavement or play cards to while away rainy afternoons. I never resented entertaining my little sister. I enjoyed spending time with her.

If the weather was good (or at least, not chucking it down), Mum would think nothing of shooing me and Annie out of the house on a Saturday morning with a bit of money in our pockets to buy snacks, and not expect to see us back till dinnertime. Mostly, it was a good thing. We had freedom. We had our imagination. And we had each other.

———

AS I HIT MY LATE TEENS things changed. I found myself with a new group of "mates." Stephen Hurst and his gang. A rough group of kids that an awkward misfit like me had no place being friends with.

Perhaps Hurst mistook my outsider status for being tough. Perhaps he just saw a kid he could easily manipulate. Whatever the reason, I was stupidly grateful to be part of his gang. I'd never had a problem with being a loner before. But a taste of social acceptance can be intoxicating for a teenager who was never invited to the party.

We hung around and did the usual things gangs of teenage boys do: we swore, smoked and drank. We graffitied the playground and tangled the swings over the top of the bars. We egged the houses of teachers we didn't like and slashed the tires of those we really hated. And we bullied. We tormented kids feebler than us. Kids who were, I tried not to admit, just like me.

Suddenly, hanging out with my eight-year-old sister was not cool. It was mortally embarrassing. When Annie asked to come down to the store with me I'd make excuses, or leave before she saw me go. If I was out with my new gang, I'd turn away when she waved.

I tried not to notice the hurt in her eyes or the way her face fell. At home, I worked doubly hard to make it up to her. She knew I was overcompensating. Kids aren't stupid. But she let me. And that made me feel worse.

The stupid thing is, looking back, I was always happier hanging out with Annie than with anyone else. Trying to act hard isn't the same as being hard. I wish I could tell my fifteen-year-old self that, along with a shitload of other things: girls don't actually go for the quiet ones, numbing your ear with an ice cube to pierce it doesn't work, and Thunderbird is not a wine, nor a suitable drink to consume before a wedding reception.

Mostly, I wish I could tell my sister that I loved her. More than anything. She was my best friend, the person I could truly be myself with and the only one who could make me laugh until I cried.

But I can't. Because when my sister was eight years old she disappeared. At the time I thought it was the worst thing in the world that could ever happen.

And then she came back.

4

I prepare for my first day at Arnhill Academy in my usual way: I drink too much the night before, wake late, curse at the alarm and then, reluctantly and resentfully, limp across the landing into the bathroom.

I turn the shower over the bath to max—which elicits a half-hearted trickle of water—then clamber in and catch a few spurts of warmth before struggling out again, toweling myself dry and pulling on some clean clothes.

I choose a black shirt, dark-blue jeans and my tattered old Converse. There's first-day smart and there's being in your boogie shoes. Stupid phrase, I know. I picked it up from Brendan, my old roommate. Brendan is Irish. That means he has any number of sayings for any given situation. Most make absolutely no sense whatsoever, but that one I always understood. Everyone has a pair of boogie shoes. The ones they sling on when they want to feel comfortable and at ease. Some days you need them more than others.

I drag a comb through my hair and leave it to dry as I head downstairs for black coffee and a cigarette. I smoke it lurking just outside the open back door. It's only marginally colder outside than in. The sky is a hard slab of gray concrete and a faint, mean drizzle spits in my face. If the sun has got his hat on, it's definitely a rain hat.

I REACH THE SCHOOL GATES just before eight thirty, along with the first dribble of students: a trio of girls, tapping away on smartphones and flicking their rigorously straightened hair; a group of boys, pushing and shoving in the jokey way that can turn into a genuine fight in the blink of an eye. A couple of emo kids with heavy fringes from under which to glower at figures of authority.

And then there are the solitary arrivals. The ones who walk with their heads down and their shoulders hunched. The slow, ragged walk of the condemned: the bullied.

I pick out one girl: short, with frizzy red hair, bad skin and an ill-fitting uniform. She reminds me of a student from my own school-days: Ruth Moore. She always smelled a little of BO and no one ever wanted to sit next to her in class. The other kids used to make up rhymes about her: "Ruth Moore, she's so poor, gets free meals and begs for more." "Ruth Moore, ugly and poor, licks up shit from the toilet floor."

Funny how creative kids can be when they're being cruel.

Not far behind I spot victim number two—tall and skinny with a shock of dark hair standing up almost vertically from his head. He wears glasses and walks with a stoop, partly because of his height, partly because of the heavy backpack slung over his back. I bet he's bad at football and all the sports but on his PlayStation he's a king among geeks. I feel a personal stab of recognition.

"Hey, Marcus, you fucking pussy!"

The cry comes from a group of boys sauntering up the street behind him. Five of them. Year 11, I would guess. They walk toward the skinny boy with the fluid swagger of a gang. Passive-aggressive. The leader—tall, good-looking, dark hair—slings an arm around Skinny Boy's shoulders and says something to him. Skinny Boy tries to look relaxed, but everything about his posture screams tension and nerves. The rest of the gang forms a loose circle. Preventing escape. Sealing off his route into the school or away from them.

I hang back a little. They haven't seen me yet. I'm on the opposite side of the road. And of course they don't know I'm a teacher. I'm just a scruffy bloke in a duffel coat and Converse. I could continue to be that bloke. It's not officially school hours. We're not even inside the school gates. And it's my first day. There will be other days, other times, to sort out issues like this.

I reach into my pocket for my Marlboro Lights and watch as the gang force Skinny Boy against a wall. The nervy smile has fled. He opens his mouth to protest. Leader Boy presses an arm against his throat as one of the gang slips the backpack from his shoulder, and the rest fall upon it like a pack of feral dogs, pulling out books and textbooks, ripping out pages, stamping on his plastic-wrapped sandwiches.

One of them gleefully extracts what looks like a new iPhone. *Why?* I think. Why do parents send them off to school with this crap? At least in my day the worst thing a bully could steal would be your lunch money or your favorite comic book.

I look longingly at my cigarettes. Then, with a sigh, I slip them back in my pocket and walk across the road, toward the altercation.

Skinny Boy tries to grab his phone back. Leader Boy knees him in the groin and takes it from his associate.

"Ooooh, new. Nice."

"Please," Skinny Boy gasps. "It was a present . . . for my birthday."

"I don't think we got an invite to your party." Leader Boy looks around at his cronies. "Did we?"

"Nah. Must have got lost in the mail."

"Not a text, nothing."

Leader Boy raises the phone high above his head. Skinny Boy reaches for it, but it's halfhearted. He's got several inches on his tormenter but he's already defeated. It's a look I recognize.

Leader Boy smirks: "I really hope I don't drop—"

I grab his raised wrist. "You won't."

Leader Boy twists his head around. "Who the fuck are you?"

"Mr. Thorne, your new English teacher. But you can call me sir."

A collective murmur runs through the group. Leader Boy's face falters, just a little. Then he smiles, in a way I'm sure he thinks is charming. It makes me dislike him even more.

"We were just having a laugh, sir. It was only a joke."

"Really?" I look at Skinny Boy. "Were you having a laugh?"

He glances at Leader Boy and gives a small, slight nod. "Just joking around."

I release Leader Boy's wrist—reluctantly—and hand Skinny Boy back his phone.

"If I were you, Marcus, I'd leave this at home tomorrow."

He nods again, doubly chastised now. I turn to Leader Boy. "Name?"

"Jeremy Hurst."

Hurst. I feel a small tic flutter by my eye. Of course. I should have realized. The dark hair threw me but now I can see the family resemblance. The hereditary glint of cruelty in his blue eyes.

"Is that all, *sir*?"

The "sir" is stressed. Sarcastic. He wants me to bite. But that would be too easy. *Another day*, I remind myself. *Another day*.

"For now." I turn back to the others. "All of you, get out of here. But if I see you so much as drop a bit of chewing gum in the future, I'll be on you like a bad case of chlamydia."

A couple almost let slip a smile, despite themselves. I jerk my head toward the school gates and they start to saunter away. Hurst stands his ground longest, before finally turning and loping casually after them. Marcus lingers uncertainly.

"You too," I tell him.

He still doesn't move.

"What?"

"You shouldn't have done that."

"You'd rather I let him get away with smashing up your new phone?"

He shakes his head wearily and turns away. "You'll see."

5

I don't have to wait long.

Lunch break. I'm at my desk, writing up some lesson notes and congratulating myself on having got through the morning without boring my classes to death or throwing a student—or myself—out of a window.

As Harry quite rightly pointed out, it has been a while since I last taught. I admit I felt a little rusty. Then I remembered something an old colleague told me: Teaching is like riding a bike. You never really forget. And if you feel like you're about to wobble or fall off, always remember that there are thirty kids waiting to laugh at you and steal the bike. So keep pedaling, even if you have no idea where you're going.

I kept pedaling. By the end of the morning I was feeling pretty smug with my own success.

Obviously, this can't last.

There's a knock at the classroom door and Harry pokes his head in.

"Ah, Mr. Thorne? I'm glad I caught you. Everything okay?"

"Well, no one's fallen asleep in my classes yet, so I'd have to say yes."

He nods. "Good. Very good."

But he doesn't look like it's very good. He looks like a man who has lost a tenner and found a wasps' nest. He walks into the room and stands awkwardly in front of me.

"I'm sorry to have to bring this up on your first day, but something has come to my attention that I can't ignore."

Crap, I think. *This is it. He's followed up on my references and I've been found out.*

It was always a gamble. Debbie, the school secretary from my previous school, had a bit of a crush on me, and a bigger crush on expensive handbags. For old time's sake (and a small clutch), she intercepted Harry's request for a reference and forwarded it to me, along with some official headed paper. Hence my glowing credentials. All well and good, unless Harry dug a little deeper.

I brace myself. But that's not it.

"Apparently, there was an incident with one of our students outside the school gates this morning?"

"If, by 'incident,' you mean bullying, then yes."

"So you didn't assault a student?"

"*What?*"

"I've had a complaint from a pupil, Jeremy Hurst, that you assaulted him."

The little shit. I feel a pulse begin to beat at the side of my head.

"He's lying."

"He said you violently grabbed his arm."

"I caught Jeremy Hurst and his little gang bullying another student. I intervened."

"But you didn't use unreasonable force?"

I look him in the eye. "Of course not."

"Okay." Harry sighs. "I'm sorry, but I had to ask."

"I understand."

"You should have come to me about this incident. I could have nipped it in the bud."

"I didn't see any need. I thought the matter was dealt with."

"I'm sure, but the fact is the Jeremy Hurst situation is a little sensitive."

"He didn't look very sensitive when he was tormenting another kid and threatening to smash his phone."

"This is your first day, so obviously you're still new to the school dynamics, and I appreciate your stance on bullying, but sometimes things aren't so clear cut."

"I know what I saw."

He takes off his glasses and rubs at his eyes. I sense that he's not a bad man, just a tired, overworked one trying to do his best under difficult circumstances and generally failing.

"The thing is, Jeremy Hurst is one of our top students. He's the captain of the school football team . . ."

On the other hand, he could just be a prick.

"That doesn't excuse bullying, lying—"

"His mother has cancer."

I screech to a halt in my tracks.

"Cancer?"

"Bowel cancer."

It's on the tip of my tongue to say, "Shit," which would, under the circumstances, be wildly inappropriate.

"I see."

"Look, I know Hurst has some social-cohesion and anger-management issues—"

"So, that's what we're calling it these days."

Harry smiles ruefully. "But with his situation, we have to tread carefully."

"Right." I nod. "I think I understand a little better now."

"Good. I should have run through a few things like this with you personally. School handbooks can't cover everything, can they?"

"No."

They really can't, I think.

"Well, I should probably let you get on."

"Thank you, and thanks for letting me know about Jeremy Hurst."

"No problem. We'll catch up later." He pauses. "I will still have to mark this on your record."

"I'm sorry?"

"Your personal record. A complaint like this has to be noted, even if it's unsubstantiated."

The pulse beats harder. Hurst. Fucking Hurst.

"Of course." I force out a tight smile. "I understand."

He walks to the door.

"Is she going to die?" I ask. "Jeremy's mother?"

He turns and gives me a strange look.

"The treatment is going as well as can be expected," he says. "But, with this type of cancer, the odds aren't encouraging."

"Must be tough on Jeremy, and his father?"

"Yes. Yes, it is." He looks for a moment as if he wants to say something else, then he gives another of his awkward little nods and closes the door.

Tough on his father. I take out my cigarettes and smile. Good, I think. *Good. Fucking karma.*

THE ENGLISH BLOCK USED TO STAND between the main school building and the cafeteria, attached by a narrow umbilical cord of corridor that always created a heaving, sweating jam of students between classes and was hotter than the Hadron Collider in summer. We used to joke you'd end up blacker than Jim Berry (the only mixed-race kid in our school) if you stood in it for too long.

Although it was *officially* called the English block, to all the kids it was simply "the Block." Four stories of concrete ugliness prone to swaying in strong winds.

No one liked having classes in the Block, even before what happened. It was always cold, the windows leaked, and one particularly vicious winter I remember a class where we all wore hats and scarves, ice flakes frosted on the inside of the panes.

After Chris Manning plummeted from the top it was closed and then reopened with "new safety precautions," which basically meant making sure that the door to the roof was kept padlocked.

At some point in the last two decades it has been demolished. Where the Block once stood there is now a small, paved square with three benches arranged around a meager circle of half-dead plants. One bench bears a small plaque: "In Memory of Christopher Manning."

I sit down on one of the other ones and sneak a cigarette out of my pack. I twist it between my fingers and stare at the paving slabs, wondering which ones hide the spot where he landed.

He didn't make a sound. Not as he fell. Even when he hit the ground. It was soft, a dull thud. It didn't seem hard enough. I could almost have believed he was still alive, just lying there, taking in the fading autumn sunshine, if it hadn't been for the fact that his body looked oddly deflated, like someone had let all the air out. And of course, there was the blood, spreading out slowly from beneath him, a ruby-red shadow lengthened by the dying sun.

"Bloody shame, isn't it?"

I start. A short girl with dark hair in a messy ponytail and an abundance of silver in her ears stands in front of me. I didn't hear her approach, but then she's so thin she could have blown in on the wind.

For a moment I think she's an especially forward student, then I notice the lack of uniform (unless a Killers T-shirt, skinny jeans and Doc Martens is the new uniform) and the lines around her eyes that belie the initially youthful impression.

"Sorry?"

She gestures at the cigarette I have been fingering restlessly. "Bloody shame they create the perfect smoking area and then ban you from lighting up on school premises."

"Ah." I look at the cigarette and slip it back into the pack. "Truly a tragedy."

She grins and sits down beside me without asking. Normally, that type of unasked-for intimacy would annoy the fuck out of me. For some reason, with Miss Multiple Piercings, it only irritates the hell out of me.

"Sad about the kid who jumped too." She shakes her head. "You ever lost one?"

"A student?"

"Well, I don't mean a sock."

"No, I don't think I have."

"Well, you'd remember. I hope." She pulls out a box of mints, unwraps one and pops it in her mouth. She offers me the box. I want to refuse but find myself taking one.

"A student of mine died. Overdose."

"I'm sorry."

"Yeah. She was a really nice kid. Hard worker. Popular. Seemed to have everything going for her and then . . . two packets of acetaminophen and a bottle of vodka. Put herself in a coma. A week later they had to turn off her life support."

I frown. "I don't remember hearing about that."

"Well, you wouldn't. Kind of got overshadowed by Julia and Ben Morton." She gives a shrug. "Always a bigger tragedy, right?"

"I suppose."

A pause.

"So, aren't you going to ask?"

"What?"

"The usual? 'Did you know them? Did you suspect anything was wrong? Did you see any signs?'"

"Well, did you?"

"Not well. No, and yes. Did I not mention? Julia came into school wearing a great big placard around her neck: 'I intend to kill my son and myself. Have a nice day.'"

"Well, politeness costs nothing."

She chuckles and sticks out a hand. "Beth Scattergood. Art."

I shake it. "Scattergood? Really?"

"Oh yeah."

"Bet the kids have fun with that one?"

"Miss Shag Her Good is the current odds-on favorite, just ahead of Miss Fatter Guts."

"Nice."

"Yeah. Kids, eh? Gotta love 'em, or you'd get a real job."

"I'm Joe—"

"I know. Joe Thorne. The replacement."

"I've been called worse."

"So, which are you?"

"How d'you mean?"

"Only two types of teachers end up at Arnhill Academy. Those who want to make a difference and those who can't get a job anywhere else. So, which are you?"

I hesitate. "I like to think I make a difference."

"Right." Her voice is heavy with sarcasm. "Well, nice knowing you, Mr. Thorne."

"Thanks. Encouraging on my first day."

She grins. "We aim to please."

I like her, I realize. The emotion surprises me more than it should.

"So, which are you?" I ask.

She stands. "The hungry sort. I was on my way to the cafeteria. You coming? I can introduce you to some of the other misfits who teach here."

I HEAR THE HUBBUB of the cafeteria long before we approach it. Once again, it takes me back. The wafting aroma of frying, stale oil and something indefinable that you never see served but only ever smell drifting from the extractor fans of schools or old people's homes.

Inside, it hasn't changed as much as I expect. Parquet flooring. Plastic tables and chairs. The kitchen looks like it's had something of an overhaul since I used to line up for my burger, fried onions and chips. Now it's all chicken and rice, vegetable pasta and salad. I blame Jamie Oliver.

"That's some of our group over there. C'mon."

Beth leads me in the direction of a table in a far corner. The teachers' table. Four people sit around it. She rattles through the introductions:

Miss Hardy, Susan—a wispy lady with long gray hair and thick glasses—history.

Mr. Edwards, James—a good-looking young man with a hipster beard—math.

Miss Hibbert, Coleen—a strong-jawed woman with a military haircut—PE.

And Mr. Saunders, Simon—a lanky figure in a Pink Floyd T-shirt and faded cords; receding hair yanked back into scraggy ponytail—sociology.

For some reason, I dislike him instantly. Perhaps because he introduces himself by saying: "How's it going, man?"

Unless you are in a band or an American surfer, do not use the term "man." It makes you look like a dick, as does a ponytail with a receding hairline—you're not fooling anyone.

I sit down and he points at me with his fork.

"You look familiar, man. Have we met?"

"I don't think so," I say, carefully unwrapping my tuna sandwich.

"Where were you teaching before you came here?"

"Abroad."

"Whereabouts?"

It takes me a moment to remember the lie. "Botswana."

"Really? My ex-girlfriend taught out there for a while."

Of course she fucking did.

He smiles. "Wareng?"

I consider the odds. *Wareng?* Not a place. Too obvious. Must be an introduction. Not "Hello," as we've already done that, so it must mean . . .

"I'm good, thanks," I say pleasantly. "You?"

The smile recedes faster than his hair. I take a bite of sandwich and wonder if anyone would care if I dragged him outside and threw him under the nearest bus.

"I hear you're from Arnhill?" Coleen asks, thankfully changing the subject.

"I grew up here," I say.

"And you came back?" James asks incredulously, and only half joking.

"For my sins."

"Well, we're glad to have you," Susan offers. "It's been difficult finding a replacement after . . . well, after Mrs. Morton."

"Yeah," Simon says. "You don't have to be mad to work here, but it helps." He chortles at his own joke.

Beth eyes him coldly. "Julia suffered from depression. She wasn't mad."

He sneers at her. "Right. Because smashing your own kid's face in is completely sane?" He takes a hearty bite of pasta and chews noisily.

I turn to Beth: "Did everyone know about Julia's depression?"

"She was quite open about it," Beth says. "She went through a bad spell after her separation from Ben's dad. I think moving here was supposed to be a fresh start."

Some fresh start, I think.

"She was on medication," Susan adds. "But apparently, she'd stopped taking it."

"How did she get hold of a gun?"

"Her family owns a farm near Oxton. It was her father's."

"Obviously," James says, "if any of us had suspected there was anything wrong—"

What? I think. What would you have done? Asked her if she was okay and smiled with relief when she said that she was fine. Job done. Concern-box ticked. The truth is, none of us wants to know. Not really. Because then we might have to care, and who has the time for that?

"Obviously," I say.

Simon snaps his fingers and points at me again: "Stockford Academy."

My stomach lurches.

"*That's* where I remember you from," he says. "I worked there as a supply teacher before I got the job here."

And now that he's said it I vaguely recall a skinny bloke with bad dress sense and halitosis. We weren't in the same department. But still. *Really?*

"Well, I wasn't there very long, so . . ."

"Yeah. You left kind of suddenly. What happened? You piss off the head?"

"No. Nothing like that."

Pissing off didn't even come close.

"Weird, though." He frowns, and nods at my bad leg. "I don't remember you having a limp back then."

I stare at him. "Then you must be confusing me with someone else. I've had the limp since I was a kid."

The moment lingers a little longer than is comfortable. Susan intervenes:

"What happened? If you don't mind me asking?"

Actually, I do. But I kind of brought this one on myself.

"I was fifteen. I was in a car accident with my dad and my little sister. We came off the road and hit a tree. Annie and my dad died instantly. My leg was crushed. Took half a dozen bits of metal to put it back together again."

"Oh God," Susan says. "I'm so sorry."

"Thank you."

"How old was your sister?" Beth asks.

"She was eight."

They regard me with sad, sympathetic eyes, apart from Simon, who, I'm pleased to see, can't meet my gaze.

"Anyway," I say, "it was a long time ago. And fortunately I had my heart set on being a teacher, not a tap dancer, so here I am."

They laugh, a little nervously. The conversation moves on. I've played it well. I'm a good man; an honest man. A man who has faced tragedy, bears the scars, but still has a sense of humor.

I am also a liar. I didn't lose my sister in a car crash, and I didn't have the limp back then.

6

People say time is a great healer. They're wrong. Time is simply a great eraser. It rolls on and on regardless, eroding our memories, chipping away at those great big boulders of misery until there's nothing left but sharp little fragments, still painful but small enough to bear.

Broken hearts don't mend. Time just takes the pieces and grinds them to dust.

I sit back in one of the cottage's creaky armchairs and take a deep swig of beer. It's been a long day. The first full day I've taught for a while. I'm feeling it, both mentally and physically. My bad leg throbs, and even the four codeine tablets I've taken are doing little to ease the insistent dull ache. I won't sleep tonight, so my solution is to get drunk enough to pass out. Self-medication.

The room is dim, lit only by a single table lamp and the crackling wood-burning stove. I made it to an out-of-town supermarket and stocked up on the essentials: pizza, frozen dinners, coffee, cigarettes and alcohol. On the way back, I spotted a farmhouse/B&B selling logs. No one answered the door when I knocked, even though a battered Ford Focus sat outside. There were two child seats in the back and a sign in the rear window: LITTLE MONSTERS ON BOARD.

A basket had been left beside the logs: "£5 per bag—pay here."

There looked to be about thirty pounds in the basket. I stared at the crumpled notes for a moment, thought about the child seats and chucked in a fiver. Then I picked up a bag and drove back to the supermarket for firelighters.

It's taken me half a dozen of these and a lot of swearing to get the damn thing lit. However, now, for the first time since I moved in, the room is filled with a pleasant dry heat. I can practically see the damp retreating from the walls. Aside from the ramshackle furniture, lack of any personal mementoes and the fact that two people died here, I almost feel at home.

A notebook is open on my lap. On the first page I've written four names, with scribbled notes beside them: Chris Manning, Nick Fletcher, Marie Gibson and, of course, Stephen Hurst. The old gang back together, on paper at least. The ones who were there when it happened. The only ones who knew.

Fletch, I have discovered, now runs a plumbing business in Arnhill. Hurst is on the council. Marie, I couldn't find anything about online, but she may have married, changed her name. Beside Chris's name I have simply written: "Deceased." Although that doesn't really cover it. Not at all.

At the top of the next page are two names: Julia and Ben Morton. Beneath, I've jotted more notes, mostly gleaned from the Internet and the newspapers—neither wholly reliable, I know. If newspapers are the place where facts become stories, the Internet is the place where stories become conspiracy theories.

What I do know is this: Julia had a history of depression. She'd just finalized her divorce from Ben's father (Michael Morton, a solicitor). She had stopped her medication, requested a leave of absence and taken Ben out of school. Oh, and after she bludgeoned her son to death—before she blew her own head off—she wrote three words in blood on the wall of Ben's bedroom.

Not My Son.

In summary—hardly the actions of a balanced mind.

I've printed off two pictures and paper-clipped them inside the notebook. The first is of Julia. It looks like it was taken at a work event. She wears a smart suit, hair tied in a loose ponytail. Her smile is wide but her eyes are tired and guarded. *Take your picture and leave me alone*, her face says. I wonder if that's the reason the newspaper chose it. This is a woman about to break. A woman on the edge. Or maybe just a woman irritated at being forced to pose for a stupid photo.

Ben's is a school photo. His smile is wide and engaging, front two teeth slightly crooked, tie done up neatly for (probably) the first time ever. The reporters have trotted out all the usual platitudes: popular, a good student, plenty of friends, a bright future. They say nothing of the real boy. Simply a cut-and-paste job from their stock "dead child" folders.

Only one article hints at something more. A shadow skimming beneath the sun-dappled surface of Ben's imagined existence. In the weeks before he died an unnamed school source claimed that Ben had been acting strangely; getting into trouble, absent from classes: "He was weird. Not himself."

I think about the words Julia wrote: NOT MY SON. An icy fingernail caresses the top of my spine.

I chuck the notebook onto the coffee table. My phone rings, "Enter Sandman" piercing the cozy silence. I tense, then pick it up and glance at the screen. Brendan. I press Accept Call.

"Hello?"

"How's it going?"

"Good question. Still working on the answer."

I wait. Brendan is not the type of friend who calls just to inquire about my well-being. If there are no reports to the contrary, he presumes I am alive, which is good enough.

"Someone was asking about you in the pub the other night," he says.

"Someone?"

"A woman. Small, blond. Pretty, but kind of hard."

My stomach cramps, my bad leg throbs harder.

"Did you speak to her?"

"Feck, no. I slipped out as soon as I saw her. Some women just radiate bad news."

"Okay. Don't go back."

"But they serve the finest steak-and-kidney pie outside of my dear old mammy's kitchen."

"Get a cookbook."

"Are you shitting me?"

"No shitting. Don't go back."

"Christ." There's the click of a lighter and the sound of inhaling. "What did you do? Pawn her jewelry? Run off with her life savings?"

"Worse."

"You know what my dear old mammy would say?"

"I have a feeling you're going to tell me."

"The quickest way to bury a man is to give him a spade."

"Meaning?"

"When the feck are you going to stop digging?"

"When I find the treasure?"

"The only thing you are going to find, my friend, is an early grave."

"I love our little chats. They're so uplifting."

"If you want uplifting, watch Oprah."

"I have a plan—"

"You have a death wish."

"I just need a bit of time."

He sighs. "Have you ever thought you need professional help?"

"When I've sorted this out, I'll think about it."

"You do that."

He ends the call. I do think about it. For about ten seconds. I owe Brendan that. We've known each other for around three years, shared an apartment for a year and a half. He was there for me when no one else was. But Brendan is a recovering alcoholic. That means he is into things like confession, forgiveness and redemption. While I am more into keeping secrets, bearing grudges and holding on to resentment.

Sometimes, I wonder how the hell we even became friends. I guess, like a lot of relationships, it was a mixture of circumstance and alcohol (on my part, at least).

We used to see each other regularly in a pub close to where I lived. Casual hellos morphed into conversation one night. We began to sit together and chat over a drink—orange juice for Brendan, Guinness or whiskey for me.

Brendan's company was easy, undemanding. About the only thing in my life that was. The foundations of my comfortable middle-class existence were fast crumbling beneath my feet. My job was hanging by a thread and I was struggling to make the rent on my apartment. When I was six months in arrears, my landlord came around with his two burly brothers, kicked me out and changed the locks.

My choices of accommodation were suddenly limited. Should I choose the studio apartment with the suspicious stains on the walls, or the basement flat with mold and what sounded like a tap-dancing ensemble living upstairs? Not to mention, I was restricted to looking in the sort of neighborhoods that Batman might think twice about sauntering around on a dark night.

That was when Brendan suggested I move in with him.

"Feck. I've got a spare room that's just wasting gas and electricity."

"That's a kind offer, but I can't afford much in the way of rent."

"Forget the rent."

I stared at him. "No. I can't."

He gave me a look. "As my dear old mammy would say: 'You can't fight the wolves at your door when you're wrestling a lion in your living room.'"

I considered. I thought about my other options. Forget lions; I might well wake up to find rats nibbling my eyeballs.

"Okay. And thanks."

"Thank me by sorting yourself out."

"My losing streak can't last forever."

For a moment his face clouded. "It better not. From what I've heard you owe money to people who don't take installments—they take kneecaps."

"I'm working it out. And I'll pay you back. I promise."

"Too feckin' right you will." He grinned. "I enjoy a nice back rub before bed. Don't hold back on the massage oil."

I REACH FOR MY BEER, realize it's empty and crumple the can in my hand. I stand to get another then decide a visit to the bathroom might be in order. I walk across the living room and flick on the hallway light. It grudgingly ebbs into life. I place my foot on the first stair. It creaks, predictably. As I climb the narrow staircase I try not to think about Julia Morton dragging her son's body up here, step by creaking, laborious step. An eleven-year-old boy is heavy. And deadweight is heavier. I remember.

The landing is cold. There's no radiator up here. But that's not it. This isn't normal cold. Not the cold I experienced when I first walked into the cottage. This cold is different. *Creeping cold.* A phrase I haven't thought about since I was a kid. The type of cold that wraps itself around your bones and settles, like a lump of ice, in your intestines.

I can hear something too. Faint but persistent. An odd rustling, clicking sound, like air in the pipes. I stand and listen. It's coming from the bathroom. I push open the door and pull on the tattered old light cord. The light flickers on with an irritating low hum, like a dying mosquito.

The cold is worse in here. The noise is louder too. Not air in the pipes. No. That *clicking, skittering* sound is something else. Something more familiar. Something more . . . *alive.* And it's coming from the toilet.

The seat and lid are down. Not because I am in touch with my feminine side but because I have a slight phobia of open holes. Drains, overflows. Any hole in the ground. Last night, before bed, I went around and placed all the plugs in the plugholes. Now, I reach forward and tentatively lift the toilet lid.

"*Shit!*"

I leap back, so fast I almost lose my footing and crash to the floor. Somehow, I manage to grab hold of the sink and keep my balance. I don't have such great control over my full bladder. A spurt of warm urine trickles down my leg.

I barely notice. The inside of the toilet bowl is moving. Teeming with a mass of small, shiny black bodies. *Clickety-click-clicking* as they scurry around, like a moving sea of excrement.

"Christ."

A shiver of revulsion ripples through me. Along with the faint echo of a memory:

It's the shadows. The shadows are moving.

I lean on the sink, breathing heavily. Beetles. Fucking beetles.

After a moment I step forward and raise the lid again. The

swarming increases, like they sense I'm here. A couple make a break for it and start to scramble up toward the rim. I hastily slam the lid back down, trapping them between the two bits of plastic. They crack with a satisfying crunch.

How the hell did they get in there? The bowl must be dry so they've come up the pipes, but still? I reach for the bleach, take a deep breath, flip the lid once more and squirt the whole bottle down the toilet, drenching the scuttling insects.

The chittering and skittering increases. Some scramble up the side of the bowl. I grab the toilet brush and force them back down. Then I flush the toilet. Again and again until the cistern groans and there's nothing left in the bottom but a small scum of water and a few floating black corpses. Just for good measure I grab some toilet paper and stuff it down the waste pipe to plug it up.

I sit down on the edge of the bath, or rather my legs give and the edge of the bath rises to greet me with a hard bump. *Beetles. Fuck, fuck, fuck.* My heart is hammering. I'm sweating, despite the cold. I need a drink, and a cigarette. But more than that, I need a fix. For the first time since I arrived here. For the first time in a long while. I need something to calm my nerves and steady my shaking hands.

I fumble in my pocket for my phone. BT isn't coming to install broadband until next week, but I have 3G. Just. Online is second, even third best. But like an alcoholic reaching for the rubbing alcohol when every other bottle has been drained, needs must.

I bring up a web page. "Vegas Gold," it declares in appropriately glittery gold writing. The irony of playing "Vegas Gold" while sitting on the edge of a mold-encrusted bath in jeans wet with urine is not lost on me. My thumb hovers over the link.

And that's when I hear the crash from downstairs.

"What the *hell*?"

I hobble as fast as I can back down the narrow staircase and into the living room. A blast of cold evening air smacks me around the face. The curtains tussle and grapple in the wind. A jagged hole gapes in the living-room window and shards of glass litter the floorboards. Tires squeal, an engine revs and the high-pitched whine of a moped fades into the distance.

In the middle of the room I spot the source of the damage. A brick with a piece of paper wrapped around it, secured with a rubber band. How original.

I walk forward, kicking the slivers of glass out of my way, and pick up the brick. I unpeel the paper. It's thin and lined, torn from an exercise book. As welcome messages go, it leaves something to be desired: FUCK OFF CRIPLE.

7

You know you're getting older when the police are getting younger. I'm not sure what it says about you when the police are getting smaller.

I stare down—way down—at PC Cheryl Taylor. At least, I think that's what she said her name was. Her tone is brusque, her demeanor cool. I get the impression she would rather not be here. Perhaps I'm keeping her from a major heist, or the evening takeaway run.

"So, you say someone threw the brick through your window at approximately 8:07 this evening?"

"Yes."

Approximately one hour ago, so whoever did it is long gone by now. Still, at least it gave me the chance to change my jeans.

"Did you see anything?"

"I saw a large red house brick in the middle of my newly air-conditioned living room."

She gives me a look. It's one I'm familiar with. I seem to get it a lot from women.

"I meant anything else?"

"No, but I heard a moped accelerating away."

She makes some more notes then she bends down and picks up the house brick.

"Do you need to bag that or something, check for fingerprints?"

"This is Arnhill, not *CSI*," she says, putting it down again.

"Oh, right. Of course. Sorry, for a moment there I thought you were interested in catching whoever did this."

She looks like she's going to retort then bites back whatever comment she was about to make and simply says, "The note?"

I hand it to her. She studies it. "Not so hot on spelling."

"Actually," I say, "I don't think that's a mistake. I think it's deliberate. To throw me off track."

One thin eyebrow rises. "Go on."

"I'm an English teacher," I say patiently. "So I see bad spelling a lot. This isn't one of those words that students get wrong, and if they do then they get the whole thing wrong. They don't just miss a 'p.'"

She considers this. "Okay. So can you think of anyone who would do something like this? Any enemies, people with a grudge."

I almost laugh out loud. You have no idea, I think. Then I consider. I'm pretty sure Hurst or one of his mates is responsible. But I've no witnesses, no evidence and, bearing in mind the little chat I had with Harry this morning (Christ, was it only this morning?), I don't want to put my job in jeopardy. Not yet, anyway.

"Mr. Thorne?"

"To be honest, I only moved in recently. I've not had time to piss too many people off yet."

"But it seems you're working on it."

"Obviously."

"Right, well, we'll look into this, but it's probably just kids. We've had some trouble with kids from your school before."

"Really? What sort of trouble?"

"The usual. Vandalism. Trespass. Disorderly behavior."

"Ah, takes me back."

"If you want, an officer can come to the school, give them a bit of a talk on social responsibility, that type of thing."

"Will that do any good?"

"Last time my sergeant did it he came back to find someone had let all the air out of his tires."

"Maybe not then."

"Okay. Well, here's your crime number, for insurance purposes. Any more trouble, call us right away."

"I will."

She pauses at the door, seems to debate something. "Look. I don't want to make your night even worse—"

I think about the skittering, scuttling beetles.

"It'd be hard."

"But did anyone tell you about this place?"

"You mean, what happened here?"

"You know?"

"It came up."

"And it doesn't bother you?"

"I don't believe in ghosts."

She glances around and can't quite disguise the shudder of distaste that scurries across her face. Something clicks.

"You found them, didn't you?"

She hesitates before answering: "My sergeant and I were first on the scene, yes."

"That must have been difficult?"

"It's part of the job. You deal with it."

"But you still wouldn't want to live here?"

A small shrug. "You can never really clean away blood. Doesn't matter how much bleach you use, how hard you scrub. It's always there, even if you can't see it."

"Comforting. Thanks for that."

"You asked."

"Can I ask you something else?"

"I suppose," she says cautiously.

"Could there be any other explanation, for what happened here?"

"No sign of a break-in, no evidence of a third party involved. Believe me, we looked."

"What about Ben's father?"

"At a client dinner that night."

"So you think that Julia Morton just cracked, killed her son and herself?"

"I *think* you're asking a lot of questions for someone not bothered by it."

"Just curious."

"Well, don't be. It won't do you any favors here." She tucks her notebook into her pocket. "And I was only letting you know about the cottage in case the rental agent hadn't informed you of all the facts."

"Thanks . . . but I don't think the cottage is a problem."

"No." She gives me another look, one I can't quite read. "I think you're probably right."

THE GLAZIER ARRIVES fifteen minutes later. He whacks up a board over the broken window, informs me, "Thar'll b'fifty quid," and that a new window will take "abarru week."

I tell him that's fine. I can live without the view of the road.

He also gives me an odd look. Not my audience.

After he's gone I sink a couple more bourbons, smoke a cigarette leaning out of the back door then decide I've had enough, more than enough, for one day and head back upstairs to bed.

The cold has gone. It's just the normal chill of the cottage. I approach the bathroom gingerly, but the toilet is still empty. I remove the toilet paper and relieve myself, wash and brush my teeth, flick the light switch and shut the door.

Then I have second thoughts. I walk back downstairs and pick up the house brick. I carry it back into the bathroom and place it on top of the toilet lid.

Just in case.

I DON'T DREAM.

I have nightmares.

Normally, the alcohol helps with that.

Not tonight.

I'm walking up the stairs in my childhood house, except—in the way that dreams are—it isn't my childhood house, not quite. The stairs are much narrower and steeper and they wind around in a spiral. I can hear a noise below me in the darkness: a skittering, chittering noise. Shadows swarm around the bottom. Above me, I can hear another noise. A terrible high-pitched keening sound, like an animal in pain, interspersed with cries: "*Abbie-Eyes. Abbie-Eyes. Kiss the boys and make them cry.*"

I don't want to climb the staircase but I have no choice. Every time I glance back I see a few more of the stairs have disappeared into darkness. The shadows are creeping, just like the cold, and they're gaining on me.

I keep climbing, the stairs winding endlessly up ahead of me and then, suddenly, I'm on the landing. I look back. The stairs aren't there anymore. The shadows have crept up and swallowed them. Now they mill and scuttle restlessly, inches from my feet.

There are three doors, all closed. I push open the first door. My dad is inside. He sits on the bed. Well, "sits" isn't quite the word. He lolls, like a puppet with its strings cut. His head lies on his shoulder, as though it's having a rest from the business of being on top of things. Glistening tendons and stringy red strips of muscle barely hold it to his body. When the car hit the tree a jagged sliver of windshield pretty much decapitated him.

He opens his mouth and a strange wheezing noise hisses out. I realize it's my name: "*Joe-eeeeee.*" He tries to stand. I pull the door shut again, heart thumping, legs trembling. I move on to the next door. This one will be worse, I know. But just like a character in a bad horror movie, I know I'm going to open it.

I push at the door then step back. The room is filled with flies. Bluebottles rise in a dark, buzzing cloud. Somewhere among them I can see two figures. Julia and Ben. At least, I think it must be Julia and Ben. It's hard to tell as Julia is missing most of her head and Ben has no face. Just a red-and-white mass of blood, bone and gristle.

They stand, shadowy figures amid the flies . . . and then I realize they're made of flies themselves. As I stare at them, they dissolve and pour toward me. I throw myself through the door and slam it shut. I can hear the flies batting themselves against the wood in a furious swarm.

Wake up, I think. *Wake up, wake up, wake up.* But my subconscious is not about to let me off so easily. I turn toward the last door. My hand reaches out and twists the handle. It swings slowly open. This room is empty. Except for a bed and Abbie-Eyes. She lies in the center, eyelids closed. I walk forward and pick her up. Her eyes snap open. Pink plastic lips twist into a smile: *She's behind you.*

I turn. Annie stands in the doorway. She's wearing her pajamas. Pale pink, decorated with small white sheep. The clothes she was wearing the night of the crash. Except that's wrong. That wasn't what my sister was wearing when she died.

"Go away," I say.

She shuffles toward me and stretches out her arms.

"Go away."

Then she opens her mouth and a swarm of beetles pours out of it. I try to run but my bad leg gets tangled and I crash to the floor. Behind me I can hear the chittering, skittering of hard shells and busy little legs. I can feel them crawling up my ankles, burrowing into my skin. I try to swat and brush them off. They scuttle up my arms and neck, into my mouth and down my throat. I can't breathe. I'm choking on stinking, black bodies . . .

I wake, sweating and shaking, batting at my bedclothes, which are tangled and knotted around my naked body.

Shards of daylight poke through the semi-drawn curtains and jab at my eyeballs. I squint at my alarm clock, just as it starts to ring, sending peals of agony through my pounding head.

I roll over and groan. Time for school.

8

S ir?"
     "Yes, Lucas?" I point wearily at the arm waving in the air, and
then, before he can say anything, I raise my own hand.

"If this is another question about Tinder, I think we've already
covered the fact that dating apps weren't exactly a thing in Romeo
and Juliet's time."

Another hand shoots up.

"Josh?"

"What about Snapchat?"

The class ripples with laughter. I smother a smile.

"Okay. You've given me an idea."

"I have, sir?"

"Yep. Take one of the chapters we've read and rewrite it as if it
were set in the modern day. Pay particular attention to parallels and
the themes of tragedy and calamity."

More hands shoot into the air. I pick one.

"Aleysha?"

"What's a parallel?"

"Something similar or corresponding to."

"What's a calamity?"

"This class."

The bell rings for lunch. I try not to wince at the noise.

"Okay. Get out of here. I look forward to reading those essays to-morrow."

Chairs scrape and clatter as the children hastily make their escape. Doesn't matter how interesting you make your lessons or how enthusiastic the students, the ringing of the bell always sends them scattering from the classroom like inmates released from prison.

I start to gather my books and stuff them into my satchel. A familiar dark head pokes around the classroom door.

"Hey!"

"Hi."

Beth saunters in—Nirvana T-shirt, ripped jeans and Vans today—and perches on the edge of my desk.

"So, I hear someone threw a brick through your window last night?"

"News travels fast in Arnhill."

"Yeah, but it never leaves."

I chuckle. "Who told you?"

"One of the teaching assistants' cousins works part-time with a woman whose brother works for the police."

"Whoa. Better sources than CNN."

"More accurate, usually."

She cocks an eyebrow, which I presume is my cue to confirm or deny reports.

I shrug. "I guess someone didn't like my lesson plans."

"You think it was one of the kids here?"

"It seems most likely."

"You have a prime suspect?"

"You could say that." I hesitate. "Jeremy Hurst."

"Oh."

"You don't sound surprised."

"St. Jeremy? No. I heard you had a run-in."

"You really do have great hearing. If you ever hear what the winning lottery numbers are . . ."

She grins. "Like I'd tell you."

"So what do you know about—"

There's a knock on the half-open door. We both look up. A slightly overweight girl with streaked blond hair and too much makeup for a school day peers in. "This Mr. Anderson's class?"

"No, next door," Beth says.

"Right." She huffs and storms off.

"You're welcome!" Beth shouts after her. She looks back at me. "Why don't we take this conversation out of the classroom? I believe it's lunchtime."

"The cafeteria?"

"Screw that. I was thinking more like the pub."

THE WORN CHAIRS AND BENCHES are gone. The migraine-inducing multi-colored carpet has been replaced by shiny wooden floorboards. Tasteful lamps are arranged on the windowsills and an array of fine wines and bourbons are available at the bar. There's also an exciting new "gastropub" menu.

Actually, none of that is true.

The Fox hasn't changed at all, not since the last time I was in here, twenty-five years ago. The same old jukebox sits in the corner, probably stacked with the same old tunes. Even some of the patrons don't look as if they have changed, or moved, since the last century.

"I know," Beth says, catching me surveying the pub. "I take you to all the best places."

"Actually, I was just thinking that you can probably still smell my vomit in the toilets."

"Nice. I forgot you grew up here. Well, not literally in *here*."

"Well, I don't know."

"So, this was your local?"

"Kind of. Officially, I wasn't old enough to drink. Unofficially . . . the landlord wasn't too stringent about that sort of thing."

I turn to the bar. I half expect to see Gypsy still serving behind it, but instead a young woman with huge hooped earrings and hair in a ponytail so tight her eyebrows look like they are being held against their will scowls invitingly at me.

"Getcha?"

I look at Beth.

"Just a Diet Coke, thanks."

I glance longingly at the whiskey, then say reluctantly, "Two Diet Cokes, please. Oh, and a menu."

"Cheese bap, ham bap, pork pie or chips."

"Heston Blumenthal is quaking in his loafers."

She stares at me and chews her gum.

"Chips and a cheese bap, please," Beth says.

"Same, thanks."

"Ten pounds sixty."

Say what you like about her attitude, her mental arithmetic isn't bad.

Beth starts to fumble in her bag.

"No, don't worry," I say. "I'll get these." I reach in my pocket and frown. "Shit. I've left my wallet at home."

"No worries," Beth says. "It's hardly going to break the bank."

I smile, feeling a little guilty. But only a little.

We pay and find a seat—not too difficult—in a corner near one of the windows.

"So," I say to Beth as she sips her Diet Coke, "you were going to tell me about Hurst?"

"Right. Well, there's probably not that much to tell. The boy is smart, athletic, good-looking and a sadistic little shit. And he gets away with it because of his dad."

"Stephen Hurst."

"You know him?"

"We went to school together."

"Ah, right."

"I hear he's on the council now?"

"Yeah. And you know the sort of people that end up being councillors—"

"People that genuinely want to help their community?"

"And arseholes that get off on being in a position of power and use it to further their own ends."

"Gosh, I can't think which Stephen Hurst could be."

"Yeah, he's a piece of work. But then you probably already know that. You've heard about the plans for the old colliery?"

"The council wants to turn it into a country park?"

"Yep. Well, one of the reasons it has taken so long to get off the ground is because of Hurst."

"How come?"

"Well, officially, because of difficulties with funding. Unofficially, Hurst has ties to a property company that wants to build houses on the land instead."

"Housing? On an old mining site? That would take years for the council to approve—" And then it hits me. "Ah, I see."

"Yup. Basically, Hurst Junior is a chip off the old block. And Daddy is on the school board, so every time Jeremy does something that would get any other kid suspended Hurst Senior waltzes in, has a chat with Harry, probably about funding for the new sports center or the extra science block we need, and guess what? Nothing happens."

I feel a familiar anger start to stir in my gut. Same as it ever was, I think.

Barmaid of the Year approaches again, brandishing our cutlery like weapons. She plonks it down on the table.

"Chips'll take a mo." We're out of ketchup."

"Okay."

She stares at me for a moment longer than is comfortable and I wonder if saying, "Okay," has somehow offended her. Then she stalks away again.

Beth looks at me. "You really do know how to make friends and influence people, don't you?"

"My natural charm?"

"Don't kid yourself."

I take a sip of Diet Coke then I say, "Julia Morton was Hurst's form tutor last year, wasn't she?"

She nods. "But I wouldn't read anything into it."

"No?"

"No. Julia could deal with Hurst. She didn't take any shit and he didn't give her too much. She was a tough cookie. She didn't crumble easily."

And yet she did, I think. She beat her own son to death. And why not use the gun? A moment of madness? Or something else?

As if she can read my mind, Beth says, "That's why what happened just doesn't make any sense."

"You said she was depressed?"

"She'd *suffered* from depression, in the past."

"But depression doesn't just go away. She'd stopped taking her medication. Maybe she had some sort of relapse, a breakdown?"

She sighs. "I don't know. Maybe. And *maybe* if she had just killed herself, I could understand it. But to kill Ben? She doted on him. I'll *never* understand that."

"What was Ben like?"

"Bright enough, plenty of friends. Maybe a little easily led. That got him into trouble a couple of times. But a good kid. Until he went missing."

"Ben went missing? When?"

"A couple of months before he died. Turned up after twenty-four hours, and after the whole village had been out looking for him. Wouldn't say where he'd been. It was out of character, not like him."

I let this sink in. Missing. But he came back.

"I never read anything about that."

She shrugs. "Kind of got swept under the carpet with everything else that happened. Anyway, afterward . . ." She pauses. "He was different."

"How?"

"Withdrawn, distracted. He stopped hanging out with his friends, or they stopped hanging out with him. This sounds awful, but he smelled, like he wasn't washing. Then he got into a fight. Hurt the other kid quite badly. That's when Julia asked for some time off and took him out of school. Said he was having 'emotional issues' because of the divorce."

"Why did no one else mention this?"

"Seriously? Who's going to say anything bad about a dead kid? Besides, everyone just blamed Julia for his behavior. His mother was nuts. Must all be her fault, right?"

I think about that unnamed school source. I want to ask more but, right on cue, our charming waitress emerges back at the table.

"Cheese baps, chips."

"Thanks."

She thuds the plates down and glares at me again.

"Sorry," I say. "Is there something wrong?"

"You're renting the Morton cottage?"

"Yes."

"You know what happened there?"

This seems to be the question of the week.

"Yes."

"So, what are you?"

"Sorry?"

"Some kind of ghoul?"

"Erm, no? Actually, I'm a teacher."

"Right."

She considers this, then she reaches into her pocket, takes out a card and holds it out to me.

Not wanting to incur further wrath, I take it: "Dawson's Dust Busters."

"What's this?"

"My mum. She's a cleaner. She used to clean the cottage for Mrs. Morton. You might want to give her a call."

Possibly the strangest sales pitch I've ever had.

"Well, I'm not sure I can stretch to a cleaner right now, but thanks."

"Suit yourself."

She wanders off again. I look at Beth. "Whoa."

"Yeah, she's a little—"

"Rude? Weird? Scary?"

"Actually, Lauren is on the spectrum. So normal social conventions can be difficult for her."

"Right. And someone employed her as a barmaid?"

"You don't think every kid should be given an equal chance?"

"I'm just saying that the hospitality industry might not be the best career match."

"Judgmental."

"Practical."

"Tomayto, tomahto."

"Actually, it's tomahto. I'm very judgmental on that one."

She grins. She grins a lot, I think. Makes me want to do the same, use muscles I haven't exercised in a while.

"Anyway," I say, sticking the card in my pocket, "you were saying?"

"Nope." She jabs her fork at me. "Your turn. So why *are* you renting the Morton cottage?"

"You too?"

"Well, it *is* a bit weird."

"It's convenient, it's cheap. And years ago it wasn't the 'Morton' cottage, it belonged to a little old lady who used to throw scraps of bread to the birds and swear at the schoolkids who cycled past. It's just a building. It has history. Most places do."

Although most places do not have an infestation of beetles in the waste pipes. I fight down a shudder.

Beth regards me curiously. "So, talking of history—is it odd, coming back here?"

I shrug. "It's always odd coming back to the place where you grew up."

"Not being funny, but I can't imagine ever wanting to come back to Arnhill. As soon as I can, I'll be getting away."

"How long have you been here?"

"One year, one day and about"—she checks her watch—"twelve hours, thirty-two minutes—"

"Not that you're counting?"

"Oh, I'm counting."

"Well, I know it's small, parochial, a bit backward."

"It's not that . . ."

"Then what?"

"Have you ever been to Germany?"

"No."

"I went once, just after college. Had a friend working in Berlin. She took me to one of the concentration camps."

"Fun."

"It was a beautiful sunny day. Blue skies, birds singing, and buildings are just buildings, aren't they? But the place still had a feel, you know? Like it was in the very air, in the atoms. You knew a terrible thing had happened there, without even being told. Even while you walked around with the guide, nodding and looking all sad, a part of you just wanted to run away, screaming."

"That's what you think of Arnhill?"

"Nope. I'd go back to Germany." She pops a chip in her mouth, then asks, "What's the deal with you and Stephen Hurst?"

"Deal?"

"I sense you two weren't exactly best buddies back in the day?"

"Not exactly."

"Something happen?"

I spear a chip. "Just the usual teenage-boy stuff."

"Right."

Her tone implies she doesn't believe me, but she doesn't push it.

We both chew our food. The chips are all right. The cheese bap tastes like plastic, if someone had tried to make plastic less flavorsome.

"Harry told me Hurst's wife is ill?" I say.

She nods. "Cancer. And whatever your feelings about Hurst, that's gotta suck."

"Yeah."

And sometimes, what goes around comes around.

"They've been married a long time?"

"Teenage sweethearts." She looks at me. "In fact, if you went to school with Hurst, you might remember her."

"I went to school with a lot of people."

"Her name's Marie?"

Time slows and stills.

"Marie?"

"Yeah—can't tell you her maiden name, I'm afraid."

She doesn't have to. Another chunk of my ground-down heart crumbles to dust.

"It was Gibson," I say. "Marie Gibson."

9

Marie and I grew up on the same street. Our mums were friends, so we got thrown together a lot when we were small, shooed off to play while they drank tea and gossiped. We played catch and hide-and-seek and sat on the curb and ate chocolate ices when the ice-cream van came around. This was before Annie was born, so I guess we'd have been about four or five at the time.

I quietly worshipped Marie. She quietly tolerated me—the only other kid her age on the street. At school she would quickly abandon me in favor of more popular playmates. I suppose I took this as my lot. Marie was pretty and fun. I was the weird, insular kid nobody liked.

By the time we reached senior school I had started to notice that Marie was a bit more than pretty. She was beautiful. Her shiny brown hair—she wore it in pigtails when she was little—had been cut into a short, swingy bob. Sometimes she crimped it like her heroine, Madonna. She wore stone-washed jeans and baggy sweaters with sleeves that hung down to her fingers. She got her ears pierced twice in each lobe and at school she rolled up the waistband of her skirt so that it hovered above her knees, revealing a tantalizing glimpse of toned flesh between the hem and her over-the-knee socks.

Of course, by this point Marie barely noticed me at all.

She wasn't unkind or cruel. At least not on purpose. Occasionally she would walk past me on the street and it was like she was seeing someone she vaguely remembered or couldn't quite place. She would offer a distracted "Hiya," and I would glow for hours at the acknowledgment.

Annie used to tease me sometimes: "Oooh, look. It's your girlfriend." And make kissy, kissy noises. "Joey and Marie, sitting in a tree, K I S S I N G."

It was the only time I used to get properly annoyed at Annie. Perhaps because it hit a nerve. Marie was not my girlfriend; she would never be my girlfriend. Girls like Marie did not go out with boys like me: skinny, awkward nerds who read comic books and played computer games. They went out with *proper* boys who played football and hung around the playground, spitting and swearing for no reason.

Boys like Stephen Hurst.

They started going out in the third year. In a way, it was sort of inevitable—Hurst was the village bad boy, Marie was the prettiest girl in school. It was just the way things were. I wasn't particularly jealous. Well, maybe a bit. Even then, I knew Marie was better than Hurst. Brighter, nicer and, unlike a lot of girls at our school, she had ambitions greater than to get married and have babies.

When I found myself accepted into Hurst's gang—and Marie began to notice me again—she would tell me how she wanted to go to college and study fashion design. She was good at art. She dreamed of moving to London, planned to support herself with a bit of modeling. She had it all planned out. There was no way she was staying in a dump like Arnhill. As soon as she could she would be on the first bus out. The one that got away.

Except, she never did. Something changed. Something stopped her. Something tore her from her dreams, trampled those ambitions underfoot and ground them into the dirt. Something kept her here.

Or someone.

I STAND AT THE CORNER of my old street, staring up the road and smoking. I intended to walk straight back to the cottage after school. But it seems my subconscious has other ideas.

The street has changed, and it hasn't. The same red-brick terraces stand shoulder to shoulder, facing each other defiantly across the road, like they're squaring up for a fight. But there are new additions: satellite dishes and skylights, PVC windows and doors. More cars are bumped up along the narrow pavement. Shiny Golfs, 4x4s and Minis. In my day, not every family had a car. Certainly not a new one.

Some things remain the same. A group of youths stand around a half-dismantled motorcycle, smoking and drinking from cans of Carlsberg. A couple of dogs bark loudly and incessantly. Music drifts from one of the windows: heavy on bass, short on tunes or lyrics. A gang of young kids kick a ball around.

My old house, number 29, is halfway along the street, a few houses up from the amateur mechanic's, a few down from the wannabe Rooneys. Of all the houses, it's the one that looks the least changed. The door is the same black-painted wood I remember, although the old brass knocker has been replaced by a smarter silver one. The wrought-iron gate still hangs a little lopsidedly, there are a couple of tiles missing from the roof and the brickwork around the front could do with repointing.

My room was at the back, next to Annie's. She got the box room, the shorter straw. When we were younger we used to knock on the wall between us before we went to sleep. Later, after she came back, I used to lie in my room with my headphones on and the covers over my ears so I wouldn't have to hear her.

Mum sold the house soon after I came out of the hospital, after the accident. Her excuse was that we needed somewhere that was easier for me—still hobbling on crutches—to get around. The narrow row house with its steep stairs wasn't really practical.

Of course, that wasn't the real reason. There were too many memories. Nearly all bad. Mum bought a small bungalow not too far away. We lived there together until I was eighteen. Mum stayed until the day they took her to the hospital to die, just ten years later, at the meager age of fifty-three. They said it was lung cancer. But that wasn't all of it. Part of Mum died the night of the crash. The rest of her just took a while to catch up.

I turn away. The light is failing now, the air getting cooler and, if I lurk here much longer, there's a good chance someone might call the police. The last thing I want is to draw any attention to myself. I pull up the collar of my jacket and start to walk back down the street.

THERE'S A LINE PEOPLE SPOUT, usually people who want to sound sage and wise, about wherever you travel, you can never escape yourself.

That's bullshit. Get far enough away from the relationships that bind you, the people that define you, the familiar landscapes and routines that tether you to an identity, and you can easily escape yourself, for a while at least. Self is only a construct. You can dismantle it, reconstruct it, pimp up a new you.

As long as you never go back. Then, that new you falls away like the emperor's new clothes, leaving you naked and exposed, all your ugly flaws and mistakes revealed for the world to see.

I don't mean to walk back to the pub. But somehow that's the way I end up going. I linger outside for a few moments, finishing a cigarette, trying to convince myself that I am not going to walk inside. Definitely not. I don't need to start another school day with a hangover. I'm going to go back to the cottage, make some food and have an early night. I stub the cigarette out, congratulate myself on being so sensible and walk inside.

I can already tell that the pub is different from lunchtime. A lot of pubs are like that. They change at night. It's darker, the ancient fringed lamps providing dusty pools of illumination. The atmosphere is—if possible—even more unwelcoming. The smell is different too. Stronger, wheatier and, if I didn't know it was illegal, I'd swear people had been smoking in here recently.

The place is also busier than at lunchtime. A few young men loiter around the bar, holding pints, despite the fact there are plenty of free seats. It's the possessive behavior of the steadfast local. Claiming territory, like dogs pissing on a tree (and I wouldn't be surprised if they had done that against the bar too).

The rest of the tables are filled by groups of older men and women. They hunch over their drinks like animals guarding a kill. The men sport signet rings and rolled-up shirtsleeves revealing blurry gray tattoos. The women are all brassy streaks and crinkly arms poking out from ill-advised vest tops.

I know pubs like this, and not just from my childhood. They might have been in bigger cities, fancied themselves as being a tad more sophisticated, but the clientele and the vibe are just the same. These are not pubs for family meals or a nice glass of chilled Chardonnay with your girlfriends. These are locals' pubs, drinkers' pubs and, in some cases, gamblers' pubs.

I walk toward the bar, trying not to look as out of place as I feel. I might know these types of pubs, but here—despite growing up in the village—I am still an outsider. It's not quite the saloon-bar doors swinging open and the piano player falling silent, but I swear, for a moment, the general hubbub of conversation stills and eyes crawl over me as I walk toward the bar.

Little Miss Scary isn't serving tonight. Instead, a balding man with inky black bags beneath his eyes and several missing teeth scowls at me.

"Worr canna getcha?"

"Erm, pint of Guinness, please."

He starts to pour the pint silently. I thank him, pay and, while the Guinness settles, I scan the room again. I spot a free table in a far corner. After he's topped up the pint I walk toward it and sit down. I have my schoolbooks with me, so I take them out and do some marking while I sip my Guinness. Despite the staff, the lighting, the smell and the decor, the beer is well kept. It goes down quicker than I intended.

I saunter back up to the bar. The barman is at the other end. He's obviously undergone some miraculous personality makeover and is smiling and laughing with the group of men I noticed as I came in. In fact, he's looking so gregarious I wonder momentarily whether he has an identical twin.

I wait. One of the young men glances my way and says something. The barman laughs louder and continues talking. I wait some more, trying to look relaxed, trying not to feel annoyed. He carries on talking. I clear my throat, loudly. He looks over, the smile falls from his face and he lurches reluctantly across the bar toward me. As if pulled by an invisible magnetic force, two of the young men follow him.

I hold up my empty glass. "Thanks," *for finally doing your job.* "Another Guinness, please."

He takes a glass and jabs it under the pump.

I'm aware that the two young men have moved unsociably close. One is short and stocky with a shaved head and a sleeve of tattoos. The other is taller and skinny with bad skin and the type of gelled hairdo I thought went out with white socks and too-short trousers. They're not quite invading my personal space, not yet. Just gathering on the border. I can smell the unpleasant aroma of stale sweat only partially masked by cheap deodorant. Something about the pair feels strangely familiar, or perhaps it's just the threat of confrontation that I'm familiar with.

I wait, watching the Guinness being slowly poured. And then I hear the shorter, stockier one say: "Not seen you in here before, mate."

If there's one thing I hate more than being called "man," it's being called "mate" by someone who is not and never will be.

I turn and smile. "Only moved here recently."

"You're that new teacher," Unwise Hair says.

"That's right."

I do love it when people tell me things I already know.

"Joe Thorne." I hold out a hand. Neither takes it.

"You're living in the old Morton cottage?"

Again. The "Morton" cottage. Tragedy—especially bloody, violent tragedy—stamps its identity on everything around it.

"That's right," I say again.

"Bit fucking weird, isn't it?" Unwise Hair has moved closer.

"How d'you mean?"

"You know what happened there, right?" Stocky asks.

"I do."

"Most people wouldn't want to live in a place where a kid died like that."

"Unless they're weird," Unwise Hair adds, in case I haven't got the subtle subtext.

"Guess I must be weird then."

"Are you being funny, mate?"

"I guess not."

He presses closer.

"I don't like you."

"And I was about to ask for your number."

I see him clench his fist. I grip the empty glass, ready to smash it on the bar if needed, and in the past, at least once, it has been needed.

And then, when it seems that violence is inevitable, I hear a familiar voice say: "All right, lads. Nothing wrong here, is there?"

The Chuckle Brothers turn and melt away. A tall, burly figure walks up to the bar. Maybe I do believe in ghosts, I think. Bad ones that no amount of time, distance or holy water will exorcise.

"Joe Thorne," he says. "Long time."

I stare at Stephen Hurst. "Yeah. Yeah it is."

10

If some kids are born victims, are others born bullies?

I don't know the answer. I do know it's not acceptable to say that these days. Not the done thing to suggest that some kids, some families, are simply bad. It's nothing to do with class, or money, or deprivation. They're just wired differently. It's in their genes.

Stephen Hurst came from a long line of bullies. The joy of picking on those weaker was something that was passed down through the generations, like a classic heirloom, or hemophilia.

His dad, Dennis, was a foreman down the pit. The men loathed him, feared him and loathed him some more. He wielded his power like a coal axe, cutting down those who opposed him, forcing his enemies on the hardest shifts, taking a delight in refusing leave to spend with newborns or ill family members.

When the strike was on he could be seen at the front of the picket line, waving his placard, hurling abuse at the working miners and stones and bottles at the police. I'm not saying all the pickets were in the wrong, nor would I ever judge those who went to work, like my dad. They both thought that they were doing the best for their families, to save their livelihoods. But Hurst wasn't on the picket line for his politics or his beliefs, he was there because he loved the confrontation, the aggravation, the ugliness and, most of all, the violence.

It was never said at the time but, looking back, I realized that it was probably Dennis who was behind the graffiti, the intimidation, the brick through our window. It was his style. Go for the soft target. Rather than attack Dad directly, he attacked his family.

Stephen's mum often sported a black eye or a cut lip. Once, she had a cast that ran all up one skinny arm. Most people knew the injuries weren't because she was "a bit clumsy" but due to Dennis being a bit free with his fists after a pint or ten. But no one ever said anything. Back then, in a small village like Arnhill, that sort of stuff was between a husband and wife. And their son.

Stephen was tall like his dad, but he had his mum's fine features and blue eyes. Poster-boy handsome. Pretty, even. He could be charming and funny too, when he felt like it. But everyone knew that was a front. Stephen was a Hurst through and through.

Of course, there was one big difference between him and his dad: while Dennis was a blundering thug, his son was not stupid. He was clever and manipulative as well as being violent, brutal and sadistic.

I had seen him force a kid's head down a toilet full of piss, make another eat worms, beat, humiliate, torture—mentally and physically. Sometimes I hated him. Sometimes I felt scared of him. Once upon a time, I would happily have killed him.

And I was never one of his victims. I was one of his friends.

THE BLOND HAIR IS SPARSER, the once-chiseled features softer, bloated by age and good living. He wears a polo shirt, dark blue jeans, and too-white trainers. Like many middle-aged men, he turns "casual clothes" into an oxymoron.

He looks uncomfortable, more used to lording it in a suit and tie. He also looks exhausted. The two-holidays-a-year tan cannot quite disguise the dark circles beneath his blue eyes or conceal the flaccidness of his skin, like worry is dragging it from the very bones.

Surprisingly, this does not make me feel better. Over the years, I've wished many terrible things on Stephen Hurst. And now his wife is dying, and I don't feel any satisfaction. This may well mean I am a better man than I give myself credit for. Or maybe it's just the opposite. Maybe it's still not terrible enough. Maybe it means, as always, that life is unfair. Marie should not be the one being slowly eaten away from the inside by cancer. It should be Hurst. I'd say it was proof that the devil does indeed look after his own, if I didn't suspect that Hurst actually *is* the devil.

We sit, on opposite sides of the small, rickety table, and regard each other appraisingly. My Guinness is half drunk. He has barely touched his whiskey.

"So what brings you back to Arnhill?" he asks.

"A job."

"Simple as that, eh?"

"Pretty much."

"I have to say, you're the last person I thought would come back."

"Well, things never work out quite like we imagine when we're kids, do they?"

He glances down. "How's the leg?"

Typical Hurst. Straight for the weak spot.

"It bothers me sometimes," I say. "Like a lot of things."

He regards me shrewdly. Despite the amiable act, I can still see the cold light in those eyes.

"Why are you really back?"

"I told you, a job came up."

"I'm sure jobs come up all over the place, all the time."

"This one appealed to me."

"You have a way of making bad choices."

"Got to be good at something."

He smiles. Unnaturally white. Completely false. "If Harry had informed me who he was interviewing, you'd never have got the job. Arnhill is a small village. People here look after their own. They don't like outsiders coming in, causing trouble."

"Firstly, I'm not an outsider and, secondly, I'm not quite sure what trouble I've caused."

"The fact you're here at all is trouble."

"Guilty conscience? No, wait, that would imply you *had* a conscience."

I see him shift. Just a little. A reflex action. He'd like to punch me in the face, but he restrains himself. Just.

"What happened here, it was a long time ago. Isn't it time you put it behind you?"

Put it behind me. Like it was schoolboy high jinks or a first crush. I feel anger simmer.

"What if it's happening again?"

His face gives nothing away. Maybe he's a better bluffer than I am.

"I don't know what you mean."

"I mean Benjamin Morton."

"His mother was depressed, had a breakdown. Worrying, the type of people who become teachers, don't you think?"

I don't bite.

"I heard Ben went missing, not long before he was killed?"

"Kids run off sometimes."

"For twenty-four hours? Like you said, Arnhill isn't a big village. Where was he?"

"I've no idea."

"Do kids still play up on the old colliery site?"

The eyes spark. He leans forward. "I know what you're implying. And you're wrong. It's nothing like—" He breaks off as an older man with a halo of white hair and brown flared slacks walks past and raises a hand: "All right, Steve?"

"Not bad. You here for quiz night tomorrow?"

"Well, someone needs to whup your arse again."

They laugh. The man wanders off to another table. Stephen turns back to me. The smile snaps off like someone flicked a switch.

"I'm sure a man with your qualifications can find himself another teaching job somewhere better than this shithole. Do yourself a favor. Leave, before there's any more unpleasantness."

"Any *more* unpleasantness?"

So he knows about the vandalism.

"Tell me," I say. "Does your son own a moped?"

"You leave my son out of it."

"Well, I would, but it seems he has this *unpleasant* habit of throwing bricks through my window."

"That sounds like slander."

"I thought it was criminal damage. And don't you need to be sixteen to legally ride a moped?"

"I think we're done here." He starts to push his chair back.

"I'm sorry about Marie."

Something in his face changes. His lip trembles. One eye droops. For a moment, he looks very old. And for the merest sliver of a second I almost feel bad for him.

"Must be tough—you've been married a long time."

"Jealous?"

"Disappointed, actually. I always thought Marie would leave this place. She had dreams."

"She had *me*."

Somehow, he makes this sound like a burden, rather than a reason.

"And that was all?"

"What else could there be? We were in love. We got married."

"Happily ever after."

"We *are* happy. Probably difficult for you to understand. We have a good life here. We have Jeremy. We have a big house, two cars, our own villa in Portugal."

"Nice."

"It fucking is. And no one, especially not some third-rate teacher at some shitty school, is going to screw that up."

"I thought the cancer already had."

"Marie's a fighter."

"So was my mum. Right until the end."

But that's not true. At the end, she didn't fight. She just screamed. The cancer that started in her lungs—nurtured by a twenty-a-day Benson & Hedges habit—had spread to her liver, kidneys, bones, invaded everywhere. Even the morphine couldn't contain the pain, not all the time. She screamed because she was in agony and then, in those tiny moments of respite, she screamed because she was terrified of succumbing to the only thing that could take the pain away for good.

"Yeah, well, this is different. Marie is going to beat the cancer. And those NHS doctors, barely fucking old enough to shave, they don't know everything."

He stares across at me, blue eyes blazing, cheeks flushed a deep red, spittle gathering at the corner of his lips.

"They've said she's dying, haven't they?"

"*No!*" He slams his hand down on the table. The drinks jump. I jump. "Marie is *not* going to die. I will *not* let that happen."

This time the pub really does falter and fall quiet; the very air seems to still. All eyes are upon us. Hurst must feel it too. After a moment, a very long moment, during which I half expect him to roar, tip up the table and wrap his hands around my throat, he glances around, composes himself and stands.

"Thanks for your concern but, like your presence here, it's unnecessary."

I watch him go. And that's when I feel it. A sudden wave of dread, like vertigo, that hollows out my stomach from within and saps the strength from my bones.

I will not *let that happen.*

It's happening again.

AFTER HURST HAS LEFT I finish my pint—more to prove a point than any real desire to drink more or stay in the pub—then walk home. My leg does not thank me. My leg calls me a sadist and dumb moron who should just swallow his pride and use his damn cane. It's right. Halfway along the lane I pause and breathe deeply, massaging the lumpy, twisted limb.

It's almost nine and most of the light has faded from the day. The sky is a dusty gray; the moon a pale, naked shadow behind shifting curtains of cloud.

I realize I have stopped beside the old colliery site. The remains of the reclaimed mine rise behind me, the dark humps of the old slag heaps like dormant dragons.

It's a huge site. At least three square miles. New fencing has been erected on this side, along with a sturdy, padlocked gate. A sign attached to it reads: ARNHILL COUNTRY PARK, OPENING JUNE.

Bearing in mind it is now September, I would say that this is optimistic at the very least. There were plans even when I was a kid to redevelop the area. All the old tunnels and shafts were supposed to have been filled in when the mine closed. But there were rumors this was done too quickly. Corners cut. Plans not altogether strictly adhered to. There were issues with subsidence. Sink holes. I remember a story about one that almost swallowed up a dog walker.

Tonight, the area looks as much of a wasteland as ever. A dead, desolate place. One solitary digger sits halfway up one of the slopes, unmanned, seemingly abandoned. The sight of it still sends cold claws skittering down my spine. *Digging into the land, disturbing things.*

I turn away and resume my slow, uneven progress. I hear a noise behind me. A car is approaching along the lane. Not too fast, for once. In fact, it's really crawling. I glance around. Headlights blind me. They're on full beam. I raise a hand to shield my eyes. What the hell?

And then I realize. The car pulls up and a voice says: "All right, mate?"

Unwise Hair sits in the beaten-up Cortina next to his stocky mate, who is driving. The lane is deserted. No other cars. No other houses. The cottage is still a good quarter of a mile away. There are two of them, in a car, and I don't have anything I could use as a weapon, not even a damn walking stick.

I try to keep my tone even. "I'm fine. Thanks."

"Need a lift?"

"No, I'm good."

I continue lurching along. There's a crunch of gears and the car crawls along beside me.

"Got a bad limp there, mate. You should get in."

"I said, no thanks."

"And I said, get in."

"I don't think you can afford my rates."

The car squeals abruptly to a stop. *Stupid, Joe. Really stupid.* Sometimes it's like my mouth just goes out there looking for a fight. Or perhaps it's just trying to speed up what is bound to happen anyway.

The doors open and they both climb out. I could try to run, but that would be pointless and pathetic. However, I'm not averse to a little begging:

"Look, it was a joke, mate. I just want to get home."

Unwise Hair takes a step toward me. "This ain't your home. You're not wanted here."

"Okay—I get the message."

"No, you don't. That's why he sent us."

There is often an inevitability to life. Like I say, not fate exactly, but a sequence of events that are unavoidable. In the moment before the first blow strikes me in the face, I realize how stupid I've been. *He sent us.* These are Hurst's lackeys. That's why they slunk away like obedient pups when he walked into the pub. Then, when I wouldn't back down, he sent them after me. Same, I think, as another blow causes me to double over and fall to my knees, as it ever was.

I curl into a ball and take a kick to the ribs. They erupt in fiery pain. I wrap my arms around my head. Sadly, I've been in this position before. If I could speak, which I can't, because I'm trying to hang on to my teeth, I would tell these thugs that I've been beaten up by better hired muscle than them. That, in the beating-up stakes, they are amateur league. A kick thuds into my back. Fire shoots up my spine. I scream. On the other hand, even amateurs get lucky. I doubt Hurst will have told them to kill me, but it's a fine line. One I'm not sure these morons are capable of understanding the subtleties of.

A boot connects with the side of my head. My skull explodes and my vision wavers. And then, distantly, I hear something. A shout or scream? I am dimly aware of muffled curses, a cry of pain that is not, for once, my own. And then, to my amazement, the sound of doors slamming shut and a car accelerating away. I'd like to feel relieved, but I'm in too much pain and barely managing to grasp on to consciousness.

I remain lying on the cold, hard ground, my body one throbbing mass of agony. It hurts to breathe, let alone move. My head feels worryingly numb. I also have a vague feeling that I am not lying here alone.

I sense a movement to one side. Right or left, I can't tell anymore. I feel someone touch my arm. I try to focus on the face leaning over mine, swimming in and out of vision. Blond hair. Red lips. And the last thing I realize, before the blackness finally claims me, is that I hope I'm dying.

Because the alternative is far worse.

11

The squeal of rubber-soled shoes on shiny linoleum. The smell of cabbage, disinfectant and something else that the disinfectant can't quite mask: feces and death.

If this is heaven, it stinks. I blink my eyes open.

"Ah, you're back with us in the land of the living."

A vision clarifies in front of me. A woman, in doctor's scrubs. Tall and thin with short blond hair and a strong face.

"Do you know where you are?"

I take in the thin blue curtain half pulled around the narrow bed; the harried-looking nurses hurrying past the end; the nearby cries and moans . . . and take a wild stab:

"Hospital?"

"Good." She walks forward and shines a light into my eyes. I squint and try to move away as a fresh bud of pain blooms in one corner of my sore brain.

"Ooo-kay." I can smell her breath. Coffee and mints. She cradles my head, moves it from side to side. "And can you tell me your name?"

"Joe Thorne."

"And the date, Joe?"

"Erm . . . the sixth of September, 2017."

"Good . . . and *your* date of birth?"

"The thirteenth of April, 1977."

"Good."

She draws back again. Smiles. It obviously doesn't come naturally. She looks like someone who spends a lot of time being efficient and the rest of it sleeping. But not enough.

"Do you remember what happened?"

"I—" My brain still feels fuzzy and tender around the edges. If I think too hard, it hurts. "I was walking home from the pub and . . ."

The car. Hurst's thugs. And there was something else. I pause. "I don't really remember."

"Had you been drinking?"

"A couple of pints." The truth, for once. "It all happened pretty quickly."

"Okay. Well, you've obviously been assaulted, so the police will want to speak to you."

Great.

"Am I okay?"

"You've sustained severely bruised ribs and some more deep bruising to your lower torso."

"Right."

"You have some nasty abrasions and two impressive lumps on your head but, miraculously, no fractures, and you don't seem to be showing any signs of concussion, but we'd like to keep you in overnight, just for observation."

She is still talking, but I'm not listening. Suddenly it comes back to me. The figure looming over me.

"How did I get here?"

"A good Samaritan found you. A woman, driving past. She saw you on the pavement, stopped and brought you here. You were very lucky."

"What did she look like?"

"Petite, blond. Why?"

"Is she still here?"

"Yes. In the waiting area."

I swing my legs over the side of the bed. "I have to get out of here."

"Mr. Thorne, I really don't think it would be wise—"

"I don't give a shit whether you think it's wise or not."

A small flush on her pale, drawn cheeks. Then a nod. She flicks the curtain open and stands to one side. "Very well."

"I'm sorry . . . I . . ."

"No. Your call."

"You're not going to stop me?"

A tired smile. "If you're well enough to walk out of here, there's not much I can do."

"I promise I'll try not to drop dead."

She shrugs. "Between you and me, we've got more beds in the morgue anyway."

I USE THE BATHROOM, splash some water on my face. It doesn't do much to wash away the dried blood, but it does make me feel a tiny bit more human. Then I limp slowly back out into the corridor. It's a big hospital. Lots of ways in and out. I turn away from the signs directing me to the Main Exit and head inward, into the maze of bluey-gray corridors. Eventually, I see another sign, for North Exit. It will do.

It takes me a while. My bruised ribs protest at just about every breath. My back feels like someone has inserted a hot spike at the base of my spine and there is a constant dull ache in my skull. Still, it could be worse. She could have found me.

I reach the North Exit and push open the doors. The night air greets me with an icy slap around the face. After the suffocating warmth of the hospital it sends my body into a paroxysm of shivers. I stand for a moment, trying to contain them, gulping in the freezing air. Then I take out my mobile phone with trembling hands. I need to call a taxi. Need to get back to the cottage before . . . and that's when the truth strikes me with a dull, hollow thud.

If she is *here.* If she was driving along Arnhill Lane this evening, then she already knows where I live.

I lower the phone, just as I hear the rumble of an engine. And I know it's her, even before the sleek silver Mercedes pulls up in front of me and the window slides down.

Gloria smiles at me from the driver's seat. "Joe, sweetheart. You look terrible. Hop in. I'll drive you home."

THERE'S A MOMENT. Most addicts know. When you realize that your vice—whether it be alcohol, drugs or, in my case, gambling—has become a real problem.

My moment of enlightenment came when I met Gloria. In fact, you might say that Gloria saved me from myself.

Up until then I think I had just about been able to pretend that it was all still a hobby, a game, a distraction. Despite losing my job, my friends, my savings, my car and pretty much every night to the lure of the green baize and the crisp shuffle and flip of the cards, I had it under control.

Funny how the biggest bluffs are the ones you pull on yourself.

My grandparents taught me to play cards. Gin rummy, Pontoon, Newmarket, Sevens and, finally, poker. We played for pennies, which they kept in a big glass jar. Even at age eight, I found it fascinating, and addictive. I loved the faded swirly red pattern on the backs of the cards, the different suits, the two-faced ace (now I'm high, now I'm low), the imperious kings and queens and the slightly sinister, caddish-looking jacks.

I loved watching my grandad deal, flicking out cards as fast as lightning with his yellow, callused fingers; fingers that looked rough and clumsy yet could be so dexterous and light with a pack of playing cards.

I tried to copy the shuffles, the cuts, the sleight of hand. Some of my happiest times as a child were spent sitting at the chipped Formica table in their tiny, grease-stained kitchen, a glass of flat cola in front of me, stout for my grandad, lager and lime for Nan, staring at our cards as their cigarettes burnt down to the filters in the ashtray.

I taught Annie some of the same games. Mum and Dad never had time to play so it wasn't quite the same. You usually needed a minimum of three people, but we still whiled away many rainy afternoons playing Snap or Patience.

After the accident, I stopped playing. I concentrated on my studies. Decided to enroll in teacher-training. I liked English, it seemed a decent job (one that might even make my mum proud) and perhaps a part of me thought that it was a way to do something good. To help kids and make up for all the stuff I had done wrong as a kid myself.

To my surprise, I was a good teacher. There was even talk, in one school, of promotion: head of year, progression to deputy head. I should have been happy; at the very least, content. But I wasn't. Something was missing. There was a void inside me that nothing, not work, friends or girlfriends, could fill. Some days, my whole life felt unreal. As if reality had ended when Annie died and everything since had just been a bad copy.

Somewhere along the way I picked the cards up again. I would usually find some like-minded acquaintances to play a few hands with in the pub after work. Like drinkers, other gamblers manage to seek each other out. But soon the friendly games, betting pounds or fivers, weren't enough.

I met a man. There's always a man. A game-changer. A devil who appears at your shoulder. I was getting ready to leave one night, a little worse for wear, when one of the regulars—a thin, pasty individual whose name I never knew or asked—motioned me over and whispered: "Fancy a real game?"

I should have said no. I should have smiled, pointed out that it was already late and I had work in a few hours, not to mention piles of neglected homework to mark. I should have reminded myself that I was a teacher, not a card shark. I drove a Toyota, bought my coffee from Costa and my sandwiches from M&S. That was my world. I should have walked away, got a cab home and got on with my life.

That's what I should have done. But I didn't.

I said: "Where?"

And later, much later, when I realized I was out of my depth, when the debts had begun to pile at my feet like unexploded grenades, when I had sold the Toyota, left my job, been turned down by every lender; when I was dragged into the back of a van one night, to find Gloria sitting there, smiling her American cheerleader meets American Psycho smile . . .

That's when I said, "No. *Please, no!*"

I don't limp these days because of a car accident twenty-five years ago, although I did, for a while. But that limp had gone, the scars long

healed, when Gloria placed one candyfloss-pink nail against my lips
and whispered sweetly:

"Don't beg, Joe. I can't bear a man who begs."

I stopped begging. And started screaming.

SHE TAPS HER NAILS against the steering wheel—a glittery red tonight.
Human League blasts out of the stereo.

Every atom cramps in terror. The other thing Gloria likes, aside
from hurting people, is eighties music. I can't listen to Cyndi Lauper
without rushing to the toilet to vomit. It makes eighties nights something of a no-no.

"How did you find me?"

"I have my ways."

My heart stalls. "Not Brendan?"

"Oh, no. Brendan's just fine." She gives me a chiding look. "I don't
go around hurting people for no reason. Not even you."

I feel relief and, stupidly, gratitude. Then something occurs to me.

"What about the other two? The ones who attacked me?"

"Ah, Dumb and Dumber. Dislocated shoulder and a broken nose.
I went easy. Didn't take much for them to run off."

No, I think. I bet it didn't. Gloria might look like a delicate china
doll. But the only doll she has anything in common with is Chucky.
Rumor has it she was a child gymnast who changed her specialty to
martial arts. She was banned from competitions after putting an
opponent in a coma. The woman is fast, strong and knows every
vulnerable spot in the human body. Some, even anatomists haven't
discovered yet.

She glances at me. "They'd have killed you if I hadn't intervened."

"And saved you a job."

She tuts. "You're no good to me dead. Dead men do not pay their
debts."

"Reassuring."

"And the Fatman still wants his cash."

"Do people really call him that, or is it just a name he got from a
comic book?"

She chuckles throatily. "You see, that's exactly the type of comment that makes him hire people like *me* to hurt you."

"Nice chap. I must meet him one day."

"I wouldn't recommend it."

"I'm working on getting the money. I have a new job."

"Joe, forgive me for being blunt, but a few quid here and there is not going to cut it. Thirty grand. That's what the Fatman wants."

"*Thirty?* But that's way more—"

"Next month he'll want forty. You know how this works."

I do. I nod. "I have a plan."

"I'm listening."

"There's a man here. He wants me to leave the village. Badly."

"This wouldn't be the same man who got those thugs to beat you up tonight."

"Yes."

"And now he's going to hand you a big wad of cash?"

"Yes."

"And why is he going to have this change of heart?"

Because of what happened. *Because of what he did.* Because, as he said himself, he has a nice life here, and I could screw it all up, just like that.

"He owes me," I say. "And he really doesn't want me stirring up trouble for him."

"Interesting. Who is this man?"

"A councillor and successful businessman."

She signals to turn into the village. "I like a public figure. There are just so many ways to fuck up their lives, don't you think?"

"I've never given it that much thought."

"Oh, you should. They're the easiest ones to hurt. The ones with the most to lose."

"In that case, I should be unbreakable."

"Well, no one is that. But physical pain is the easiest to recover from."

Right now, just about every part of my body would beg to disagree, but I don't reply. Talking about pain with Gloria is a bad idea. Like taking a poacher on safari.

We drive along in silence for a while. She sighs. "I like you, Joe—"

"You have a funny way of showing it."

"I sense a hint of sarcasm."

"You crippled me."

"Actually, I saved you from being a cripple." She pulls up outside the cottage and yanks on the handbrake. "The Fatman wanted me to ruin your *good* leg."

She turns and rests a hand gently on my thigh. "Luckily for you, being a daft little woman from Manchester, I got a bit confused."

I stare at her. "You want me to thank you?"

She smiles again. It would be a nice smile, if it made it anywhere near her dead blue eyes. If the eyes are the windows to the soul, Gloria's reveal nothing but empty rooms covered in blood-spattered sheets.

She runs her hand down my thigh to my knee. And then she squeezes, hard. For a tiny woman, she has a powerful grip. In other circumstances this might be a good thing. Right now, all my breath is sucked out of my diaphragm. I'm in too much pain to even scream. Just when I think I might pass out, she releases me. I gasp and fall back in my seat.

"I don't want you to thank me. I want you to get me that thirty grand, because next time I won't be so fucking forgiving."

12

"Don't tell me," Beth says. "I should see the steamroller?"

I try to raise an eyebrow. It hurts. Just about everything hurts this morning. The only consolation is that it makes the pain in my leg bearable by comparison.

"Very funny." I sit down at the cafeteria table next to her. "Excuse me if I don't laugh, but I don't want to rupture anything."

She regards me with a smidge more compassion. Either that or she has something stuck in her throat. "What happened?"

"I fell down the stairs."

"Really?"

"They're very steep stairs."

"Right."

"Easy to trip."

"Uh-huh."

"It's almost like you don't believe me?"

She shrugs. "I just wondered if you'd managed to piss someone else off."

"You have a very low opinion of me."

"No. I just have a very high opinion of your ability to be annoying."
I chuckle. Predictably, it hurts.

"Well," she says, "at least you can laugh about it."

"Barely."

Her face softens. "Seriously, are you okay? If there's anything you want to talk about . . ."

Before I can respond, I catch a whiff of halitosis mixed with bad aftershave. I cough and push my sandwich to one side. To be fair, I wasn't very hungry anyway.

"Joey, man."

I thought I couldn't hate him any more, but the addition of an "ey" on the end of my name has just made it possible.

Simon drags out a chair and sits down. Today he wears a *Magic Roundabout* T-shirt over maroon cords. *Maroon.*

"Wow, what happened to your face, man? Or should I see the other guy?"

"He has really badly bruised knuckles," Beth quips.

Simon gives a feeble laugh. I sense he doesn't really like women who are smart or funny. Makes him feel inferior. Rightly so. And actually, my face got off lightly. Just a bruised eye and a cut lip.

"I fell down the stairs," I say.

"Really?" He shakes his head. "I thought it might have something to do with Stephen Hurst."

I stare at him. "What?"

"I saw you two talking in the pub last night."

"You were there?"

"Just having a quiet pint."

And spying on me. The thought leaps into my head unbidden. Paranoid. Maybe. But why not introduce himself?

"I didn't want to interrupt," he says. A rehearsed lie if ever I've heard one.

"What does talking to Stephen Hurst have to do with anything?" I ask innocently. If we're going to play Pretty Little Liars here, I bet I can win.

Simon smiles. I really wish he wouldn't.

"Well, between you, me and the lamppost . . . Stephen Hurst might give the impression of being a respectable councillor, but rumor has it he isn't averse to using less professional methods when people upset him."

"Meaning?"

"Meaning," Beth says, "Jeremy Hurst had a run-in with our last head of PE. Before the guy resigned, he had a run-in with someone's fists on the way home one night."

She glances at me and I realize: she knows. She knew from the minute I sat—painfully—down.

"Well, you shouldn't listen to rumors," I say evenly.

"Good point," Simon says, opening his chicken sandwich noisily and taking a bite, noisily. I bet he even sleeps noisily.

"Reminds me, though," he mumbles, "d'you remember Carol Webster?"

"Sorry?"

"At Stockford Academy. She was deputy head."

I try to keep a neutral face, even as my heart picks up pace, like a jogger with the finishing line in sight. Except I'm not quite so happy about where this road is leading.

"Afraid not."

Actually, I do. She was a vastly overweight woman with a huge halo of curly dark hair and a face that looked permanently disappointed—with herself, the school or the world in general, I was never sure.

"Well, she and I keep in touch on Facebook."

Of course you do, I think. Facebook is the place where people with no friends in real life keep in touch with people they'd never want to be friends with in real life.

"That's nice."

"She remembers you, or rather, she remembers you leaving."

"Yeah?"

"It was about the same time all that money from the school safe went missing."

I regard him steadily. "I think you've got your facts wrong—I heard the money was returned."

He makes a pretense of stroking his chin. "Oh yeah. I suppose that's why the police never got involved. Got kind of hushed up."

Beth looks at Simon. "Are you accusing Mr. Thorne of something here? Because you're being about as subtle as a frigging tank."

He holds up his hands in mock-surrender. "Oh no. Not at all. Just saying that's why she remembered him. Timing. Talking of which"—he glances at his watch—"I have a kid I need to see about a detention." He stands, grabbing his sandwich. "Catch you later."

"Yeah," I say. "Catch you later."

"Not if we get immunized against you first," Beth mutters, smiling sweetly.

I watch Simon's departing back and wish for a crater to suddenly open up beneath him or perhaps for the ceiling to cave in, or an instance of spontaneous human combustion.

"Don't let him get to you," Beth says.

"He hasn't."

"Bullshit. Simon is a bloody awful teacher, but one thing he excels at is getting under other people's skin. If you have an Achilles' heel, he'll find it and nip at it like a starving terrier."

"Thanks for the mental image."

"You're welcome." She pops a piece of pasta into her mouth: "Not true, is it?"

"What?"

"You didn't really steal all the money from your last school?"

"No."

I intended to. I really had sunk that low. But when it came to it, I couldn't.

Because someone else had got there before me.

"Sorry," Beth says. "Shouldn't have even asked."

"It's okay."

"I mean, I know Harry was desperate for a new English teacher, because, let's face it, the position is a bit of a poisoned chalice—"

"Like I said, forget it."

"But even Harry wouldn't—"

"*Forget it.*"

I've snapped. She stares at me. I don't want to piss off the one ally I have here.

"I'm sorry," I say. "I'm just in a bit of pain and—"

"No, it's fine." She shakes her head. Silver earrings glint. "Sometimes I don't know when to shut up."

"It's not that—"

My phone buzzes in my pocket. I'd like to ignore it. But then again, it might be Gloria. Gloria made it pretty clear last night that she isn't about to be ignored.

"Sorry," I say again. "I just need to—"

"Go ahead."

I slip the phone out of my pocket and glance at the screen. It's not Gloria. I stare at the text message. My skin prickles with a million tiny, icy pitchforks.

"Something wrong?"

Yes.

"No." I slip the phone back into my pocket. "But I've just remembered, I have to be somewhere."

"Now?"

"Right now."

"You've got class in thirty minutes."

"I'll be back."

"Good to know, Arnie."

I shrug on my jacket, and wince. "I'll see you later."

"Watch your step."

I frown. "Why?"

She cocks an eyebrow. "You don't want to fall down any more stairs, now, do you?"

13

St. Jude's is a small soot-crusted building that looks more like a run-down scout hut than a village church. There is no spire, just an uneven and pitted roof, tiles missing, holes in places. The windows are grilled, the door boarded up. The only congregations filling its pews and raising the rafters are the nesting crows and pigeons.

I push open the gate and walk up the rutted pathway. The churchyard is similarly neglected. It hasn't been used for burials for a very long time. My sister and my parents were cremated at the large crematorium in Mansfield.

The headstones here are chipped and cracked, the inscriptions eroded by the weather and the passing of the years, some completely worn away. Tree roots have undermined a few of the oldest graves, toppling them over to be reclaimed by the grass and weeds.

We try so hard, I think, to mark our place on this earth. To leave something of ourselves. But in the end, even those markers are transitory, impermanent. We can't fight against time. It's like trying to run uphill on an ever-accelerating descending escalator. Time is always moving, always busy, always cleaning up after itself, removing the detritus of the old and sweeping in the new.

I walk slowly around the church to the rear. The ground rises a little; there are fewer headstones. I stand and look around. For a moment, I can't see her. Maybe she's gone. Maybe the text was just some . . . and then I spot her, lurking at the far end of the graveyard. Half hidden, overgrown with ivy and creepers.

The Angel. Not a memorial or a headstone. Apparently, she was placed here in the Victorian era by the owners of the mine. Some say it was after the family's twin daughters died as infants, but the grave was once exhumed (something to do with the church being worried about it being unmarked) and no human remains were discovered beneath.

No one really knows where she came from or to what purpose. She doesn't even look much like an angel these days. Her hands are broken stumps and her head has gone. She tilts a little, unsteady on her square stone feet. The once gracefully flowing robes are chipped and broken, crusted with furry moss, as though nature has wrapped an extra layer around her to keep her stony bones warm.

I bend down—a new and interesting burst of pain reminding me that I need to take some more painkillers soon—and brush away moss and grass from the base. The inscription is a little faded but still legible.

But Jesus said, "Suffer little children, and forbid them not, to come unto me: for of such is the kingdom of heaven."

I look again at the message on my phone:

Suffocate the little children. Fuck them. Rest in Pieces.

A long time ago a gang of teenagers sprayed graffiti all over the Angel. The same ones who brought a shovel and scythed off her head and hands, decapitating and maiming her. There was no real reason for the attack. Just mindless vandalism, spurred on by cheap cider and teenage bravado.

The dismemberment and spray cans had been Hurst's idea. But the words, I am ashamed to say, were mine. At the time, with a bladder full of booze and the jeering encouragement of the rest of our gang, I had felt pretty pleased with myself.

Later, hanging over the toilet, spewing out bile and shame, I had felt like shit. I wasn't religious, none of my family was, but I still knew what we had done was wrong.

Even twenty-five years later I feel discomfort at the memory. Funny how the good memories flit by like butterflies: fleeting, fragile, impossible to capture without crushing them. But the bad ones—the guilt, the shame—they hang on in there, like parasites. Quietly eating you away from the inside.

Four of us were here that day. Hurst, me, Fletch and Chris. Marie was absent. She hung around with our gang more and more—much to the irritation of Fletch, who resented a girl in our midst—but not all the time. Hurst probably told her about it, though. And in a school word gets around; rumors spread. Just because we were the only ones here that day doesn't mean that no one else knew.

Still, it *does* mean that whoever sent the text must have been at school with us back then. Perhaps the same person who sent the email? I tried to call the number. It went to voicemail. I sent a text. I'm not expecting a reply. I don't think the sender wanted a conversation. They wanted me to come here. But why?

I straighten and stare at the headless angel. She steadfastly refuses to offer me any divine enlightenment. I wonder what happened to her head and hands. The church probably stored them away, or maybe some weirdo took them for a memento, to keep under their floorboards. Better than a real head, I suppose.

I'm missing something. Something obvious. I regard the Angel's oddly tilted posture. And then it comes to me. I walk around the back and crouch down again.

Where the roots of the creepers have started to push her from the ground there's a hollow. A recess in the damp earth. Something has been wedged underneath. I stick my hand in, grimacing at the feel of the cold, dank soil. There's a package of some sort in there, bound up in plastic. It takes a couple of tugs and I pull it out, shaking off dirt and a few slugs and earwigs. I study the package, turning it over in my hands: letter-sized, about half the thickness of an average paperback. It's been wrapped in a trash bag and secured with electrical tape. I'm going to need scissors to open it. Which means I need to get back to school.

I slip the package inside my satchel (along with my notebooks and some essays I should probably be marking right now). I buckle the satchel up, stand and walk more briskly back around the church. I'm almost at the gate when I realize I'm not alone. A figure is sitting on the church's only small bench, beneath an aged sycamore. A familiar skinny, hunched figure. My heart sinks. Not now. I need to get back to school. I need to open the package. I don't need to play the concerned teacher or the good bloody Samaritan.

But then, another part of me, the irritating part—the part that actually gives a shit about kids and got me into teaching in the first place—gets the better of me.

I walk over to the bench. "Marcus?"

He starts and looks up, flinching slightly. The reaction of someone who only ever expects an insult or a blow.

"What are you doing here?" I ask.

He shifts, embarrassed, red-faced. "Nothing."

"Right."

I wait. Because that's what you have to do sometimes. You don't push to get kids to tell you things. You pull back, let them ease it out on their own.

He sighs. "I come here to eat my lunch."

It's on the tip of my tongue to ask why, but that would be stupid. Why did Ruth Moore eat her lunch in the bus shelter down the road from school every day? Because it was safer. A place to hide from the bullies. Better a urine-stinking shelter or a damp bench in a cold graveyard than the ritual humiliation of the cafeteria and the playground.

"Are you going to scold me for being off school premises?" Marcus asks.

I sit down beside him, trying not to grimace at the fresh twinge in my back. "No. Although I'm curious as to how you found a way past the security gates."

"Like I'd tell you."

"Fair point." I look around. "Isn't there a better place to hang out?"

"Not in Arnhill."

Also a fair point.

"Are you here to avoid Hurst?"

"What d'you think?"

"Look—"

"If you're going to give me some lecture about how I should stand up to Hurst because bullies respect you if you stand up to them, then you can take that crap and stuff it right back in your stupid satchel, along with your copy of the *Guardian*."

He glares at me defiantly. And he's right. Bullies don't respect you if you fight back. They just beat you harder. Because there are always more of them. A simple equation of numbers.

I try again. "I'm not going to tell you that, Marcus. Because it *is* crap. The best thing you can do is keep your head down, keep away from Hurst, and get through as best you can. You won't be at school forever, even though it feels that way now. But you *can* come to me. I'll deal with Hurst. You can count on that."

He stares at me for a moment, trying to decide whether I'm feeding him a line or he really can trust me. It could go either way. Then he gives a very small nod:

"It's not just me. Hurst picks on loads of kids. Everyone's shit scared of him . . . even the other teachers."

I think about what Beth said in the pub. About Hurst being in Julia Morton's form group. About Ben going missing.

"What about Mrs. Morton? She was his class adviser last year, wasn't she?"

"Yeah, but she wasn't scared of him. She was more . . . like you."

Bearing in mind she killed her son and blew her own head off, I'm not sure whether to take that as a compliment.

"Did you know Ben Morton?" I ask.

"Not really. He was only a first-year."

"What about Hurst? Did Hurst bully Ben?"

He shakes his head. "Hurst didn't pick on Ben. Ben was popular. He had mates—" He hesitates.

"But there was something?"

He throws me a sideways glance. "A lot of the younger kids, they want to impress Hurst. Be on his good side. Be one of his gang."

"And?"

"Hurst would make them do stuff . . . to prove themselves."

"Like an initiation?"

He nods.

"What sort of stuff?"

"Just stupid dares and things. Pathetic, really."

"On school premises?"

"No. There's this place Hurst knows about . . . up on the old colliery site."

My blood slows and chills.

"*On* the old colliery site? Or *under* it? Did he find something up there—tunnels, caves?"

My voice has risen. He stares at me. "I don't know, okay? I never wanted to be one of Hurst's fucking gang."

I've pushed too hard. And he *does* know. He's just not ready to say yet. I already have a pretty good idea anyway. For now, I let the moment slide. We can come back to it another time. With kids like Marcus there is always another time. Hurst might be indiscriminate in his bullying but, like parents, every bully has a favorite, even if they don't say so.

I glance around the graveyard again. "You know, when I was a kid we used to hang around here sometimes."

"You did?"

"Yeah, we'd . . ." *vandalize angels* ". . . drink, smoke, other stuff. I probably shouldn't be telling you this."

"I like to look at the old graves," he says. "The people's names. I like to imagine what their lives were like."

Short, hard and miserable, I think. That's what most people's lives were like in the nineteenth century. We romanticize the past, with our period dramas and glossy film adaptations. A bit like we do with nature. Nature isn't beautiful. Nature is violent, unpredictable and unforgiving. Eat or be eaten. That's nature. However much Attenborough and Coldplay you wrap it up in.

"Most people had hard lives back then," I say to Marcus.

He nods, suddenly enthused. "I know. Do you know the average age people lived to in the nineteenth century?"

I hold up my hands. "English, not history."

"Forty-six, if you were lucky. And Arnhill was an industrial village. Lower-class, manual workers died younger. Lung infections, mine accidents and, of course, all the usual diseases—smallpox, typhoid, et cetera."

"Not the best time to be born."

His eyes light up. I sense we have found his chosen subject. "That's the other thing. In the eighteen hundreds women had an average of eight or ten children. But many would die in infancy or before they reached their teens." He pauses to let this sink in. "Ever noticed something weird about this place?"

I look around. "You mean, aside from all the dead people?"

His face closes again. He thinks I'm making fun of him.

"Sorry. Flippancy. Bad habit of mine. Tell me?"

"What's missing from the graveyard?"

I look around. There *is* something. Something obvious. Something I should have noticed before. I can feel it at the back of my mind, but I can't quite grasp it.

I shake my head. "Go on—"

"There's not one baby or young person buried here." He stares at me triumphantly. "Where are all the children?"

14

When Annie was about three, she asked me: "Where are all the snowmen?"

It wasn't quite so random. It was November and it had snowed quite heavily a couple of days before. All the kids in the village had run outside, chucking snowballs around and rolling them into huge misshapen lumps that looked nothing like the snowmen you see in films or on Christmas cards. Real snowmen never do. They're usually far from round and the snow is never white, mixed in with a fair bit of mud, grass and, occasionally, dog shit.

Still, that weekend there were lots of these oddly formed, ugly snowmen leaning lopsidedly around. In every park, garden and yard. From Annie's window, you could see quite a few outside other people's houses. We made one of our own, of course, and although it was small, it wasn't that bad. It had coal for its eyes and mouth, and an old woolen hat of mine perched on its head. The arms I made from two school rulers—there weren't any trees or twigs around on our street.

Annie loved our snowman and would get up excitedly in the morning to peer out of her window and check he was still there. Then, on day three, the temperature rose, it started to rain and, overnight, the snow and all the snowmen pretty much disappeared.

Annie rushed to look out of her window and her face fell at the sight of the scattered lumps of coal, sodden hats and dismembered makeshift limbs.

"Where are all the snowmen?"

"Well, the snow has gone," I said.

She looked at me impatiently. "Yes, but where are all the *snowmen*? Where did *they* go?"

She couldn't understand that, when the snow melted, the snowmen went too. To her, they were a separate thing. Real, solid, substantial. Snow*men*. Once created, they couldn't just disappear. They had to go *somewhere*.

I tried to explain. I told her we could make another snowman when it snowed again. But she just said: "It won't be the same. It won't be *my* snowman."

She was right. Some things are like that—unique, transient. You can copy, re-create, but you can never bring them back. Not the same.

I just wish Annie hadn't had to die for me to realize that.

I SIT ON THE SOFA in my coat, the mysterious package on the coffee table in front of me. I didn't have a chance to open it at school. When I got back I was already late for my next class. I had to use the break to catch up on grading, and by the time I made it through the last period I just wanted to get out of the building.

I even declined the offer of a Friday-night drink with Beth, Susan and James in the Fox. Something I'm now regretting. Good company and a cold pint in a warm pub, even if it is the Fox, suddenly seems a much better option than a cold cottage with no TV and the only company my skittering, chittering bathroom buddies.

I stare at the package. Then I pick up the scissors I found in a kitchen drawer and carefully slit open the plastic bag. Inside is a folder bulging with papers and held together with two elastic bands.

Scribbled on the front in black ink, just one word: "Arnhill."

I reach for my drink and take a large gulp.

Every town, village and city has a history. Often more than one. There's the official history. The bone-dry version collated in textbooks and census reports, repeated verbatim in the classroom.

Then there's the history that is passed down through generations. The stories exchanged in the pub, over cups of tea while babies squirm in buggies, in the work cafeteria and the playground.

The secret history.

In 1949 a cave-in at Arnhill Colliery buried eighteen miners beneath several tons of rubble and suffocating dust. It became known as the Arnhill Colliery Disaster. Only fifteen bodies were ever recovered.

Locals would recall how the bellowing tremor shook the whole village. At first people thought it was an earthquake. People ran, panicking, out of their houses. The teachers ushered children quickly out of their classes. Only the older villagers didn't run. They remained, supping their pints and exchanging troubled looks. They knew it was the pit. And when the pit roared like that, you were probably already too late.

After the roar came the dust: black, billowing clouds that filled the sky and eclipsed the sun. The high-pitched wail of the colliery alarm shrieked to the dark heavens, followed by the sirens: ambulance, fire and police.

There were reports and inquiries. But no one was ever held to account for the accident. And the three lost miners remained buried, deep beneath the ground.

Officially.

Unofficially—because who would ever tell such things to an outsider or a newspaper?—many swore, my grandad included (especially after a few pints), that they had seen the missing men, up on the colliery site, at night. One urban legend—retold with fresh embellishments each time—had it that a few of the surviving crew were sitting drinking in the Bull after hours one night when the door burst open and Kenneth Dunn, the youngest of the men lost that day, at just sixteen, walked right up to the bar. Bold as day and black as the night with coal dust.

Allegedly, the barman put down the glass he was drying, looked the dead lad up and down and said: "Get out of here, Kenneth. You're under age."

A good ghost story, and every village has plenty of those. Of course, no miner would admit to being in there that night. And when asked about it, the barman (long retired by then) would just tap his red-veined nose and say: "You'd have to buy me a lot of drink to tell you that tale."

No one ever did buy him enough drink. Although plenty tried.

Just off the high street stood the Miner's Welfare. Not the original building. That was demolished in the sixties when subsidence caused a wall to collapse, crushing several miners and their families. Two women and one toddler died. People claimed that the little boy still roamed the new building, and sometimes you'd see him in the long, dark corridor between the main bar and the toilets.

As a kid, left to sip soda while Dad downed beer and Mum drank half a lager and lime while rocking Annie in her pram (because Friday was Family Social Night at the Welfare), I would will my bladder to hold until we got home. If I absolutely had to go, I'd run as fast as I could down that dingy corridor to the toilets and back, terrified that one night I might feel a cold hand around my wrist and turn to see a tiny boy, face still smeared with dust, clothes ragged and torn, a bloody red dent in his head where his skull had been crushed.

In 1857 a man by the name of Edgar Horne stabbed his wife to death and was hanged from a lamppost by a lynch mob, his body left in a shallow grave on unconsecrated ground. Legend had it that he was still alive when he was buried. He clawed his way out and could sometimes be seen, dirt crusted on his hair and clothes, sitting by his wife's headstone. On Bonfire Night, instead of a guy, for years the tradition in Arnhill was to burn an effigy of Edgar Horne. To make sure that, this time, he was really dead.

My dad would always scoff at such things. If he heard Grandad telling the story about Kenneth Dunn, his face would darken and he'd say: "Leave it, Frank. There's more hot air spouted out your mouth than out the pit stack."

But sometimes, the way he said it made me think he wasn't angry but afraid. His words not derision but a defense, against stuff he'd rather not think about.

Even my dad couldn't deny that Arnhill was a village plagued by misfortune. There were never any more fatal accidents down the pit, but several smaller ones claimed time, money and, in one case, a miner's legs. The pit gained a reputation for being jinxed. Some miners were reluctant to send their sons down there. Despite still being profitable—with tons of coal beneath the surface—in 1988 the decision was made to close Arnhill Colliery for good.

Whatever remained down there would be left, abandoned and undisturbed.

I FLIP THROUGH PAGE AFTER PAGE of the folder. It makes for morbidly fascinating reading. Some of it I know, or thought I knew. There are details I wasn't aware of. Facts obscured in the retelling. I had always imagined Edgar Horne as a boorish monster. In fact, he was a doctor, respected in the community. Until one hot summer night he went to church, ate a supper of potato broth and cut his wife's throat with a scalpel as she slept.

Remarkably, no villagers were ever held accountable for his lynching. All covering each other's backs. I wonder how many of their descendants still live in Arnhill today and how many know—or care—about the blood on their forefathers' hands.

Further back, the history of the village becomes vaguer: the usual tales of poverty, disease and untimely death. A lot of death. Some pages have been highlighted. I lift one of them out:

NOTTINGHAMSHIRE'S SALEM

During the sixteenth century witch hunts were prolific across Europe. The trials in Arnhill began when a young man by the name of Thomas Darling accused his aunt of consorting with devils to bring babies back from the dead. According to Darling, Mary Walkenden took ill babies up to caves in the hills and exchanged their souls for eternal life.

The name Darling doesn't ring a bell, but I remember a Jamie Walkenden at school. The bus really does never leave, I think. Generation after generation. Born, living, dying here.

I place the page to one side and pick out another.

EZEKERIAH HYRST—MIRACLE MAN (1794–1867)

Hyrst was a renowned spiritual faith healer, alleged to have performed many miracles. Witnesses claim that Hyrst cured a young boy of paralysis of the legs, banished the devil from a woman and gave breath to a stillborn baby. Most of these took place in Nottinghamshire, in a small village called Arnhill.

Hyrst? Hurst? Not a coincidence, surely? And a charlatan healer seems to fit the family tradition. Miracles and tragedies. Tragedies and miracles. You can't have one without the other.

I turn over the next page. My breath feels like it's been sucked from my lungs.

SEARCH FOR MISSING EIGHT-YEAR-OLD CONTINUES

Annie's face smiles back at me. Wide, gappy smile, hair in a high ponytail. Mum always tried to plait it, but Annie would never sit still for long enough. Always wanting to be off doing something else. Always looking for adventure. Always following me. I don't need to read this story. I lived it. I push the folder away, reach for my drink and realize the glass is empty. Odd how that happens. I stand. And then I pause. I thought I heard something. A creak from the hallway. A floorboard? *Shit.* Gloria?

I turn, and my legs almost give out on me. Not Gloria.

"Heyup, Joe."

15

Life is not kind. Not to any of us, in the end.

It adds weight to our shoulders, a heaviness to our stride. It tears away the things we care about and hardens our souls with regret.

There are no winners in life. Life is ultimately all about losing: your youth, your looks. But most of all, those you love. Sometimes I think it's not the passing of the years that really ages you but the passing of the people and things you care about. That kind of aging can't be smoothed away by needles or plumped out with fillers. The pain shows in your eyes. Eyes that have seen too much will always give you away.

Like mine. Like Marie's.

She sits awkwardly upon the sagging sofa. Knees together, hands clasped tightly on top. She is thinner—much thinner—than the blossoming teenage girl I remember. Back then, her cheeks were round, with deep dimples when she smiled. Her limbs were long and lithe, cushioned with the firm flesh of youth.

Now, the legs in skinny jeans are stick thin. Her cheeks are hollow. Her hair is still thick, dark and shiny. It takes me a moment to realize that it must be a wig, her eyebrows artful pencil lines.

I hover, equally awkwardly. I swept up the papers I had been reading back into the folder, which I clutch beneath one arm. I don't know how much Marie saw. I don't know how long she had been standing there, after she let herself in when I didn't hear her knock. At least, she *said* she knocked.

"Can I get you a drink? Tea, coffee, something stronger?"

The sentence makes me wince a little. *Cliché*, I mentally note, in red pen.

She tilts her head; her hair falls to one side, just like it used to. "How strong?"

"Beer, bourbon? Of course, you haven't tried my coffee—"

A tiny hint of a smile. "Beer, thanks."

I nod and walk into the kitchen. My heart is pounding. I feel a little faint. It's probably just my hollow stomach. I really should eat something. Or have a soft drink. More alcohol is just going to make me feel worse.

I open the fridge and take out two beers.

Before I return to the living room I open the cabinet beneath the sink and chuck the folder inside. Then I walk back and place a can on the coffee table in front of Marie. I pop mine open and take a deep swig. I was wrong. It doesn't make me feel worse. It doesn't make me feel better either, but that's not really the point.

I sit heavily in the armchair. "So, it's been a long time," I say, like the cliché-spouting machine I am tonight.

"It has. Are you going to tell me I haven't changed a bit?"

I shake my head. "We all change."

She nods, reaches for her drink and pops the tab. "Yeah. But we're not all dying of cancer."

The bluntness of her words takes me back. And then, as she tips back the beer, I realize. This is not her first drink.

"I presume you know," she says. "This is Arnhill, after all."

I nod. "How's the treatment going?"

"Not working. Tumor is still spreading. More slowly. But it's just delaying the inevitable."

"I'm sorry."

Cliché after fucking cliché. After the crash, I used to hate it when people told me how sorry they were. Why? Did you cause the crash? No? Then what are you sorry for, exactly?

"What have the doctors said?"

"Not a lot. They're too scared of Stephen to give me a straight answer. He says they don't know everything anyway. Reckons he can get me into a clinical trial in America. The Bardon-Hope Clinic. Some new miracle treatment."

Ezekeriah Hyrst—Miracle Man, I think, and then, hot on its heels: *Marie is not going to die. I will not let that happen.*

"Did he say what the treatment is?" I ask.

She shakes her head. "No, but I'd try anything." She fixes her sunken eyes on mine. "I want to live. I want to see my boy grow up."

Of course. And we'd all do the same. Even though there are no miracles. Not without a price.

I look away. We both swig our beer. Funny how the more you share, the less you have to say.

"You're teaching at the academy?" she says eventually.

"That's right," I say.

"Must be a bit weird?"

"A little. Now I'm one of the guards, not one of the inmates."

"What made you come back?"

An email. A compulsion. Unfinished business. All of those and none of those. Basically, I always knew I would.

"I don't know, really. The job came up and it seemed a good opportunity."

"For what?"

"How d'you mean?"

"It was just a surprise, hearing you were back. I never thought I'd see you again."

"Well, you know me—a bad penny."

"No," she says. "You were one of the good ones, Joe."

I feel my cheeks redden and suddenly I'm fifteen again, basking in the glow of her approval.

"What about you?" I say. "You never left?"

A small, lifeless shrug. "Things always seemed to get in the way, and then Stephen proposed."

"And you said yes?"

"Why wouldn't I?"

I think about a fifteen-year-old girl crying on my shoulder. A bruise around her eye. A promise that she would never let it happen again.

"I thought you had plans?"

"Well, they don't always work out, do they? I didn't get the grades I wanted. Mum was made redundant. We needed extra money so I got a job and then I got married. End of."

Not quite, I think.

"And you have a son?"

"You know I do."

"Yeah—real chip off the old block. Bet his dad's proud."

A glance so sharp I feel it sting.

"We're both proud of Jeremy."

"Really?"

"You don't have kids?"

"No."

"You don't get to judge then." She crumples her can. "Got another?"

"Are you sure?"

"Well, it's hardly going to kill me."

I stand and fetch two more cans from the kitchen. Then I pause. Marie must have driven here. I saw her slip her car keys into her handbag. She probably shouldn't drink any more and drive home.

Not my problem, though. I walk back through and hand her a beer. She looks around and shivers.

"This place is cold."

"Yeah, the heat doesn't work very well."

But that's not it.

"Why here?"

"It just came up."

"Like the job."

"Yeah."

"You're so full of shit."

And there it is. The bitter ball she's been waiting to cough up since she arrived.

"If you've come back to start stirring up the past—" she says.

"What? What are you scared of? What's Hurst scared of?"

She takes a moment to reply. When she does, her voice is softer. "You went away. The rest of us, we're still here. I'm asking you, just leave things be. Not for Stephen. For me."

And I get it.

"He sent you, didn't he?" I say. "His thugs didn't work, so he thought you might tug at my heartstrings, persuade me, for old times' sake?"

She shakes her head. "If Stephen wanted you gone, he wouldn't send me. He'd send someone to finish the job Fletch's boys started."

"*Fletch's* boys?"

Of course. Stocky and Unwise Hair. That's why they seemed familiar. I should have guessed. Fletch was always the brainless muscle when we were kids. Now, his offspring are carrying on the tradition.

"I really should have spotted the family resemblance," I say. "The way their knuckles dragged on the floor."

Her face flushes. And I do feel a tug inside. But it's not my heartstrings. It's the depressing yank you get on your guts when your worst fears about someone are confirmed.

"You knew about my welcome party?"

Which explains why she didn't ask about my bruised face when she arrived.

"Not until afterward. I'm sorry."

"Me too."

She stands. "I should go. This was stupid, a waste of time."

"Not completely. You can give Hurst a message."

"I don't think so."

"Tell him I have something of his."

"I doubt there's anything you have that Stephen wants."

"Call it a memento. From the pit."

"For Christ's sake—it was twenty-five years ago. We were just kids."

"*No*, my sister was just a kid."

It probably says something about me that I feel pleased when her thin, sallow face falls.

"I'm sorry about Annie," she says.

"And what about Chris?"

"That was his choice."

"Was it? Why don't you ask Hurst something else—ask him if Chris really jumped."

16

C hris found it. That was his knack. Finding stuff.
     Like me, he was an unusual addition to Hurst's gang: tall and
lanky with white-blond hair that stuck up like electrified straw and a
stutter that got worse when he was nervous (and like most awkward,
nerdy kids, Chris spent a lot of his schooldays being nervous).

No one could fathom why Hurst took him under his wing. But I
got it. Hurst may have been a bully, but he was also smart. He had a
way of knowing who to crush, and who to keep. And Chris had his
uses. I guess we all did.

While Hurst's casual associates were the usual mixture of posers
and brawlers, his inner circle was a little different. Fletch was the
muscle. The brainless thug who would laugh at Hurst's jokes, lick his
arse and smash heads. Chris was the brains. The misfit, the misun-
derstood genius. His flair for science helped us create the best home-
made stink bombs, ingenious booby traps for unsuspecting victims
and, once, a chemical explosion that caused the whole school to be
evacuated at the expense, and job, of a stand-in science teacher.

But Chris had another useful quirk. A feverish curiosity. A desire
to find out stuff, and to find stuff. A way of seeing things that other
people couldn't. If you wanted to get hold of some exam papers, Chris

would find a way to get them. A spot to stand in the fields to see into the girls' changing rooms, Chris could calculate the best vantage point. A way to break into the store and steal sweets and fireworks, Chris could devise a plan to do it.

If his skull hadn't smashed open in the schoolyard and his brilliant brains spilled all over the stained gray concrete, Chris would have grown up to be a billionaire entrepreneur . . . or a criminal mastermind. That's what I had always thought.

When he blustered into the kids' playground that Friday evening, late as usual, because Chris was always late—not fashionably, but red-faced, tie askew, food down his shirt and apologetically so—he was even more flushed and frantic than normal. Straight off, I knew something was up.

"All right, Chris?"

"The site. F–f–f–found. G–g–g–ground."

When nervous, Chris's stutter worsened; he became almost entirely incomprehensible.

I glanced over at Hurst and Fletch. Marie wasn't with us that evening, as she had to help her mum with some chores, so there was just the three of us, killing time, talking shit. In a way, it was a good thing. As much as I liked Marie . . . well, that was the problem. I *liked* Marie. Too much. And when she was with us, she was with *Hurst*, his arm slung proprietorially around her shoulders.

Now, he dropped his half-smoked cigarette to the ground, jumped down from the climbing frame and regarded Chris in the hazy evening twilight.

"All right, mate. Calm down. Fuck's sake, you sound like a fucking Speak & Spell."

Fletch chortled like someone had just filled his cigarette with laughing gas.

Chris's face flamed harder, cheeks fire-engine red in his pale face. His hair was tousled and tufted like a particularly windswept haystack and his sweatshirt was creased and crusted with dirt. But the thing I noticed most about him was his eyes. Always a startling blue, that night they blazed. Sometimes, though I didn't like to admit it, because it made me sound a bit weird and gay, Chris looked like some kind of beautiful crazed angel.

"Leave him," I said to Hurst.

I was the only one who could get away with speaking to Hurst like that. He listened to me. I guess that was my use. I was his voice of reason. He trusted me. The fact that I often did his English homework for him didn't hurt either.

I ground out my own cigarette. I never really liked them that much. Just like beer. The taste made me want to spit and wipe my tongue. Of course, I have grown older, wiser and more addicted since then.

"Breathe," I said to Chris. "Speak slowly. Tell us."

Chris nodded and attempted to rein in his manic huffing and puffing. He clutched his hands together tightly in front of him, trying to get control over his nerves and his stutter.

"Fucking retard," Fletch muttered, and spat a huge gob of phlegm onto the ground.

Hurst gave me a look. I reached into my pocket, pulled out a slightly melted Wham bar and held it out to Chris, like offering a treat to a puppy.

"Here."

Contrary to what is believed nowadays, a sugary snack was about the only thing that could calm Chris down. Perhaps that was why he nearly always had a constant supply of them.

Chris accepted the Wham bar, chewed a bit and then, still half chewing, said:

"Been up . . . up at the old mine."

"Okay."

All of us kids went up there and messed around sometimes. Before they started to demolish the old buildings we would sneak in and steal stuff. Useless stuff. Bits of old metal and machinery. Just to prove we'd been. But Chris went up there a lot. On his own, which was odd. But then everything about Chris was odd, so much so that it just became normal after a while. When I asked him once why he went up there so much, he said:

"I have to look."

"For what?"

"I don't know yet."

Conversations with Chris could be frustrating. I fought my irritation down as he struggled to find his words without them breaking into pieces on his tongue.

Finally, he said: "I found something. In the g–g–ground. C–c–could be a way in."

"A way into what?"

"The pit."

I stared at him, and it was weird. I felt like I had heard the words before. Or had been expecting them. A strange shiver ran around my body, like when you touch a shopping cart and your hand tingles with static. *The pit.*

Hurst loped over. "You found a way into the old mineshafts?"

"Fucking ace," Fletch added.

I shook my head. "No way. They were all blocked off and, anyway, those shafts are, like, hundreds of feet down."

Hurst looked at me then nodded. "Thorney's right. Are y'sure, Doughboy?"

Doughboy was Hurst's nickname for Chris because he was "soft as dough."

Chris looked between us, helpless as a giant rabbit caught in our headlights. He swallowed and said, "I d–d–don't know for sure. I'll show you."

It was only later, when I really thought about it—and I had plenty of opportunity to think about it—that I realized he never answered Hurst's question.

"A way into the old mineshafts?"

We presumed that's what he meant. But I don't think he did, even then. He meant The Pit. Like he already knew what it was. And The Pit was something very different indeed.

THE LIGHT WAS LOSING ITS GRIP on the day by the time we got up there. It was late August, the tail end of the summer holidays, and "the nights were drawing in," as my mum would say (which always made me think of someone taking a great big piece of charcoal and scribbling out the day).

I think we all had that feeling of stuff ending, like you always do when you're a kid and six weeks of holidays is almost over. I guess we also knew that this was our last summer of really being "kids." Next year we had exams, and plenty of our classmates, even in the nineties, would leave school straight for work, although not straight down the mine, like they used to.

By this point the old colliery site was just a great muddy scar on the landscape. Grass and scrubby bushes were starting to take a grip. But the place was mostly still black with coal dust and littered with rocks, rusted machinery, sharp fragments of metal and lumps of concrete.

We hauled ourselves through a gap in the ineffectual security fencing around the outside where signs like DANGER, FORBIDDEN and NO TRESPASSING might as well have read: WELCOME, COME IN and DARE YOU.

Chris led the way. Well, sort of. He scrambled and slid and tripped then stopped, looked around and scrambled and slid and tripped some more.

"Fuck, Doughboy—you sure you're going the right way?" Hurst panted. "The old shafts are back that way."

Chris shook his head. "This way."

Hurst looked at me. I shrugged. Fletch made a whirling motion at the side of his head.

"Give him a chance," I said.

We continued our awkward progress. At the peak of one steep, muddy summit Chris paused and looked around for a long while, like a large dog sniffing the air. Then he plunged down the almost sheer incline, scrabbling and skidding through the gravel and rubble.

"Fuck's sake," Fletch muttered. "I'm not going down there."

I admit I was tempted to turn back, but I also felt a strange, bubbling excitement. Like when you see a fairground ride and you don't want to get on it because it looks scary as fuck but another part of you *does* want to, really badly.

I glanced at Fletch and couldn't resist: "Scared?"

He glared at me. "Fuck you!"

Hurst grinned, never happier than when there was discord within the troops.

"Pussies!" he cried, and then, with a wild whoop, he plunged down the slope. I followed, more cautiously. Fletch swore again then did the same.

At the bottom I almost slipped on my arse but just managed to keep my footing. I felt gravel lodge in my trainers and dig into the soles of my feet. Overhead, the sky seemed to hang lower, heavy with impending darkness.

"We're not going to be able to see fuck all now," Fletch moaned.

"How much further?" Hurst asked.

"We're there!" Chris called back, and disappeared.

I blinked, looked around then spotted a flash of gray. He was crouched down in a hollow formed by a small overhang. If you looked quickly you wouldn't even see him in the dip. We scrambled down after him. Patchy grass and bushes had started to make a tentative hold on the ground nearby, offering further camouflage. There were several large rocks scattered around. Chris moved a couple and I realized he had placed them there on purpose, as markers.

He shoved away dirt and smaller stones with his hands. Then he sat back on his heels and stared at us triumphantly.

"What?" Fletch spat in disgust. "I can't see nothing."

We all squinted at the uncovered patch of earth. Maybe a bit more uneven and a slightly different color from the surrounding earth, but that was it.

"Are you putting us on, Doughboy?" Hurst snarled. He grabbed him by the neck of his sweatshirt. "Because if this is some kind of prank—"

Chris's eyes widened. "No prank."

I would think later that, even then, half choked by Hurst, he still didn't stutter. Not here.

"Wait," I said. I bent closer to the ground, brushed away a bit more dirt and felt my fingers touch something colder. Metal. I sat back. And suddenly, I saw it.

A circular shape in the earth, rusted almost the same color, but not quite. It looked a bit like an old hubcap, but if you looked closer you could see it was too large for a hubcap and too thick. There were small round lumps around the edge, like rivets. In the middle was another circle, slightly raised, with grooves in it.

"There," I said. "Can you see it now?"

I pointed at the ground and looked back at the others.

Hurst dropped Chris. "What the fuck is it?"

"It's just an old hubcap," Fletch said, echoing my first thought.

"Too big," Hurst said immediately, echoing my second thought. He looked back at Chris. "Well?"

Chris just stared at him, as if the answer was obvious. "It's a hatch."

"A *what*?"

"It's like an opening," I said. "To underground."

Hurst's face broke into a wide grin. "Fucking ace." He looked back at the circular shape in the ground. "So, what? Some sort of escape shaft for the mines or something. I think I've heard of those."

I never had, and my dad had worked down the mines most of his life, but I knew mines did have air shafts, to ventilate them. I didn't see how that would help us much, though. Those shafts were the equivalent of chimney stacks. They ran all the way up to the surface. A drop of around three hundred feet straight down. That wasn't a way in. That was suicide.

I was about to point this out when Hurst spoke again. "Go on, then," he said to Chris. "Open it."

Chris looked pained. "I can't."

"You can't?" Hurst shook his head in disgust. "Oh, for fuck's sake, Doughboy."

He bent and tried to grasp the edges of the metal, wedging his fingers underneath. But it was so big and heavy I could see he was having difficulty getting any traction. He grunted and heaved then yelled at the rest of us: "Well, come on, fucking help me, you bunch of twats."

Despite my trepidation, I complied, along with Fletch. We all dug our fingers into the dirt and tried to grasp the metal around the edges, but it was impossible. It was just too thick and too deeply embedded into the earth. It had probably been untouched for years. However much we pulled and twisted and tugged, it just wouldn't budge.

"Fuck this," Hurst gasped, and we all fell gratefully back onto the hard ground, arms aching, chests heaving.

I looked back at the strange metal circle. Yes, it was stuck fast in the earth, but if it was some kind of smoke or escape hatch, surely there ought to be a handle or lever so you could get it up quickly if necessary. That was the whole point of a hatch. But there was nothing, except that odd second circle, almost as if it wasn't put there to be opened at all. Not to let anyone in, or out.

"Right," Hurst said. "We need to get some proper tools and get it up."

"Now?" I said. The light had faded so fast I could only just make out the ghostly circles of their faces.

"What's the matter? You *wimping out*, Thorney?"

I bristled. "No. I'm just saying, it's almost dark. We're not going to have much time. If we're going in, we should be prepared."

Not that I wanted to go in at all, if indeed there even was an "in" to go to, but it seemed the best argument for now.

I thought he was going to argue back. Then he said, "You're right. We'll come back tomorrow." He looked around at us all. "We'll need flashlights." He grinned. "And a crowbar."

WE COVERED THE HATCH roughly with dirt and rocks and then, as a marker, Hurst left his school tie in a loose knot on the ground. No one casually walking past would think anything of it. Ties, like trainers and socks, were often scattered around the old colliery site.

Then, as the final trace of light withered from the sky, we started to trudge home. I'm not sure, but I think I glanced back once, a strange feeling of unease tickling the base of my neck. I couldn't have possibly seen anything from that distance, but in my mind I could still just make out the strange rusty hatch.

I didn't like it.

A crowbar. I didn't like that either.

17

After Marie has gone I can't settle. My leg is hurting again, and even the addition of a large bourbon and two codeine tablets can't ease the twitching nerves.

Sitting makes it ache. Pacing makes it throb. I curse and rub at it viciously. I try to distract myself with a book, some music, then I stand and smoke at the back door. Again.

My mind is also working overtime. *Suffocate the Little Children, Rest in Pieces.* It's happening again. The sender of the text must be the same person who sent me the email. And if they know about the Angel, then they must have known me all those years ago. Not Hurst, or Marie. *Fletch?* I'm not sure Fletch is capable of sending a coherent text message, not with the lack of opposable thumbs. So, who else? And more to the point, why, why, why?

My general state of befuddled confusion has not been helped by Marie's impromptu visit tonight. I'm not sure if I have done the right thing. If I have shown my hand too soon. A good gambler knows never to do that. Not without being damn certain what cards the other player is holding.

But then, I don't have much time. Certainly not as much as I thought. Because Gloria is here. Waiting. Impatiently. Tapping those glittery red nails. If I don't satisfy her demands soon, the game will be over. Because I will be dead, quite possibly with no hands at all. Or feet. Or anything that could be used to identify my body.

I chuck my cigarette out into the darkness and watch the glowing red tip dim and die. Then I turn, limp back into the kitchen and take the folder out from beneath the sink. Because who am I kidding? I was always going to read it. I pour another drink, walk into the living room and place it on the coffee table in front of me.

The twitching nerves in my leg aren't the only things that are restless tonight. I can feel the cottage shifting around me. The lights seem to ebb and dim occasionally—nothing new with a village electricity supply—but I can hear something too. A noise. Familiar. Troubling. That same faint chittering sound. It makes my fillings hum and the hairs on my skin bristle. Grating, external tinnitus.

I wonder if Julia sat here and tried to tune out the same insidious noise. Night after night. Or if it only came later? Chicken and egg. Did what happened to Ben somehow change the cottage? Or was the cottage already a part of it? The skittering in the walls and the creeping cold feeding Julia's fear and paranoia?

I drag my hands through my hair and rub at my eyes. The chittering seems to have grown louder. I try to ignore it. I thumb through the folder until, once again, Annie's face beams out at me.

SEARCH FOR MISSING EIGHT-YEAR-OLD CONTINUES. The headline. But not the whole story. Not even close.

Dad put her to bed that night. About eight. Or so he thought. He was drunk. As he was most evenings by then. Mum was at Nan and Grandad's house because Nan had had a "nasty fall" a few days before and broken her ankle and wrist. I was out with Hurst and his gang. It wasn't until the next morning that Mum discovered Annie wasn't in her bed, or her room, or anywhere in the house.

The police were called. There were questions, searches. Uniformed officers and local men, including my dad, spread out in uneven lines across the old colliery site and the fields beyond, hunch-shouldered against the pummeling rain, dressed in long black waterproofs that made them look like giant vultures. They trod slowly and wearily, as though in time to some somber internal beat, and brushed at the ground with branches and sticks.

I wanted to go with them. I asked, begged, but a kind-faced officer with a beard and bald crown placed a hand on my shoulder and said gently: "I don't think that's a good idea, son. Best you stay here, help your mum."

At the time, I was angry. Thought he was treating me like a child, a nuisance. Later I would realize he was trying to protect me. From finding my sister's body.

I could have told him it was too late to protect me. I could have told the police a lot of things, but nobody wanted to listen. I tried. I told them how sometimes Annie would follow me when I went out with my mates, sneak out of the house. I'd brought her back before. They nodded and took notes, but it didn't really change anything. They *knew* Annie had sneaked out of the house. They just didn't know where she'd gone.

The one thing I *couldn't* tell them was the truth, not the *whole* truth, because nobody would have believed me. I wasn't even sure I believed it myself.

Every second, minute and hour that passed the terror and guilt grew. I have never been more aware of what a coward I am than in the forty-eight hours that my sister was missing. Fear battled conscience, tearing up my insides. I'm not sure which would have won in the end if the impossible hadn't happened. I turn the page:

MISSING EIGHT-YEAR-OLD FOUND—
Parents' joy!!

I was in the kitchen making toast for Mum and Dad when Annie came back. The bread was stale and a bit moldy. Nobody had gone shopping since last week. I scraped off the mold and stuck it under the grill. It didn't matter. They wouldn't eat it anyway. I would just end up throwing it in the trash can with the previous day's uneaten meals.

There was a knock at the door. We all looked up, but no one moved. Three knocks. Did that mean news? We listened like it was Morse code. *Knock, knock, knock.* Good or bad?

It was Mum who broke first. Maybe she was the bravest, or maybe she was just tired of waiting. She needed release, one way or another. She shoved her chair back and staggered to the door. Dad didn't move at all. I hovered in the hallway. I could smell the toast burning, but neither of us moved to take it off the grill.

Mum pulled open the door. A policeman stood there. I couldn't hear what he was saying, but I saw Mum wilt and clutch the doorframe. My heart stuttered to a halt. I couldn't swallow. I couldn't breathe. And then she turned and screamed:

"*She's alive! They found her! They found our baby!*"

We went to the police station together (Arnhill had its own back then), squashed into the back of a blue-and-white police car: Mum and Dad wet-eyed with joy and relief and me a sweating mass of jangling nerves. As we climbed out of the car my legs gave and Dad had to catch my arm. "It's all right, son," he said. "It's going to be all right now."

I wanted to believe him. I really did. I used to think my dad was right about everything. Always trusted his word. But even then I knew. Things weren't all right. Things would never be all right again.

"She hasn't said very much," the officer told us as we walked down a long, pale blue corridor that smelled of sweat and urine. "Just her name, and she asked for a drink."

We all nodded.

"Did someone take her?" Mum blurted out. "Did someone hurt her?"

"We don't know. A dog walker found her wandering up on the old colliery site. She doesn't seem to have any physical injuries. She's just cold and a little dehydrated."

"Can we take her home?" Dad asked.

The officer nodded. "Yes, I think that would be best."

He held open the door to the interview room.

"Joe." Mum nudged me and, before I had a chance to gather myself, or make sense of anything, we walked inside.

Annie sat on a plastic chair, next to a lady police officer who obviously didn't have much to do with children, and looked awkward and uncomfortable.

There was a small cup of juice on the table and some uneaten cookies. Annie stared straight past them at the dirty, scuffed wall and swung her legs back and forth. Her pajamas were muddy and torn in places. The police had wrapped her in a blue blanket that was too big and no doubt intended for the adult prisoners who normally frequented the cells. Her feet were bare. And black with coal dust.

She clutched something to her chest, half hidden by the blanket. I could just see dirty-blond curls, pink plastic, one blue eye. My scalp prickled. Abbie-Eyes. *She brought her back.*

"Oh, Annie."

Mum and Dad ran over and wrapped her in their arms. They smothered her in kisses, getting covered in dirt and coal dust themselves but not caring because their daughter was back. Their little girl was home, safe and sound.

Annie remained still, face impassive, only her legs swinging back and forth. Mum slowly drew away, her face tear-streaked. She reached out and smoothed a hand down Annie's cheek.

"What happened, sweetheart? What happened to you?"

I hovered by the door, hoping that the officers would mistake my reticence for teenage awkwardness. Perhaps I was even trying to convince myself it was the reason I hadn't moved any closer.

Annie looked up. Her eyes found mine.

"Joey."

She smiled . . . and that was when I realized what was wrong. What was so terribly, horribly wrong . . .

I STAND. The closeness of memory feels suffocating, like it's choking me. I can taste bitter bile at the back of my throat. I stagger upstairs, making it to the bathroom just in time. I spew sour brown liquid into the stained sink. I pause, breathing raggedly, and then my stomach convulses again. More vomit forces its way out of my throat and down my nose. I clutch at the cold porcelain, trying to catch my breath and stop myself from shaking. I lean there for a while, waiting for my legs to regain some solidity, staring at the vomit-splattered basin.

Eventually, I turn on the tap and wash the lumpy brown contents of my stomach down the plughole. I spit a few times and breathe, slowly and deeply. The water from the sink gurgles noisily down the pipes.

That's not all I can hear. Now that I've finished vomiting, I'm conscious again of that invasive chittering, skittering sound. Closer. Insistent. All around me. I shiver. The cold is back too. *Creeping cold.*

I look over at the toilet. The brick still squats on top of it. I carefully lift it off. Then I reach for the plastic toilet brush and use the scraggy end to flip up the lid. I inch forward and peer inside. Empty. I look around. The shower curtain is closed. I grab the moldy edge and yank it to one side. The only thing lurking behind it is a scum of shower gel and a dirty sponge.

I walk out of the bathroom. The chittering, skittering seems to move with me. In the pipes, the walls? I advance along the landing, still brandishing the toilet brush. I glance in my bedroom. Nothing to see here. Something about this niggles at me. And then it's gone. I keep moving forward, toward Ben's room.

There's a smell. Not the toilet brush. This smell is rich, metallic. I've smelled it before. Another house. Another door. But the same feral scent, the same *creeping cold*, slithering through my guts like an icy parasite.

I grip the handle. Then I push open the door and quickly flick the switch. The bare bulb spews out a jaundiced yellow light. I look around. It's not a big room. Just enough space for a single bed, a wardrobe and one small chest of drawers. The room has been decorated. Several coats, I imagine . . .

I see all of this, but I don't really see it. Because all I see is red. Soaking the new mattress, running down the wall. Slippery, ruby rivulets slithering down from the words painted there.

Her writing. His blood.

NOT MY SON.

When did she decide? When did she realize? Was it a slow accumulation, the horror and dread building every minute, every hour, every day until she could no longer take it? The smell, the creeping cold, the noises. She already had the gun. But she didn't use the gun on Ben. She killed him with her bare hands. Consumed by fear, rage? Or did something happen that left her with no other choice?

I force myself to close my eyes. When I open them the blood and words have gone. The walls are bare and clean, the same shade of bland off-white as the rest of the house. Malevolent magnolia. I give the room a final glance. Then I back out and close the door. I rest my forehead against the wood, breathing deeply.

Just the cottage. Just playing with your mind.

I turn. My heart stops.

"Jesus!"

Abbie-Eyes sits on the carpet, halfway down the landing.

Pudgy plastic legs poke out in front of her, blond curls stick out in disarray, her wonky eye gazes off toward a dusty cobweb in the corner. The good blue eye stares up at me mockingly.

Hey, Joey. I came back. Again.

I stare around, as if I might spot some cheeky doll-depositing burglar creeping down the stairs, giggling at his little joke. But no one is there.

On unsteady legs I walk over and pick Abbie-Eyes up. The loose eye rattles. Her cheap polyester dress rustles stiffly. The weight of her, the feel of the hard, cold plastic in my hand, makes my skin squirm.

The urge to hurl her out of a window, into the overgrown back garden, is almost overwhelming, but I'm seized by an even more unpleasant image of her crawling back to the house, her plastic, rosy-cheeked face pressed to the glass, peering in from the darkness.

Instead, holding her at arm's length, like an unexploded bomb, I walk back down the stairs and into the kitchen. I open the cabinet under the sink, stuff her inside, along with the toilet brush, and slam the door shut.

Shit. My whole body is shaking. I'm not sure if I'm about to faint or about to have a heart attack. I pour a glass of water and gulp it down greedily.

I try to rationalize. Maybe I moved Annie's doll myself and forgot—some kind of alcohol blackout. I remember Brendan telling me how, in his drinking days, he suffered from hallucinations and memory loss. Once, he woke to find he had pushed a wardrobe down the stairs. He had no recollection of doing it or any idea why.

"'Course, I was a lot bigger back then." He winked. "Alcohol weight."

Brendan, I think. I need to talk to Brendan. I try his number. It goes to voicemail. This isn't comforting, despite Gloria's assertion that he is fine. Gloria is not, I don't think, a liar. But it would be good to hear his voice, even if it is just telling me to "feck off." It occurs to me that I have come to count on Brendan being around when I need him, his presence as familiar and comforting as an old pair of jeans, or my boogie shoes. Worry gnaws at my already ragged edges.

I limp back into the living room. The folder is still open on the coffee table. I haven't finished it. Some pages I skimmed. But I'm done for tonight. I get the message: Arnhill is a grim little village where a lot of bad things have happened. Jinxed. Cursed. Abandon hope all ye who enter here.

I start to pile the pages back into the folder. One of them catches my eye. It's another newspaper cutting:

TRAGIC DEATH OF PROMISING STUDENT

The picture: a smiling teenage girl. Pretty, with long dark hair and a glinting silver nose ring. Something about her smile reminds me of Annie. Despite myself, I scan the story. Emily Ryan, thirteen, a student at Arnhill Academy who killed herself with an overdose of alcohol and acetaminophen. Described as "bright, fun and full of life."

"You ever lost one?"

Beth's voice pops into my head. The student she talked about. Must be. But something about that is wrong. I sit down. It takes me a moment, my frazzled brain taking a while to haul itself up to speed. Finally, it clunks rustily into place.

I couldn't tell you what day it is most of the time, but I could recite whole passages from Shakespeare (if you were very unlucky. And I really didn't like you). I can memorize reams of text and random words. Just the way my mind works. I collect useless information like dust.

"One year, one day and about twelve hours, thirty-two minutes."

That's how long Beth said she had worked at Arnhill Academy. Which would put her start date at September 2016. According to this story, Emily Ryan died on March 16, 2016.

Of course, maybe Beth was wrong. Maybe she had her dates confused. But I don't think so.

"Oh, I'm counting."

Which means that Beth wasn't a teacher here when Emily Ryan killed herself. Emily Ryan certainly wasn't one of her students. So why did she lie to me?

18

I wake early the next morning. This is uncalled for. I half open one eyelid, groan and roll over. Annoyingly, my brain refuses to slip back into oblivion, even though the rest of my body feels like it has molded itself to the bed overnight.

I lie there for several minutes, willing myself back to sleep. In the end, I give up, peel myself from the mattress and swing my legs out, onto the cold floor. Coffee, my brain instructs. And nicotine.

It's a gray, blustery day, the wind herding clouds across the sky like a parent hurrying along recalcitrant children. I shiver and finish the cigarette quickly, eager to get back inside to the relative warmth of the cottage.

Already the events of last night have become indistinct, blurred in my memory. I take Abbie-Eyes out of the cabinet. In daylight, she looks harmless. Just an old, broken doll. A little worse for wear, a little unloved. You and me both, I think.

I feel bad now about sticking her beneath the sink. So I take her through to the living room and place her on an armchair. I sit down on the sofa and finish my coffee. Abbie-Eyes and me, enjoying a little morning downtime.

I try Brendan's number twice more. Still no reply. I re-read the newspaper article about Emily Ryan again. It makes no more sense this morning than it did last night. I try to distract myself by taking out a pile of papers to grade. I get about halfway through before I realize I have just written, "Feck, no!!!" beside one particularly clunky paragraph and give up.

I glance at my watch. It's 9:30 a.m. I have no real desire to hang around the cottage all day. And nothing else to occupy my time.

There's nothing else for it.

I decide to go for a walk.

THE FIRST TENTATIVE EXCAVATIONS in Arnhill began sometime back in the eighteenth century. The mine grew, expanded, was demolished, rebuilt and modernized over a period of two hundred years.

Thousands of men and families built their livelihoods around the mine. It wasn't a job. It was a way of life. If Arnill was a living organism, then the mine was its beating, smoke-bellowing heart.

When the mine closed it took the council less than two years to rip out that heart, although by that time it had long stopped beating. Soot and smoke no longer circulated around its steel arteries. The buildings had crumbled and been vandalized. Thieves had stolen a lot of the metal, fixtures and fittings. In a way, it was a mercy when the bulldozers moved in.

Finally, there was nothing left. Nothing except a deep wound in the land—a constant reminder of what had been lost. Some families moved, to find work elsewhere. Others, like my dad, adapted. The village limped its way back to a sort of recovery. But some scars don't ever really heal.

The rugged landscape rises in front of me, grown thick and abundant with wildflowers and grass. Hard to believe that once, in this same place, stood great industrial buildings. That beneath the earth there are still shafts and machinery, abandoned because it was too costly to remove.

But that's not all that lies beneath the earth. Before the mines. Before the machines that bore into the ground, there were other excavations here. Other traditions upon which this village was built.

I start to ascend, glad I brought my cane to aid my progress along the uneven ground. I found a way in through a narrow gap in the perimeter fence. From the trampled-down grass and bare earth on the other side, I guess it is a well-used entrance.

As a kid, I knew this place well. Now, it is foreign to me. I can't place exactly where I am or even where the old shafts used to be. And the hatch doesn't exist anymore. That was lost, along with our way in, thanks to Chris. For good, I thought. But I should have known. Some things won't stay buried. And kids will always find a way.

I stand at the crest of one steep hill to catch my breath. Even if I didn't have a crippled leg, I am not a man used to hiking and hill-climbing. I'm built for sitting at tables and perching on bar stools. I have never even run for a bus. I try to force my lungs to drag in some much-needed oxygen. And then I give up, pull out my cigarettes and light one. I thought that when I got out here I would feel some instinctive recall, a twinge, like an internal divining rod. But there is nothing. The only twinge I am feeling is from my bruised ribs. Perhaps I have worked too hard to forget. I am not sure if that makes me disappointed or relieved.

I stare around at the undulating lines of brown and green. Scraggy grass and hard thorny bushes, slopes of slippery gravel and deep hollows filled with muddy marsh water and swaying reeds.

I can almost hear them whispering to me: *You thought you could just stroll up here and find your way back? It doesn't work like that, Joey-boy. Haven't you learned anything by now? You don't find me. I find you. And don't you fucking forget it.*

I shiver a little. Perhaps this little hike up memory hill, like many of my actions, is a fruitless exercise. Perhaps the email isn't important either. Or the text. Or any of it. Maybe the best thing to do would be to get what I'm due and get out. I'm not the hero type. I'm not the guy in the film who goes back, solves the mystery and gets the girl. If anything, I'm the deadbeat friend who never makes it past the second act. What happened here was a long time ago. I've lived twenty-five years without having to revisit it. Why bother now?

Because it's happening again.

Who cares? It is not my problem. Not my battle. With any luck, the excavators will cause the whole rotten village to fall into the earth, and that really will be the end of it.

I start to turn but something catches my eye. Something fluttering on the ground. I stare at it for a moment. Then I crouch down and pick it up. A Wham bar wrapper. I'd recognize that bright blue and red anywhere. Chris's pockets used to be stuffed with them. If he had made it to adulthood, I doubt his teeth would have done the same.

I straighten and look down the hill. I'm sure it isn't steep enough. But still, I tuck the wrapper into my pocket and scramble down the slope. It's actually steeper than I gave it credit for at the top and half-way down my bad leg gives, my feet slip out from under me and I skid the remaining few yards on my backside.

I lie at the bottom for a moment, winded and shaken. Getting vertical again seems like an effort. I close my eyes and take a few deep breaths.

"You never called my mum."

I start and sit up. A young woman, her pale face framed by a hooded parka, stares down at me. She's holding a small, scruffy black dog on a lead. Something about her is familiar, and then it clicks. The charming barmaid from the pub. *Lauren.*

If she notices that I am lying prone, covered in dirt, it doesn't register on her face.

"I'm fine," I say. "Thanks for asking."

"Old bloke fell up here last year. Died of hypothermia."

"Thank God a good Samaritan like you found me."

I grab my cane and force myself clumsily to my feet. The dog sniffs around my boots. I like dogs. They're uncomplicated. Easy. Unlike people. Or cats. I reach to chuck him under the chin. His lips draw back and he snarls. I snatch my hand back.

"He doesn't like being stroked," Lauren says.

"Right."

There's a patch of missing fur, almost like a ring, around his neck: an old scar.

"What happened to him?"

"He got caught on some barbed wire, slit his throat open."

"Amazing he survived."

A shrug.

"Is he your dog?"

"No. Mum's. She's had him years."

"You walk him up here a lot?"

"I suppose."

"Many other people walk up here?"

"A few."

The words "blood" and "stone" come to mind.

"I hear some of the kids from school hang around here too."

"Some of them."

"When I was a kid, we used to do that. We'd look for ways into the old shafts."

"Must have been a long time ago."

"It was. Thanks for rubbing it in."

She doesn't smile. "Why haven't you called Mum?"

"I don't need a cleaner right now. Sorry."

"Okay."

She turns to go. I realize I am missing an opportunity.

"Wait."

She looks back.

"Your mum—she cleaned the cottage for Mrs. Morton?"

"Yeah."

"So she knew her?"

"Not really."

"But she must have spoken to her?"

"Mrs. Morton kept herself to herself."

"Your mum never mentioned Mrs. Morton acting oddly—seeming upset, disturbed?"

A shrug.

"I heard Ben went missing. You think he ran away?"

Another shrug. I try one last time.

"Was Ben one of the kids who came up here? Did they find something? Maybe a tunnel, a cave?"

"You should call Mum."

"I told you, I don't—" Then I catch myself. "If I call your mum, will she talk to me?"

She stares at me. "She charges ten pounds an hour. Fifty pounds for a deep clean."

I get the drift. "Right. I'll bear it in mind."

The dog edges toward my boots again. Lauren gives it a little tug on the lead. It wrinkles its gray muzzle at her.

"He must be pretty old," I say.

"Mum says he should be dead."

"I'm sure she doesn't mean it."

"Yeah, she does." She turns. "I have to go."

"See you then!" I call after her.

She doesn't return the farewell, but as she walks away I hear her murmur, almost to herself: "You're in the wrong place."

Weird doesn't really cover it.

A WHITE VAN IS PARKED outside the cottage when I get back. There's a picture of a large tap on the back. I make a wild guess that it belongs to a plumber. Bearing in mind my current bathroom issues, this would be fortuitous. If I had called a plumber.

As I draw closer my worst fears are confirmed. The name on the side reads: Fletcher & Sons Plumbing and Heating. I watch as the doors swing open. Unwise Hair climbs out of one side. Another figure, less familiar these days, climbs out of the driver's side. He spits yellow phlegm on the ground.

"Thorney. Fuck me. Never thought I'd see you back here."

I can't say the same. I always knew Fletch would never leave. Some kids, you just do. It's not that they don't want to move somewhere else. It's just that the thought that there *is* somewhere else has never even occurred to them.

"What can I say?" I hold out my arms. "I missed the warm welcome."

Fletch looks me up and down. "You've not changed."

Again, I can't say the same. If the years have not been kind to any of us, they've been really hard on Nick Fletcher. Always a blunt-faced youth—one of those kids who probably looked old even in nappies— he has lost the sinewy muscle that once made him such a formidable bouncer for Hurst. Now, he is thin to the point of skeletal. His shorn hair is a dirty nicotine yellow and his face is crisscrossed with deep creases that only illness or a lifetime of drinking and smoking can carve.

He walks up to me, Unwise Hair lurking behind in a way that I presume is supposed to be menacing but just makes him look a bit constipated. I note the swollen look of his nose and bruises beneath both eyes. Gloria. I wonder if his brother is still nursing his injured shoulder. I feel a sliver of satisfaction.

Fletch himself has the gait of a man—not dissimilar to me— battling some kind of pain or stiffness in his joints. Arthritis, maybe? The malformed knuckles of his hands are a further giveaway. I guess pounding heads takes its toll after a while.

As he draws nearer I can smell him. Juicy Fruit and cigarettes. All Fletch ever smelled of was Juicy Fruit and cigarettes. Perhaps he hasn't changed that much.

"You're not wanted here, Thorney. Why don't you do everyone a favor and fuck off back to whatever shitty stone you crawled out from."

"Wow. That was a long sentence for you. A bit clichéd. A slight mix of adjectives and verbs, but not bad."

His face darkens. Unwise Hair lumbers forward. I can sense the barely contained violence. He's not just ready to beat the crap out of me. He's eager for it. Slavering like a dog eyeing a juicy bone.

Like father, like son. Fletch always preferred to punch first and ask questions later. He didn't need an excuse to hurt someone, but Hurst helpfully gave him one. Fletch enjoyed smashing teeth and blacking eyes. He was a mean and dirty little fighter. And he didn't give in. I'd seen him take on bigger lads than himself and wear them down with sheer viciousness and persistence. If Hurst hadn't held his leash, I think, even then, he could have easily beaten someone to death.

He holds up one misshapen hand to his son, who stumbles to a halt.

"What do you want?"

"World peace, fair wages for all, a better future for our children."

"Still think you're funny?"

"Someone has to."

The hand wavers.

"I want to see Hurst," I say quickly. "I think we can come to an arrangement that will suit both of us."

"Really?"

"I have something he wants. I'm happy to give it to him. For a price."

He snorts. "You know, Hurst said to take it easy on you the other night. Maybe he's not feeling so generous now that you're threatening him."

"I'm willing to take the gamble."

"Then you're more fucking stupid than you look."

"Really? Because it looks to me like your son took a pretty good beating last night too." I smile at Unwise Hair. "How's your brother's shoulder?"

His face reddens. "You got lucky, cripple."

"Yeah," Fletch says. "No big mates around to help you now—"

Big mates? So his sons couldn't admit to being beaten up by a woman.

"And no one fucks with my lads," Fletch snarls. He lowers his hand.

Unwise Hair lunges. But this time I'm prepared. As he raises a fist I swing the cane. It catches him hard above his ear and he drops to the ground. I jab the cane into his stomach then smash it across his back. He folds like a particularly ugly piece of origami.

Fletch starts toward me. But he is older and slower than his son. I sidestep and bring the cane up between his legs. He yelps and crumples to his knees. I've picked up a few hints on causing pain myself over the years. I lean over him, panting slightly.

"You were wrong," I say. "I *have* changed."

He squints up at me, eyes full of tears. "You are so fucking dead."

"Says the man clutching his balls. Now you tell Hurst I want a meeting. He can choose the night. But it has to be this week."

"You have no idea what you're getting yourself into."

Unwise Hair starts to rise. He looks dazed, and is younger than I first assumed. I feel a twinge of guilt. But only a twinge. I swing the cane and smash it across his swollen nose. Blood spurts out. He screams and clutches at his face.

"No. *You* have no idea what I'm getting myself out of. You've got five minutes to get out of here or I call the police."

I turn and stagger toward the cottage. Now that the adrenaline is fading, my battered body is complaining loudly at my exertions.

Fletch shouts after me: "Your sister's dead. You can't bring her back . . ."

The sentence hangs. He doesn't finish it. He doesn't need to.

19

1992

We had agreed to meet back at the pit at 9 p.m. No one went up there that late and we didn't want anyone to catch us and ask what we were doing.

I planned to sneak out sometime after dinner. Mum was busy with a pile of ironing and Dad would be down at the pub. There was just something I needed to do first. I crept out of the kitchen door and over to the shed in the backyard. It was where Dad kept his tools and his old mining equipment.

I had to delve a bit, brushing aside cobwebs and dead spiders. Then I found it. An old work jacket, sturdy boots, rope, a flashlight and . . . *yes* . . . a miner's helmet. I picked it up, wiped off some dirt and fiddled with the light at the front. I half expected it not to work but, to my surprise, a robust yellow beam flared out.

"What are you doing?"

I jumped and spun around, almost dropping the helmet.

"*Shit!* What are *you* doing, sneaking up on me?"

Annie stood in the doorway, skinny silhouette framed by the fading evening light. She was dressed in her pajamas—pink, with a picture of a Care Bear on—and her long dark hair was pulled back in a ponytail.

My little sister. Eight going on eighteen. Funny, feisty, stubborn, silly. Stupidly intelligent, annoyingly sweet. Hilarious, frustrating, entertaining. The boniest yet somehow also the softest little body to ever envelop me in a gangly web of arms and legs. A toothy smile that could shatter the hardest heart. A tough little tomboy who still wanted to believe in Santa Claus and magic. But then, who doesn't?

"You shouldn't swear," she said.

"Okay, okay. I know. But you shouldn't sneak up on people."

"I didn't. You just weren't listening properly."

One of many pointless things in life is arguing with an eight-year-old. Doesn't matter how smart you are, eight-year-old logic always wins.

"Well, I was busy."

"Doing what? Is that Dad's?"

I hurriedly put the helmet back down. "Yeah. So?"

"So, what are you doing with it?" She suddenly noticed the backpack in my other hand. "Are you taking Dad's stuff?"

I loved my sister. I really did. But, at times, she was an unbearable pain in the neck. She was like a terrier. Once she had hold of something, she just wouldn't let go.

"Look, I'm just borrowing it, okay? Not like he uses it anymore."

"What are you borrowing it for?"

"None of your business."

She folded her arms and narrowed her eyes. A look I knew meant trouble. "Tell me."

"No."

"Tell me or I'll tell Mum."

I sighed. I was feeling tense and on edge. I didn't really want to go back to that weird hatch in the ground. Didn't really know why we were doing this, but I had to go through with it or I'd look like a chicken in front of the others, and now my eight-year-old sister was giving me grief.

"Look, it's just boring shi— stuff, okay. We're just going up the old mine for a bit."

She sidled closer. "So why d'you need Dad's stuff?"

I sighed again. "Right, if I tell you, you have to promise not to tell anyone else, okay?"

"Okay."

"We've found this hole that leads all the way to the center of the earth and we're going to climb down it because we think there's a lost world full of dinosaurs down there."

She glared at me. "You are so full of shit."

So much for not swearing. "Fine. Don't believe me then."

"I don't."

"Fine."

A pause. I stuffed the hat, clothes, rope and boots into my backpack, zipped it up and hefted it onto my back.

"Joey?"

I hated being called Joey by anyone except my sister, not least because it was such an easy insult.

"What?" I said.

"Be careful."

And then she ran back toward the house, feet bare and dirty, ponytail bouncing up and down.

I watched her go, and I'd like to say I had some shiver of premonition. That a cloud scudded across the sky carried by an ill wind. That birds rose and shrieked from the trees or a sudden crack of thunder broke the still of the evening.

But there was nothing.

That's the problem with life. It never gives you a heads-up. Never offers you even the slightest clue that this might be an important moment. You might want to take some time, drink it in. It never lets you know that something is worth holding on to until it's gone.

I watched Annie skip away—happy, innocent, carefree—and I had no idea that it would be the last time I would ever see her like that.

And I didn't realize that she had taken the flashlight.

WE STOOD AROUND THE HATCH. Me, Fletch and Chris. Hurst hadn't turned up yet. A part of me—a big part—hoped he wouldn't.

We all had on boots, dark clothes and heavy jackets, aside from Chris, who looked like he had ambled along for a day at the park, in a denim jacket, jeans and trainers. I was the only one who had brought

along a miner's helmet (and the backpack with the rope in) but everyone had flashlights. We were ready. Still, without any tools to prise
open the hatch, we were ready for nothing.

"Where the crap is he?" Fletch moaned, taking out a packet of
B&H.

I shrugged. "Maybe he's not coming."

Then we could all go home and forget about this stupid plan without feeling bad or looking chicken.

Chris scuffed his trainers. Fletch smoked his cigarette down to
the glowing butt. I pretended to look pissed off, checking my watch
but all the while feeling more and more relieved. I was just about to
suggest we call it a day and leave when I heard a familiar voice call
out: "All right, lads?"

We all turned. Hurst loped down the slope. He wasn't alone.
Marie scrambled down after him.

"What's she doing here?" Chris asked.

"She's my girlfriend, that's what."

I felt my heart slide down to my oversized boots. As well as the
fact that Marie was hardly dressed for pot-holing—in stonewashed
jeans and stilettos—she was also clutching a carrier bag with a bottle
of Diamond White poking out of the top.

"So, we all set then?" Hurst grinned and brandished the crowbar.
His voice sounded a little slurred.

"Ready." Fletch threw his cigarette butt to one side, where it glared
hotly like a resentful red eye.

Chris shuffled again, like he needed the toilet or was wearing too-
small shoes. He looked nervous, but not the same nervous that I felt.
A sense of restless agitation radiated off him.

"She shouldn't be here," he muttered, almost to himself.

Marie glared at him. "Are you talking about me?" she asked.

Despite the situation—and agreeing with Chris—I couldn't help
but notice that she looked really good tonight. Her hair was all kind
of tousled and the walk here (probably the cider too) had given her
cheeks a flattering pink flush. I swallowed and shuffled a bit myself.

She advanced toward Chris. "Are you saying I shouldn't be here
cos I'm a girl? Like I'm too pathetic to do the same stuff you guys do?"

Marie could be feisty, but there was something about her that night—again, possibly the cider—that had given her an even more confrontational edge.

Chris shrunk back. "No. It's just—"

"What?"

"Nothing," I said quickly. "Chris was just looking out for you. We don't know what's down there. It could be dangerous."

She looked as if she was about to argue again. Instead, her face softened.

"Well, that's nice, but don't worry. I can look after myself." She took the Diamond White out of the bag, twisted the cap off and took a swig.

"And if she can't, *I'll* take care of her," Hurst said, grabbing first her arse and then the cider and pouring several glugs down his own throat.

"Let's ger'on then," Fletch muttered. I could tell he wasn't happy about Marie being here either. But for different reasons. Fletch always thought of himself as Hurst's best mate. With Marie here, he moved down a notch in the pecking order.

"Fucking right," Hurst said, handing the cider back to Marie.

He swaggered over and wedged the crowbar under the metal rim of the hatch. On the first attempt, he stumbled; the crowbar slipped from his grip.

"Shit!"

He snatched it up and stuck it under the hatch again. Again, it slipped.

"Maybe it's stuck," I said.

He scowled at me. "You think so, *Brainiac!*" He looked between Fletch and me. "Help me, then?"

Reluctantly—certainly on my part—we both moved forward. Fletch got there first. He grasped the crowbar just below where Hurst was gripping it and they both bore down.

I stared at the hatch, willing it not to move. But this time there was a squeal. Rusted metal giving way after years of disuse.

"More," Hurst groaned, through gritted teeth.

They pushed down again, and now I could see the hatch rising. A few inches of darkness appeared between metal and earth. My bad feeling rose with it.

"Again," Hurst growled. Fletch roared, properly roared, and they shoved down once more.

The hatch rose further.

"Grab it!" Hurst yelled.

Chris and I bent down and grabbed the edges of the metal. Marie joined us. We all pulled. It was heavy, but not as heavy as I expected.

"One, two, three."

We hefted together and this time it gave, suddenly and unexpectedly. We staggered backward as it hit the ground in a cloud of dirt and dust, with a thud that I felt resonate up through the soles of my boots.

Hurst whooped in triumph. He threw the crowbar down and high-fived Fletch. Marie grinned like a loon. Even I felt a momentary rush of adrenaline. Only Chris stood by silently, his face impassive.

We all stepped forward and peered down into the hole. Fletch flicked on his flashlight. I adjusted the light on the miner's helmet. I expected to stare into darkness. A pitch black barely penetrated by our lights; a long straight drop into nothing.

That wasn't what I saw. What I saw was worse. Steps. Metal rungs stuck into the rock, like a ladder, and going straight down, way down. I couldn't even see the bottom of them. An icy chill slithered down my spine.

"Shit," Hurst muttered. "You were right, Doughboy. It *is* a way in."

But to what? I thought. What the hell did we think we would find down there?

Hurst looked back up. His eyes gleamed. I knew that look. Flat, dangerous, crazy.

"So who's going first?"

A pointless question. Because—

He turned to me. "Thorney, you've got all the gear."

Of course. I looked back down the hole. My guts churned. I didn't want to go down there. Nothing we could find at the bottom of that long, dark shaft could be good. Nothing about any of this was good.

"We don't know where it goes," I said. "Those rungs look old, rusted. They could give way. It could be a massive drop."

Fletch made a long, slow clucking noise. "What's the matter, Thorney? Chicken?"

Yes. I was. Pure, feathered, egg-laying chicken.

There are times in life when you need to make a choice. To do what is right or to bow to peer pressure. If I turned and walked away now, I would be doing the sane, sensible thing—the others might even follow—but I could forget about being part of Hurst's gang anymore. I could look forward to spending the remainder of my schooldays eating lunch in a bus shelter.

Still, at least I would be alive to eat my lunch.

"Joe?" It was Marie. She rested her hand on my arm. She smiled, a drunk, lazy smile. "You don't have to do this, if you don't want to. It's okay."

That decided it. I reached up and tightened the strap on my dad's helmet.

"I'll go," I said.

"Ace." Hurst clapped me on the back. He glanced around at the others. "All ready?"

Nods and murmurs of agreement. But I could see the nerves on Fletch's face. Only Hurst looked confident, buoyed up by booze and manic excitement. And Chris. Chris looked as calm as if he were taking a stroll to the shops.

"Right. Let's do this shit." Hurst grabbed his tie from the ground. He knotted it around his head and grinned. "First blood." Then, as an afterthought, he bent down and picked up the crowbar.

I stared at it, a strange, tight ball forming in my stomach. "What are you taking that for?"

He grinned again and slapped the crowbar against the palm of his other hand. "Just in case, Thorney. Just in case."

THE RUNGS *WERE* RUSTED, and narrow. I could just about get my toe on each one. They groaned and sagged as I placed my weight on them. I clung on desperately, praying that I could hold on for long enough to reach the bottom.

Above, I could hear the others coming after me, showering bits of metal and dirt down on my miner's helmet. Even though I'd felt a bit stupid putting it on, I was glad now of the protection, and the fact that it left both my hands free for gripping.

As I descended, I counted. *Ten, eleven, twelve.* At nineteen, my foot missed a rung. It flailed in the air and then found purchase on solid ground. Relief flooded through me. I stepped down. I'd made it.

"I'm at the bottom!" I shouted.

"What can you see?" Hurst's voice called down.

I looked around, the light from the miner's helmet casting a pale, yellow glow. I was standing in a small cave. Barely big enough to hold more than half a dozen people. Aside from what looked like a few animal bones on the ground, it was empty. I wasn't sure if I felt relieved or disappointed.

"Not much," I said.

Hurst landed beside me with a thud. Fletch, Chris and Marie followed. She clambered down awkwardly in her stilettos, still clutching the carrier bag of cider.

"Is this it?" she said.

Fletch panned his flashlight around then spat on the ground. "Just a shitty hole."

"Guess this was a waste of time," I said, trying not to sound pleased.

Hurst scowled. "Fuck this. I need a piss."

He turned to the wall. I heard him unzip his pants and the gush of urine hitting the floor. The acrid smell, strong with cider, filled the small space.

Chris was still staring around, frowning.

I glanced at him. "What is it?"

"I thought there'd be something more."

"Well, there's not, so—"

But he wasn't listening. He started to circle the cave, like a dog sniffing out a bone. Suddenly, he stopped, at a point in the rock where the shadows seemed to coalesce and deepen. He bent down.

And then he was gone. I blinked. What the hell?

"Where'd he go?" Marie asked.

Hurst zipped up his jeans and turned. "Where's Doughboy?"

"Here," a disembodied voice called.

I trained my light in the direction of the voice. And now I saw it.
A gap in the rock. About four feet high, and narrow. Easy to miss,
unless you were looking hard. Or you knew it was there.

"It goes deeper!" Chris called from the darkness. "There are more
steps."

"That's more fucking like it!" Hurst exclaimed.

He shoved me out of the way and squeezed straight through after
Chris. After a moment's hesitation, and another swig of cider, Marie
followed, and then Fletch.

I sighed, inwardly cursing Chris, and bent down to go after them.
My head clanged against the rock. The miner's helmet. It was too
wide. The light wavered and went out. Crap. I must have knocked the
battery. I edged backward and took the helmet off. I'd have to carry
it sideways. I started to shuffle through and then hesitated. I thought
I'd heard something. A scraping and a rattle of stones. The sound
had come from behind me, from the metal rungs we'd climbed down.

I looked around, but without the light all I could see were shadows and dancing spots in front of my eyes.

"Hey?" I called. "Anyone there?"

Silence.

Stupid, Joe. There was no one there. The noise was probably just
the wind, gusting down the open hatch. How could there be anyone
here? No one knew about the hatch. No one knew *we* were here. No
one at all.

Ain't nobody here but us chickens, I thought, a little crazily, remembering an old song my nan used to play. *Ain't nobody here at all.*

I gave the darkness a final searching glance. Then I turned,
squeezed through the gap and started down after the others.

20

"G ood weekend?"

Beth emerges at my side from amid a throng of pupils.

She is looking fresh-faced and perky and all the things I generally hate to see in someone at just before eight-thirty on a Monday
morning.

I look at her from beneath eyelids weighted with lead. "Just dandy."

She squints at me more closely. "Really? Cos you look like crap."

I shuffle along the corridor. "That's what a good weekend will do
for you."

"Yeah. Guess when you get to your age the hangovers take longer
to get over."

"*My* age?"

"You know, the middle. Stuff of crisis, spread and prostate exams."

"You really are a little ray of sunshine on a dismal Monday morning, aren't you?"

"Oh, I haven't got to my best stuff yet."

"Let's pretend you've peaked."

She winks. "Oh, you'd know when I've peaked."

"Doubtful. At *my* age."

She chuckles, low and hearty, and actually, it does go a tiny way to
lightening my current dark mood.

So why did she lie?

I'm just trying to work out a way to ask her when a Year 9 with boy-band hair and a uniform on the borderline of acceptable skids around the corner, almost colliding with us, before he manages to gather in his momentum and screech to a halt.

"Anyone mention no running in the corridors?" I say briskly.

"Sorry, sir, miss, but you need to go to the toilets."

"I already went, thanks."

Beth throws me a look.

"What's up?" she asks.

He fidgets nervously. "I think you should just go and see, miss."

"We need more than that," I say.

"It's Hurst—he's got some kid in there and—" He falters. No student likes being a snitch.

"Okay. We're on it." I nod my head to indicate he can go. "And don't worry—you never saw a thing."

Gratefully, he hurries off down the corridor.

I look at Beth. She sighs. "There goes my coffee."

I CAN HEAR MUFFLED SHOUTS and laughter as we approach. I push at the door. Someone is holding it shut from the other side.

"Piss off. It's engaged."

"Not anymore it isn't."

I shove the door with my shoulder and we burst in. The kid holding the door stumbles into the urinals. I take in the scene. Three of Hurst's cronies stand in a loose semicircle. Hurst kneels over a kid on the floor, a Tupperware box at his side. I grab his arm and haul him up.

"You. Stand over there."

I turn to the kid on the floor. My heart sinks. Marcus. Of course it is.

"Are you okay?"

He nods. Tries to sit up, can't quite make it. I hold out a hand but he doesn't take it. There's something odd about his mouth.

"Marcus. Talk to me. Are you okay?"

Suddenly, he clutches his stomach, lurches over and retches. Half-eaten toast spews onto the cracked and stained tiles, along with something else. A mangled mess of dark bodies and stringy legs. One of them drags itself up and tries to crawl away. I feel my own stomach give a lurch. Daddy-long-legs.

I pick up the Tupperware box. It is still half full of the spindly insects. They've been making Marcus eat them. For a moment, I can't see. White spots flood my vision.

"Whose idea?" I ask. Like I don't know.

More silence.

"I said—*whose idea?*"

My voice reverberates off the tiled walls.

Hurst steps forward, lips curving into a smirk. The desire to rip it from his face is overwhelming.

"It was mine, sir. But I was provoked."

"Really?"

"Yeah. Marcus has been calling my mum names. About the cancer. Ask anyone."

He glances at his band of boneheads. They all nod.

"You're a liar," I say.

He steps forward to meet me until we are almost nose to nose.

"Prove it, *sir.*"

Before I can stop myself I have shoved him hard up against the sink. I grab his hair and ram his head into the rusted taps, again and again. Blood sprays up the tiled walls and decorates them in abstract patterns of red. I feel his skull splinter and crack. Several teeth shoot from his mouth and hit the floor. And I can't stop. Can't stop until—

Beth lays a hand on my arm. "Why don't I deal with this, Mr. Thorne?"

I blink. Hurst still stands before me, still smirking. My right hand has formed a fist at my side. But I haven't touched him.

Beth takes the Tupperware box from my other hand.

"Hurst—I'm *this close* to suspending you on the spot. One more word and I will. All of you—headmaster's office. Now."

"I should come with you," I say.

"*No,*" she says firmly. "You should stay right here and take care of Marcus."

She yanks open the door and they all file through, even Hurst. She turns and gives me an odd look.

"We'll discuss this later, Mr. Thorne."

"I had it under control."

Her only reply is the slam of the door. I stare at it for a while, then look back down at Marcus. He remains half curled on the floor, breathing heavily.

"Can you stand up?"

He nods faintly. I hold out my hand and this time he takes it. I haul him up and point at the sink. "Why don't you wash your face, rinse out your mouth?"

Another dazed nod. I look back down at the pile of regurgitated toast and daddy-long-legs. The half-dead insect has given up and sprawls on the floor.

I sigh. A teacher's work. I walk into one of the cubicles and grab some toilet paper (being school regulation, it takes several sheets to constitute a safe handful that won't disintegrate upon contact with anything wet or solid). I notice there's something in the toilet, as well as a vast quantity of sour-smelling urine. A black object bobs in the center of the bowl. A mobile phone. I flush the toilet, taking the chance it's too big to go down the pipe, then fish it out gingerly and dry it on the toilet paper. I look at the old Nokia and walk back out of the cubicle.

Marcus turns off the tap, wipes his face on the sleeve of his blazer and blinks at me. His eyes are red-rimmed.

"This yours?" I hold up the phone.

He nods. "Yeah."

"What happened to your iPhone?"

He stares down at his shoes. "What d'you think?"

Anger burns in my chest. You can't protect them all the time. I know that. You do your best while they are in school. But you can't be there on the way home, in the park, the playground, by the shops. Bullies don't stop being bullies when the bell rings.

"Marcus—"

"I'm not going to the head."

"And I'm not going to make you. Beth and I both saw what happened. With any luck, Hurst will be suspended."

"Yeah. Right."

I'd like to contradict him but find I haven't got the will.

"You never know," I say.

"Yes, I do. And you do too."

I don't reply.

"Can I go now, sir?"

I nod wearily. He slings his bag over his shoulder and shambles off. I remain, staring down at the vomit on the floor. Marcus is not my problem, I tell myself. I won't even be here much longer. But still, my irritating good side wants to help him. I try to ignore it and grab some more toilet paper. As I do, I realize I still have his phone. I slip it into my pocket. I'll find him later and hand it back. I clean up the vomit—grimacing, my own stomach turning—and limp from the toilets.

I could go to Harry's office, but my gut tells me that my presence may only hinder the situation. Besides, I already know what will happen. I can see it now. A slap on the wrist. Detention. A deep sigh from Harry as he explains that his hands are tied; to suspend Hurst now wouldn't be appropriate, bearing in mind his mother's condition, not to mention the upcoming exams. And after all, kids will be kids.

The problem is, if you let kids be kids, then before you know it they're smearing their faces in pigs' blood, pushing each other off the edge of cliffs and smashing their mates' heads in with rocks. Our job as teachers, adults and parents is to stop, at every level, kids being kids, or they'll tear the fucking world down around our ears.

I shuffle slowly along the corridor, empty now, except school corridors never really feel empty. They echo with the laughter, shouts and screams of students long departed. Their ghosts remain, milling around me, shoving past with cries of *"Hey, Thorney!"* and *"We're gonna get you, Doughboy!"* The bell rings again and again as trainers now rotted to dust squeal around corners to classes that never end. Once or twice I think I catch a reflection other than my own in the glass of the windows. A shock of blond hair, a small skinny kid with a mass of red where his face used to be. And then they are gone again, consigned to the register of memory.

"Mr. Thorne?"

I jump. Miss Grayson stands in front of me, clutching a pile of blue folders to her chest and staring at me coolly through her glasses.

"Shouldn't you be in class?"

Her tone makes me feel like I should be in short trousers.

"Err, yes, I'm just on my way."

"Is everything all right?"

"Just one of those mornings. You know, the ones that make you wonder why you became a teacher."

She nods. "You're doing a good job, Mr. Thorne."

"Really?"

"Yes." She rests a hand on my arm. Through my shirt her fingers feel cold. "You're needed here. Don't give up."

"Thank you."

Something that looks remarkably like a smile slips briefly across her features. And then she is gone, padding away in her sensible moccasins, cardigan and beige skirt, like the ghost of schooldays past.

MY YEAR 10 PUPILS are waiting for me when I finally reach the classroom. And when I say "waiting," I mean that they are sitting around, glued to smartphones, feet on desks. Some make a halfhearted attempt to pocket their phones or sit up as I enter. Most don't bother, barely glancing around as I sling my satchel onto my chair.

I stare at them. Despite Miss Grayson's words, I suddenly feel depressed with the futility of my job, my life, my return here. I walk around the room and hand out well-thumbed copies of *Romeo and Juliet*.

"Phones away before I confiscate them. And I should warn you, I often get mixed up between the school safe and the microwave."

There is a small avalanche of activity.

"Okay," I say as I return to the front of the class. "Today's lesson—how you can all get at *least* a B for the lackluster essays you turned in last week."

A murmur runs around the room. One foolhardy suspect shoots their hand up:

"How's that, sir?"

I sit down and take out the mountain of homework that I should have graded over the weekend.

"You can sit quietly and pretend to revise, while I pretend to actually read them."

I take out my red pen and look meaningfully around the room. They open their books.

CLASS ENDED, PUPILS RELEASED and grading complete—contrary to what I may have said, I read most and some even deserved a B—I pack up my bag, turn on my phone and check for messages. Nothing. No reply from my cryptic courier. Not that I was really expecting one. That's not how these things work. Still, ever one for pursuing the futile, I try the number one more time.

It rings. I frown. Another phone is ringing too. In perfect synchronization. In this room. In my pocket. I slip my hand inside and pull out the old Nokia. Marcus's phone. I stare at the handset. My number flashes up. The ringing stops and an automated voice informs me that I have reached the Vodafone voicemail, blah, blah.

I'm still staring at the phone, trying to make sense of things—*anything*—when someone raps loudly on the classroom door. I stuff the Nokia back in my pocket.

Beth strolls into the room and perches on a desk. "Hey."

"Come in, sit down."

"Thanks. I will."

"What happened with Hurst?"

"A week's detention."

"That's it?"

"More than I expected. I've met amoebas with more backbone than Harry."

"So, all Hurst's mates backed his story?"

"Oh, they sang to his chorus like the world's ugliest boy band."

"Right."

A pause. "Look, about what happened—"

"You were right," I say. "I almost lost it."

"That's what I thought."

"Sometimes, with Hurst, it's a bit too much like history repeating."

"I know it's probably none of my business—"

"Probably."

"But is there something more going on with you and Hurst Senior? With you coming back here?"

"Why d'you ask?"

"I'm not the only one asking."

"Meaning?"

"Word has got back to Harry that you two have history. I think he's worried it's going to cause him problems. And by problems, I mean work."

"No need for him to worry. That particular history is ancient."

"No such thing in this place."

She's right. Arnhill has more secrets than shared genes.

"Anyway," she continues, "if you fancy a chat over a beer, tomorrow night?"

I consider. I don't really want to talk about Hurst. But I *would* like to talk to Beth.

"Okay."

"Good. You're buying."

"Oh. Good."

She grins and slips off the desk. There's something else I need to ask her.

"Beth—do you know much about Marcus and his family?"

"Why?"

"Just curious."

"Well, his mum is a cleaner. Lauren gave you her card in the pub the other day."

I hear a dull clunk at the back of my mind. The penny dropping. I take out my wallet and fish out the card.

"Dawson's Dust Busters?"

"There you go," says Beth.

Which would make Lauren—Sullen Barmaid, Reluctant Dog Walker—Marcus's sister. And now I can see the resemblance. The gangly awkwardness. The social weirdness. I consider. The text came from Marcus's phone. He was in the graveyard that day. Not a coincidence. But how did he get hold of my number? And how would he know about the graffiti, about my sister? No. There's something more. Something I'm missing.

"Marcus's mum—has she lived here all her life?"

"Haven't most people in Arnhill?"

"What's her first name?"

"Ruth."

And *now* something stirs at the back of my mind. Just like it did on my very first day at the school gates. An old memory reawakened.

"Is Dawson her maiden name?"

Beth rolls her eyes. "Jesus! What d'you think I am? The marriage register for every person in Arnhill? I do have a life outside this crappy village, you know."

"Right. Sorry."

She folds her arms and glares at me. "Why d'you need to know anyway?"

Because I do. Because I need answers.

"I think I may have gone to school with her."

She sighs heavily. "Actually, *no*, it's not. Her husband died several years ago. No loss—he was a nasty piece of work, by all accounts. Lauren won't even use his surname."

"And you know this how?"

"I helped Lauren fill in some job applications. Noticed the surname was different. She told me she uses her mum's name—"

"Which is?"

"Moore."

I almost palm slap my forehead.

Ruth Moore, she's so poor, gets free meals and begs for more. Ruth Moore, ugly and poor, licks up shit from the toilet floor.

Another awkward, socially impaired kid. Another victim. And yet, sometimes, those are the kids that see the most. Unnoticed, they absorb everything that goes on—the stories, the gossip, the detritus of school life, catching it like a log bobbing in a busy river current. And no one ever realizes how much they know. Because no one ever asks.

Beth is frowning. "You okay?"

"Yeah. I was just thinking, maybe I could talk to her . . . about Marcus."

Among other things.

"You could try. But she's a little odd." She looks at me and reconsiders. "On second thought, you two will probably get on fine."

"Thanks."

"No problem." She strolls to the door. "I'll see you later."

I wait until the squeak of her shoes has faded then I take out Ruth's card. Dawson's Dust Busters. On the back, a number and a slogan: "No job too small. No mess too big."

If only that were true. Unfortunately, there are some things you can't just scrub away with a scouring pad and a bucket of bleach. Like blood, they remain, festering beneath the surface.

I know what happened to your sister.

And sometimes, they come back.

21

The row house is small and neatly kept. It does not look poor by any means. New PVC windows, smart wooden door, a bright hanging basket outside. A blue Fiesta is parked on the curb, "Dawson's Dust Busters" written along the side in shiny silver lettering.

I walk up the short pathway. A fat tabby cat lounges on the windowsill. It eyes me with a lazy contempt. At the door, I pause. Even though I've had all day to think about it, I'm still not sure exactly how to approach this. Those messages were anonymous for a reason. If Ruth sent them, she doesn't want to talk. The question is, *why* did she send them?

I don't know Ruth. I never really knew her all those years ago. No one did. At school, she was never part of any group. Never friends with anyone. Never included. Never picked first unless the team sport was humiliation and torment.

I remember one day some of the other girls stole her panties in PE. A gang of kids—boys and girls—armed with sticks and rulers followed her out of school. They surrounded her as she tried to escape home, jeering, calling her names and lifting her skirt to reveal her nudity. It was cruel and horrendous and not even sexual. It was brutal and simple degradation. I'm not sure quite how far it would have gone if Miss Grayson hadn't spotted what was going on out of a window, intervened and taken her home.

Not that home was much better. Her mum liked a drink and her dad had a temper. Not a good combination. Apparently, you could hear them screaming at each other all the way down the street. About the only companion she had was a mangy old dog she used to walk up over the old colliery site.

I wasn't one of the kids who bullied her. Not that day. But that's nothing to be proud of. I didn't help her either. I just stood by, watching her torment. And then I walked away. Not for the first time. Or the last.

Ruth was one of those kids you try hard not to think about after you have left school, because to do so makes you feel just that little bit worse about yourself. And I had far bigger things to feel worse about.

I raise my hand to knock on the door . . . and it swings open.

A short, stocky woman stands in front of me. She is dressed in a magenta cleaner's smock, the company name neatly embroidered on the chest. Her thick, dark hair has been cropped short. For practical rather than aesthetic reasons, I presume. Beneath the blunt fringe her square face has the stoic look of someone who has become accustomed to disappointment. A face battered by life's small blows. They are often the ones that hurt the most.

She regards me suspiciously, arms folded.

"Yes?"

"Erm, Mrs. Dawson? I left a message earlier. I'm Joe Thorne. I'm a teacher at—"

"I know who you are."

"Right."

"What do you want?"

The lack of social niceties evidently runs in the family.

"Well, like I said in the message, I wanted to return Marcus's phone. He lost it at school today. Is he here?"

"No." She holds out her hand. "I'll give it to him."

I hesitate. If I give her the phone now, I'm pretty sure I will be continuing this conversation with a closed door.

"Could I come in?"

"Why?"

"There's something else I'd like to talk to you about."

"What?"

I debate with myself. Sometimes you need to show your cards. Others, you need to play the long game.

"A cleaning job."

I wait. For a moment I think she's still going to slam the door in my face. Instead, she stands to one side.

"Kettle's on."

THE HOUSE IS AS PRISTINE INSIDE as out, a little unnervingly so. It smells of disinfectant and air fresheners. I feel my sinuses swell and a dull throb begin in my temple.

"Through here." Ruth leads me into a small kitchen. Another cat squats on the kitchen counter: gray, fluffy, malevolent-looking. I wonder where the dog is. Perhaps Lauren is out walking him.

I take Marcus's phone out of my pocket and place it on the kitchen table.

"It got a bit wet but I think it still works."

Ruth glances at it. Her face betrays nothing.

"Marcus has an iPhone."

"Not anymore, I'm afraid. It got broken."

She gives me a sharper look. "Broken or smashed?"

"I couldn't say."

"Of course not. No one ever can."

"If Marcus wants to make a complaint about bullying—"

"What? What will you do? What will the school do?"

I open my mouth then flounder like a grounded fish.

Ruth turns to the cabinet and takes out two mugs. One has a picture of a cat on it. The other proclaims: "Keep calm. I'm a cleaner."

"I've been up to the school. Loads of times," she says. "Talked to your head."

"Right."

"Fat lot of good that did."

"I'm sorry."

"I thought things might have changed. Schools don't put up with that type of thing no more. They crack down on bullying."

"That's the idea."

"Yeah. Nice idea. Crap, though." She turns to the kettle. "Tea?"

"Um. I'd prefer coffee."

I'd prefer to tell her that she is wrong. That schools *do* crack down on bullying now. That they don't brush it under the gym mats for the sake of a decent inspection report. That who someone's daddy is has no effect whatsoever on their treatment by the teachers. That's what I *want* to tell her.

"We don't have any coffee."

But we can't always get what we want.

"Tea is fine."

She fills the mugs with boiling water, adds milk.

"I remember you from school," she says. "You were part of Hurst's gang."

"For a while."

"I never thought you were like the rest."

"Thanks."

"Didn't say it was a compliment."

I wonder how to respond. I decide to say nothing, for now.

She finishes making the tea and brings the mugs over. "Are you going to sit down or what?"

I plonk my backside down in a chair. She takes the seat opposite.

"I heard you were renting the cottage."

"Word gets around in Arnhill."

"Always has."

She reaches for her tea and takes a sip. I look at the brown liquid stewing murkily in my mug and decide against doing the same.

"You cleaned the cottage for Julia Morton?"

"That's right. Though I doubt she'll be giving you a reference."

"You must have gotten to know her and Ben?"

She wraps her hands around her mug and regards me shrewdly. "Is that why you're really here? You want to know about what happened?"

"I have a few questions."

"It'll cost you."

"How much?"

"A deep clean."

I remember Lauren's price list. "Fifty pounds?"

"Cash."

I consider. "I'll live with the dust. Twenty-five pounds—and it will have to be a check."

She sits back in her chair and folds her arms. "Go on."

"What was Julia like?"

"All right, as teachers go. She wasn't too up herself. But she thought she was better than this place. Most of them do."

And most probably are.

"But she wasn't depressed?"

"Not that I saw."

"And Ben?"

"A good lad. At least he *was*, before he went missing."

"What happened?"

"Didn't come home one day after school. Had everyone out looking for him." She pauses. "And then he came back."

For the first time, I sense discomfort, a crack in the hard façade.

"And?"

"He was different."

"How?"

"He'd always been a polite, tidy lad. After, he'd leave the toilet unflushed. His bed was always stained with sweat, and other stuff. His bedroom stank, like something had crawled in there and died."

"Maybe he was just going through a phase," I say. "Kids can turn from sweet youngsters into smelly teens in the blink of an eye."

She looks at me, swigs some of her tea. "I used to clean there last on my rounds. Sometimes Ben would be home from school. We'd chat. I'd make us both tea. After he came back, I'd turn around and find him standing there, just staring. It used to make my skin crawl. The way he looked at me. The way he smelled. Sometimes, I could hear him muttering under his breath. Foul words. It didn't even sound like him. It wasn't right."

"Did you say anything to Julia?"

"I tried. That was when she said she didn't need me anymore. Gave me my notice."

"When was this?"

"Just before she took him out of school for good."

I glance at my mug and wish I had a strong coffee. Strike that. I wish I had a bourbon and a cigarette.

"Open the back door," Ruth says.

"What?"

"You want a smoke. I wouldn't mind one neither. Open the back door."

I stand and walk over to the door. It opens onto a small backyard. Someone has tried to brighten it with a few wilting plants in pots. At the far end, there's a kennel. I walk back inside and sit down. I slip two cigarettes out of my pack and offer one to Ruth, then light both.

"What do you think happened to Ben?" I ask.

She takes a moment to reply: "When I was a kid, we had a dog. I used to walk him up at the old pit site."

"I remember," I say, wondering where this is going.

"One day he ran off. I was gutted. I loved that dog. Two days later he came back, coat matted with dirt and dust, a huge bloody scar around his neck. I bent down, fussed him. He wagged his tail and bit my hand. Right through to the bone. Dad wanted to throttle him right there and then. 'Once a dog turns bad,' he said, 'that's it. There's no going back.'"

I stare at her. "You're comparing Ben Morton to a *dog*?"

"I'm saying *something* happened to that boy and it was so bad his mother couldn't live with it anymore." She drags on the cigarette, blows out a thick cloud of smoke.

"Did you tell any of this to the police?"

She snorts. "And have them call me crazy?"

"But you're telling me."

"You're paying me."

"And that's all?"

She drops the cigarette butt into her mug. "Like I said, you weren't like the rest."

"Is that why you sent me the email?"

She frowns. "What email?"

"The one about my sister—*it's happening again.*"

"I never sent you any email. Today's the first time I've set sight on you since we were kids."

"I know you sent the text." I pick up the Nokia from the table.

"It came from this phone. I'm guessing it's an old one of yours that Marcus borrowed."

"I never sent you any bloody text neither. And that's not my phone."

The confusion on her face looks genuine. My head throbs harder. Right on cue, the front door slams. Marcus shuffles into the kitchen.

"Hi, Mum." Then he spots me. "What's he doing here?"

"I brought your phone back," I say, holding up the Nokia.

His face falls.

"Where did you get it?" I ask.

"I've had it ages."

"Really? So, does this mean anything to you—*Suffocate the little children. Fuck them. Rest in Pieces?*"

Guilt radiates off him like body heat.

"Marcus?" Ruth prompts.

"It was just a joke. A prank."

"All your idea then?"

"Yeah."

"I don't believe you."

"It's true."

"Did someone make you send the text?"

"It wasn't like that. No one *made* me do anything." He juts out his chin defiantly.

"Fine." I tuck the phone into my pocket. "I think I should let the police deal with this."

I take a step toward the door.

"Wait!"

I turn. "*What*, Marcus?"

He looks at me desperately. "She won't lose her job, will she?"

22

1992

More steps. Different from the first. These were carved out of the rock and they curved gradually downward, like a staircase. A slippery, treacherous staircase. Some of the steps crumbled a bit when you stood on them, sending bits of rock skittering down below. It sounded a long way down.

The walls on either side were jagged, the roof above me low. I had to crouch a bit. I'd adjusted the battery on my helmet but, because of the curve, the light only illuminated one or two steps at a time, so sometimes it seemed like the third step was straight out into darkness. Ahead of me, I could see the other two flashlights bobbing up and down, but they only provided odd, abstract patches of illumination. However, they did at least confirm that nobody had fallen off the edge of a precipice and broken their neck. Yet.

Occasionally, I heard one of the others curse, usually Marie. I had no idea how she was managing in stiletto heels. Beneath my miner's overalls I was coated in sweat. It slid down my brow and trickled around my eyebrows. My heart hammered and my breath was growing more ragged. Not just because of tension and exertion. My dad once told me there's less oxygen in the air the deeper down you go.

"How much fucking further?" Fletch grumbled, because, if I was finding it hard going, Fletch—with his ten-smokes-a-day habit—must *really* be struggling.

I expected Hurst to reply, but Chris got there first. "We're close," he said calmly, and I could swear he didn't sound breathless at all, didn't sound as if he was even breaking a sweat.

We resumed our unsteady, stumbling progress. After a few more minutes I realized something. I wasn't bending over quite so much. I could stand upright. The roof was getting higher. The quality of the light seemed to be changing too. Even the air felt a little more breathable, as if there was more of it around us.

Getting close, I thought. But to what?

"Be careful," Chris called back now. "There's a drop."

He was right. We rounded the next corner and the narrow passageway opened out into a much larger cavern. It was big. Really big. I looked up. The ceiling rose high above us in a rough dome shape. Thick wooden beams formed supports. They crossed and curved in a way that reminded me of the vaulted roofs in barns or churches. Similar but more rudimentary. The steps continued but there was no wall to our left anymore. Just a straight plummet down.

"*Shit!*" Marie suddenly yelped. Glass shattered, brittle and abrupt in the darkness. "The cider."

I jumped. My concentration wavered. The foot I was poised to place on the next step slipped. My ankle buckled beneath me. I yelped in pain and grabbed for the wall but, of course, it was gone. No wall, just air.

Fear snatched the scream from my throat. I tried to grab hold of something—anything—but it was too late. I was falling. I closed my eyes, prepared for the long drop . . .

. . . and I hit the ground almost immediately with a sudden, spine-cracking thump.

"*Owwww. Shiiit.*"

"Joe?" Chris's voice called down. "Are you okay?"

I attempted to sit up. My back hurt a bit. It felt bruised, but it could have been worse—a lot worse. I looked up. I could see flashlights and vague silhouettes. Only a few feet above me.

We had found it, I realized. We were here.

I pushed myself to my feet. My ankle twinged again.

"Shit."

I clutched at it. It already felt a bit swollen. I hoped I'd just twisted it and not broken anything. I still had to climb back up those frigging steps.

"I'm okay!" I shouted back up. "But I've hurt my fucking ankle."

"Boo hoo. What can you see? What's down there?" Hurst's voice. As caring and compassionate as ever.

My helmet had been knocked sideways. I propped myself against one rocky wall, relieving the weight on my bad ankle, and adjusted it. I looked around. More wooden beams were set into the walls. They ran straight up from the ground. Between them I could see other shapes and patterns. They looked like they had been made by white sticks embedded into the rock. They formed intricate designs. Stars and eyes. Odd-looking letters. Stick men. I fought back a small shiver. On some of the walls there were fewer patterns. Instead, piles of sticks and yellow rocks were stacked tightly in large arched alcoves.

I didn't like it. Any of it. It was creepy. Weird. Wrong.

I heard the others descending. Chris stepped slowly down into the cavern. Hurst jumped and landed beside me with a thud, almost immediately followed by Marie and Fletch. There was a pause as they all looked around, taking it in.

"Whoa. This is well cool," Marie said. "It's like something out of *The Lost Boys*."

"Is it summat to do with the pit?" Fletch asked, displaying his usual abundance of imagination.

"No." The word came from Chris, but he snatched it from the tip of my tongue.

This wasn't something forged by miners. Mines were hacked, punched and hewn from the rock; it was clumsy and rough and industrial, done with heavy tools and machinery.

This was something different. It had not been formed by necessity or stoic workmanship. It had been created by, I sort of wanted to say, passion, but that wasn't quite right either. As I gazed around, another word thrust itself into my head. *Devotion*. That was it—devotion.

"Shine your flashlight round, fuckwit," Hurst said to Fletch, who duly obliged.

He turned in a circle, pointing the flashlight around the cavern. It only just reached the far walls, and rather than illuminating it seemed to accentuate the deep hollows and corners filled with blackness. It was probably just some weird effect of the light, but if you glanced quickly, out of the corner of your eye, it almost looked like the shadows were moving, shifting and ebbing restlessly.

"This is really weird," Hurst muttered. "Doughboy's right. This ain't no mine." He turned to me. "What d'you think, Thorney?"

I was trying, but thinking was hard down here. Even though the cavern was big and far less stifling than the narrow tunnel, I was still finding it laborsome to breathe. Like the air was wrong. Like the oxygen had been replaced with something else. Something heavier and sort of foul. Something no one should breathe, ever.

Poisonous gases, I thought suddenly. My dad had often spoken about the fumes released from deep down in the earth. Was that it? Were we slowly being poisoned while we stood here? I glanced over at Chris.

"Chris, what is this place?"

He still stood near the steps, venturing no farther. His face in the grimy gloom was pale, streaked with dirt, not scared exactly but tense. He looked much older than his fifteen years, like the man he would never become. Then his vivid eyes met mine and I understood. He hadn't found this place. It had found *him*, and now he desperately wanted it to let him go again.

"Don't you know yet?" he said. "Don't you get it?"

I looked back around the cavern. At the high, vaulted roof. The wooden beams. And that was when something in my head clicked. Because when you looked again, it was obvious. Air that shouldn't be breathed. A huge underground chamber. Like a church but not.

"Get what?" Hurst asked.

And right on the heels of that thought came another. The white sticks in the walls and the rocks piled in the alcoves. I limped forward, toward the nearest wall. The light on my helmet illuminated a star, a symbol like a hand and a stick figure. Up close, they weren't pure white. And they weren't sticks. They were something else.

Something you would expect to find in a place like this.

In a grave, a burial chamber.

"Thorney, are you going to tell me what the fuck is going on?" Hurst snarled dangerously.

"Bones," I whispered, horror leaching the strength from my voice. "The rock—it's full of bones."

23

Sometimes, it takes a while for you to realize that something is wrong. Something is off. It stinks. Like when you stand in dog shit and it's not until you're sitting in the car, wondering where the bad smell is coming from, that it sinks in: the stink is coming from you. You brought it along for the ride.

When I get back to the cottage I notice that the front door is ajar, just a little. I'm sure I remember closing and locking it. As I get closer, I see that the frame is splintered and cracked. Someone has forced it. I push the door all the way open and walk inside.

The cushions on the sofa have been thrown off and sliced open, spilling their foamy guts all over the floor. The coffee table has been tipped up, the drawers from the small cabinet yanked out. My laptop is in pieces.

The cottage has been ransacked. I frown, my mind taking a while to assess the situation. And then it dawns on me. Fletch and his sons, probably on instruction from Hurst. I guess he didn't want to negotiate after all. Typical Hurst—if someone won't give you something, you take it, by any means.

Except, I know damn well that they won't have found what they were looking for.

I walk wearily upstairs. My mattress has been slashed and

eviscerated, the clothes in the wardrobe pulled off hangers and dumped in a heap on the floor. I bend down to pick up some shirts and I can immediately tell, from the dampness and acrid smell, that they have been liberally pissed upon.

I check in the bathroom: shower curtain yanked down for no apparent reason, the top taken off the cistern and smashed. I could have told them that nothing they could do in here could disturb me more than the things I've already encountered.

Finally, I check the spare room. Ben's room. I open the door. I stare at the lacerated mattress, the ripped-up carpet, and feel a slow burn of anger. I limp back downstairs.

I find Abbie-Eyes in the wood-burning stove, along with the folder that I discovered beneath the Angel. I crouch down and take them both out. They're dusty and black but they haven't been set alight. I wonder why? I place Abbie-Eyes on the coffee table. After a moment's consideration I slip the folder inside one of the slit-open cushions, just to be on the safe side. Something is bothering me. Why didn't Fletch's lads burn them? Had they got bored of their destruction by this point? Seems unlikely. Did they run out of time?

Or was it something else? Were they disturbed, interrupted?

I suddenly have a very bad feeling. There's a creak from the kitchen. I straighten and turn.

"Evening, Joe."

I SIT ON THE CUSHIONLESS SOFA. Gloria perches delicately on the armchair. Flames crackle noisily in the wood-burning stove. This is not as homely as it sounds. Gloria wears black leather gloves and holds a poker in one hand.

"What are you doing here?"

"Checking up on your welfare."

"I find that hard to believe."

She laughs. My bladder cramps.

"I saw you had some visitors today."

"You met them?"

"They were leaving just as I arrived. We didn't have a chance to chat."

She glances around. "It strikes me that they were searching for something. Perhaps the same thing that you were hoping your old friend might stump up a wad of cash for."

"They didn't find what they were looking for."

"You're sure."

"Yes."

"Why?"

"Because I don't have what they're looking for. Not here."

She considers this. "I have found, in my line of work, that it is beneficial to be in possession of all the facts."

"I've told you—"

"*You've told me FUCK ALL!*"

She slams the poker down on the coffee table. Abbie-Eyes flies into the air and lands near my feet. A crack splits her plastic features. Her loose eye spills out of the socket. It stares up at me from the floor. Sweat gathers at the base of my spine.

"Fortunately," Gloria continues, "I've done a little research of my own. It was interesting."

She stands, walks over to the wood-burning stove, bends down and opens it.

"Let me take you back twenty-five years. Five schoolfriends. You, Stephen Hurst, Christopher Manning, Marie Gibson and Nick Fletcher. Oh, and your little sister, Annie. Never told me about her."

She sticks the end of the poker into the stove, wedging it deep inside the logs. The flames crackle louder.

"One night, when you were out with your friends, she went missing. Disappeared from her own bed. There were searches, appeals. Everyone thought the worst. And then, miraculously, after forty-eight hours, she came back. But she couldn't, or wouldn't, say what had happened to her . . ."

"I don't see—"

"Let me finish. Happy ending, except, two months later, Daddy crashes his car into a tree, killing little Annie and himself and leaving you critically injured. How am I doing so far?"

I stare at the poker. In the fire. *Out of the frying pan*, I think wildly.

"Like you said, you've done your research," I say.

Gloria begins to pace. "Oh, I left a bit out—a few weeks after your sister's return your friend Christopher Manning falls from the school English block. Tragic coincidence, don't you think?"

"Life is full of tragic coincidences."

"Fast-forward to now, and you return to the village where you grew up. You plan to blackmail your old schoolfriend Stephen Hurst for a large amount of cash. What do you have on him? What is he hiding?"

"Someone like Hurst has plenty of secrets."

"I'm beginning to think you do too, Joe."

"Why do you care?"

"Because I like you."

"You have a very odd way of showing it."

"Put it another way then—you interest me. Not many people do. For a start, you're one of the least likely teachers I've ever met. You're a drunk, a gambler. But you have a vocation. You choose to impart knowledge to children. Why is that?"

"You get a lot of holidays."

"I think it's because of what happened here, twenty-five years ago. I think you're trying to make amends for something."

"Or just trying to make a living."

"Flippancy is a flimsy defense mechanism. Trust me, I should know. It's one of the first things to fall away when people are in fear for their lives."

"Is that a threat?"

"You wish. Actually, what I'm giving you is a lifeline."

She walks over. I flinch. She bends down and holds something out. A card. Blank, except for a phone number.

She reaches down and slips it into the pocket of my jeans, patting me gently on the crotch.

"You can reach me on this for the next twenty-four hours if you need my help."

"Why?"

"Because, deep down, I have a soft spot for you."

"That's comforting to hear."

"Don't take it to heart."

My eyes flick back to the poker. The fire spits.

"The Fatman is getting impatient."

"I told you—"

"Shut up."

The sweat is now trickling down between my arse cheeks. My stomach is a tight ball of cramp. I want to be sick, to shit and to piss all at once.

"He gave you extra time. Now, he wants his money."

"He'll get it. That's why I'm here."

"I know, Joe. And if it were just up to me?" She gives a dainty shrug. "But it looks to him like you ran. That doesn't inspire faith. The Fatman wants to be sure you understand how serious he is."

"I do. Really."

She takes the poker out of the stove. The tip glows red. I glance toward the door. But I know I'd be in a headlock before my backside left the armchair.

"Please—"

"Like I said, Joe, I have a soft spot for you."

She walks over and crouches down next to me. She holds up the poker. I can feel the heat.

Gloria smiles. "So, I'm going to spare your pretty face."

I LIE ON THE SOFA. I have taken four codeine tablets and finished the bottle of bourbon. My left hand is bound in an old tea towel and resting on a pack of frozen fish fingers. It is now only mildly agonizing. I am not expecting to be playing a violin concerto anytime soon.

My skin feels hot and feverish. I drift in and out of consciousness. Not sleep. Just an illusory gray-and-black place peppered with strange visions.

In one, I'm back at the old colliery site. I'm not alone. Chris and Annie stand on the crest of a hill. The sky hangs above them like a bag of mercury, swollen with silvery light and fluid with black rain. The wind rages and tears with invisible claws.

Chris's head is oddly misshapen, caved in at the back. Blood runs from his nose and eyes. Annie holds his hand. And this Annie, I know, is my Annie. The ugly gash is there on her head, deep and ruinous. As I watch, she opens her mouth and says softly:

I know where the snowmen go, Joe. I know where they go now.

She smiles. And I feel happy, calm, at peace. But then the clouds above them lower and swell, and instead of rain a cascade of shiny black beetles pours down. I watch my friend and my sister fall to the ground, engulfed in the scuttling mass of bodies until all I can see is a swarm of blackness. Devouring them, swallowing them whole.

My phone starts to ring. Saved by the bell, or rather Metallica.

I roll over and pick it up with my good hand. I squint at the screen. *Brendan.* I press Accept with a shaky finger.

"You're alive?" I croak.

"Last time I checked. You sound like shit."

"Thanks."

"You love my honesty."

"Don't forget your pert arse."

"Healthy eating, no booze. You should try it."

"I've been calling you for days," I say.

"Lost my phone charger. What's so urgent?"

"I just . . . wanted to check you were okay."

"Aside from missing my favorite pub, dandy. When can I go back?"

I look at my bandaged, burnt hand. "Not yet."

"Feck."

"It might be an idea to move out of the apartment for a while as well."

"Jesus! Is this to do with your habit of owing money to unpleasant people?"

Guilt stabs my insides. Brendan has been good to me—more than good. He's let me share his apartment, rent free. He has never lectured me on my gambling. Most people would have given up on me. But not Brendan. And now I'm paying him back by putting him in danger.

"Have you got somewhere to stay tonight?"

"*Tonight?* Well, there's my sister. I'm sure her husband will be bloody delighted about that."

"It shouldn't be for long."

"I should feckin' hope not." He sighs. "You know what my dear old mammy would say?"

"'I'm losing my voice,' hopefully?"

"When does a hare stop running from the fox?"

I groan. "When?"

"When it hears the hunter's bugle."

"Meaning?"

"Sometimes you need someone bigger—like the police—to sort out your problem."

"I am sorting it. Okay?"

"Like you sorted it before—stealing money from the school safe."

"I never took a penny."

True. But only because Debbie—the secretary with the handbag addiction—got there before me. When I found this out we came to an agreement. I would say nothing if she paid the money back. I would also leave quietly (I was on my final written warning for tardiness, sloppy work and general shittiness of attitude by that point anyway). Oh, and she would owe me.

"That was different."

"I remember. I was the one who brought you grapes every day in the hospital when you couldn't pay your debts and someone made papier-mâché out of your knee."

"You visited me twice in the hospital and you never brought me grapes."

"I sent you texts."

"You sent me porn."

"Well, who needs feckin' grapes?"

"Look, I really will sort this."

"Did I mention that I'll have to share my sister's spare room with feckin' hamsters that squeak their wheels all night?"

"I'm sorry."

"Or that she has two young kids who think five o'clock in the morning is a perfectly acceptable time to play trampoline on their uncle's stomach?"

"I'm *sorry*."

"'Sorry' will not help my hernia."

"I just need a few more days."

A deep, deep sigh. "Fine. But if you don't sort it, or if you run into anything you can't handle—"

"I'll call you."

"*Jesus, no.* Call the police, you moron. Or the A Team."

24

"So then I said to this student that, while I respected her right to express herself by throwing the shoe . . ."

Simon is drawling on. It says something about my current state of mind that the soporific nature of his voice is vaguely bearable this lunchtime. Or perhaps I have just managed to tune him out to white noise. Irritating but ignorable.

It's just me, Simon and Beth at lunch today. I am not hungry. Not in the slightest. But I force down some chips in the vague hope they might help my hangover. I also have my second can of full-fat Coke in front of me.

Simon has gone through the obligatory and predictable drinking-on-a-school-night "jokes." I smile politely and just about manage not to punch him in the face. It would hurt my hand, for one thing. I have made a relatively professional-looking bandage out of a cut-up pillowcase and told people that I burnt myself on the oven. Drunken cooking, et cetera. Beth occasionally gives me knowing looks. She doesn't believe me. I don't care. Right now, I am more preoccupied by last night. By what Marcus told me. By my encounter with Gloria. By what a mess I am in and how it would be difficult for things to get any worse.

"Mr. Thorne?"

I look up. Harry is standing by the dining table. His face is grim.

"Could we have a word in my office?"

Difficult but not impossible.

"Of course."

I wait for some sort of snide comment from Simon. None is forthcoming. He seems intent upon his lunch. Too intent. I scrape back my chair.

Beth raises her eyebrows. "Catch you later."

"Yeah."

I follow Harry along the corridor.

"Can I ask what this is about?"

"I'd rather wait until we reach my office."

His tone is hard, noncommittal. I don't like it. I have a very bad feeling about this. Which, considering my starting point this morning, is impressive.

Harry pushes open the door and steps inside. I follow him. And stop. Dead.

A visitor sits in front of Harry's desk.

As we enter, he stands and turns.

I'd say my heart sinks, but I'm not sure it could dive much further without a mask and oxygen. In fact, I almost laugh. Really, I should have expected it. I'm a gambler. You're supposed to think about all possible outcomes before you act—work out your strategy—but I suddenly feel as though I've been flapping around like a tasty bit of tuna at a table of sharks.

Harry closes the door and looks between the pair of us. "I believe that you two know each other."

"We both grew up in Arnhill," Stephen Hurst says. "Other than that, I wouldn't say I really 'know' Mr. Thorne at all."

"Well, I was picky about my friends even then," I say.

Hurst's smug expression falters momentarily. Then he spots my bandaged hand. "Been picking fights again?"

"Only with the oven. But if you're offering?"

"Mr. Thorne, Mr. Hurst," Harry interrupts curtly. "Can we all sit down?"

Hurst lowers himself into his seat. I walk over and reluctantly do the same. It feels a lot like how we used to sit in front of the headmaster twenty-five years ago.

"So," Harry says, and shuffles some papers in front of him. "Some things have come to my attention that I think we need to discuss."

I try to adopt a pleasant tone. "Is this regarding Jeremy Hurst and the incident with Marcus Dawson in the toilets yesterday, because—"

"No." Harry cuts me dead. "It is not about that."

"Oh."

I'm back-footed. I glance at Hurst. His face has resumed its former self-satisfied expression. I would like to smash it from his jowls. I would like to leap from my chair, grab him around the throat and choke him until his eyes bulge and his tongue turns blue.

Instead I say, "Then I suppose you had better enlighten me."

"Prior to taking the position with us here at Arnhill you worked at Stockford Academy."

"That's right."

"You supplied a reference from your former head—Miss Coombes?"

I can feel sweat starting to dampen my underarms. "Yes."

"Except that's not entirely true, is it?"

"I'm afraid I don't understand."

"Miss Coombes did not supply that reference."

"She didn't?"

"She denies any knowledge of it."

"Well, I think there may have been some miscommunication."

"I doubt it. Miss Coombes was quite clear—you left Stockford Academy suddenly, not long after a substantial amount of money went missing from the school safe."

"That money was recovered."

Hurst can't contain himself any longer. "Apparently, you like to play cards, Joe?"

I turn. "Why—fancy a game of Liar? And what exactly does any of this have to do with you?"

"In case you've forgotten, I'm on the board of governors. When it is brought to my attention that one of the teachers here is not fit for the job—"

"Sorry—'brought to your attention.' By whom?"

His lips purse. And then it comes to me. Simon Saunders. He was in the Fox the night I ran into Hurst. He knows him. (Doesn't everyone in Arnhill?) Why go running to Harry when he could go over his head and tell all to someone on the board of governors? Someone who already hates my guts. Get Hurst on his side and maybe store up some favors for himself. Two birds—one poisonous little toad.

"You should be careful who you listen to," I say.

"You're not denying it then?"

"I would say that the version presented here bears only a vague resemblance to the truth. Something which I would prefer to discuss with my superior in private."

Hurst's eyes flash. "The *truth* is that you accepted this position under false pretenses and you left your previous position under a cloud. This, on top of the fact that you have some vendetta against my son, no doubt based upon your imagined prior history with me. Your demeanor and performance as a teacher are entirely unsuitable. Oh, and you stink of booze."

He straightens his tie and sits back triumphantly. Harry stares at me wearily from across the desk.

"I'm sorry, Mr. Thorne. This will go before the board. You are entitled to union representation, but in the light of these revelations—"

"Accusations. Unproven for the most part."

"Still, I have no choice but to temporarily suspend you from teaching duties while we come to a decision about your future with the academy."

"I understand."

I stand, trying to contain the trembling in my body. Partly the hangover, mostly anger. I mustn't let it show. Mustn't let Hurst know he has gotten to me. Always keep the game face on.

"I'll just collect my things."

I walk toward the door. And stop. You also need to let them know you still hold the winning card. I glance at Hurst.

"Nice tie, by the way."

The look on his face is all I need.

I DON'T RETURN TO THE CAFETERIA. I gather my coat and satchel from the staff room—which is mercifully empty—and head out of the school. I don't trust myself to face Simon again. Even though I am already under suspension, an assault charge isn't something I particularly want to add to my CV.

When I reach reception I pause. Miss Grayson is not in her usual place in her small glass cubicle. Instead, a younger clone—short dark hair, glasses, although no hairy mole—is sitting in her seat, tapping at a computer.

"Excuse me, where's Miss Grayson?"

"She has a cold."

"Oh."

"Did you need to speak with her?"

"Well, I'm leaving, and I was hoping to say goodbye. Do you know when she'll be back?"

"I'm afraid not."

"Right. Thanks for your help."

I start to turn.

"Oh, Mr. Thorne—"

"Yes?"

"Mr. Price requested you hand in your front-door pass when you leave."

My pass. The pass that allows me to enter the school. Harry really isn't taking any chances.

"Worried I might sneak back in and steal the school lunch money?"

She doesn't smile. I wonder how much she knows. How much they all know.

"Fine." I take it out of my pocket and just about manage not to slam it on her desk.

"Thank you."

"You're welcome. And pass on my regards to Miss Grayson."

"Of course."

She offers an efficient smile. Then she picks up the pass and, as if I was in any doubt about my suspension being temporary, produces a pair of scissors, cuts it neatly in half and drops it in the bin.

THE COTTAGE EYES ME RESENTFULLY upon my return, its one good window glowering darkly. *Look*, it seems to hiss from between the splintered wood of the front door. *Look what you have done. Are you happy yet?*

No, I think. Because I am not done yet. I push at the door. It sticks and then gives with a reluctant groan. I'm not entirely sure the cottage is on my side in all of this. It is too much in cahoots with the past, too much a part of the village. It does not want me here. It has no intention of making me comfortable. But that's fine too. I don't plan to be here for very much longer.

I walk inside and throw my bag on the sofa. The room is still in much the same state as when I returned last night. Internal injuries. I consider tidying up and sorting out some of the mess. Then I go and smoke a cigarette.

Perhaps Hurst has done me a favor. Speeding up the inevitable. After all, I never intended to stay, did I? I never intended to settle back down in a place that holds such dark and painful memories. The wounded animal doesn't escape the trap only to throw itself back into the metal jaws and wait for them to pulverize its bones.

Not unless it has a damn good reason.

I'd like to say the reason was Annie, or the message. But it's not that simple. Even all that guilt and recrimination weren't enough to drag me back here. Not on their own.

The truth is, I was desperate. I needed to get away and I saw an opportunity—to settle bad debts and old scores at the same time. Perhaps it had always been at the back of my mind. I knew I had something that could screw up Hurst's life. The idea he might pay money for it came later.

I hadn't expected him to be quite so determined to hound me out of the village. But despite all his threats and manipulations, ultimately, Hurst has played his hand. He doesn't have anything left. There is only one way to get rid of me now and, although I've no doubt that Hurst is capable of murder, the stakes are higher. Is he willing to risk his career, his comfortable life, his family?

I'm hoping the answer is no. But on the other hand, I wouldn't bet on it.

I close the back door and walk inside. The feeling of coldness is on me again. I can hear the walls chittering. I am starting to become used to both the cold and the incessant tinnitus of the cottage. I'm not sure whether, like tuning out Simon's monotonous drone, this is a good thing. Once you become accustomed, you become complacent and then you become either complicit or consumed.

I wander back through to the living room and take out my phone. I pull up Brendan's number. He answers on the second ring.

"What do you want now?"

"Isn't it enough to hear the dulcet tones of your voice?"

"You'd better be wearing underwear."

"I need a favor."

"Seriously? You know, right now, I have gerbil shit in my beard."

"I thought it was hamsters."

"Gerbils, hamsters, who gives a feck? The little bastards spent all last night kicking crap onto my head. How long do I have to stay here?"

"Do you still have that holdall I asked you to look after?"

"Holdall? What holdall?"

"Sides literally splitting."

"Yes, I've got it."

"Can you courier it to me overnight?"

"Joe—"

"Look, I just want to say, you've been a good friend. Thank you."

"Don't go all mushy on me."

"Well, I thought I'd say it in case I actually do."

There's a pause and then Brendan says with heartfelt emotion: "Just feck off before I end up doing an Ozzy Osborne on one of these feckin' gerbils."

He ends the call. I glance at my watch. It's 3:30 p.m. I stare around the wrecked living room. I pick up Abbie-Eyes from the floor and place her back on the armchair. She observes me with one cold, blue eye. The hollow socket yawns darkly. I look around but can't see her other eye anywhere. I have a sudden mental image of it being carried away on the backs of scuttling beetles. I thank my imagination. I really needed that.

My phone starts to ring, making me jump. I press Accept.

"Hello?"

"Were you going to mention playing hooky? I might have joined you."

Beth. Of course.

"How did you get my number?"

"From Danielle on reception. I know her brother. He's in my pub-quiz team."

"So I suppose you know what happened?"

"Harry told me that you were taking a leave of absence."

"That's what he called it?"

"What would you call it?"

I hesitate.

"You're leaving, aren't you?"

"I think I might have already left."

"Jesus—that's got to be a world record."

"I'm glad my brevity impresses you."

"Don't tell everyone. Is this about yesterday, with Jeremy Hurst?"

"No."

"Then what?"

"It's a little complicated."

"How complicated?"

"Well—"

"A few pints complicated or several glasses of bourbon complicated?"

I consider. "Definitely the latter."

"Right, I'll see you in the Fox at seven. Line your stomach first."

She ends the call without saying goodbye. *Why do people keep doing that?*

I should have said something. I have questions. But I suppose they can wait. I sit down heavily on the hard sofa frame and think about making coffee. Then I glance at Abbie-Eyes, or maybe that should be Abbie-*Eye*. I shake off a shudder. Decision made.

I head back out the door and walk down to the fish-and-chip shop.

25

The Fox looks even more run-down and dilapidated tonight. It's decaying, I think. As if my presence here has started some sort of chain reaction. As if this small, shriveled place has been held in some mummified state and now a crack has appeared, a little bit of oxygen admitted into the rarefied environment, and suddenly everything is rotting from within.

I push open the doors and walk inside. A quick appraisal informs me that Hurst is not here and nor are any of his goons. A few elderly patrons—probably the same ones from the other night—vegetate at tables, staring into their pints of ale and lager tops.

Beth isn't here yet but I spot one familiar face. Lauren is back behind the bar, which, while not exactly evoking rainbows, sunshine and tweeting birds, is at least better than Nosferatu's surly countenance.

I smile. "All right?"

She stares at me as though she has never seen me before in her life.

"Joe Thorne. Teacher. We bumped into each other up at the old colliery site."

"Oh. Yeah. Right." Her face moves a little. Could be a smile. Could be a twitch of annoyance—hard to tell. "So, what can I get you?"

"Erm, bourbon, please. Double."

"Make that two."

I turn. Beth stands at my side. Her hair is loose for once and falls around her shoulders in semi-dreadlocks. An oversized leather jacket swamps her small frame and makes her legs, in sprayed-on black jeans and DMs, look even skinnier.

A nose ring glints as she grins at me. "You are the talk of the staffroom, Mr. Thorne."

"Really? Might explain why my ears are burning."

"Yeah, well, that might also be the effigy Simon has of you that he is sticking pins into."

"I imagine he is overcome by sorrow at my premature departure."

"If singing 'Oh, What a Beautiful Morning' is evidence of his sorrow, then yes."

Lauren plonks both glasses down upon the bar. The delivery is abrupt but, just by glancing at them, I can tell she has been generous with the measures.

"Nine pounds, please."

"Thanks." I pay with my last twenty, wondering how far over my overdraft I currently am and how long before the bank stops all my cards.

Beth picks up her glass. "Shall we?"

We walk toward a table in a far corner. One thing the Fox does have going for it is plenty of dim, dusty corners in which to lurk if you would rather not be seen or overheard.

Beth sits herself down on one of the hard wooden chairs and I follow suit. We both take sips of our drinks—mine a bit larger than hers.

"Soooo," she says meaningfully. "Want to tell me what really happened?"

"What's Harry said?"

"You have taken a leave of absence for personal reasons."

"What does the grapevine say?"

"Oh, you've had some kind of breakdown, Hurst Senior got you sacked, you've been abducted by aliens—that type of thing."

"Right."

"So which is it?"

"Aliens, naturally. They have taken over my body and my real self is in a cocoon in the cottage."

"Hmmm. Almost believable . . . except everyone saw Hurst with Harry today."

I look down into my glass. "I lied to get the job here. I faked a reference from my old school. I did not leave under a halo so much as under a cloud. Harry found out."

"O—kay. What did you do at your old school that was so bad?"

"Nothing, actually. But I *intended* to steal money from the school safe to pay a debt."

I watch her take this in. "But you didn't?"

"No."

She nods, considering. "So how did Harry find out—?" Then she holds up a hand. "No, wait. *Simon.* Didn't Simon mention he knew you from somewhere?"

"Yeah. And I'm guessing Simon knows Hurst."

"I didn't realize he did . . . but then Simon is just the sort of bum bogie who would stick himself up anyone's arse to get a bit further up the ladder."

"*Bum bogie?*"

She raises her glass. "And that's being kind to him."

"Well, obviously being a bum bogie works. Because here I am— currently and probably permanently—jobless."

"I wouldn't be so sure. Harry likes you. The kids seem to like you. Harry knows he'll have a hell of a job filling that post."

I shake my head. "Hurst won't let Harry take me back on."

"You and Hurst aren't really ancient history, are you? What is it between you two?"

I put my glass down and look at her across the table. In the dim light she looks younger again. It softens the faint lines around her mouth and on her forehead. Her dark eyes seem very wide and her skin very soft and pale. I feel a tug. I wanted one thing about this place to be good and honest. Just one thing.

Beth frowns. "What are you staring at? Have I got something on my face?"

"No . . ." I pause. "Nothing."

She continues to stare at me, suspiciously. Then she says: "So you were about to tell me about you and Hurst."

"Was I?"

"You were."

"The truth, the whole truth and nothing but the truth?"

"Something like that."

"We fell out, badly, in our teens. Stupid, looking back. Over a girl, as these things usually are."

"Was the girl Marie Gibson?"

"Yes."

The lie comes easily.

She sips her drink. "I wouldn't have had her down as your type."

"Why? What do you think is my type?"

"I mean, she's pretty but—"

"But what?"

"Don't take this the wrong way—"

"Okay."

"I know this seems a shitty thing to say with the cancer and everything, but she always seemed a bit of a bitch."

I'm slightly taken aback. "Well, she could be tough when she wanted to be."

"I don't mean tough. I mean a bitch. She would throw her weight around because of Hurst. I've seen her reduce a teacher to tears at a parents' evening. Once, she went around to another mother's house because their kid had accused Hurst Junior of bullying. This woman worked part-time for the council. Next day—contract terminated."

I frown. I suppose Marie could be a bit of a firecracker. And a mother can't always see their offspring's faults. Still, it doesn't sound like the Marie I remember.

"Well, people change, I suppose."

"Not that much."

"And I was young and foolish back then."

"What are you now?"

"Old and cynical."

"Join the gang."

No, I think. She puts on a good front. But I don't believe that. I can see it in her eyes. The light hasn't gone out. Not completely. Not yet.

"That reminds me," I say. "You never told me which one you are?"

Her forehead creases. "Which one of what?"

"Want to make a difference or can't get a job anywhere else?"

"Well, obviously, who wouldn't want *this*?" She spreads her arms.

"So, you want to make a difference?"

"Is this an interview now?"

"No, I was just wondering."

"About me?"

"About Emily Ryan."

Her face changes. The softness is gone.

"She was the student you were talking about, wasn't she? The one who killed herself?"

"You really know how to ruin a mood."

"You said she was a student of yours. But you weren't teaching here when she died."

"Been doing your research?"

"Just call me Columbo."

"I can think of other names. And I don't have to tell you anything."

"True."

"I barely know you."

"True."

"You're fucking irritating when you're agreeable."

"Also—"

She holds up a hand. "*Okay*. You're right. Emily wasn't my student." A pause. "She was my niece."

"MY SISTER WAS A FEW YEARS OLDER than me. No dad around and Mum wasn't exactly Mum of the Year, so we were close. We grew up in Edgeford—you know it?"

"I've heard of it—not the best area of Nottingham."

"Anyway, Carla—my sister—she got pregnant pretty young. Following the family tradition, the dad didn't hang around, but she was a brilliant mum. She brought Emily up while training to be a nurse. Emily was a sweet kid; she grew up into a pretty okay teenager."

"That's a feat."

"I was teaching at a school in Derby, so I couldn't come and see them that much. But Emily and I would text or FaceTime. She came to stay with me a few times. We'd go shopping, to the movies and stuff. I was the cool auntie, I suppose."

"Well, that's what cool aunties are for."

A tiny smile. "Don't get me wrong. She was thirteen, she could be moody sometimes but overall she was good to be around—bright, funny, inquisitive."

I feel my heart give a little. I wonder what sort of teenager Annie would have been. Loud, outgoing, funny, sporty? Or would she have reverted into herself, like so many do?

"Then, Carla got a job. A good job. They moved. Emily had to change schools."

"Let me guess. They moved to Arnhill?"

She nods. "The job was at the hospital in Mansfield. Arnhill wasn't far, houses were cheap and the school was within walking distance. It seemed to make sense."

Most bad decisions do at the time.

"Moving schools—to any school—is tough when you're thirteen," I say.

"To start with, it seemed okay—"

"But?"

"It was too hunky-dory. You know—when everything is so frigging fine, it just can't be."

"What did your sister say?"

She sighs. "She didn't get it. I mean, don't get me wrong. She loved that girl's bones, but it was like she just didn't see the problem. Or she didn't want to."

I nod. We're all too busy, too distracted by the sheer effort of getting through each day—working, paying the bills, the mortgage, shopping—that we don't *want* to look deeper. We don't dare. We want things to be fine. To be "hunky-dory." Because we simply haven't got the mental energy to deal with it if they're not. It's only when something bad happens, something irretrievable, that we see things properly. And then it's too late.

"Did you try and talk to Emily?"

"I tried. I even drove over to see her. Took her for pizza, like we used to, except it wasn't the same."

"How d'you mean?"

"You done with those?"

We both glance up. Lauren hovers over the table.

"Err, yes, thanks," I say. "And could we get a couple more?"

She nods. "S'pose." She wanders back to the bar.

Beth glances at me. "She must really like you. She doesn't do table service for just anyone."

"My natural charm. So, you were saying?"

Her face darkens again. "We went to her favorite pizza place, but she didn't eat much. She was just moody, sarcastic. It wasn't her."

"Kids can change in senior school," I say. "It's like someone flicks a switch, their hormones crank up to eleven and all bets are off."

"No shit. I'm a teacher too, remember? I know what it's like. *Invasion of the Body Snatchers.*"

She picks up a beer mat and begins to peel it apart. "But even when Emily was going through a 'teenager' phase before, she still talked to *me*. I thought our relationship was different."

"Did she say anything about school, stuff that was bothering her?"

"Nope. And when I asked she just clammed up."

Lauren returns and plonks down two more bourbons. If they are doubles, then the optics are malfunctioning. Maybe Beth was right. Maybe she does like me.

Beth takes a sip. "Now, I think I should have pushed her. Made her talk to me."

"It doesn't work like that. Push teenagers too hard and they'll just go scuttling back into their shells."

"Yeah. But you know the shit thing? I didn't even hug her goodbye. We always hugged. But this time she just walked away. And, I thought—cool auntie—I'll let her go. Give her time. Turns out we didn't have time. Two weeks later she was dead." She sniffs, wipes angrily at her eyes. "I should have hugged her."

"You couldn't have known."

Because life never gives you a heads-up.

"Well, *I should have.* I'm a teacher. I should have realized this wasn't the usual moody teen. I should have spotted the signs of depression. She was my niece. And I let her down."

Guilt washes over me in a wave. I feel crippled by it for a moment. I swallow.

"What happened to your sister?"

She shakes her head, gathering herself. "She couldn't stay. Not in that house, where it happened. She moved back to Edgeford, nearer to Mum. She's still having a hard time, dealing. I go back as often as I can, but it's like Emily's death is this barrier between us and we can't seem to work our way around it."

I know what she means. Grief is personal. It isn't something you can share, like a box of chocolates. It is yours and yours alone. A spiked steel ball chained to your ankle. A coat of nails around your shoulders. A crown of thorns. No one else can feel your pain. They cannot walk in your shoes because your shoes are full of broken glass and every time you try and take a step forward it rips your soles to bloody shreds. Grief is the worst kind of torture and it never ends. You have dibs on that dungeon for the rest of your life.

"Is that why you came here?" I ask. "Because of Emily?"

"When the job came up a couple of months later it seemed like it was meant to be."

Funny how that happens.

"Why didn't you tell me at the start?"

"Because Harry doesn't know. I didn't want him to think I was here for the wrong reasons."

"Like?"

"Revenge."

"And you're not?"

"At the start, maybe. I wanted *someone* to be held accountable for Emily's death." She sighs. "But I couldn't find anything. At least, not anything specific. Just the usual friendships and fall-outs."

"What about Hurst?"

"She never mentioned him—"

"But?" I prompt.

"*Something* isn't right in that school, and Hurst is a part of it. When you let a kid like Hurst get away with the stuff he does, you create a place where cruelty is the norm."

I wonder if that's all. I remember what Marcus said: about Hurst taking kids up to the old colliery site. Kids who wanted to fit in. Perhaps even a young girl desperate to be accepted in a new school. The pit could get to you in more ways than one. Like it did with Chris.

"You've gone quiet."

"Just thinking that history has a shitty habit of repeating itself," I say bitterly.

"But it shouldn't. The only way schools like Arnhill Academy change is from the inside. Teaching is not all about rankings and inspection reports. It's about helping our young people to become decent, rounded human beings, and getting them through their teens in one piece. If you lose them at this age, you lose them forever." A small shrug. "You probably think that sounds naive."

"No, I think it sounds brave and commendable and all the stuff that is going to make you give me a one-fingered salute any second now and . . . yep, there it is."

She lowers her finger. "For all your cynical, world-weary crap, you almost sound like you understand."

"I do. I mean, don't get me wrong, my reasons for being here are far less worthy."

"So what are they?"

I hesitate. Of all people, it is Beth that I would like to tell the truth to. But then, of all people, it is Beth whose opinion I care about.

"Like you said, only two types of teachers come to Arnhill—I couldn't get a job anywhere else."

"I thought we were being honest here."

"I am."

"No." She shakes her head. "There's something you're not telling me."

"There really isn't."

"I can see it in your face."

"That's just my face. It's a curse."

"Fine. Don't tell me."

"Okay."

"So, there *is* something?"

"All right—I used to gamble. I ended up owing a lot of money. I needed to lie low somewhere until I could clear my debts. There is no noble reason for my return. I am a poor gambler, a mediocre teacher and a questionable human being. Happy?"

She glares at me. "Bullshit. You might be a twat, but you're a twat who's here for a reason. Something important to you. Otherwise, you would have turned tail the minute Hurst's cronies beat you up. But if you don't want to tell me, then fine. I thought we were becoming friends. I was obviously wrong."

She stands and grabs her jacket.

"You're going?"

"Nope. I'm storming out."

"Oh."

"Leaving *you* looking like a sad loser."

"Hate to break it, but I don't need you for that."

She slings on her jacket. "You need somebody."

"Everybody needs somebody."

"Meaningful."

"*Blues Brothers*."

"Piss off."

And with that, she turns and stomps out of the pub. Nobody so much as glances up from their drink.

I remain sitting at the table, like a sad loser. But at least a sad loser with two half-full glasses of bourbon. Every cloud. I pour Beth's glass into mine and take a large swig. Then I reach into my pocket and take out a piece of paper. I have scribbled an address on it.

Time to make a house call. Brighten someone else's evening.

IN A CARD GAME there is always a moment where you can see the other players' hands, as though the cards are transparent. You know what they are holding. You can see the odds in your head. The next moves. It's all there, as clearly as if someone had written it in fluorescent marker in the air in front of you.

And usually, you are wrong.

If ever you think you have got a handle on everyone else in a game, that you know how it is going to play out, the moves you should make, the bluffs you should call, you are in big trouble.

Because that is the point when it will come crashing down around your head.

I thought I had been clever working out the Ruth and Marcus connection. Thought I knew what was going on. Ruth lived here back then, she knew me, she knew Arnhill. She also knew Ben and Julia. It was *possible* that she somehow got hold of my email and phone number and sent those messages. It was all *possible*. But why?

Now I have another explanation. It doesn't make a lot more sense. I do not know what cards the other player is holding. But at least I know who I am playing.

I step forward and ring the doorbell. Then I stand back again.

It takes a moment. There are no lights on behind the curtains in the front room, but I'm sure she is here. I'm right. Seconds later, through the glass of the front door, I see a light come on in the hall.

The blurry outline of a figure approaches; I hear a cough, a sniff, and then the sound of a key in the lock, and the door edges open . . .

"Mr. Thorne."

She doesn't seem surprised to see me. But then, she has spent a lifetime perfecting a calm and unemotive exterior. What else has she spent a lifetime doing? I wonder.

I smile politely. "Hello, Miss Grayson."

26

1992

*B*ones!!"

Hurst's face lit up with so much joy it was like someone had yanked his pants down and given him a blow job right there and then.

It took me a moment to realize what it reminded me of. The look of ecstasy, the glow of the miner's light illuminating his features. And then I got it. It reminded me of that scene in *Raiders of the Lost Ark* where the Nazis are staring into the Ark . . . just before all the demons pour out and their faces start melting right off their skulls.

I thought I couldn't feel any more afraid. As usual, I was wrong.

"Bones!" The word shuddered around the group like a dark echo.

They stared at the bones laid into the rock. Some were more yellow, up close. Older, maybe. They were also small. Although some had obviously been broken or cut to form the symbols and shapes, others were still whole. They looked delicate, fragile even.

Hurst stretched out a hand and touched one, surprisingly gently. Then he dug his fingers in and pulled it from the rock. It gave, far more easily than I expected, in a small cloud of dust and rock fragments that crumbled to the ground. Hurst stared at the bone. An arm, I thought. A small arm.

"Jesus fuck!" Fletch yelled. "Have you seen this?"

We turned. He was holding up one of the yellowed rocks, except it wasn't a rock. It was a skull. Tiny. It barely filled his hand. Not an adult's. A child's. Nearly all of these dismembered skeletons were children.

"I think we should go," I said, but my voice sounded distant and weak.

"Are you joking?" Hurst said. "This place is the balls. And it's ours."

That was when I understood what truly deep shit we were in. You didn't own something like this. You could never own a place like this. If anything, it owned you.

Fletch grinned and chucked the skull at Marie.

"Dickhead." She ducked and the skull hit the ground and split neatly in two.

"Gross," Marie moaned. She didn't look so great. Maybe it was the sight of all the bones, maybe it was the effects of the cider kicking in, but her face had gone a pallid gray color.

Hurst was prowling around the cave now, gouging out more bones from the walls with the crowbar, whooping each time. Actually whooping.

Fletch grabbed some more skulls and started to boot them across the cavern, like he was playing football. My gut twisted in horror. But I didn't do anything. I just stood by. Like I always did.

"Here!" Hurst yelled, brandishing the crowbar. Fletch picked up a skull, clasping it like a bowling ball with his fingers in the empty sockets. He lobbed it toward Hurst. Hurst swung the crowbar. The metal and skull connected with a crack. The skull shattered. My stomach rolled.

I looked over at Chris for some help, some backup, but he just stood, arms hanging at his sides, staring blankly. As though, now that we were here, now that he could see what he had found, the trauma had shunted him into catatonia.

My voice finally broke: "For fuck's sake, these are the bones of dead kids."

"So?" Fletch turned to look at me. "Not like they're gonna complain."

Hurst just grinned. "Lighten up, Thorney. We're just having fun. Besides, finders keepers, right?"

He picked up the half-skull from the ground. "What's that Shakespeare shit? 'To be or not to be'?"

He threw the skull into the air and whacked it with the crowbar. Fragments of bone flew across the cavern.

I winced, but I was distracted. I thought I had heard something. Coming from the walls. A weird sort of sound. Not scratching, exactly. More like a *skittering, chittering* sound. I thought about bats. Could there be bats down here? Or rats even. They liked dark underground tunnels, didn't they?

"Did you hear something?" I asked.

Hurst frowned. "Nope."

"Are you sure? I thought I heard something—bats or rats?"

"Rats!" Marie's head whipped round. "Shit!" She bolted for a far corner and loudly threw up.

"Fuck," Fletch said. "I knew we shouldn't have brought her."

Hurst's face tensed. I wasn't sure if he was going to have a go at Fletch or shout at Marie. But then there was another noise. This time more distinct. A small cascade of stones rattling down from the steps above.

We all spun around (aside from Marie, who was making heaving, groaning noises in the corner). The cavern hung heavy with the smell of vomit and sweat. Still, it seemed to me that the air felt cooler. Cold even. But not normal cold. Weird cold. *Creeping cold*, I suddenly thought. Like the shifting shadows. Not static. Moving, alive.

We swung our flashlights back in the direction of the noise. Toward the steps. They rose unevenly up into darkness.

"Hey!" Hurst called. "Anybody up there?"

Silence, and then another small fall of stones.

"You'd better get down here or I will come up and . . ."

His voice tapered off. A shadow reared up on the wall. Tall and spindly, clutching something in its elongated fingers, something that looked like a baby . . .

We all fell quiet, even Marie's moans subsiding. I could hear the other sound again. The *skittering, chittering* sound. Closer. The shadow rounded the corner. My scalp tightened. Hurst raised the crowbar. Slowly, the shadow shrank and melted into a solid figure. A small figure in a gray hoodie, pink pajama bottoms and trainers. In one hand, she held a flashlight. In the other, a plastic doll.

"For fuck's sake." Hurst lowered the crowbar.

"You are shitting me," Fletch muttered.

I stared at Annie. "What the hell are you doing here?"

27

We sit, the pair of us, in the back room. It is dimly lit, furnished only with two sturdy leather armchairs, a desk and a reading table. A faded but probably once expensive rug covers the bare floorboards. Tall bookshelves take up most of the wall space, jam-packed with books whose spines are all pleasantly cracked and worn.

Never trust a person whose bookshelves are lined with pristine books, or worse, someone who places the books with their covers facing outward. That person is not a reader. That person is a shower. *Look at me and my great literary taste. Look at these acclaimed tomes that I have, most probably, never read.* A reader cracks the spine, thumbs the pages, absorbs every word and nuance. You might not be able to judge a book by its cover, but you can definitely judge the person who owns the book.

"So," Miss Grayson says, placing a cup of coffee on the table beside me then sitting down in the other armchair with a mug of Theraflu. "You have some questions."

"Just a few."

She sits back. "Probably the first being am I a crazy old woman with too much time on her hands?"

I reach for the coffee and take a sip. Unlike the slop she first served me at the school, this is rich and strong.

"It's up there."

"I imagine it is."

"You sent me the email?"

"Yes."

"How did you find me?"

"Process of elimination. I knew you'd become a teacher. I tracked you down to your last school, explained you were applying for a position here and I'd lost your contact details."

"But that was *before* I applied for the job here."

"That's right."

Something else occurs to me.

"Did the school mention how I left?"

"It came up."

"So you knew I faked the reference I gave Harry."

A glint in her eye. "I was impressed with your inventiveness."

I let this sink in. All along, she has been playing me.

"And the folder?"

"I collated it. Marcus left it for you—I thought it would attract less attention."

"But the text came from Marcus's phone?"

"An old one he didn't use. But then his iPhone was smashed and he needed a spare."

"*Why?* Why go to all this trouble? This pantomime? You didn't think to just *call* me? I hear that the mail even delivers such things as letters?"

"Would you have come back if I had just called?"

"Maybe."

"We both know that's not true."

Her voice is sharp. And I feel rebuked. Like a child caught in a lie.

"I learned a lot," she continues, "working with children all these years. One—never ask anything outright. They will only lie. Two—always make them think it is their idea. And three—make something interesting enough and they will come to you."

"You missed out four—never let them light their own farts."

A small smile. "You always used sarcasm as a defense mechanism, even as a boy."

"I'm surprised you remember me as a boy."

"I remember all my students."

"Impressive. I can barely remember my last class."

"Stephen Hurst—sadistic, amoral but clever. A dangerous combination. Nick Fletcher—not a bright boy, an excess of anger. A pity he couldn't have found a better way to channel it. Chris Manning—brilliant, damaged, lost. Always searching for something he could never find. And you—the dark horse. Deflecting blows with words. The closest thing Hurst had to a real friend. He needed you, more than you realized."

I swallow. My throat feels like sandpaper.

"You forgot Marie."

"Ah yes—a pretty girl, cleverer than she made out. A girl who knew how to get what she wanted, even back then."

"But we're not children anymore."

"We're all still children inside. The same fears, the same joys. We just get taller, and better at hiding things."

"You're pretty good at hiding things yourself."

"I didn't mean to deceive you."

"Then what exactly *did* you mean to do?"

"Persuade you to return. In which I succeeded." She starts to cough, pulls a tissue out of her sleeve and covers her mouth. Once the coughing has subsided, she says: "I presume you found out through Marcus."

I nod. "He was worried you'd get into trouble. I promised him you wouldn't . . . as long as you told me the truth."

She nods. "Marcus is a good boy."

"He thinks a lot of you."

"He's my godson, but I suppose he told you that as well?"

"Yes. I never realized you knew his mum—"

"Ruth suffered terribly at school. I rescued her from the bullies one day and became something of a confidante."

I think about the children I would see in her office. The ones she tried to help. It wasn't much. But, in school, when you are scared and bullied, a small kindness is everything.

"Anyway," she continues, "Ruth and I stayed in touch after she left school. When she had Lauren and Marcus she asked me to be their godmother.

"I would look after them sometimes when she was working, in the holidays. We remained close, especially Marcus. He still visits me for tea twice a week. He's a very smart young man and we share a lot of the same interests."

"Local history?"

Another thin smile. "Among other things."

"So you used him?"

"He wanted to help. He doesn't know everything, if that's what you're thinking."

"Oh, you have no idea what I'm thinking."

"Then tell me."

I open my mouth and realize *I* have no idea what I'm thinking.

"You read the folder?" she prompts, taking a sip from her mug.

"Most of it."

"Did you find it interesting?"

I shrug. "Arnhill has a grim history. A lot of places do."

"But most places aren't as old as this village. People presume Arnhill grew up around the mine. Not true. It was here long before the mine."

"So?"

"Why does a village grow up in the middle of nowhere?"

"Nice views?"

"Villages grow in certain places for a reason. Clean water, fertile land. And sometimes, there are other reasons."

Other reasons. I feel a sudden draft. A cool waft of icy air.

"Such as?"

"Did you read the articles about the witch trials and Ezekeriah Hyrst?"

"Myth, urban legend."

"But there is often a grain of truth."

"And what's the truth about Arnhill?"

She wraps her hands around her mug. Strong hands, I think. Competent. Steady.

"You visited the graveyard. You noticed what was missing?"

"Children. Babies."

She nods. "That's what is *obviously* missing."

"Obviously?"

"Arnhill has a grim history, as you said. A lot of death. But there are just ninety souls buried in the graveyard."

"Don't they reuse old graves after a while?"

"They do. But even taking that into account—and the fact that most people were buried in other churchyards after about 1946, or cremated in more recent years—there's a shortfall. Put bluntly, there are not enough graves for the dead. So, where are they?"

I suddenly understand what she has done. She has led me here, slowly and carefully, taking the long road so I didn't see exactly where we were going. Until now.

"I think that they were taken to another place," she says. "A place that the villagers believed was somehow special." She lets the sentence hang for a moment. "And twenty-five years ago, I believe that you and your friends found it."

Places have secrets too, I think. Like people. You just need to dig. In land, in life, in a man's soul.

"How did you know?"

"I've seen a lot of young people in my time, here in the village. Seen them grow up, marry, have children of their own. Some never make it that far. Like Chris."

I think about a soft thud. A ruby-red shadow.

"He used to sit in my office sometimes. Before Hurst took him under his wing."

"I don't remember—"

"You were probably too busy scurrying past, hoping I wouldn't tell you off for your untucked shirt, or for wearing trainers."

I almost smile. The past, I think. Never more than a few careless words away. Except I don't think any of Miss Grayson's words are careless. She has spent a long time waiting to speak them.

"A few days before he died," she says, "Chris came to see me. He wanted to talk to someone. About what you found."

"He told you what happened?"

"Some of it. But I think there's more, isn't there, Joe?"

There's always more. *You just need to dig.* And the deeper you go, the darker it gets.

I nod. "Yes."

"Why don't you tell me?"

28

1992

Annie looked around the cavern, eyes huge hollows in her small face.

"I followed you."

"No shit. What were you thinking?"

"I wanted to see what you were up to. Are they skulls? Are they real?" Her voice trembled a little. She clutched Abbie-Eyes to her narrow chest.

"You have to go." I walked—hobbled—forward and grabbed her arm. "C'mon."

"Wait." Hurst moved to block us.

"What?"

"What if she blabs?"

"She's eight."

"Exactly."

"I won't say nothing," Annie muttered.

"See? Now let me get her out of here."

We locked eyes. I'm not really sure what I would have done if Marie hadn't moaned from the corner: "I don't feel good, Steve. I want to go home."

"Stupid cow," Fletch spat, but it sounded halfhearted.

I saw Hurst debate with himself. He looked at Annie and me, then back at Marie.

"Fine," he growled. "We'll go. But we're coming back. And I ain't leaving without some mementos."

"No!" Chris spoke for the first time. "You can't. You can't take anything from here."

Hurst advanced on him. "Why the fuck not, Doughboy? This is ours now. We own it."

No, I thought again. You didn't own this place. It might let you think so. Might even *want* you to think so. But that was how it got you. That was how it drew you down here. That was how it owned *you*.

"Chris is right," I said. "We can't take anything. I mean, what if someone asks where we got human bones from?"

Hurst turned to me. "No one tells. And no one fucking tells me what I can and can't do, Thorney."

He raised the crowbar again. I felt Annie flinch. I gripped her tighter.

A slow smile spread across Hurst's face: "Give me your backpack."

Without waiting for a reply, he yanked it from my back and threw it to Fletch.

"Let's grab some booty. We can stick some candles in these and scare the shit out of people on Halloween."

Fletch caught the bag and knelt to gather up some more skulls. Hurst returned to the wall and began hacking at it with the crowbar, gouging out bones in a frenzy.

Annie clutched my arm. "Abbie-Eyes doesn't like it down here."

"Tell Abbie-Eyes it's okay. We're going, soon."

She shivered against me. "Abbie-Eyes says it's not okay. She says it's the shadows; the shadows are moving." She turned sharply. "What's that noise?"

There was no mistaking that *skittering*, *chittering* now. It was all around us. Not rats. Or bats. They were both too large. Too cumbersome. This was a brittle, busy sound. The sound of something small but multitudinous. A mass of bristling shells and scuttling legs.

I understood a moment before it happened. *Insects*, I thought. *Insects*.

Hurst stuck the crowbar into the rock, gouging at a stubborn bit of bone. "Gotcha!"

The wall exploded in a mass of shiny black bodies.

"Fuck!!"

Beetles poured out in a glistening wave, like living oil. Hundreds of them. They swarmed out of the hole and down to the floor. Some scurried along the crowbar and up Hurst's arms. He dropped the bar and started shaking himself, like he was doing some kind of crazy dance.

On the other side of the cave Fletch yelped. The skull he was holding swiveled in his hand and more beetles poured from the eye sockets and gaping mouth. The skulls on the ground shifted, pushed around by thousands of tiny insect legs.

Fletch threw the skull to one side and scrambled to his feet. In his haste to get up he dropped the flashlight. It hit the floor and went out, plunging half of the cave into darkness.

Marie screamed, shrill and hysterical. "I can't see. *Shit, shit, shit.* They're all over me. Help me. *Help me!*"

A scream welled in my own throat but I needed to think about Annie. She clung to me, paralyzed into silence. I wrapped my arms around her, whispered into her hair.

"It's okay. They're just beetles. We're going to get out of here."

I tried to shuffle us backward, toward the steps, where Chris still stood, flashlight hanging uselessly from his hand, illuminating a small patch of moving ground. Beetles cracked and crunched under our feet. *Snap, crackle and pop.* I felt glad of my heavy boots, jeans tucked in the top, even though I could feel my swollen ankle pressing painfully against the leather. Annie whimpered beside me like a scared animal.

We were almost there when a figure charged out of the darkness. Hurst. In the glow of the miner's light his face was sallow and slick with sweat. Panicked. And that scared me more than anything.

"Give me your helmet."

He grabbed for it, knocking me back into the wall. I lost my grip on Annie.

"Get off me!"

"Give me the light."

He shoved me hard, smashing my head back against the rock. My skull clunked inside the helmet. I heard something crack. The light wavered, clung on tentatively and then faded to nothing. Blackness enveloped us in a dank cloak.

"You *fucking* moron!" I shoved Hurst away. Desperation clawed at my throat. We needed to get out of here. *Now.* "Annie?"

"Joey? I can't see you." Her voice was full of held-back tears. Still trying so hard to be brave.

I limped in the direction of her voice. "I'm right here. Turn on your flashlight."

"I can't. I've lost it."

"It's okay—" I reached out my hand; my fingers glanced hers.

From the darkness, Marie screamed: "*Nooooo!*"

I felt a whoosh of air as something sliced past my face. I dived to the floor, landing hard on my elbow. The helmet flew off my head. Pain tore up my arm. But I didn't have time to focus on it because right then I heard another scream, high-pitched, agonizing, terrible.

"*ANNIE?!!*"

I scrambled across the ground, scrabbling among the hard shells and scurrying legs. My fingers brushed metal. Annie's flashlight. I grabbed it, realized a battery was hanging out of the back. I shoved it in, flicked the switch and pointed the light around.

My mind went into free-fall. My heart seemed to fold and expand and shatter all at once. Annie lay on the ground in a small, crumpled heap, still clutching Abbie-Eyes. Her pajamas had ridden up, revealing thin, dirt-smeared legs. Her face and hair were both covered with something dark, red and sticky.

I crawled over to my sister and gathered her awkwardly in my arms. She felt so bony, all angles. She smelled of shampoo and cheese-and-onion chips. Around us, the beetles that had been swarming everywhere had started to retreat, to dissipate and melt back into the walls, their work here finished.

"It was an accident . . ."

I raised the flashlight. Hurst stood a few feet away, Marie clinging to his arm. The crowbar lay at his feet. I remembered the *whoosh* past my face. I looked back down at Annie, blood seeping from her head.

"*What the fuck have you done?*"

Rage rose like burning black bile in my throat. I wanted to charge at him and smash his head into the rock until it was nothing but splintered bone and jelly. I wanted to take the crowbar and drive it into his guts.

But something stopped me. *Annie.* My ankle was still throbbing. It would be a struggle to get up those steps on my own. I couldn't carry Annie too. I wasn't even sure we should move her. I needed Hurst and the others to get help.

"Give me something for the blood."

Hurst fumbled the tie off his head and threw it to me. His face was slack. He looked like he was waking from a bad dream and discovering it wasn't a dream.

"I didn't mean to . . ."

Didn't mean to hurt Annie. Just meant to hurt me. But I couldn't process that now. I pressed the tie against the wound on Annie's scalp. It sunk in. Not good. Not good.

"Is she dead?" Fletch asked.

No, I thought. *No, no, no. Not my little sister. Not Annie.*

"You have to get an ambulance."

"But . . . what do we tell them?"

"What does it matter?"

The tie in my hand was sodden. I threw it to one side.

"Fletch is right," Hurst muttered. "We need a story. I mean, they're gonna ask stuff—"

"A story?" I stared at him. "For fuck's sake."

Out of the corner of my eye I saw Chris move. He bent down and picked something up from the ground. Then he shifted back into the shadows.

"Tell them anything," I said desperately. "Just get help. Now."

"What's the point if she's dead?" Fletch again. *Fucking* Fletch. "I can't hear her breathing. She's not breathing. Look at her. Look at her eyes."

I didn't want to look. Because I had already seen. She was just unconscious, I told myself. Just unconscious. *So why weren't her eyes rolled back? Why was her frail body already feeling colder?*

Hurst ran a hand through his hair. Thinking. That was bad. Because if he started to think, started to worry about saving his own neck, we were screwed.

"They'll ask questions. The police."

"*Please*," I begged. "She's my little sister."

"Steve." Marie touched his arm. I had almost forgotten she was there.

Hurst looked at her. Something seemed to pass between them. He nodded. "Okay. Let's go."

I looked at Marie, tried to signal my thanks, but she wouldn't meet my eyes. She still looked pale, ill. They all shuffled toward the steps. No one offered to stay with me, not even Chris. But that was okay. I didn't want them here. Just me and Annie. Like it always had been.

At the bottom of the steps, Hurst paused. He looked like he was about to say something. If he had, I think I would have run at him and torn out his heart with my bare hands. But he didn't. He turned silently and disappeared into the darkness.

I remained kneeling on the cold ground, cradling Annie's limp body on my lap. I propped the flashlight up against the rock, like an uplighter. Squashed, dead beetles surrounded us. I could still hear the rest of them faintly, in the walls. I tried not to think about that. Tried to listen to the sounds of the others ascending. Tried not to listen to what was lacking.

She's not breathing.

They weren't going quickly enough. *Faster*, I thought. *Go faster*. After a while their stumbling steps grew distant. They must be near the opening now, I thought. Must be. Then it wouldn't take them long to run back to the village, to a house, a phone box. To call 999. The hospital was a good twelve miles away but the ambulances would have lights and sirens and if they knew it was a child, if . . .

A sound. More like an echo. Distant but still loud enough to carry. *CLUNG*. Like something heavy dropping. *CLUNG*. Or a metal door slamming. *CLUNG*.

Or a hatch closing.

CLUNG.

I stared up into the darkness.

"No," I whispered.

They couldn't. They wouldn't. Not even Hurst. Surely?

No one tells. We need a story. They'll ask questions.

CLUNG.

And who would know? Who would find us? Who would tell?

I tried to rationalize. I might be mistaken. Maybe they had just closed the hatch to keep us safe, or to make sure that no one fell in. I tried. I tried really hard to convince myself, but all I came back to was that heavy metallic sound:

CLUNG.

In that moment I understood things no fifteen-year-old should. About human nature. About self-preservation. About desperation. Panic rose in a tidal wave, filling my throat, making it hard to breathe. I clutched my little sister tighter, rocking her back and forth.

Annie, Annie, Annie.

CLUNG.

And now I could hear another sound. *Skittering, chittering.* The beetles. They were coming out of the walls again. Coming back for us.

The thought broke my paralysis.

We couldn't wait here. Hoping for help that might never come.

We had to move. We had to get out.

I laid Annie gently on the ground and forced myself to my feet. If I put most of my weight on my left foot I could just about stand. I bent and lifted Annie under the arms, then realized I had no hands free to hold the flashlight. I dithered. The beetles skittered. I grabbed the flashlight and gripped it between my teeth. Then I picked up Annie again and staggered backward up the first few steps, balancing myself against the rocky wall, dragging her limp body after me. She was slight, but so was I. Her hoodie kept hitching up, her soft skin chafing against the rough stone steps. I kept stopping to try and pull it down, which was stupid. I was wasting effort, and time.

I heaved her up three more steps. My ankle twinged. My head swam. I paused, tried to breathe, readjusted my grip. Then I stepped backward. The stone crumbled beneath my heel. My foot slipped, my legs went out from under me. I was falling. Again. I held on to Annie, but with no way to break my fall my skull cracked hard against the rocky step behind me. My vision wavered and darkness folded in on me.

It was different this time. The darkness. Deeper. Colder. I could feel it moving.

around and inside me. Crawling over my skin, filling my throat, burrowing right down into . . .

My eyes shot open. My hands flailed, rubbing and slapping at my head and face. I was dimly aware of things retreating. A whispering tide of glistening shells receding once more into the rock. The flashlight lay beside me, emitting a sickly, feeble glow. It didn't have much life left in it. How long had I been out for? Seconds? Minutes? Longer? I was sprawled on the next-to-last step. My body felt oddly light. A weight removed.

Annie.

She wasn't lying on me. I sat up. She wasn't next to me, or near me, or at the bottom of the steps. What the—

I picked up the flashlight and scrambled to my feet. My ankle still hurt, but not as badly. Perhaps it was just numb, or I was becoming inured to the pain. The back of my head felt sore. I touched it. A tender bump. No time to think about that.

Annie.

I stepped cautiously back down into the cavern. Bones and skulls still lay scattered across the ground. Small pieces cracked beneath my feet.

"Annie?"

My voice reverberated back at me. Hollow. Empty. *Nobody here but us*, the empty echo seemed to reply. *Nobody here but us chickens.*

Impossible. And yet, if she wasn't here, there was only one explanation—she must have gotten out.

I tried to think back. I never saw her getting struck. Yes, there was a lot of blood and she was unconscious, but head wounds bled a lot, didn't they? I read that somewhere. Even a small cut could bleed loads. Maybe she wasn't hurt as badly as I had thought.

Yeah? What about how cold she felt? What about her not breathing?

A mistake. My mind exaggerating. We were all shit scared. It was dark. I panicked, overreacted. And there was something else, wasn't there? I stared around the cavern again. *Abbie-Eyes.* Abbie-Eyes was missing. I had left the doll down here but now she was gone. Annie must have taken her.

I took one last look around the cavern and headed back to the steps. I scrambled up them more quickly this time—urged on by hope and desperation—and squeezed through the gap in the rock. A quick scan of the small cave revealed it was also empty. The flashlight flickered. Maybe enough battery life to get me home, maybe not.

Home. Could Annie have made it home?

It was barely a ten-minute walk from our house up to the old mine. If she had made it out, maybe she had made it back? Maybe she was there now, telling Dad everything, and I could look forward to a good belting when I got home. Right then, I would have welcomed it.

I pulled myself back up the ladder. The hatch was partly open (so maybe I had been wrong about that too). Not all the way, but enough for Annie to have squeezed through, enough for me to squeeze through. I stood up in the cool, fresh night air. It stung my throat as I breathed it in. I felt myself wobble slightly, my vision blur. I bent and rested my hands on my knees. I needed to keep it together. Just long enough to get back.

I scrambled over the slag heaps and slipped through the gap in the perimeter fence. Halfway down the street the flashlight finally gave up. But that was okay because now there were streetlights and the occasional glow of lamps through living-room curtains. How late was it? How long had we been down there?

I hurried down the alley that ran along the back of our house, and through the gate. In the yard, I paused. I still had Dad's jacket and boots on. *Shit.* I shed them quickly, shoved them in the shed and then limped, in my holey socks, over to the back door. I turned the handle. Unlocked. It usually was, because Dad was usually too drunk to remember to lock it.

In the kitchen, I hesitated. A light glowed in the living room. The television. Dad half sat, half sprawled on his armchair in front of it, snoring. A small collection of lager cans nestled on the floor beside his feet.

I tiptoed over to the stairs, placed a hand on the banister and dragged my flagging body up the staircase. I felt exhausted, sick. But I needed to see Annie. I needed to make sure that she was home. I eased her door open.

Relief. Huge. Overwhelming.

By the light from the hall I could just see a small Annie-shaped mound curled up beneath the My Little Pony duvet. Poking out of the top, a crown of tousled dark hair.

She was here. She made it home. It was all okay.

In that moment, I could almost have believed that everything that had happened before was just some terrible dream.

I started to pull the door closed . . .

And then I paused. Did I think, for a second, how strange it was that Annie had gone straight to bed and not even tried to rouse Dad, to get help for me? Did I consider, even briefly, going into her room to check if she was all right? After all, she had a head injury. I should have woken her, made sure she was conscious, coherent.

Should have, should have, should have.

But I didn't.

I pulled the door shut and stumbled into my own room. I took off my dirty clothes and chucked them into the laundry basket. It would all be all right, I told myself. We would sort it all out in the morning. Make up some story about what happened tonight. I would tell Hurst I didn't want to be part of his gang anymore. I would spend more time with Annie. I would make it up to her. I really, really would.

I collapsed into bed. Something fluttered briefly, like a soft gray moth, in my mind. Something about Annie, in her bed. Something important that was *missing*. But, before I could grasp it, it was gone again. Dissolved into dust. I pulled the duvet up to my chin and closed my eyes . . .

29

"And in the morning, she was gone?"

"She never made it back. The lump in the bed was a pile of toys. The hair—a doll." I shake my head. "A pile of *fucking* toys. I should have seen it. I should have checked."

"You sound like you were concussed yourself, not thinking straight."

But I should have noticed what was missing. *Abbie-Eyes.* Abbie-Eyes wasn't on the bed. Annie would never have left her down there. She would have brought her back.

"What happened then?" Miss Grayson asks.

"The police were called. Search parties sent out. I tried to tell them. Tried to explain how Annie would follow me sometimes, up to the pit. How they should look up there."

"But you didn't tell them what happened?"

"I wanted to. But by then Hurst had told the police we were all at his house that night. His dad backed him up. No one would believe me. Not my word against his."

Miss Grayson nods and I think: *She knows.* She knows I am a liar and a coward.

"You didn't go back to look for her?"

"I couldn't get near and the police wouldn't let me join the search parties. I just kept thinking they would find the hatch. They would find her. They had to."

"Sometimes, some places, like people, have to *want* to be found."

I would very much like to dismiss this as crazy. But I know she's right. Chris didn't find the hatch. It found him. And if it didn't want you inside, you'd never find it again.

"I was going to confess," I say. "I was going to go down to the police station and tell them everything."

"What stopped you?"

"She came back."

And they all lived happily ever after.

Except, there's no such thing. My little sister came back. She sat in the police station, swinging her legs, an oversized blanket wrapped around her shoulders, Abbie-Eyes clutched tightly in her arms. And she smiled at me.

That was when I knew. That was when I realized what was wrong. So terribly, horribly wrong.

Annie's head. Where was the wound? The blood? All I could see was a small red scar on her forehead. I stared at it. Could it have healed so quickly? Had I been wrong? Had I imagined the blow being worse than it was? I didn't know. I didn't know anything anymore.

"Joe?"

"*Something* happened to my sister," I say slowly. "I can't explain what. I just know that, when she came back, she wasn't the same. She wasn't *my* Annie."

"I understand."

"No, you don't. No one does. And I've spent twenty-five years trying to forget it." I look at her angrily. "You said you know what happened to my sister. You know nothing."

She stares back at me, her gaze cool and appraising. Then she stands and walks to the desk. She opens a drawer and takes out a bottle of sherry and two glasses.

She fills both to the brim, hands one glass to me and sits back down, clutching the other. I'm not really a fan of sherry but I take a sip. A large one.

"I had a sister once," she says.

"I didn't know—"

"She was stillborn. I saw her, just afterward. She looked just like she was sleeping, except, of course, she didn't breathe, didn't make a sound. I remember the village midwife—an older woman—wrapping her up and placing her in my mother's arms. And then she said something I'll always remember: 'It doesn't need to be like this. I know a place you can take her—you could bring your baby back.'"

I want to make an acerbic comment. Something pithy, something puerile. I want to tell her that she was a child and misinterpreted the words. I want to tell her that memories become soft over time. As malleable as putty in our minds—we can shape them into anything we want.

But I find I can't. That cold draft is back. A window open somewhere.

"What did your mother do?"

"Told the woman to get out. To never speak of such things."

"Did you ever ask her about it?"

"My parents never talked about my sister. But then, very few of us talk about death, do we? It's a dirty secret. And yet, in a way, death is the most important part of life. Without it, our existence would be unthinkable."

I throw back the rest of the sherry. "Why did you want me to come back?"

"To stop history repeating itself."

"You can't. That's what history does. We like to pretend we learn from our mistakes, but we don't. We always think it will be different this time. And it never is."

"If you really believed that, you wouldn't be here."

I bark out a laugh. "Right now, I have no idea what I believe, or why I'm here."

"Then let me help you—I believe that Jeremy Hurst has found another way into the cave you discovered. He has been taking children down there. I think he took Ben and something happened to him, just like your sister."

"And I'm *sorry* about that, okay? I'm sorry about Ben. I'm sorry about Julia. But I don't know what you expect me to do—"

"This isn't just about Ben and Julia."

"Then what the hell *is* it about?"

"Stephen Hurst."

Instinctively, my jaw clenches.

"What has he got to do with any of it?"

"He's been obstructing the progress of the country-park scheme for months. Stopping developers getting access to the land."

"I thought he wanted to build houses."

"That's what he *wants* people to think. I think he's protecting what's beneath the ground."

"Why?"

"Marie is very ill."

"Cancer. I know."

"*Terminal* cancer. She has months, maybe weeks, left. She is dying."

I remember the wave of dread I felt in the pub.

Marie is not *going to die. I will* not *let that happen.*

"No." I shake my head. "Not even Hurst is *that* insane."

"But he *is* desperate. And desperate people will try anything. They're looking for a miracle." She leans forward and rests a cool, dry hand on mine. "Of course, that is seldom what they find. Do you understand now why I wanted you to come back?"

I do, and the understanding carves a deep, cold chasm out of my insides.

"He wants to save her," I say.

"And I think you are the only person who can stop him."

30

I sit on the sofa, a glass of bourbon and the pack of playing cards on the coffee table in front of me. I haven't touched either yet. The fire isn't lit and the room is in darkness. I still have my coat on. It's cold, but then it always is.

In the faint moonlight shining through from the kitchen window I can see Abbie-Eyes on the opposite armchair, regarding me with her new—and even more nightmarish—gaze.

She is not my only company. I can sense them, close by. Not just the *skittering*, *chittering* sounds I have become almost accustomed to. Other companions. Silent, but watching. I open the pack of cards—for the first time in a long time—and start to shuffle them.

"It's not my problem, okay?"

I spit the words out into the darkness and wait for it to challenge me. It doesn't reply, but I feel eyes upon me, full of blackness.

"I tried to stop it before. It didn't work."

The darkness bristles, the chittering increases, like I have said something that annoys it. I deal the cards out. Four hands for my invisible players. Then I reach for my drink and throw it back. Dutch courage. Stupid phrase. False courage, no matter what the tongue.

"I don't owe Hurst anything. So, let him go ahead. Let him learn. I don't care."

Except, the darkness chides, like a parent to a tantrum-throwing child, *that's not true, is it, Joe? Because this isn't just about Hurst. It's about Marie. A girl you once had feelings for. A woman who is dying. Who deserves to do that in some sort of peace. Because there are things worse than death. Because what comes back isn't always what left. And you're the only person who can stop it.*

I try to stare the darkness down. But the darkness doesn't budge, doesn't blink. If anything, it seems to draw closer, pressing itself against me like an unwelcome lover. And now, I can see something else lurking in its folds. Figures, shadows within shadows. Because the dead never really leave us. We carry them inside. In everything we do. In our dreams, our nightmares. The dead are a part of us. And maybe they are part of something else too. This place. This earth.

But what if the earth is rotten? What if the things you plant there grow back full of poison? I think about how you can never build the same snowman, or how the tapes that Dad's mate copied were always fuzzy and corrupted. There are some things—some beautiful, perfect things—you can never re-create without ruining them.

I hear movement. The creak of a door, the soft tread of footsteps. I'm ready.

"What do you want from me?" I ask. "What do you want me to do?"

"Well, for a start, you could turn the feckin' lights on."

I jump and spin around, just as the living room floods with light.

"Jesus." I shield my eyes, like a vampire exposed to the burning rays of the dawn.

I squint through my fingers. Brendan stands near the doorway, resplendent in army jacket, baggy sweater, cords and tattered Green Flash trainers. A large holdall is slung over his shoulder.

He regards me from within his nest of tangled hair and beard. "What the feck are you doing here, sitting in the dark, talking to yourself?"

I just stare at him. Then I shake my head.

"Am I the only person who knocks on a door anymore?"

BRENDAN MAKES TERRIBLE COFFEE. It is also past midnight—not my preferred coffee-drinking hour. But I am too tired, confused and wrung out to argue the case against it.

He emerges from the kitchen with two mugs, plonks one down in front of me and looks around for somewhere to sit with his.

"I love what you've done with the place."

"It's called deconstructed."

"It's called something."

I nod toward the armchair. "Sit. Abbie-Eyes loves company."

He eyes the doll. "This is probably stating the obvious but sitting here talking to a one-eyed doll is even more bloody creepy than talking to yourself."

He removes Abbie-Eyes and places her on the floor with a shudder, then sits and clasps his mug. The holdall rests at his feet. I look down at it.

"I was expecting a courier, not personal delivery."

"Yeah, well, I figured the petrol was cheaper."

"You haven't got a car."

"I borrowed my sister's."

"What about work?"

"I can give it a miss for a couple of days. And I'm glad I did. Because you look like shit, my man. Countryside air does not agree with you."

I rub at my eyes. "Well, I won't be breathing it much longer."

One way or another.

"Your plan is coming to fruition."

"Something like that."

"Is that why you've got a pack of playing cards out?"

I glance at the hands of cards I have dealt on the table.

"I was just killing time."

"You're not planning on winning your money back?"

"*No*. Of course not."

"Thank feck for that. Don't take this wrong, but you're a shit card-player."

"And you couldn't have told me that *before* someone made matchsticks out of my leg?"

"You've got to want to hear it." He looks down at the holdall. "So, presumably—and I don't think I'll be stepping on Sherlock's toes when I deduce this—it has something to do with what's in this bag?"

"Bravo, dear Watson."

"So?"

I raise an eyebrow. Or at least, I try. The effort is a little too much tonight.

"Someone is going to pay me a lot of money *not* to take that to the police." I lean forward and lift the holdall onto the coffee table. "Have you looked inside?"

"I figured if you wanted me to know, you'd show me."

I unzip the top and carefully take out a bulky shape wrapped in an old sweatshirt. I unfold the sweatshirt, revealing two items carefully preserved inside a clear plastic bag:

A crowbar, and a dark blue school tie, darker in places, where it soaked up the blood. My sister's blood. Just visible, a name sewn into it: S. Hurst.

"What the feck is this?" Brendan asks.

"Payback."

31

F alling doesn't kill you. Stopping kills you.
   That's what Chris told me.

People think that when you fall from a great height your brain shuts down before you hit the ground.

Not true. It's possible, because of the speed at which your brain processes information, that it may not have time to consciously comprehend the actual impact. But that doesn't mean it isn't furiously working all the way down.

Right until the final crunch.

I HAD ENGLISH IN THE BLOCK, last period, the day that Chris fell. We read from *Animal Farm*. I never liked that novel. I was not then, or now, a fan of overly heavy-handed symbolism.

In my fifteen-year-old opinion, you could just as easily have told the story with people instead of dressing it up with animals. I didn't see the point. I didn't like the conceit. It was like the author thought he was being clever and no one could see through his book pretending to be one thing when it wasn't. But you could. And it wasn't clever. It was like a magic act, where you could see the trick but the magician still thought they were all that.

Orwell wasn't all that. But *Nineteen Eighty-Four* was good. It didn't pretend. It was just harsh and scary and brutal.

To be fair, I wasn't thinking much about the book during this particular lesson. I was distracted. I'd been distracted a lot over the previous few weeks.

Annie had been back for almost a month. The initial euphoria and attention had faded. But it still should have been a happy time. Things should have been getting back to normal. But they weren't. I wasn't even sure I knew what normal was anymore.

For the first few days I tried to talk to Annie. To coax out of her what had happened that night. But she just stared at me with eyes that were muddy with incomprehension. Occasionally, she smiled or giggled for no reason. The sound of her laughter, which had always made me feel warm inside, now set my teeth on edge like nails down a blackboard.

Mum still wasn't around much because she was spending most of her time caring for Nan, who "wasn't doing so well" after the fall. Dad had taken leave from work to help look after Annie until she was ready to go back to school. Or so he said. It wasn't true. I had seen a letter sticking out of his jacket pocket one evening. At the top, it read: "P45." I knew what that meant. That he had left his job or been fired. I tucked the letter farther into his pocket and didn't say a word to Mum.

There were a lot of things I wasn't telling Mum. *Couldn't* tell her. Because I didn't want to worry her. Because I didn't want to make her unhappy. Because I was scared she wouldn't believe me.

I didn't tell her that I had started to dread going home after school because Dad would already be drunk and the house would stink. Not just of booze. Of something worse. Something fetid and sour. The sort of smell you might get when something has crawled under the floorboards to die. Mum even sent Dad and me looking for a dead mouse one night. When we couldn't find anything she rolled her eyes and said, "I'm sure it will pass."

I didn't tell her she was wrong. That the smell wasn't a dead mouse. It was something else that had come to nest in our home.

I didn't tell her that I lay awake most nights listening to the noises from Annie's room next door. Sometimes it would be the same song, over and over:

"She'll be coming round the mountain when she comes, She'll be coming round the mountain when she comes."

Other nights, there would be terrible shouts and screams. I would put my Walkman headphones on or jam my pillow over my head, anything to muffle the sounds. In the morning I would go into Annie's room, pull the urine-soaked sheets off her bed and stuff them in the washing machine, sticking it on before I went to school. Mum probably thought I was trying to help Dad. And to be fair, if I hadn't done the washing, it wouldn't have got done. But that wasn't the real reason.

I did it because I felt responsible. This was my lot. Penitence. Punishment for what I had done. Or what I hadn't done. I hadn't saved her.

I didn't tell anyone that sometimes I changed my own sheets too. That I twitched at every creak in the house because I might turn and find Annie standing there, clutching Abbie-Eyes; not speaking, just smiling and staring at me with those eyes that were too dark and old for an eight-year-old.

I didn't want to admit, even to myself, that sometimes I was scared to death of my own little sister.

The bell rang for the end of class. I stuffed my books into my bag and scraped my chair back. The seat next to me was empty. Chris used to sit there. But now he had taken to sitting on his own, at a spare desk near the back.

I was relieved. Not just because I didn't want to speak to him, didn't want to hear him make excuses or give apologies for what they did that night. But also because something was going on with Chris. And it wasn't good. His appearance was more unkempt than ever. His stutter was worse. He had taken to humming and murmuring to himself. Sometimes he would suddenly stop and brush manically at his arms, like he was brushing off invisible dirt. Or insects.

Normally, he scuttled out of class first. That way he could avoid the name-calling, the deliberate tripping and shoving. Now that he wasn't hanging around with Hurst anymore (neither of us was), he was devoid of his invisible shield.

I didn't stick up for him. I had my own problems. My own worries. So, when I saw that this afternoon he had lingered behind, and when he fell into a shambling step beside me as I hurried down the stairs, I was pissed off.

"What is it?"

"I–I n–n–need to sh–sh–sh–show you s–s–something."

His breath smelled stale, like he hadn't brushed his teeth. His shirt stank of BO.

"What?"

"C–c–can't t–t–tell you here."

"Why?"

"T–t–too many p–p–people."

We reached the ground floor. I pushed open the door to the courtyard outside. Other students thronged around us, the usual hustle and bustle of hometime. Chris's face was flushed. I could see him trying to force the words out. I felt bad for him, despite myself.

"Just try and breathe, okay?"

He nodded and took several deep breaths. I waited.

"The g–graveyard. M–m–m–meet me there. Six p.m. Important."

I wanted to come up with an excuse. But what was the alternative? Make sure Dad hadn't set the house on fire after falling asleep with a cigarette? Check my sister was still there? Still not being Annie?

"Okay." I sighed. "It better be good."

Chris nodded, put his head down like he was running for cover and scurried around the corner.

I adjusted my bag on my shoulder and heard laughter behind me. I glanced around. Hurst had emerged from the English-block doors, Fletch following him like a greasy shadow. Hurst looked over, smirked then whispered something to him. I saw them both chortle.

I clenched my fists, dug my nails into my palms and forced myself to turn away. I'd just get into more trouble. Mum would be upset. Dad would belt me. Hurst would win. Again. What was the point? I put my head down and marched resolutely toward the gates.

I didn't head straight back home. I never did now. I walked the streets, ate chips in the bus shelter, hung out in the playground (if Hurst and Fletch weren't there), anything to delay the moment I would have to push open the door and be confronted by the smell, the cloying darkness, the *creeping* cold that would wrap itself around me . . .

I only had a few pence in my pocket today. I couldn't go for fish and chips or to the sweetshop, so I dawdled along the high street, kicking at an empty soda bottle. I wandered past the small patch of grass where the brass statue of a miner stood. There was a bench beside it. Usually it was empty. Today, a solitary figure sat there, hunched over in an oversized army jacket, head down, dark hair falling over her face. Marie.

We hadn't spoken since the night down the pit. To be honest, I wasn't sure she remembered a lot of it. I'd like to say this made me think less of her. That she had slipped from the pedestal I'd put her upon. But that wasn't true. The sight of her still tugged at my heart, and other places.

I hovered awkwardly.

"Are you okay?"

She looked up through her hair. "Joe?"

She sniffed and rubbed at her nose. I realized she was crying. I hesitated and then I slung my bag off my shoulders and sat down next to her.

"What's wrong?"

She shook her head, voice clogged by tears and snot. "I've been an idiot."

"Why?"

"I'm sorry. About what happened, with your sister."

"It's okay," I said, even though it wasn't.

"It was so crazy down there. I mean, I can't believe we thought she was, y'know—"

I swallowed a hard lump in my throat. "I know."

She shook her head again. "You don't know how much I wanted to talk to you, but I was scared."

"Scared? Of what?"

She pulled her hair across her face self-consciously. "Nothing."

But it didn't seem like nothing. The tremor in her voice. The way she was shielding her face with her hair. I suddenly had a feeling:

"Is something the matter with your eye?"

"No, it's—"

I leaned forward and brushed her hair behind her ear. She didn't stop me. Her right eye was blue-black and swollen.

"What happened?"

"We argued. He didn't mean it."

Anger swelled into a hot ball in my throat. "*Hurst* did this?"

Hurst was a bastard, but I'd never known him to use his fists on a girl.

"Just leave it."

"He *hit* you. You have to tell someone."

"Please, Joe. You mustn't say anything." She grabbed my hands. "Promise."

I didn't have much choice. "Okay. But promise me you won't let it happen again."

"Okay."

"Why were you arguing?"

"It was about Chris."

"Chris?"

"Steve is scared he's going to say something about the pit. He's acting so weird. Steve said he's got something he shouldn't and he needs to be straightened out. I told him to leave Chris alone. And then I said I wanted to split up and that's when—"

"When he hit you?"

"He called me a bitch and said no one leaves him, ever."

Fresh tears welled in her eyes. I wrapped my arms around her and drew her close. Her hair was scratchy; it smelled of hairspray and smoke.

"Joe," she whispered, "what do we do?"

"I'll fix it," I said. "I'm meeting Chris at six in the graveyard. I can warn him."

She pulled away a little. "Maybe you could talk to him. Tell him not to say anything. Stop with all the crazy shit."

"I don't know."

"You're good at talking to people."

"Okay, I'll try."

"Thank you." She leaned forward and pressed her lips against mine. Then she hopped up. "I should go."

I nodded, numb with shock.

"D'you want to walk back with me?" I asked.

"I can't. I have to get some shopping for my mum."

"Oh. Okay."

"I'll see you later."

"See you."

I watched her go, the memory of her kiss tingling on my lips, thinking about what I'd like to do to Hurst.

Perhaps that's why I never thought about what I had just said.

DAD WAS SEMICONSCIOUS in front of the TV when I got back. Annie must have been in her room. Mum had left some meals in the freezer. I got one out and stuck it in the microwave. I wasn't that hungry but I forced myself to eat a bit of the lasagne, downed a Coke then shouted to Dad that there was food in the kitchen and headed upstairs to change.

At the door to Annie's room, I paused. I used to like hovering at her door sometimes, watching her unawares as she engaged in some imaginary play with her Barbie dolls and my old Action Men, putting on different voices. Now, her door was always closed and the voices inside were different.

This evening I couldn't hear anything. The silence was worse. I hesitated. But it was dinnertime, Annie must be hungry. I couldn't rely upon Dad to feed her.

I raised my hand and knocked on the door. "Annie?"

No reply.

"Annie?"

The door opened a couple of inches. I pushed it further, trying not to recoil at the smell. Annie stood on the far side of the room, staring out of the window. She must have run over to the door, opened it and run back. But I couldn't be sure of that. I couldn't be sure of anything anymore.

I stepped into the bedroom.

"I've just heated up some lasagne."

She remained still. I suddenly realized that she had on an old sweatshirt but no jeans or panties.

"Well, let me know if you want some—"

She turned. I flushed. Annie was still only a kid, but I hadn't seen her naked since she was a baby. As if sensing my awkwardness, she smiled. A sly, dreadful thing. She took a step forward, parted her feet and a stream of hot yellow urine gushed from between her legs and onto the carpet.

I felt bile rise in my throat. She started to laugh. I bolted from her room, slammed the door behind me and ran down the stairs. I didn't care about changing. I just wanted to get away, away from my little sister.

Her laughter chased me out of the house, but now it sounded more like screams, snapping at my heels.

CHRIS WASN'T IN THE GRAVEYARD. I pushed open the gate and walked down the overgrown path. I wandered around the church in a circle, in case he was hiding somewhere, which would be weird but not unthinkable.

No Chris. No sign of any living soul. I sighed. Typical. He was losing it. Seriously losing it. But then, I wasn't exactly coasting along on an even keel at the moment.

I couldn't get the image of Annie out of my mind. Her nakedness. The urine streaming between her skinny legs. I couldn't go back. Not tonight. The thought of ever going back seemed beyond comprehension.

Maybe she needed to see a doctor again. Maybe the blow to her head—and there *had* been a blow to her head, I was sure—had done something to her brain. I mean, she had lost her memory. She couldn't remember where she had been for those forty-eight hours. Maybe there was something else wrong. Something that was making her act so weird. I should try and talk to Mum. She could take her to the hospital. Maybe they could fix her. Make her better. Make her *Annie* again.

The thought gave me some comfort, even though I'm not sure I really believed it. But then, maybe that's what churches are for. To give comfort even when, deep down, you know it's just a pack of lies.

I sat on the rickety bench in the graveyard and stared out over the lopsided gray headstones. I leaned forward, resting my elbows on my knees, tucking my feet beneath me. That's when I realized that there was something under the bench. I bent over and hauled it out. A bag. I knew right away it was Chris's. While the rest of us had Adidas or Puma, Chris had an old, unbranded holdall covered with *Doctor Who* and *Star Trek* stickers.

This evening there was something else stuck on it. An envelope, taped to the top, with my name scrawled on the front. I ripped it off and opened it. Inside, a torn-off sheet of textbook paper was covered in Chris's straggly scrawl:

> *Joe, the stuff in this bag is for you. You'll know what to do. The other things—I think you might need them sometime. I'm not sure why. Just in case.*
>
> *This is all my fault. I wish I had never found it. That place is bad. I know that now. Maybe you do too.*
>
> *I'm sorry. About Annie. About everything.*

I stared at the note, like the words would rearrange themselves into something that made sense. Something that didn't sound batshit crazy. Why had he left it for me? Why wasn't he here himself?

I unzipped the holdall. The first thing I saw was a stack of fireworks, big fuck-off ones. The sort you needed ID to buy. Unless you were good at finding a way to get stuff.

I frowned and delved deeper. Underneath was something else. Something heavier, wrapped carefully in a clear plastic bag. I took it out and my stomach flipped. I knew what this was immediately. I stared at the two items inside. Then I carefully put the bag back and zipped the holdall up.

CHRIS'S HOUSE was on the other side of the village. I slung the holdall over my shoulder and started to walk. I needed to talk to him.

For some reason, it felt urgent. I had this weird, jittery feeling in my stomach, like I was already late for something important. I picked up my pace. Bits of the note kept fluttering around my mind:

That place is bad.

I walked past the bench where Marie had pressed her lips to mine. Something flared, like a dark shadow on the walls of my mind, and then it was gone again.

Maybe you could talk to him.

I found myself at the gates of the school. They were usually left open back then, until all the after-school clubs had finished and the teachers had gone. It was quicker to cut through the school grounds to Chris's house and slip out of the fence on the other side, so long as the caretaker didn't catch me.

I hurried across the parking lot, past the science wing and toward the Block. It rose before me, a dark monolith against the silvery sky. As I rounded the corner a gust of wind slapped me in the face and snatched at my hair. I shivered. And then I paused. I thought I'd heard something. Voices. Carrying on the wind. From the playing fields? No. Closer. I looked around. And then . . . I looked up.

I SAW HIM. ALREADY FALLING. I felt the *whoosh* as he cut through the air. Heard the dull thud as he hit the ground. The distance between, an eternity and the blink of an eye. I wondered if he felt it. The final crunch.

MY FIRST INSTINCT was to run. To get the hell away. But I couldn't. I couldn't just leave him, lying there. What if he was still alive?

I walked over on shaking legs. His eyes were open and a small trickle of blood ran down the side of his mouth. More blood spread out beneath him, forming a crimson halo around his blond head. The weird thing was, for perhaps the first time ever in his short life, he looked calm, like he had finally found the thing he was always looking for.

I let the bag slip from my shoulders and sank to the ground. I stayed there, kneeling beside him on the cold concrete, in the fading warmth of the day. Tears slipped down my cheeks. I gently stroked his soft, shaggy hair. I told him it wasn't his fault.

Later—because it had always been too late for Chris; perhaps, for some kids, it always is—I got up, brushed the dirt from my trousers and walked down the road to a phone box. I called an ambulance. I told them a kid had fallen. I didn't tell them who. I didn't tell them my name.

And I didn't tell them—or anyone—what else I saw that evening.

A second figure, running away from the Block. No more than a dark shadow. But I knew. Even then.

He needs to be straightened out.

Stephen Hurst.

32

The next day, I make plans. This is out of character for me. I'm not someone who believes in planning ahead. I've seen first-hand how planning is a predictor of disaster, an invitation for fate to screw with you.

But for this, I need to be prepared. I need to have a course of action. And, without a job, it's not like I have much else to do.

Brendan left the cottage just before two this morning. I offered him the spare room, but he declined.

"No offense, but this place gives me the feckin' creeps."

"I thought you weren't superstitious."

"I'm Irish. Of course I'm superstitious. Along with guilt, it's in our DNA." He shrugged his coat on. "I've booked into a B&B down the road."

The farm, I think, something momentarily flitting across my mind then flitting out again, before I can grasp hold of it. It was important, I think. But, like most important things in my life, now it's gone.

I make strong black coffee with the dregs of water in the kettle and smoke two brisk cigarettes before getting down to work. I sit at the small kitchen table and start making notes. It doesn't take long. My plan is not complicated. I'm not quite sure why I felt the need to write it down at all. But then, I'm a teacher. I find comfort and stability in the written word. Pen and paper. Something tangible to cling on to. Or perhaps it's just procrastination. Unlike plans, I'm good at procrastination.

Next, I pick up my phone and I make some calls.

One goes to voicemail. I leave a message. The second is a little trickier. I'm not even sure if she will answer. My deadline has been and gone. Then I hear her voice. I explain what I need. I do not know whether she will say yes. I am not really in any position to be asking favors.

Gloria sighs. "You realize this will take time. As well connected as I am, I'm not your fucking fairy godmother."

I fidget, fingering a cigarette. "How long?"

"A couple of hours."

"Thank you," I say, but the phone is already dead. I try not to take this as an omen.

The third call is to an international number. This one took a bit of research. Maybe it isn't entirely necessary. But now that the seed has been planted I have to know. I put on my most professional voice. I explain who I am and what I would like to confirm. I listen as the very polite American receptionist tells me to get lost in a very polite American way. I accept her wishes for a nice day—although it seems unlikely—and end the call.

I stare at the phone for a while, my heart just that little bit heavier. Then I get up to make more coffee. The final call I will make later. This isn't procrastination. I don't want to give him too much time to plan, or to rally his goons.

I'm waiting for the kettle to boil when my phone rings. I snatch it up.

"Hello."

"I got your message."

"And?"

"I've got classes."

"You've never played truant?"

"You want me to skip school?"

"Not regularly. Just this afternoon. It's important."

A deep sigh. "Is this why they fired you?"

"No. That was for something far worse."

I wait.

"Okay."

I SIT ON THE SCRUBBY GRASS, staring out over the coarse landscape. A place like this will never be pretty or picturesque, I think. It doesn't matter how many saplings you plant or wildflowers you seed; build all the playgrounds and visitor centers you like, something about it will always remain barren and unyielding.

A place like this does not want to be reclaimed. It is happy being forsaken, lying dormant and dead. A graveyard of lost livelihoods, lost dreams, coal dust and bones. We only skim the surface of this earth. But it has many layers. And sometimes, you shouldn't dig too deep.

"You're here."

I turn. Marcus stands behind me, on the incline of the small hill.

"Yep. And twice as ugly," I say.

He doesn't smile. I get the feeling that humor, being happy, just isn't in his repertoire of emotions. But that's fine. Happiness is overrated; it's far too short-lived, for a start. If you bought it on Amazon, you'd demand a refund. *Broke after a month and impossible to fix. Next time will try misery—apparently that shit lasts forever.*

He walks over and stands awkwardly beside me. "What are you doing?"

"Admiring the view, and eating this—" I hold up the Wham bar I have been chewing. And chewing. "Want one? I brought two."

He shakes his head. "No, thanks."

I regard the shiny pink candy. "A friend of mine used to eat them. You remind me of him."

"In what way?"

"He was a misfit. We both were. He liked finding out about stuff. And *finding* stuff. I think you might be good at that too, Marcus. Like how you found a way past the school security gates."

He doesn't reply.

"You told Miss Grayson that Jeremy found the cave?"

"He did."

"No." I shake my head. "I don't think so. Some places have to *want* to be found. It takes someone special to do that. Not someone like Hurst. Someone like you."

He debates, and then says: "Hurst knew about the cave. A lot of the kids had heard rumors. He knew I came up here. He wanted me to help him look for a way in."

I nod. "And you did."

"I just kind of stumbled over it."

"Yeah. That happens."

He sits down beside me.

"You want me to take you."

"Not really. But I *need* you to take me."

"You said it was important."

"It is."

He seems to notice the backpack for the first time. "What's in there?"

"Probably best if you don't know."

Silence for a moment. Then he stands. "Let's go."

I push myself to my feet. As I follow him down the hill he says, "You know, you shouldn't offer sweets to strange kids."

Maybe he does have a sense of humor after all.

THERE IS NO HATCH THIS TIME. Instead, I find myself staring at a thick, semicircular grille beneath a low, rocky overhang. The metal is rusted almost the same color as the earth and camouflaged by overgrown weeds and thorns. Marcus pushes them aside and carefully removes the grille. It's heavy and I can see gouge marks on the edges where it must have been forced open.

At some point the villagers tried to seal off all the entrances, I think. But they couldn't silence the pit. Couldn't stop it calling. To Chris. To Marcus.

I take out the flashlight I brought and point it into the hole. I can see that this tunnel is less steep than the one from my youth. But it's small, barely two feet high. I will have to crawl. This is not a comforting thought.

"It's about five minutes till it opens up and you reach some steps," Marcus says. "They take you all the way down."

"Thanks."

"Are you going to stop people going down there?"

"That's the plan. You okay with that?"

"I suppose." He stares at me. "You know, you're a weird sort of teacher."

"I'm a weird sort of human. But weird isn't always bad. Remember that."

He gives a small nod. And I'm not sure, but it looks like a smile momentarily grazes his lips before he turns and lopes away.

The thin sun catches him on the brow of the hill. It illuminates his hair in a lighter halo. For a second, he looks like the ghost of a boy I once knew. Then he descends into shadow and both ghost and boy are gone.

MY PROGRESS ALONG THE TUNNEL is slow and crablike. My bad leg throbs constantly. Several times I stop and consider turning back. But turning itself is an issue, so I crouch and shuffle onward, fighting the cloying claustrophobia rising in my throat and wincing every time the backpack on my back bumps against the tunnel roof.

After what seems like several decades—during which my knees have been scraped raw and my spine has developed a permanent hunch—the tunnel widens enough for me to stand, albeit bent over. Steep steps lead down to what appears to be a solid rock wall. I run the flashlight over it. The light reveals a narrow gap, almost hidden in the depths of the shadows. Of course. Another way in, or out. It explains how Annie disappeared. Why I couldn't find her. I squeeze through.

Twenty-five years fall away. I'm standing in the cave from my childhood nightmares. It feels slightly smaller. Shrunk by my adult perspective. The ceiling is not so high or cathedralesque. The space not so vast. This doesn't stop my scalp from bristling with ice.

A few skulls lie on the ground, along with some crushed cans of Woodpecker and cigarette butts. There are holes in the walls where

Hurst and Fletch wreaked their wanton destruction but, higher up, the rock is still intricately inlaid with yellow and white bones. I stare at them. *The ones who didn't come back.* Left to be used as macabre decorations, or perhaps some kind of offering.

I wonder how long this place has been here. Hundreds, thousands of years? Amazing that the mining didn't destroy it. Or was it the other way around? I think about the Arnhill Colliery Disaster. Despite all the investigations, never fully explained. No one ever held accountable. And what about the other accidents? There must be mine shafts beneath the cave. Did the miners get too close? Did they threaten the ancient excavation that came before them? A place that had been here for centuries, lying dormant, waiting.

I walk slowly around, breathing deeply, trying to keep myself calm. This is just a cave. The dead cannot hurt us. Bones are just bones. Shadows are nothing but shadows. Except shadows are never just shadows. They are the deepest part of the darkness. And the deepest part of the darkness is where the monsters hide.

I need to do this quickly.

I take the item that Gloria brought me out of my backpack. My hands are shaking, I am slick with sweat. I fumble, swear, catch myself. I have to do this right. Fuck this up and I will take *myself* apart. I place it carefully—oh so carefully—in the center of the cave, my bandaged hand making me feel stupidly clumsy. Then I back away. I force myself to turn. I can hear them chittering now. A warning. A threat. I squeeze through the gap and hobble as fast as I can up the steps. I tell myself to be careful, that hurrying, careless steps are what they want. A trip, a fall—like before—would send me plunging back down.

I reach the tunnel and crawl along it. At least my backpack is now empty. The thought of what I carried down there—and a sudden paranoia that I have no guarantee it will work as planned—spurs me on and out.

I emerge a sodden, shaking, jelly-legged mess into the fresh air, and collapse onto the stony ground.

I lie there gasping, letting the breeze cool the sweat on my skin. After a while I sit back and fumble my cigarettes out of my pocket. I light one and suck it down like it's pure oxygen. I consider lighting

a second off the butt of the first. Then I check my watch and reluctantly slide the cigarette back into the pack.

Instead, I take out my cellphone. Getting hold of his number
wasn't difficult. I press Call and wait. He answers on the third ring.
Nearly always the third ring. Ever noticed that?

"Hello."

"It's me."

Silence. And then, feeling very much like a character in a bad
thriller, I say: "I think we should talk."

33

He's done well for himself. That's what we say, isn't it, when we see an expression of someone's wealth or success? Usually a big house, expensive suit or shiny new car.

Odd how we measure things. As if the ability to purchase a large building or the most fuel-guzzling mode of sitting in a traffic jam is the ultimate expression of achievement during our scant years upon this planet. Despite all our advancements, we still judge people in terms of bricks, cloth and horsepower.

Still, I suppose on those terms Stephen Hurst has indeed "done well for himself."

His bricks and mortar is a converted farmhouse about half a mile outside of Arnhill. The sort of conversion that takes the original character of an old building and systematically tramples on it with the addition of acres of steel, glass and bifold bloody doors.

This evening only one car sits on the gravel driveway. A brand-new Range Rover. Marie is out with Jeremy in Nottingham—shopping for new trainers and then pizza. Around the back, I can see a long garden, a hot tub and a floodlit swimming pool. A man does not own a hot tub and a swimming pool on a councillor's wages alone.

Maybe that's why Marie stayed. And yet, ultimately, it all means nothing. Because the years enjoying the hot tub and the swimming pool are fewer than she could ever have imagined. And maybe it would have been better to use the time to enjoy some freedom, a life away from this place. I guess it all depends on how much you want those bifold doors and how much you are willing to sacrifice for them.

I check my watch—8:27 p.m. I hesitate a moment longer then force myself to raise my arm and ring the doorbell.

Distantly inside I hear chimes. I wait. Footsteps. And then the door swings open.

I'd say it was impossible for a man to age in a couple of days. But I'd also swear that this is exactly what has happened. In the harsh glare of the security light Hurst looks like a much older man, pensionable even. His skin hangs from his face like a wet rag and his eyes are bloodshot slits within folds of gray skin. He does not hold out a hand or offer a greeting.

"My study's this way," he says, and turns, leaving me to close the door behind myself.

The house isn't quite as I expected. It's more tasteful, if a little chintzy. I get the feeling that the satin wallpaper and faux Persian vases are evidence of Marie's hand.

He leads me along the hallway. Ahead, I catch a glimpse of a large open-plan living-room/diner. To my right, a sleek, marble-and-chrome kitchen. Hurst opens another door on his left. His study. I feel an underlying current of resentment course through me. Hurst has all of this, with everything he has done.

And a wife who is dying of cancer.

I follow him into the room. In comparison to the rest of the house, the study is more minimalist. A large oak desk dominates. A few black-and-white pictures adorn the walls. A glass cabinet displays an array of crystal glasses and expensive whiskies.

It's like a parody of a gentleman's study, even down to a heavy glass paperweight on the desk. The study of a man who believes he has done very well for himself indeed.

Except, he doesn't look it right now. He looks like a man who is falling apart at his expensive, custom-tailored seams.

"Drink?" He walks to the cabinet and half turns. "Whiskey?"

"Fine by me."

He pours two large measures into two sparkling crystal glasses and places them on the desk.

"Sit."

He gestures to an armchair in front of the desk. I place the bag on the floor, next to the chair. I wait for Hurst to sit in his high-backed executive recliner then lower myself onto the creaky leather. It puts me lower than him. Whatever makes him feel superior. I have the winning hand.

For a moment, nothing is said, nothing is drunk. Then, at the same time, we both reach for our glasses.

"What do you want?"

"I think you know."

"You've come to beg me for your job back?"

"You'd like that, wouldn't you?"

"Not really. What I'd like is for you to go home. Leave us all in peace."

"Some people don't deserve peace."

"You always thought the worst of me."

"You always did the worst."

"I was a kid. We all were. It was a long time ago."

"How's Marie?" I ask.

I can tell the question rattles him.

"I don't want to talk about Marie."

"You're the one who sent her to see me."

"Actually, it was her idea."

Not what she told me. But this is Hurst. Lies are as natural as breathing.

"She thought she might be able to talk some sense into you. Avoid any more unpleasantness."

"Like sending Fletch's boys to beat me up? Trashing the cottage? That sort of unpleasantness?"

A thin, whip-sharp smile. "I'm afraid I don't know what you're talking about."

"Didn't find it, did they? I bet that really pissed you off."

He shakes his head and takes a sip of his drink. "You seem to think I care more about the things that happened back then than I actually do."

"You cared enough to follow Chris up the Block that evening. What happened? Did you argue? Did you push him?"

He shakes his head, like he's dealing with a sad lunatic.

"Have you heard yourself? You know, I feel sorry for you. You made some sort of life for yourself. You had a career, and yet you're willing to throw it all away. For what? To settle old scores? Search for answers where there aren't any? Just let it go. Leave now before you make things even worse for yourself."

I reach for my drink and take a long, slow sip.

"I saw you. You were there."

"I didn't hurt Chris. I tried to save him."

"Right."

"I tried to talk him down. But he was beyond reason. Rambling. Insane stuff. And then he jumped. And I ran, I admit it. I didn't want to stick around, have people leap to the wrong conclusions."

I wonder if his choice of words—"leap to"—is deliberately callous. But I don't think so. And I don't think he's lying. Deep down, I'm not sure I ever believed he pushed Chris. I wanted to. It gave me another reason to hate him. And maybe, it gave me a get-out too. Because if Chris jumped, it meant I'd let him down. Just like Annie.

Of course, I don't believe Hurst tried to save Chris either. The only person Hurst has ever cared about saving is himself. That's what I'm counting on.

"Why are you so afraid of me being here?"

"I'm not. Just sick of it."

"Yeah, funnily enough, you don't look so well."

"I'm tired. Cancer takes its toll, on everyone. There. Happy? Not such a perfect life after all. That what you want to hear?"

I stare at him. Maybe he's right. Maybe things haven't worked out so well for him. I think about what Miss Grayson said:

He is desperate . . . *You are the only person who can stop him.*

I fully intend to. But that is not why I'm here. First, I have other business. Business Hurst would understand. Saving-my-own-skin business.

I take the bag and thump it onto the desk. I see his eyes widen. He recognizes the battered, unbranded holdall. The faded and curling *Doctor Who* and *Star Trek* stickers.

"What the hell is this?"

"I think you know. But for the members of the jury—" I open it and carefully place the contents in front of him—"it's the crowbar you smashed my sister's head in with, and your school tie, coated in her blood and your DNA."

His mouth works, teeth grinding, chewing on this information like a bitter pill. "And what is this supposed to prove? Your sister was found. Alive."

"We both know that's not what happened."

"Try telling that story to the police. I'm sure they'll find you a nice comfy straitjacket to slip into."

"Fine. Try this. My sister disappeared for two days. Forty-eight hours. Where was she? What do you think the police would do if they were given this evidence? Evidence that you took her? Hurt her? How would that go down with the villagers, your councillor buddies?"

He stares at the plastic bag containing the crowbar and the bloody tie for a long time. Then he raises his eyes.

"So I'll ask you again—what do you want?"

"Thirty grand."

I wait. And then something happens to his face. I was expecting anger, denial. Maybe threats. Instead, he leans back in his chair and a sound bellows from his lips. Laughter.

In all the scenarios I played out in my mind, this is not one I expected. I glance nervously toward the window. Just darkness outside. I feel my tension rise.

"Want to share the joke?"

He straightens and gathers himself. "It's you. It's always been you."

"Fine." I pick up the crowbar and the tie and put them back inside the bag. "Maybe I'll just take this to the police right now."

"No, you won't."

"You sound very sure about that."

"I am."

"If you try to stop me, or plan on calling your thugs, I should warn you that—"

"Stop talking shit." He cuts me down. "I've no intention of hurting you. You see, that's your problem. You're always looking for someone to strike out at. Someone to blame. You never stop to think that you brought all of this on yourself."

"I don't know what the hell you mean."

"I know about the crash."

"What's to know? It was an accident. My sister and father died."

"Where were you going that night?"

"I don't remember."

"Convenient."

"The truth."

"The papers speculated that something must have happened, that your father was driving to the hospital. Not long before the crash someone tried to call 999 from your house."

I wonder how he knows this, or perhaps, more important, why he has made it his business to know.

"Why don't you just get to the point?"

"Your father didn't crash your car that night by accident."

"You're wrong. There was evidence he tried to brake. Tried to prevent the crash."

"Oh, I'm not saying it wasn't an *accident*. But your father didn't cause it."

He smiles and I feel my house of cards—my so-close-to-winning hand—fold and flutter to the ground.

"You did, Joe. You were the one driving."

34

The past isn't real. It is simply a story we tell ourselves.

And sometimes, we lie.

I loved my little sister. So much. But the sister I loved was gone. I saw her walking around the house in the strange lurching way she had now—like her body was the wrong fit—but I didn't see Annie. I saw something that looked like Annie, sounded like Annie. But it was a fake. A bad copy.

Sometimes I wanted to scream at my parents: *Can't you see? It's not Annie. Something happened and she's gone. There was a mistake. A terrible mistake, and this thing got sent back in her place. A thing that is wearing her skin and looking through her eyes but, when you look back, it's not Annie inside.*

But I didn't. Because that would have sounded crazy. And I knew it was the last thing my parents needed to deal with. I didn't want to be the straw that finally broke our family into pieces. I needed to sort this out. To put it right. So one day, before school, I picked up the phone in a trembling hand and called the doctor's. I put on my best voice and said I was Mr. Thorne and wanted to make an appointment for my daughter. The receptionist, who was brisk and efficient, but obviously not very perceptive, barked that she could fit us in at four-thirty that afternoon. I thanked her and said that was perfect.

When I got back from school I told Dad I had just remembered that Mum said she'd made an appointment for Annie at the doctor's. Fortunately, he was only on his second can. He complained, but I said that was okay, he could tell Mum he had decided to cancel it. That did the trick. Dad didn't want to risk going against Mum, making her mad. He stuck his jacket on and yelled for Annie to come downstairs. I said I'd go along too. On the way, I bought some mints from the shop. I offered Dad one. He took two.

THE DOCTOR WAS AN OVERWEIGHT MAN with a nose full of red veins and a thin scraping of dry hair over his shiny head. He was friendly enough, but he looked tired and I noticed that the case by his feet was already packed, ready to go home.

He examined Annie, shone things in her eyes, tapped her knee. Annie sat in the chair, as stiff as a ventriloquist's dummy. After performing his tests, the doctor patiently explained that he couldn't find anything physically wrong with Annie. *However*, she had suffered a trauma. Missing for two days. Lost, maybe trapped somewhere. Who knew what had happened to her? The bed-wetting, the nightmares, the strange behavior were all to be expected. We just had to be patient. Give her time. If there was no improvement, he could refer us to a therapist. He smiled. It probably wouldn't come to that. Annie was young. The young are incredibly resilient. She would be back to her old self in no time, he was sure.

Dad thanked him and shook his hand. His own hand was shaking quite a bit. I was glad I had bought the mints. We walked home again. Annie wet herself on the way.

Trauma. Give her time. He was sure.

I wasn't. I thought it was a load of bullshit and, for some reason, I felt like we were running out of time.

ON TOP OF THIS, I was dealing with Chris's death. Or rather, I wasn't. There had been a funeral, at the crematorium. It didn't feel real. I kept expecting to turn around and find Chris standing beside me, blond hair sticking up like always, pointing out that the temperature of the furnace was between 1400 and 1800 degrees Fahrenheit, the body was consumed in two and a half hours and the crematorium burnt around fifty bodies a week.

Chris's mum sat at the front. He didn't have any other family. His dad had left when he was little and his older brother had died of cancer before Chris was born.

His mum had the same wild white hair as Chris. She wore a shapeless black dress and clutched a pile of tissues. But she didn't cry. She just kept staring straight ahead. Occasionally, she mumbled something and smiled. Somehow, it was more awful than if she'd been bawling her eyes out.

I saw her a few times afterward. She was still wearing the same clothes. I felt like I should say something, but I didn't know what. Whenever I walked by Chris's house the curtains were pulled. A couple of weeks later a "For Sale" sign went up.

I found myself wandering the village aimlessly after school, always ending up beneath the Block, staring up, wondering how it felt to fall so far, so fast. People left flowers and tributes. There was even one from Hurst. The temptation to take it, rip it to shreds and stamp it into the ground was almost too much.

I never did. Just like I never told anyone how I saw him that day.

Chris's death had put me in a kind of paralysis. I had hidden the bag in the shed, but I didn't know what I was supposed to do with it. I couldn't think. Couldn't seem to get my head in order. Every time I thought about the bag I saw Chris lying on the ground, his oddly deflated body, the thick, dark blood. So much blood. And then I would think of my sister.

Sometimes, I wondered if I was the one going crazy. Maybe there was nothing wrong with Annie. Maybe the knock I'd taken to the head had done something to *my* brain. Maybe I was imagining it all.

I was finding it hard to concentrate in school. Remembering to eat, to have a bath—those things didn't seem important anymore. My long, repetitive treks around the village became longer and longer. One night, a police officer stopped me and told me to go home. It was almost midnight.

I woke several times a night, clawing at the air to escape the nightmares. In one, Chris and Annie stood on a snowy hill. The sky shimmered behind them, a dappled candy-pink. The sun was black, haloed by a silvery light, like an eclipse. Chris and Annie looked perfect again, whole. Like they did before they died.

All around them, there were snowmen. Big, round, fluffy white snowmen with long, twiggy arms and lumps of shiny black coal for their eyes and mouths. As I watched, their crooked smiles twisted into snarls.

You can't stay here. There's nobody here but us snowmen. Go back. GO BACK!

The sun plummeted below the horizon. Chris and Annie disappeared. The candy-pink sky bubbled and boiled, darkening to a deep crimson. Flakes started to fall. But not white. Red. And not flakes. Blood. Huge, fat drops of blood that burnt like acid. I fell to the ground. My skin was melting from my bones. My bones were melting into the ground. The snowmen watched with cold, black eyes as I dissolved into nothing.

THE NEXT MORNING, I knew what I had to do.

I got dressed in my school uniform, like usual. I left at the normal time. But my bag contained a few other items packed carefully under my textbooks.

I walked briskly out of the house. I didn't head down the street, toward the school. I headed up, toward the old pit. They had fixed the broken fence. Put even more warning signs up. DANGER. KEEP OUT. TRESPASSERS WILL BE PROSECUTED. There was supposed to be a man from the council who patrolled the site to make sure no other kids got in there. But I didn't see anyone this morning as I walked slowly along the perimeter. It didn't look so secure. The fence was still a bit wobbly, and there were gaps between the mesh panels. It didn't take long for me to find one that was just about big enough for me to squeeze through. Although it *was* a squeeze. My school blazer caught on a sharp bit of wire and snagged. I tugged it free and felt it rip. I cursed. Mum would tear a strip off *me* for that. Or she would have done before. Now, I realized, she probably wouldn't even notice.

I trudged on, up the hill. It looked different this morning. It was cold, but the sun was shining. It didn't exactly brighten the place but it did somehow soften its sharper, bleaker edges. It also threw me a bit. Which way was the hatch? At the bottom of the next steep rise, or was it the one after that? I stood and looked around. But the more I looked, the more uncertain I felt. Panic began to nibble at the edges of my stomach. I needed to be quick. I couldn't be too late for school.

I started one way then changed my mind and doubled back the other. Everything looked the same. Shit. What would Chris do? How did he find it? And then I remembered. He didn't find it. *It* found him.

I stood and breathed slowly. I didn't try to think, or look. I just let myself be.

And then I walked—to my left, up one rise, down and then up another, steeper hill. I scrabbled down the rocky slope. At the bottom was a small hollow, shielded by scrubby bushes. *Here*, I thought. I couldn't see it. All I could see was rubble and rocks. But I knew it was here. I could almost feel the ground humming beneath my feet.

I approached cautiously. Trying to train my eyes not to scan the ground. Not to look too carefully. And it worked. Suddenly, I made out the shape of the hatch in the earth. I crouched down. Up close, it wasn't quite closed. There was enough of a gap for me to wedge my fingers underneath and move it. I tried and, satisfied I could do it, I lowered it down again. I didn't plan on going down there right now. I couldn't turn up to school covered in dirt and coal dust. Plus, I couldn't risk someone spotting something and coming up here to investigate.

I had to come back later. When it was darker. When I could do what I needed to without anyone stopping me.

For now, I took the items I had carefully packed in my bag and hid them beneath a scrubby bit of bush. Then, because I didn't want to run the risk of not finding the hatch again when I came back later, I draped an old red sock I had brought with me around one of the branches. It would do. The first part of my plan finished, I stood and made my way back out of the site and down to school.

THE DAY DRAGGED, yet it also went too fast, in the way it always does when you're waiting for something, yet also dreading it. Like a trip to the dentist's or the doctor's. I'd happily have traded a pulled tooth for what I had to do this evening.

Finally, the bell rang and I walked out of class, worried someone might call my name or stop me, half hoping they would. No one did. I didn't hurry, though. I still had time to kill before the day started to fade to dusk.

I did my usual walk around the high street. I had some cash on me that I had nicked out of Dad's wallet the night before, so I bought some chips—even though I wasn't hungry—and picked at them in the bus shelter, before chucking half the tray in the trash.

I wandered around a bit more, then sat on a swing in the deserted playground for a while. When the streetlights started to blink on, like startled orange eyes, I began my walk up toward the pit.

I'd packed a flashlight in my bag, as well as an old woolen hat of Dad's that I pulled right down over my head, almost over my eyes. I checked out the site for any signs of security, but the street was empty and silent. I slipped through the fence before that could change.

I didn't need the flashlight just yet, even though, now that it was almost the end of October, the light was fading fast. I didn't want to draw any attention to myself. Also, for some reason, I felt that I would find my way better in the dark. Despite a couple of trips and stumbles—putting a tear in my school trousers this time—I was right. I reached the bottom of the steep incline and could just make out the red sock, a darker shadow on the bush.

I'd made it. And now that I was here, again, I was crapping myself. I knew I needed to be fast, or else I'd chicken out entirely. I heaved aside the hatch, scraping the skin from my knuckles. Then I retrieved the fireworks that I had hidden beneath the bush, stuffed them back in my bag and took out my flashlight.

After a final glance around I lowered myself into the hatch and climbed down the steps.

IT DIDN'T TAKE LONG. Once I'd lit the fuses on the fireworks I barely had time to scramble back up the steps and shove the hatch across the opening before I heard the first muffled bangs. I grabbed my bag and got to my feet. The metal hatch rose before clanging back down again, dust puffing out around it. And then it just kind of collapsed into the ground.

I backed away. I'd only taken a few steps before I felt the earth shudder, a rumbling roar that seemed to rise all the way up from the soles of my trainers to my chest. I knew that sound. There had been a rockfall down the pit when I was about Annie's age. No one was hurt, but I always remembered that rumbling roar as somewhere deep below the ground, the earth folded in on itself.

It was done, I thought. I just had to hope it was enough.

IT WAS ALMOST EIGHT when I got back home: tired, dirty, but oddly exhilarated. Just for a split second, before I pushed open the back door, I was possessed by this insane notion that suddenly everything would be okay. I had broken the spell, slain the dragon, exorcised the demon. Annie would be herself again, Mum would be cooking dinner and Dad would be reading the paper, singing along to the radio like he used to sometimes when he was in a good mood.

All crap of course. When I walked in Dad was slumped in his usual position in front of the television. I could just see the top of his curly head above the armchair and I was sure he had already passed out. Annie wasn't downstairs, so I guessed she must be in her room again. The smell in the house was worse than ever. I covered my mouth and rushed upstairs to the bathroom.

On the landing, I paused. The door to Annie's room was wide open. That never happened anymore. I walked forward.

"Annie?"

I peered inside. The room was in semidarkness, as always. Just the thinnest haze of twilight seeping through the thin curtains. The bed was unmade. If the smell downstairs was bad, up here it was almost unbearable—stale urine, sweet rot and something like bad eggs and vomit all mixed up at once. The room was empty.

I checked my bedroom. Also empty. I knocked on the bathroom door.

"Annie? Are you in there?"

Silence. There was no lock on the bathroom door. Dad had taken it off when Annie was little, after she locked herself inside one day.

Mum and I had sat outside and sung to her, to keep her calm. All the while, Dad had worked on the lock to get it off the door. When we finally burst in, Annie had gone to sleep, curled up in just a nappy and a T-shirt on the bathroom floor.

I stared at the closed door. Then I grasped the handle, which felt oddly sticky, pushed it open and pulled on the light. My world swam.

Red. So much red everywhere. All over the sink. Smeared across the mirror. Splotches trailing over the floor. Rich, glistening, fresh.

I stared, my guts heaving. I looked at my hand. The palm was stained crimson. I turned and half ran, half stumbled back down the stairs. I noticed now that the walls and banister were covered in more red smudges.

"Annie! Dad?"

I jumped the last step and into the living room. Dad was still slumped in the armchair, his back to me.

"Dad?"

I edged around the armchair. His face drew into view, eyes half closed, mouth half open, a small, rattling wheeze of breath coming from his lips. He wore an old Wet Wet Wet sweatshirt. He'd won it in some local-radio competition (he'd wanted to win the holiday to Spain). Weird the things you notice. Like I noticed that below Marti Pellow's face a huge stain had spread out from the center of my dad's chest. Like an ink stain. Like when I left the lid off my fountain pen. Except it was too big. And it wasn't blue. It was red, dark red. Not ink. Blood. *Wet, wet, wet.*

I tried to fight down the panic. Tried to think. Stabbed. He had been stabbed. Annie was missing. I needed to call the police. I needed to call 999. I ran over to the phone on the wall and picked up the receiver. I dialed with trembling fingers. It rang and rang and then a pleasant voice said: "Which service do you require?"

I opened my mouth but the words dried up. *Blood. Red. Fresh.*

"Hello? Which service do you require?"

The bathroom. Splotches on the floor. But not splotches. Shapes. One splotch, five small ones.

Footprints. Small footprints.

"Hello? Are you still there?"

I lowered the phone. From behind me, I heard a noise. A tiny giggle. I put the receiver back and turned around.

Annie stood in the doorway. She must have been crouched in the closet beneath the stairs. She was naked. Blood streaked her body and her face, like war paint. I could see gashes on her arms, her narrow chest. *She had slashed at herself too.* Her eyes glittered. In one hand, she held a large kitchen knife.

I tried to breathe, tried not to throw myself screaming out of a window.

A knife. Dad. Wet, wet, wet.

"Annie. Are you all right? I—I thought someone broke in."

I saw confusion flicker.

"It's okay. I'm home now. I'll protect you. You know that, don't you? I'm your big brother. I'll always protect you."

The knife wavered. Something in her face changed. She almost looked like *my* Annie. Like she used to. I felt my heart clench.

"Put the knife down. We can sort this out." I held out my arms, tears thickening my voice. "Come on."

She smiled. And charged at me with a growl of guttural ferocity. I was ready. I sidestepped and shoved her hard. She flew forward, tripped on the hearthrug and fell. I grabbed for the poker by the fire, but there was no need. Her head caught the corner of the fireplace. She crumpled to the floor, the knife falling from her hand.

I stood, shaking, half expecting her to leap straight back up. She continued to lie still. Because whatever was inside, it was still inside the body of an eight-year-old girl. And eight-year-olds are fragile. They break easily.

I looked back at my dad. I had to get him to a hospital. I glanced at the phone. Then I ran into the kitchen. A while ago Dad had given me a few driving lessons. Just up and down the local roads. Back then, in Arnhill, no one really gave a shit about a fifteen-year-old behind the wheel. I wasn't great. But I knew the basics.

And I knew where Dad's keys were.

DAD WAS HEAVY. He had put on weight. I dragged him to the door, inched it open and glanced out at the street. No one around. Curtains drawn. I couldn't be sure that some busybody like Mrs. Hawkins wasn't peering out of her net curtains, but I had to take the chance.

I heaved his body down the short pathway and over to the car. I propped him against the back door and opened the passenger side. Then I manhandled him in, body first and then his legs and feet. I stood back. My hands and the front of my school shirt were covered with blood. No time to worry about that. The hospital was twelve miles away, in Nottingham. I had to move quicker. I hurried around to the driver's side and stopped. I looked back at the house. Annie.

I couldn't just leave her.

She stabbed your dad.

She's still just a kid.

Not anymore.

She might die.

And?

I can't leave her. Not again. Not like before.

I ran back into the house. Half of me expected to find Annie had gone, like in horror films when you think the hero has killed the bad guy only for them to disappear and then reappear later, wielding a chain saw. But Annie still lay where she had fallen. Naked. *Shit.* I ran back upstairs, heart thudding like an internal clock, reminding me that time was running out. I flung open the small white wardrobe in Annie's room, grabbed some pajamas—pink with white sheep—and ran back down the stairs.

She didn't stir as I dragged them on her, although I could feel her breathing faintly. I lifted her in my arms, as slight as a baby deer. She felt cold. And a part of me couldn't contain a shudder of distaste.

I was almost at the gate when I saw a shadow approaching along the street and heard excited panting. A dog walker. I backed up and waited in the shadows as they passed. The dog stopped near the gate, sniffed then recoiled, tugging its owner faster down the road.

"All right, all right, got scent of a fox, 'ave yer?"

No, I thought, but it got a scent of *something.*

I bundled Annie into the back of the car. Then I ran around to the front and flung myself into the driver's seat. My hands were shaking so badly it took me three attempts to fumble the keys into the ignition.

Fortunately—miraculously—the engine started the first time. I put the car into gear. Suddenly remembered my seat belt. I clicked it in and lurched off down the street. I concentrated on trying to stay on the right side of the road, and also on not bumping the curb. It distracted me from thinking about what I would do if Dad died on the way, or what I would say if he didn't.

I needed a story. I remembered what I'd said to Annie—an intruder. Someone broke in. They would believe that. They had to. And if Dad was alive, he could tell the truth.

I was out of the village now. The black country road twisted in front of me like an oily snake. No streetlights, only cat's eyes. I couldn't find the full beam. A car emerged from a side road and pulled close behind me. Too close. The glare in the rearview mirror was blinding me. *What if it was the police? What if they had traced the 999 call and they were following me?* And then the car signaled and pulled past, horn blaring.

I glanced down at the speedometer. I was only doing 35 mph, on a 60-mph road. No wonder they were pissed off at me. And I was drawing attention to myself. Despite the blackness and my tenuous grip on the wheel, I forced myself to push my foot down harder on the accelerator. I watched the needle creep up to forty, fifty. I glanced in the rearview mirror again.

Annie stared back at me.

I swerved, the tires bumped the verge, I wrestled with the steering wheel to drag it back again. The rubber squealed but managed to regain its grip on the tarmac. Dad fell heavily against me. *Crap.* I'd forgotten to do up his seat belt. I shoved him back into his seat with one hand, trying to control the steering wheel with the other.

Annie lunged from the back seat. Her fingers clawed at my face and grabbed my hair, yanking my head back. I tried to bat at her with my free hand but her grip was surprisingly strong. I felt her nails rake my flesh; the roots of my hair screamed. I bunched my hand into a fist and struck her hard in the face. She fell back.

I grabbed the wheel again, just in time, as headlights flashed by on the opposite side of the road. *Fuck.* I pressed my foot down harder still on the accelerator. I had to get to the hospital. *Had to.* The speed crept up to seventy. I saw Annie pull herself up to a sitting position. I tried to strike back with my elbow, but she ducked past and wrapped her hands around my eyes. Her fingers dug in. I yelled. I couldn't see, my eyes were streaming. Just glimmers of darkness and light.

I let go of the wheel with one hand, tried to pull her fingers away.

My foot slipped on the accelerator. The engine screamed. I felt the car spin, the wheels leave the tarmac and hit the grassy bank.

The car bucked. Annie's fingers let go. A huge black shadow loomed ahead. A tree. I tried to grab the wheel back, stamped on the brake. Too late.

Impact. A monstrous jolt. Crunching metal. My body flew forward, nose smashing against the steering wheel. The seat belt flung me back again. Dazed. Something crashed past me out of the windshield. Pain. My chest. My face. My leg. *MY LEG!* Screaming. My own.

Blackness.

35

That was how we found you."

"We?"

"Me and Dad. We were coming back from the evening football match. Dad spotted the car, all smashed up against a tree.

"We pulled over, to see if we could help. Saw right away that your dad was dead. I found your sister's body a little way from the car. I couldn't help her..." He pauses. "I went back to the car and Dad said: 'The boy's still alive.' Then he said, 'And he's got a big problem, hasn't he?'

"I knew what he meant right away. You were only fifteen. You shouldn't have been driving.

"We decided to move you. Put you in the passenger seat and your dad in the driver's so the police would think he was driving."

"Why? Why did you care?"

"Because, whatever differences we had, Dad believed you looked after your own. You were part of my gang. Your dad was a miner—even if he was a scab. You didn't turn your own in to the pigs.

"I was supposed to come and see you in the hospital, tell you to stick to the story. But turned out you'd already got one of your own. Couldn't remember anything about the crash, a nurse told me. That true, Joe?"

I stare at him. Lies, I think. There are no such things as white lies. Lies are never black or white. Only gray. A fog obscuring the truth. Sometimes so thick we can barely see it ourselves.

To start with, I wasn't sure what I remembered. It was easier to just go along with what the police and the doctors told me. Easier to close my eyes and say I didn't know what had happened. Couldn't remember the crash.

I never told Mum. But then, she never asked. About any of it. She must have had questions. She must have cleaned up the blood. But she never said a word. And once, when I tried to talk to her, she gripped my wrist so hard it left bruises and said: "Whatever happened in that house, it was an accident, Joe. Just like the crash. D'you understand? I *have* to believe that. I can't lose you too."

That was when I understood. She thought I had done this. That I was somehow responsible. I suppose I couldn't blame her. I had been acting weird for weeks. Hardly eating, not talking, staying out as much as possible. And in a way, I *was* responsible. I had caused it. All of it.

When I returned home, on crutches, pins in my shattered leg, the house had been aired and cleaned and Annie's room had been freshly decorated. Everything was the same as it was before.

I didn't try to put Mum right, or tell her what had really happened. And she never put into words what I saw in her eyes: that the wrong child had been lost. That it should have been me. Until the day she died, Mum pretended she still loved me.

And I pretended not to know that she didn't.

I clear my throat. My head feels too full, conflicting thoughts wrestling with each other in the mud of my consciousness.

"You want me to *thank* you?" I say.

Hurst shakes his head. "No. I want you to take these"—he gestures at the crowbar and the tie—"and chuck them into the River Trent. And *then*, I want you to fuck off and never come back."

I feel sick. Loser sick. That feeling when you see the other player's cards and know you have been screwed. That you are done. Well, almost done.

"The police will ask you questions too. Why you moved me. Why come forward now? Tampering with the scene of an accident. That's a crime."

He nods. "True. But I was just a kid. It was my dad's idea. Now that I'm older and wiser, it has made me reevaluate things. I need to come clean. If I have to, I can spin this. And they'll believe me. I'm a respected member of the community. While you? Well, look at yourself. Suspended from your current job. Suspicion of theft from your old school. You're hardly a model citizen."

He's right. And what if they start asking more questions? Investigate the scene again. Question my dad's injuries.

"So," Hurst says, "I think this is what we call a stalemate."

I nod and stand. I take the carefully wrapped items and put them back into the holdall. I don't really have any other choice. I take my phone out of my pocket.

Hurst stares at it. "You're still going to call the police?"

"No."

I bring up my contacts and raise the phone to my ear. She answers on the first ring.

"Hi, Joe."

"You need to talk to him." I hold out the phone to Hurst.

He looks at it like I am holding out a grenade. And I am. In a way.

"And who exactly am I talking to?" he asks me.

"The woman who will kill your wife and son if I do not walk out of here thirty grand richer."

He takes the phone and I watch his face turn gray. Gloria can do that to people. Even before she sends him the pictures: shots of Marie and Jeremy finishing their dinner in town right now.

He hands the phone back to me.

"You'd better get that money," Gloria says. And then: "They're leaving. I need to follow them."

I end the call and look at Hurst. "Thirty grand. Transfer it now and I'll be out of your hair for good."

He just stares at me. He looks dazed. Like someone has just told him all at once that the world is flat, aliens exist and Jesus is on his way back for a visit.

Gloria can do that to you too.

"What the hell have you done?" he croaks.

"I just need the money."

His eyes find focus. They are full of tears. "I don't have it."

"I don't believe you. That car sitting out front is worth sixty grand at least."

"Contract lease."

"This house."

"Remortgaged."

"The villa in Portugal."

"I sold it, barely broke even."

The sick feeling is back. Worse now. It feels like a rat is worrying away at my insides. Chewing through my stomach lining. Heading for my bowels.

"I don't think Gloria will like to hear that."

He runs a hand through his perfectly coiffed hair. "It's the truth. I don't have thirty grand. I don't have twenty or ten or even five fucking grand."

"Bullshit."

"It's all gone. Marie's treatment in America. Do you know how much a miracle cure costs?" A bitter chuckle. "Over seven hundred and fifty thousand pounds. That's how much. It's everything I've got. I've nothing left."

"Liar." I shake my head. "Just like always. Trying to save your skin. You're a liar."

"It's the truth."

"No. I called the clinic in America. Marie told me about it. And guess what—they'd never heard of you or Marie. She isn't booked in there for a fucking ingrowing toenail, let alone a miracle cancer treatment."

I stare at him in triumph. I expect to see the usual defiant snarl. A man challenged and angry at being caught in a lie. But instead I see something else. Something not expected. Confusion. Fear.

"That can't be right. She paid them. I transferred the money."

"More lies. Do you ever stop? I *know* what you're planning."

"I can show you the bank statements. The account number."

"Right. Of course you can—" I stop suddenly. I stare at him. "*She?*"

"Marie. She found the clinic. She arranged it all. The hotels, flights."

"You transferred all the money to Marie?"

"Into our joint account. She made the payment from there."

"But you didn't talk to the clinic. You didn't check that they received the money?"

"I trust my wife. And why would she lie? She's desperate. She doesn't want to die. This treatment was her only chance."

And desperate people want to believe in miracles.

I try to stay calm, to think. "Why have you been obstructing the country-park plans?"

"Because it's more profitable to build houses on the land."

"Even with what's underneath?"

He sneers. "A rockfall sealed that place off years ago."

"That's what I hoped. But it seems your son has found another way in."

"*Jeremy? No.* And what the hell does this have to do with anything?"

"You never told him what we found?"

"I *told* him never to go up there. To stay away."

"And kids always do what their parents tell them?"

"Of course they don't. In fact, Jeremy couldn't care less what I say. But he listens to Marie. Always has. He'd do anything for her. He's a mummy's boy."

I swallow and it's like swallowing fragments of ground glass.

He'd do anything for her. A mummy's boy.

And sometimes the apple does not fall so very far from the tree.

I've just been barking up the wrong tree.

My phone starts to ring. I grab it. "Yes?"

"How's it going?"

I glance at Hurst. "Fine. How long till they get back?"

"That's why I called. They're not coming back."

"What?"

"They drove back from town. Marie dropped the boy off on the high street to meet some mates. Now she's heading along the road toward your cottage."

"*My* cottage?"

"No, wait, hang on—she's stopped. She's getting out of the car. Okay, this is weird. She's got a flashlight and a backpack."

Shit.

"The pit," I say. "She's going to the pit."

36

I do not believe in fate.

But sometimes there is an ineluctable quality to life, a course it is difficult to alter.

It all started here, at the pit. And this, it seems, is where it will end.

Not quite how I imagined. Not quite how I planned. But then, that's the problem with plans. They never work out like you think. Mine, it seems, never work out at all.

WE PULL UP in Hurst's Range Rover. He hasn't said a word throughout the short drive. But I can see the dazed look in his eyes, his jaw clenching and unclenching as he tries to digest what he's learned. Tries to comprehend how Marie could have betrayed him. Lied to him.

I expected anger. But he just looks broken. Diminished. I was wrong about him. I thought Marie was just another trophy, like the house and the car. But Hurst loves her. Always has. And, despite everything, he still wants to save her.

I spot a yellow Mini parked carelessly by the side of the road. I can't see Gloria or her car. I'm not sure if this is a concern or a relief.

We both climb out.

"Where is she?" Hurst asks.

"I don't know." I scan the fence with my flashlight, find the gap I squeezed through before. "Come on."

I slip through; Hurst follows. I hear him curse. It isn't just his wallet that is better padded these days.

"About time."

I jump. Gloria emerges from the shadows by the fence. Unusually for Gloria, she is wearing a dark coat over her normal pastel hues. Dressed for business.

I look around. "Where's Marie?"

"In the trunk of my car."

"You bitch," Hurst says.

Gloria turns to him. "Stephen Hurst, I presume? Actually, I'm joking. She set off over that hill about twenty minutes ago."

I quickly intervene. "Gloria, Marie has your money. More than thirty grand. Over seven hundred and fifty. We just need to bring her down."

She looks at Hurst. "What about him?"

"What about him?"

"You said Marie, his wife, has the money?"

"Yes."

"So what use is he?"

"Gloria—"

"That's what I thought."

She moves so fast I barely see the gun. I just hear a pop and suddenly Hurst is writhing on the floor, screaming and clutching his leg. Dark red blood is gushing—*actually gushing*—from the wound. I drop to my knees beside him. I grasp his arms.

"Jesus!"

I look around. The road beyond the fence is deserted. No one around. Even the headlights of a passing car wouldn't illuminate us, here in the shadows.

"Femoral artery," Gloria says, lowering the gun, which has a large silencer attached to the end. "Even if I apply pressure, he will bleed out in approximately fifteen to twenty minutes."

Hurst's eyes find mine. Gloria grabs my arm and hauls me up. "You're wasting time. Go and get my *fucking* money."

"But what about—"

She presses a finger to my lips. "Tick, tock."

I scramble up the hill, flashlight bobbing wildly up and down in front of me. It isn't a lot of use. I'm guided by gut instinct and fear. I didn't bring my cane, so I stumble, limp and scrabble up and down the rocky, slippery slopes. My bad leg provides a near-constant accompaniment of pain. My ribs join in on percussion. But another part of me feels disembodied from the whole experience, like I am above myself and watching as a tall, thin man with a smoker's wheeze and wild black hair staggers around the countryside like a drunken tramp.

I want to laugh at the absurdity of it all; laugh until I scream. The whole thing feels like some terrible, macabre dream. And yet, I know, deep down, that this is unremittingly real. A waking nightmare that started twenty-five years ago.

And finishes tonight.

At the bottom of the hill I see her, sitting cross-legged, at the entrance. A camping light is beside her, a backpack at her feet. Her head is swathed in a scarf and a hood is pulled up against the chill. She hunches over and for a moment I think she is praying. Then, as she straightens, I see that she is lighting a cigarette.

I flick off the flashlight and watch her. But I'm not really seeing her. I'm seeing a fifteen-year-old girl. A girl who was beautiful, clever . . . and cold. I wonder how I never saw it before, but then a pretty face can blind you to a lot of faults, especially when you are a fifteen-year-old mass of hormones yourself. You don't care what lies beneath. The darkness. The rotten bones.

I take a step forward. "Marie?"

She doesn't turn. "I knew it would be you. Always you. Since we were little kids, a thorn in my side."

"By name, by nature."

"Go home, Joe."

"Okay. If you come with me."

"Nice try."

"Try this then—if you don't come with me, a crazy lady is going to kill your husband."

"Even if I believed you, why should I care? When this is done, Jeremy and I are leaving Hurst and this shithole. For good."

"You must know that this is insane."

"It's my only chance."

"The clinic in America was your only chance. Did you ever intend to go? Or was it all just a ploy to get the money?"

Finally, she turns her head toward me. Her face, in the lamp's illumination, looks frighteningly thin and terrifyingly calm.

"Do you know what the remission rate was—thirty percent. Just thirty percent."

"I've bet on worse odds."

"Did you win?"

I don't reply.

"Thought not. And I don't want to take that chance. I don't want to die."

"We all have to die."

"Easy for you to say, when you're not about to." She blows out smoke. "Do you have any idea what it's like? Closing your eyes every night, wondering if this time will be the last. And some nights you hope it *is* because you're scared and in pain. Others, you try to stay awake, to fight it, because you're so terrified of falling into the darkness."

Her eyes find mine. The lamplight gives them a feverish glow.

"Ever thought about death? Really thought about it? No feeling, no sound, no touch. Not existing. Forever."

No, I think. Because we all try not to. That's what living is. Keeping ourselves busy, averting our eyes so we don't have to stare into the abyss. Because it would drive us insane.

"None of us knows how long we have."

"I'm not ready."

"It's not your call. We don't get to make the choice."

"But what if you could? What would you do?"

"Not this."

"Says you." She glances toward the tunnel. "We both know what's down there."

"Bones," I say, trying to keep my voice steady. "That's what is down there. Bones of long-dead people who didn't have drugs and chemo and pain relief. Who still believed in God and the devil and miracles. We know better now. It's not *real*."

"Don't fucking patronize me, Joe. You were there. We all were."

"Marie, you are ill. You're not thinking properly. Please. There is nothing down there that can help you. Nothing. Believe me."

"Fine." She stubs out her cigarette and reaches into the backpack. She takes out a bottle of vodka and a packet of sleeping tablets. "If you really believe that, then let me go. I'll take these and that will be the end of it. At least *I* get to make the choice."

I don't reply.

She smiles. "You can't, can you? Because *you know*. Because of what happened to your sister."

"My sister was hurt. She got lost. She came back."

"From where?"

I swallow the hard lump in my throat. "She didn't die."

She laughs. A horrible, brittle sound, devoid of humor or humanity. And a part of me wonders if she was always like this, on the inside. Or if something changed in her, that night, when we went down there. Maybe something changed in all of us. Maybe guilt and regret weren't the only things we brought back.

"You don't believe that," she says.

"Yes. I do."

"Bullshit." Her mouth twists: "She was dead. No way she survived that blow. I know because—"

She breaks off. I freeze. Every nerve ending suddenly humming.

"Because *what*?"

"Nothing. It was nothing."

But that's a lie. It's everything. And suddenly I can see it all again. Annie in a small, crumpled heap. Hurst a short distance away. The crowbar on the ground. Marie clinging to Hurst's arm. But Marie hadn't been standing there *before*. She had moved. She was closer; to me, to Annie.

"It was you," I say. "You were the one who hit her."

"I didn't mean to. I panicked. It was an accident."

"You let Hurst take the blame. He covered for you, protected you."

"He loves me."

And now it all makes sense. Why she stayed. Why they married. He loved her. But he also had something over her. She couldn't get away from him. And maybe the swimming pool and the bifold doors helped. Just a bit.

"Were you really going to leave us down there?"

"I tried to talk him out of it."

But that's not quite true. I remember her placing her hand on his arm. The look that passed between them. I thought she wanted to help us. But now, I'm not sure. I'm not sure of anything anymore.

"And Chris? I told you where I was meeting him that evening. Did you send Hurst after him? Was that your idea too?"

"No. It wasn't like that. You know what Hurst was like. I was scared of him."

I recall the bruise around her eye. Her right eye. And then I picture Hurst pouring my whiskey. *Right-handed.* Another chunk of the pedestal crumbles.

"He never hit you, did he?"

"Does it matter?"

"Yes."

"Fine. No, he didn't. I'd had a scrap with Angie Gordon after school."

"So you lied about that too."

"For fuck's sake, it was twenty-five years ago. What happened happened. I can't change it. I wish I could." She glances at the entrance to the cave. "Please, Joe. Just let me go."

"I can't."

"I'll do anything. I can give you money, whatever you want."

"Whatever I want?"

"Yes."

I think about Hurst bleeding to death in the dirt. I think about the money I owe. I think about Annie's wide eyes staring out of the window one bright, snowy morning and her small, crumpled body lying on the cave floor.

I think about the explosives I placed in the cave and the mobile detonator in my pocket. I look at Marie. Hatred burns bright.

"You can tell me something," I say.

"Anything."

"Where are all the fucking snowmen?"

She opens her mouth. The side of her head collapses. Bone, blood and brain matter explode into the air and rain down like confetti. Her skull is an open crater, bone torn apart like papier-mâché.

Her eyes barely widen in surprise. It is too sudden for that. There is no moment of reckoning or understanding. One minute she is alive. The next she is dead, folding to the ground in an ungainly pile, like someone pulled the switch. Cut the power. Off.

"*Jesus Christ!*" I spin around.

Gloria stands behind me, holding the gun.

"You killed her!"

"She wasn't going to give you anything. I've dealt with bitches like her before."

"Where's Hurst?"

"Turns out he was a fast bleeder."

Hurst. Dead. I try to comprehend this. For years, I thought I wanted him dead. Wished for it, even. But standing here, I don't feel anything, except sick and tired. And scared. Because now, it's just me and Gloria.

"You didn't have to let him die—"

"Afraid I did. But look on the bright side. I have two extra bodies to dispose of, so I really don't have time to kill you slowly." She points the gun at me. "Any last words?"

"Don't shoot me?"

"I wish."

There's no point begging. Not with Gloria. I could try. I could tell her that I am a teacher. Teachers do not get shot. We're not that interesting. We die slowly, several years after people presume we're already dead. I could tell her I have another plan. I could tell her I want to run away with her. I could tell her I'm not ready. It won't make any difference.

I shut my eyes.

The gun cocks. "Hope you're wearing your boogie shoes."

I close my hand around the cellphone . . . and press Call.

Not a rumble this time. A roar. It bellows up from the earth and shakes the ground I'm standing on. I open my eyes. I see Gloria stumble, the gun waver. Have I got time to run, charge her? She looks back up. The gun steadies. Her finger tightens on the trigger . . .

No reprieve. No last-minute escape. No second chance.

Gloria drops through the ground.

Like a rabbit down a hole, a penny down a well. Not even a scream.

Gone. Vanished. I stare in shock at the spot where she was standing; at the sinkhole that has just opened in the earth.

I limp over. I can just see a glimmer of pink, a strand of blond hair. The ground shakes again. Soil and grass start to fall away beneath the toes of my trainers. I stagger backward. Just in time, as the sides of the hole fold in and more gravel, earth and rocks pile on top of her body.

I peer into the deep chasm, feeling dazed and sick. My vision falters. Something warm trickles down my cheek, past my ear. My head hurts. I raise a hand to touch it. The area above my eye feels sticky and strangely soft. I don't have time to dwell on it. There's another growl from below. A warning. I need to get out of here before I join Gloria. Down there. In the darkness. Among the bones of the dead.

And other things.

IT SEEMS TO TAKE A LONG TIME to make my way back. My balance is off. I stagger and sway over the inclines and descents. Several times I fall. There's a ringing in my left ear and one eye doesn't want to focus properly. This isn't good. Not good at all.

I'm almost at the old colliery gates when I feel the final aftershock rumble through the ground. I stop and glance back. Black smoke mingles with the charcoal sky.

Something falls on my face. It feels like flakes of snow. It takes me a moment to realize that the flakes are black, not white. Flakes of coal. I stand for a second or two and let them fall around me.

And then I sit down. This is not a conscious decision. My legs simply give way, like the instructions from my brain have stopped working. Clocked off for the night. Maybe for good. I'm tired. My left eye is clouded with red. It occurs to me that I might not get up again. I don't care.

I lie back on the stony ground. I stare up at the sky, but it feels like I'm staring down, into a deep black hole. The darkness tugs at me.

Someone grabs my arm . . .

37

I'm not big on emotional goodbyes."

"Me neither."

"Should we hug?"

"Do you want to?"

Beth gives me a look. "Not really."

"Me neither."

"You know what people say about hugs?" she says.

"What?"

"Just an excuse to hide your face."

"Well, for some people, that's probably a good thing."

"Screw you."

"Missed your chance."

"I'll get over it."

"And I thought you were drowning your sorrows."

Beth raises her glass toward me. "Cheers."

I click my Coke against her pint.

"And don't think, just because you are pissing off and leaving me to deal with the fallout, that I am buying all night," she says.

"By 'the fallout,' I presume you mean your new position as deputy head?"

"Yeah, well, you know—to*mayto*, to*mahto*."

"*Tomah*to."

She gives me the finger.

Harry resigned a few days ago, along with Simon Saunders. I can't be sure, but I think it probably has something to do with some emails the police found on Stephen Hurst's computer that showed evidence of bribery and corruption. Undue influence upon Harry and payments to Simon Saunders in exchange for doctoring his son's course work. All very unfortunate.

Miss Hardy (Susan, history) has taken the role of acting head and she has appointed Beth as her deputy. I think they will make a good team. In fact, if I were an optimist I might go even further and say that I think they could really turn Arnhill Academy around, especially as it looks likely that one of its major problems—Jeremy Hurst—will not be returning.

Currently, he is living with foster parents and being counseled by a psychiatrist. He is in shock after the sudden, violent deaths of his parents. I would like to say that I feel sorry for Jeremy. But then I remember Benjamin Morton.

I'll never know for certain, but I believe Jeremy took him to the cave. Maybe a joke, maybe an "initiation." Whatever. Something happened to Ben down there. Something bad. And maybe he wasn't the first. I think about Beth's niece, Emily. Another child who changed. Another life cut tragically short.

And Jeremy didn't tell anyone. Except, maybe, his mother.

Hurst's and Marie's bodies were found on the old colliery site. Police are still investigating the circumstances of their deaths. Hurst had some questionable associates and more than his fair share of enemies, not to mention a holdall containing a bloodstained crowbar in his trunk, so getting to the bottom of it all may take some time. I have a feeling, without any further information, they may never really solve this one.

The sinkhole is due to be filled in very soon. The country-park scheme is under review. Houses will never be built on the land. No council would ever approve it.

The police came to talk to me, of course. PC Taylor and another, large—very large—sergeant, DC Gary Barnes. They could place me in Hurst's car, which I admitted—I told them he had given me a lift home one night. However, once that had been ticked off, the questions seemed perfunctory.

"So I'm not under suspicion?" I asked as they left.

Taylor cocked an eyebrow. "Not for this."

The large sergeant guffawed. Police humor.

"This looks like a professional job," he said. "I don't have you down as the hit-man type."

I could have told them that there are all types of hit men (and women). But I didn't. I smiled.

"The pen is mightier," I said.

He stared at me. Teacher humor.

BETH EYES MY COKE SUSPICIOUSLY. "D'you really need to leave today? It's not much of a goodbye drink. We could order a bottle of wine. Make an afternoon of it?"

I stare at her. I'm going to miss staring at her. And I'm glad we have made our amends. I told her that the reason I came back to Arnhill was that I blamed Hurst for Chris's suicide. I needed to lay some ghosts to rest. Partly true. Most lies are. Sometimes, it's enough.

"Appealing as that is," I say, "I have to go. Anyway, it's the company that's important."

She pulls a face. "Smooth. I'm going for a wee."

She sashays away from the table. I watch her slim figure depart. She is clad in black skinny jeans, DMs and a baggy striped sweater riddled with holes (which I presume is a fashion statement and not the work of overenthusiastic moths). I feel a small tug of regret. I like Beth. A lot. And I could almost dare to entertain the notion that she likes me back. She's a good person. But I am not. Which is why I am leaving and getting as far away from her as possible.

"Bowl of chips to share."

I glance up. Lauren plonks an overflowing bowl down on the table. I smile. "Thanks."

"You're welcome."

"Not just for the chips."

She stares at me.

"I remember," I say. "It was you who found me, up at the pit that night."

The moment stretches. Just when I think she's going to remain silent, she says: "I was taking the dog for his last walk."

An old dog, I think. *Her mum's. A dog with a chunk of fur missing from around its neck. And a tendency to bite.*

"Well, thank you again," I say. "For getting me home. For not saying anything. And for everything else. I'm a little hazy on the details."

"I didn't do much."

"I don't think that's true."

She shrugs. "How's your head?"

I raise a hand and touch my forehead. There's a small red mark on my temple and it feels a little tender, like the remains of a bruise. But that's all. "I guess I must have hit it when I fell."

"You didn't fall."

"I didn't?"

"Not all the way."

She turns and stalks back to the bar. I stare after her.

Beth sits back down at the table. "Did you say something?"

"No. Nothing." I pick up a packet of sauce. "Ketchup?"

"Thanks." She takes it, then says, "Oh, before I forget."

She reaches into her bag and slides a small shoebox across the table.

"You got it?"

"Mrs. Craddock in Biology got it."

"Thanks." I open the box and peer inside.

"Meet Fluffball," Beth says.

"She didn't . . . you know?"

"Nooo. Natural causes."

"Good. Thanks."

"Don't suppose you're going to enlighten me?"

"No."

"Man of mystery."

"Don't forget 'International.'"

"I'm going to miss you."

I smile. "Me too."

"Now, can you put that away? It's putting me off my food."

I slip the box into my satchel. "Better?"

"I meant your stupid smile."

IT'S PAST THREE by the time I climb into my car for the drive back to the Northwest. Beth and I exchange numbers and promise to stay in touch, and I know that we probably won't because we are not the type of people to be text buddies, but that's okay too.

There is no hug, there are no tears and no last-minute lustful, romantic kiss. She does not run after the car as I drive down the street. She gives me two fingers in the rearview mirror then disappears back inside the pub. It's all good.

I pull off along the high street. But I do not go far. I reach the end of the road and then I stop beside St. Jude's.

I climb out of the car and push the gate open. She is sitting on the rickety wooden bench. She looks composed in a plain gray jacket and blue dress. As I approach, she turns.

"Strange place to meet for a farewell," Miss Grayson says.

"But appropriate, I thought."

"I suppose so."

We stare out over the graveyard.

"She's not buried here, is she?" I say.

"Who?"

But she knows.

"Your sister."

"This churchyard hasn't been used for a long time."

"She's not buried at any cemeteries nearby. I checked."

"My parents had her cremated."

"No record of her at the crematorium either. In fact, there's no record of her death at all."

A long pause. Then she says:

"To lose a child, the pain is unimaginable. I think grief is a type of madness. It can make you do things you would never, under normal circumstances, ever consider."

"What happened to her?" I ask.

"My parents took her away one night. They never brought her back. Or, at least, they never brought her home."

"That's why you were so interested in the history of Arnhill and the pit? Why you said you knew what had happened to Annie?"

She nods, then asks: "Was the car crash really an accident?"

"Yes," I say. "It was."

She looks thoughtful: "People say that life finds a way. Perhaps, sometimes, death does too."

And ultimately, I think, he holds all the cards.

"I should get going." I hold out a hand. "Goodbye, Miss Grayson."

She takes it in her cool, smooth palm. "Goodbye, Mr. Thorne."

I stand and walk away. I'm almost at the gate when she calls out: "Joe?"

"Yes?"

"Thank you. For returning."

I shrug. "Sometimes, you don't have a choice."

38

The winding country lanes are dark. I negotiate them slowly and carefully. Even at my snail's pace, the journey takes less time than I expected. I've missed the rush-hour traffic and my mind is busy. Too busy.

I pull up on a side street a few doors down from the apartment I shared with Brendan. I climb out and look up and down. I walk right to the end of the road before I find it. A slightly battered Ford Focus, two child seats in the back and a sign in the rear window that reads: LITTLE MONSTERS ON BOARD.

I stare at it for a while and then I walk more slowly across the road and down two more streets to my old local. A good local. They do a mean steak-and-kidney pie.

I push open the door and spot him right away, at our usual table in the far corner. I order a beer and a pack of crisps and stroll over. He looks up. A grin spreads across his craggy face.

"Well, look what the cat dragged in."

I put my beer down on the table. He stands and holds open his arms. We hug. He cannot see my face.

Finally, we sit. Brendan raises his glass of orange juice. "Glad to have you back, and in one piece."

I take a sip of my pint. "Thanks."

"Now, are you going to tell me what the feck happened?"

"The blond woman won't be a problem anymore."

"No?"

"She's dead. An accident."

I watch him. But he's good.

"And what about your debt?"

"I think that will be written off very soon."

"Well, you know what my dear old mammy would say?"

"What's that?"

"A wise man never counts his chickens until he's killed the last fox."

"Meaning?"

"You might have taken care of the woman, but do you really think that's the end of it?"

I open the packet of crisps and offer it to Brendan. He pats his stomach and shakes his head. "Diet, remember?"

"Ah. Of course. You used to be a lot bigger, didn't you? When you drank."

He grins. "Not like the Adonis I am now."

"So you'd say you were fat back then?"

The grin fades. "What is this, Joe?"

"Something Gloria said, before she died. It was quick, if you're wondering. I know you two were close."

"Close? I have no bloody idea what you're talking about. I'm your friend. The one who has always been there for you. The one who visited you for weeks in the hospital."

"You visited me twice. But I guess you were too busy running your businesses. Gambling, extortion, murder."

"Businesses? This is *Brendan* you're talking to!"

"No. This is the Fatman I'm talking to."

We stare at each other. I see him realize it's no good. All the cards have been played. He holds out his arms.

"Fuck. You got me. Always were sharp. That's why I like you."

The thick Irish brogue has fallen away, like a snake shedding its skin.

"That's why you got Gloria to cripple me?" I say.

"Business is business. Friendship is friendship."

"What do you know about friendship?"

"You're still breathing. I'd call that friendship."

"Why? Why pretend to be my friend at all? Why let me share your apartment?"

"I was trying to help you. Give you a chance to pay. But you kept getting yourself in deeper. Also, God's honest truth, I enjoy your company. In my position, you don't have many close friends."

"Tend to have a lot of accidents, do they?"

He chuckles. "Sometimes it's necessary."

Necessary. Of course.

He leans back in his chair. "So, tell me—what did Gloria say?"

"*Hope you're wearing your boogie shoes.* It didn't register at the time, what with her pointing a gun at my head. But later, I remembered."

He shakes his scruffy head. "Should have known my words of wisdom would come back to haunt me one day."

"It wasn't just that. I could almost have dismissed what Gloria said—"

And I wanted to. I so badly wanted to. But there was something else.

"It was the car," I say.

"Car?"

"I saw a black Ford Focus with child seats parked at the B&B *before* you said you drove down to bring me the bag. It was familiar, but I couldn't quite place it. Then I remembered. I'd seen the same Ford Focus outside the apartment once before. You told me it was your sister's car that you'd borrowed."

"Ah."

"Is it?"

"Actually, no. Always hide in plain sight, my friend. Half the people in this pub have heard of the Fatman. Not one knows he's in here most nights. No one looks twice at Brendan, reformed drunkster, harmless Irish buffoon.

"Same with the car. Nobody notices another kiddie carrier. Something bad happens, you need to get out fast, the police won't stop the scruffy-looking dad trundling along in his Ford Focus to pick up the kids. Perfect disguise."

"Or maybe not."

"Well, we all make mistakes. Yours was coming back here. Because now I have a dilemma. You still owe me money. My girlfriend is dead. What am I supposed to do with you, Joe?"

"Let me walk out of here."

He laughs. "I could do that. But it would only be delaying the inevitable."

"You're not going to kill me."

"And why is that?"

"Tell me two things first—why did you tell me to go to the police?"

"Because I knew you wouldn't. Reverse psychology."

"And was everything lies? Everything else you told me?"

He considers. "Well, let's see. My mammy *is* Irish, but not so dear. I did used to be fat. I'm a recovering alcoholic. Oh, and I have a sister—"

"With two kids—Daisy and Theo."

He stares at me. A nerve twitches by his eye.

"They live in Altrincham. Their dad works at the airport. Mum is a receptionist at the doctors' office. Daisy and Theo attend Huntingdon Primary School. Your sister fetches them three days a week and a babysitter picks them up on Tuesdays and Fridays when she works late. Oh, also, it isn't gerbils they have. It's hamsters." I pick up my drink and take a sip. "How am I doing so far?"

"How the hell—"

"I haven't got a job. I had some spare time. Now, here's the thing. If you come after me, I will come after your sister and her family."

A snarl curls at the corner of his lip. "You don't have it in you."

"No?"

I reach into my pocket and pull out something small, brown and furry. I drop the dead hamster into his drink.

"As your dear old mammy said at the gang bang—you have no *feckin'* idea what I have in me."

Brendan stares at the hamster. Then back at me. I smile. His expression changes.

"Get out of here. I never want to see your ugly face again."

I push my chair back.

"Far, *far* away," he adds.

"I hear Botswana's nice."

"Book a one-way ticket. You even send a postcard, you're a dead man. Understand?"

"I understand."

I turn and walk across the pub. I don't look back.

And for some reason, I don't limp.

EPILOGUE

Henry has been told not to play up there. Ever since they moved in, it's all his mum has harped on. It's dangerous; he could get hurt, or lost, or fall into a hole in the ground. And he doesn't want to fall into a hole in the ground, does he?

Henry doesn't, but then he doesn't always listen to his mum either. Sometimes it's like her words are just a jumble of letters. He hears them, but he doesn't really understand what they mean. Apparently, this is because of his autism. It means he doesn't empathize (feel stuff properly).

That's not totally true. People, he has difficulty with. Animals, not so much. And places. He can feel those. Like the old pit. He felt that the moment they moved in. Calling to him. Like he was standing next to a room where loads of people were talking. But he couldn't quite make out what they were saying.

Henry hasn't told his mum about the voices. There are lots of things he doesn't tell his mum because "she worries." She says this a lot. She worries about keeping him safe. She worries that he spends so much time alone. That's why she was so happy when he told her about his new friends. Henry has never had friends before and he knows his mum worries about this too.

Today Mum is upstairs painting. She is redecorating the cottage.

She said magnolia on every wall made her feel like she was living in a tin of semolina. Mum said funny things sometimes. Henry thinks he loves his mum.

So, he feels a bit (guilty?) when he sneaks out. But not enough to stop himself. That's the problem. Henry doesn't stop to consider how his actions will affect other people (the doctors said). He only lives in the moment.

This moment is good. The sun is bright. But not soft, melted-butter bright, like summer. It's hard bright. Winter bright. All sharp around the edges, like it could slice your fingers if you touched it. Henry likes that. He's wrapped in a thick duffel coat and inside is secure and warm, insulated from the world around him. Henry likes that too.

He walks along the lane until he reaches the start of the security fencing. He knows where there is a gap. He's good at finding ways into places. He squeezes through and looks around.

He wonders where his friends are. They usually meet him up here. And then he spots them (as if just thinking about them has made them appear). They wave and walk down the small slope toward him. The girl is about Henry's age. The boy is a bit older, skinny with blond hair. Sometimes the girl carries a doll.

They amble around the scrubby wasteland together. Occasionally, Henry stops and picks up a bit of rock, an old screw or a piece of metal. He likes collecting things.

After a while—he's not sure how long because watches confuse him—he realizes that the sun isn't so hard and bright. It's slipped a long way in the sky. It occurs to Henry that his mum might have stopped painting, and if he isn't home she'll be *worried*.

"I should go," he says.

"Not yet," says the boy.

"Stay a bit longer," says the girl.

Henry debates. He would like to stay. He can feel that tug on his insides. Hear the pit thrumming in his head. But he doesn't want his mum to be unhappy.

"No," he says. "I'm going."

"Wait," the boy says. His voice is more urgent.

"We've got something to show you," says the girl.

She touches his arm. Her hand is cold. She's only wearing thin pajamas. The boy has on a T-shirt and shorts. Neither is wearing shoes.

It occurs to Henry that this is a bit odd. Then the thought is gone, smothered by the whispering voices.

He tries once more. "I really need to go back."

The boy smiles. Something black drops from his hair and scuttles away.

"You'll come back," he says. "We promise."

ACKNOWLEDGMENTS

Blimey—a second book. Not so long ago, I had pretty much given up hope of ever having a book published and now here we are: Book 2. I almost feel like a proper author. And there are a lot of people I'd like to thank for that:

My amazing agent, Madeleine Milburn, without whom I'd still be a dog walker in Nottingham.

My brilliant editor, Max, who quite simply "gets" my writing, and also gets how to make it that much better. Similarly, Nate—a great editor and one of the nicest people on earth.

Everyone at Michael Joseph and Crown. Plus, all my international publishers.

My partner, Neil. You already got the dedication at the front, dear.

My little girl, Betty, for giving me perspective on what's really important in life (glitter).

My mum and dad. Literally wouldn't be here without you.

The Ladykillers, for their friendship, support and the boozy lunches. Mainly the boozy lunches.

My English teacher, Mr. Webster, who once told me, "If you don't become prime minister or a bestselling author, I'll be very disappointed."

Stephen King. Constant inspiration.

My oldest friends—Kirsty, Suzanne, Julie and Clare—who know how much I've wanted to be a writer ever since we all went to comprehensive school together, in a mining village in Nottinghamshire.

And of course, YOU, for reading this book. If it wasn't for you, I wouldn't get to keep doing this stuff. Thank you. You're bloody marvelous!

THE HIDING PLACE

C. J. TUDOR

RANDOM HOUSE READER'S CIRCLE

QUESTIONS AND TOPICS
FOR DISCUSSION

1. Chapter 6 opens with the statement: "People say time is a great healer. They're wrong. Time is simply a great eraser." Do you agree with this sentiment? Why or why not? How does this connect with Joe's storyline?

2. In chapter 9, Joe thinks that if you get far enough away from the relationships that bind you, that you can easily escape yourself. "Self is only a construct. You can dismantle it, reconstruct it," Tudor writes. Do you believe that Joe was able to reinvent himself in adulthood?

3. Do you believe that places retain the weight of history? Have you ever been somewhere that felt suffused with a kind of magnetic, or repulsive, power?

4. Throughout the book, Arnhill and the mine are described like characters with a power to influence all on their own. Discuss the methods that the author uses to personify these areas.

5. The author examines how children absorb everything that goes on around them, "catching it like a log bobbing in a busy river current." What do you think the author was trying to say about the nature of victimhood and violence?

6. What do you think gives the mine its power?

7. Discuss the book's twists: Joe's role in the car accident, Marie's true character, Brendan's identity. Did you see any of them coming? How did they change your understanding of these characters?

8. What do you think the snowmen symbolize?

9. Joe is a complex character with some less-than-admirable qualities. Despite that, were you rooting for him? Do you think he finds redemption in the end?

10. Do you think what Joe and Julia did to Annie and Ben was the right thing to do? What would you have done in their places?

If you enjoyed *The Hiding Place,*
read on for a preview of C. J. Tudor's next novel,

THE OTHER PEOPLE

Coming soon from Ballantine Books

*S*he sleeps. A pale girl in a white room. Machines surround her. Mechanical guardians, they tether the sleeping girl to the land of the living, stopping her from drifting away on an eternal, dark tide.

Their steady beeps and the labored sound of her breathing are the sleeping girl's only lullabies. Before, she loved music. Loved to sing. Loved to play. She found music in everything—the birds, the trees, the sea.

A small piano has been placed in one corner of the room. The cover is up, but the keys are coated in a fine layer of dust. On top of the piano sits an ivory shell. Its silky pink insides look like the delicate curves of an ear.

The machines beep and whirr.

The shell trembles.

A sharp C suddenly fills the room.

Somewhere, another girl falls.

1

2016. M1 NORTH

He noticed the stickers first, surrounding the car's rear window and lining the bumper:

HONK IF YOU'RE HORNY. DON'T FOLLOW ME, I'M LOST. WHEN YOU DRIVE LIKE I DO, YOU'D BETTER BELIEVE IN GOD. HORN BROKEN—WATCH FOR FINGER. REAL MEN LOVE JESUS.

Talk about mixed messages. Although one thing did come through loud and clear: the driver was obviously a dick. Gabe was willing to bet he wore slogan T-shirts and had a picture at work of a monkey with its hands over its head and the caption: "You don't have to be mad to work here but it helps."

He was surprised the driver could see out of the back at all. On the other hand, at least he was providing reading material for traffic jams. Like the one they were currently stuck in. A long line of cars crawling through the M1 roadworks, which felt like they had started sometime in the last century and looked set to continue well into the next millennium.

Gabe sighed and tapped his fingers on the wheel, as though this could somehow hurry along the traffic, or summon a time machine. He was almost late. Not quite. Not yet. It was still within the bounds of possibility that he might make it home in time. But he wasn't hopeful. In fact, hope had left him somewhere around Junction 19, along with all the drivers savvy enough to take their chances with their GPS and a country lane diversion.

What was even more frustrating was that he had managed to leave on time today. He should easily have made it home by six-thirty, so he could be there for dinner and Izzy's bedtime, which he had promised, *promised* Jenny that he would do tonight.

"Just once a week. That's all I ask. One night when we eat together, you read your daughter a bedtime story and we pretend we're a normal, happy family."

That had hurt. She had meant it to.

Of course, he could have pointed out that *he* was the one who had got Izzy ready for school that morning as Jenny had to rush out to see a client. *He* was the one who had soothed their daughter and applied antiseptic cream to her chin when their temperamental rescue cat (the one *Jenny* had adopted) had scratched her.

But he didn't. Because they both knew it didn't make up for all the missed times, the moments he hadn't been there. Jenny was not an unreasonable woman. But when it came to family, she had a very definite line. If you crossed it, then it was a long time before she let you step back inside.

It was one of the reasons he loved her: her fierce devotion to their daughter. Gabe's own mum had been more devoted to cheap vodka, and he had never known his dad. Gabe had sworn that he would be different, that he would always be there for his little girl.

And yet, here he was, stuck on the motorway, about to be late. Again. Jenny would not forgive him. Not this time. He didn't want to dwell upon what that meant.

He had tried to call her, but it had gone to voice mail. And now his phone had less than 1 percent battery, which meant it would die any minute and typically today, of all days, he had left his charger at home. All he could do was sit, fighting the urge to press his foot on the accelerator and barge the rest of the traffic out of the way, tapping his fingers aggressively on the steering wheel, staring at bloody Sticker Man in front.

A lot of the stickers looked old. Faded and wrinkled. But then, the car itself looked ancient. An old Cortina or something similar. It was sprayed that color that was so popular in the seventies: a sort of dirty gold. Moldy banana. Pollution sunset. Dying sun.

Dirty gray fumes puffed intermittently out of the wonky exhaust. The whole bumper was speckled with rust. He couldn't see a man-ufacturer's badge. It had probably fallen off, along with half of the number plate. Only the letters "T N" and what could be part of a six or an eight remained. He frowned. He was sure that wasn't legal. The damn thing probably wasn't even roadworthy, or insured, or driven by a qualified driver. Best not to get too close.

He was just considering changing lanes when the girl's face ap-peared in the rear window, perfectly framed by the peeling stickers. She looked to be around five or six. Round-faced, pink-cheeked. Fine blonde hair pulled into two high pigtails.

His first thought was that she should be strapped into a car seat.

His second thought was: *Izzy.*

She stared at him. Her eyes widened. She opened her mouth, re-vealing a tooth missing right in the front. He remembered wrapping it in a tissue and tucking it under her pillow for the tooth fairy.

She mouthed: "Daddy!"

Then a hand reached back, grabbed her arm and yanked her down. Out of sight. Gone. Vanished.

He stared at the empty window.

Izzy.

Impossible.

His daughter was at home, with her mum. Probably watching the Disney Channel while Jenny cooked dinner. She couldn't be in the back of a strange car, going God knows where, not even strapped into a car seat.

The stickers blocked his view of the driver. He could barely see the top of the person's head above HONK IF YOU'RE HORNY. Fuck that. He honked anyway. Then he flashed his lights. The car seemed to speed up a little. Ahead of him, the roadwork was ending, the 50-mph signs replaced by the national speed limit.

Izzy. He accelerated. It was a new Range Rover. It went like shit off the proverbial shovel. And yet the battered old rust bucket in front was pulling away from him. He pressed the pedal down harder. Watched the speedometer creep up past seventy, seventy-five, eighty-five. He was gaining, and then the car in front suddenly darted into the middle lane and undertook several cars. Gabe followed, swerving in front of a large articulated truck. The horn's blare almost deafened him. His heart felt like it might just burst right out of his chest, like bloody *Alien*.

The car in front was weaving dangerously in and out of the traffic. Gabe was hemmed in by a Ford Focus on one side and a Toyota in front. Shit. He glanced in his mirror, pulled into the slow lane and then darted back in front of the Toyota. At the same time a Jeep pulled in from the fast lane, just missing his hood. He slammed on his brakes. The Jeep driver flashed his hazards and gave him the finger.

"Screw *you* too, you fucking wanker!"

The rust bucket was several cars in front now, still weaving, tail lights disappearing into the distance. He couldn't keep up. It was too dangerous.

Besides, he tried to tell himself, he must be mistaken. *Must be*. It couldn't have been Izzy. Impossible. Why on earth would she be in in that car? He was tired, stressed. It was dark. It must be some other little girl who looked like Izzy. *A lot like Izzy*. A little girl who had the same blonde hair in pigtails, the same gap between her front teeth. *A little girl who called him "Daddy."*

A sign flashed up ahead: SERVICES 1/2 MILE. He could pull in, make a phone call, put his mind at rest. But he was already late, he should keep going. On the other hand, what was a few more minutes? The slip road was slipping past. Keep going? Pull over? Keep going? Pull over? *Izzy*. At the last minute, he yanked the wheel to the left, bumping over the white hazard lines and eliciting more horn beeps. He sped up the slip road and into the services.

GABE HARDLY EVER STOPPED at service stations. He found them depressing, full of miserable people who wanted to be somewhere else.

He wasted precious minutes scuttling up and down, past the various food outlets, searching for a payphone, which he eventually found tucked away near the toilets. Just the one. No one used payphones anymore. He wasted several more minutes looking for some change before he realized you could use a card He extracted his debit card from his wallet, stuck it in and called home.

Jenny never answered on the first ring. She was always busy, always doing something with Izzy. Sometimes she said she wished she had eight pairs of hands. He should be there more, he thought. He should help.

"Hello."

A woman's voice. But not Jenny. Unfamiliar. Had he called the wrong number? He didn't call it very often. Again, it was all mobiles. He checked the number on the payphone. Definitely their landline number.

"Hello?" the voice said again. "Is that Mr. Forman?"

"Yes. This is Mr. Forman. Who the hell are you?"

"My name is Detective Inspector Maddock."

A detective. In his house. Answering his phone.

"Where are you, Mr. Forman?"

"The M1. I mean, in the services. On my way back from work."

He was babbling. Like a guilty person. But then, he *was* guilty, wasn't he? Of a lot of things.

"You need to come home, Mr. Forman. Right away."

"Why? What's going on? *What's happened?*"

A long pause. A swollen, stifling silence. The sort of silence, he thought, that brims with unspoken words. Words that are about to completely fuck up your life.

"It's about your wife . . . and daughter."

C. J. TUDOR is the author of *The Chalk Man* and *The Hiding Place,* and lives in England with her partner and daughter. Over the years she has worked as a copywriter, television presenter, voice-over artist, and dog walker. She is now thrilled to be able to write full-time, and doesn't miss chasing wet dogs through muddy fields all that much.

Facebook.com/CJTudorOfficial
Twitter: @cjtudor